PENGUIN BOOKS

CONFESSIONS OF A DEMENTED HOUSEWIFE

Confessions of a Demented Housewife

The Celebrity Year

NIAMH GREENE

PENGUIN BOOKS

PENGUIN BOOKS

Published by the Penguin Group
Penguin Books Ltd, 80 Strand, London WC2R ORL, England
Penguin Group (USA) Inc., 375 Hudson Street, New York, New York 10014, USA
Penguin Group (Canada), 90 Eglinton Avenue East, Suite 700, Toronto, Ontario, Canada M4P 2Y3
(a division of Pearson Penguin Canada Inc.)
Penguin Ireland, 25 St Stephen's Green, Dublin 2, Ireland (a division of Penguin Books Ltd)
Penguin Group (Australia), 250 Camberwell Road, Camberwell, Victoria 3124, Australia
(a division of Pearson Australia Group Pty Ltd)
Penguin Books India Pvt Ltd, 11 Community Centre, Panchsheel Park, New Delhi – 110 017, India
Penguin Group (NZ), 67 Apollo Drive, Rosedale, North Shore 0632, New Zealand
(a division of Pearson New Zealand Ltd)
Penguin Books (South Africa) (Pty) Ltd, 24 Sturdee Avenue, Rosebank, Johannesburg 2196, South Africa

Penguin Books Ltd, Registered Offices: 80 Strand, London WC2R ORL, England

www.penguin.com

First published by Penguin Ireland 2008
Published in Penguin Books 2008
1

Typeset by Rowland Phototypesetting Ltd, Bury St Edmunds, Suffolk
Printed in England by Clays Ltd, St Ives plc

ISBN: 978-1-844-88138-3

www.greenpenguin.co.uk

Penguin Books is committed to a sustainable future
for our business, our readers and our planet.
The book in your hands is made from paper
certified by the Forest Stewardship Council.

Annual review of life goals

Have made enormous progress in my spiritual growth since last year. In fact, I have achieved such a high level of self-awareness that I may no longer need to watch *Dr. Phil* every morning. (A huge breakthrough.)

Life lessons learnt in past twelve months

(a) *Other people cannot complete me.* Having a semi-affair with Lone Father from the mother-and-toddler group was a big mistake – especially as he turned out to be a love-rat who had no real feelings for me. Luckily I have not thought about him or his saucy sex texts in weeks. Instead I have made peace with his manipulative two-timing ways and wish him well in all his future endeavours – such as writing a ridiculous tell-all book about his secret liaisons with a married housewife.

(b) *Joe is the perfect husband and I must appreciate him more.* It was very handy when he blamed himself for forcing me into the arms of another man, then forgave me when I wrongly accused him of romping with his secretary in LA.

Plus he bought Mum and Dad's old house so we now have a private country retreat, just like Madonna and Guy. (Range Rover and tweed flat caps to follow.)

(c) *Chicken-fillet push-up bras and false acrylic nails are apparently the key to a man's heart.* Lone Father's new lover/muse, Marita, swears by them.

Goals for next twelve months

- Find my Core Self. (NB Investigate what this actually involves and whether doing anything practical to achieve life goals is absolutely necessary.)

- Reignite the passion between Joe and me. We may have moved to a whole new relationship level after our recent rocky patch but we must make sure not to stray off the path of marital harmony and bliss again. (NB It will probably be important to avoid engaging in inappropriate mother-and-toddler group liaisons at all costs. It may also be crucial to invest in skimpy new underwear sets and ditch all well-washed granny pants that come to the navel ASAP.)

- Ensure that Katie and Jack are emotionally secure and intellectually challenged at all times. Specifically, make sure they both settle into the education system without serious incident. (NB Jack violently attacking his playschool teacher with a Magic Marker counts as a serious incident.)

- Help Very Best Friend Louise accept her impending single-mother status and act as a maternal mentor. This should be easy – we have become much closer after the little spat we had when she prioritized her relationship with a total loser over her decades-old friendship with me. Our new-found closeness may be helped by the fact that the total loser, a.k.a. her ex Steve, dumped her and high-tailed it like a bat out of hell once he got wind of her surprise pregnancy. It may also have helped that she has packed on a disproportionately large amount of weight for a first pregnancy and now looks frumpy and hard-done-by instead of groomed and polished to within an inch of her life. *And* she will probably develop stretchmarks in unusual places – so we have much more in common than we ever did before.

- Persuade Mum and Dad that relocating to a plush golf resort in Portugal was an unwise decision and that they would be much happier back here, looking after their grandchildren like normal pensioners. (NB Do not entice them home until we have taken an extended break in the sun ourselves.)

- Keep Joe's mother, Mrs H, at arm's length. Should be manageable as she'll have no real excuse to drop by for coffee unannounced now that both children will be at school. (NB May consider installing hi-tech surveillance CCTV outside house just in case.)

- Learn to love my body. Luckily the size-zero obsession is on the wane and there have been loads of celebs-in-bikinis specials in *Heat* with really unflattering pics of unsuspecting A-listers letting it all hang out on the beach. Which means that the pounds I packed on over the summer are nothing to be embarrassed about. (Bonus: smock tops are hot for autumn/winter so I no longer have to worry about exposing my jelly belly over the waistband of my knock-off Rock and Republic jeans.)

It looks like quite a lot when it's written down, but if I got through last year's little difficulties, I'm sure I can easily achieve it all.

Hectic morning. If it continues like this I don't think I'll make it to half-term (worryingly, only eight weeks away, according to the handout from school – which cannot possibly be right).

Skidded up to the school gate just before nine and saw all the other mothers huddled round, whispering among themselves as a massive Range Rover Sport, with tinted windows, pulled away from the kerb.

'What's up?' I asked, wondering why they seemed so shell-shocked.

'It's Angelica Law,' a mother breathed, looking like she needed a stiff drink. 'Her little boy started today.'

'Who's Angelica Law?' I was mystified.

All the other mothers tittered in disbelief.

'Only the wife of James Law,' one piped up. 'The gorgeous American actor? He's here to shoot the new Noel Jordache film so they've relocated to Dublin for the year.'

My heart almost stopped. The son of a properly famous person, not just a Z-list celeb, was going to be in Katie's class, maybe even sitting beside her. This was big. This was HUGE. How had I not known about it? I should have been in serious celebrity training all summer, preparing to dazzle a real A-lister with my wit and glamour. Instead, I'd been lounging around eating Doritos all day and counting the hours until the kids were back at school.

'If we're lucky we'll get to see him in the flesh,' another mother was saying.

'Oh, God.' Someone sighed. 'I hope so – he's sex on legs.'

Then they all dissolved into girlish giggles.

Called Joe on the way home to tell him the amazing news.

'I hope the school's going to take the necessary precautions,' he said, sounding worried.

'What do you mean "precautions"?' I asked. Maybe he thought we were going to be frisked every morning for hidden cameras or secret recording devices – just like they do at *Hello!* celebrity weddings to stop guests leaking gossip to the press.

'Well, if this actor guy's such a big shot, his child could be ripe for kidnapping. The school will have to be very security-conscious. Does he have a bodyguard?'

'Ooh, I don't know!' I said, thrilled at the very idea that a six-foot SAS muscleman in dark glasses could be sitting in on class every day, a walkie-talkie and a Smith & Wesson in his pockets.

I hung up the phone, floating on cloud nine. Having the real-life child of a superstar around will be fantastic. Now all I have to do is cultivate a friendship with celebrity mom Angelica Law and get myself invited to the best parties in town. May well have to sex up my wardrobe just in case she takes an instant shine to me. Polo-necks and bootlegs will definitely not cut the mustard on *E! Red Carpet Style*.

PS Called Louise to fill her in on the latest celeb-watching news but it went to voicemail. Was probably for the best – suspect she wants to pin me down about being her birth partner and I'm kind of regretting agreeing to it.

2 September

Hung around the school gate for a bit, trying to spot Angelica Law, but eventually admitted defeat when the playground emptied and I was the only one left. Went home and decided to watch a snippet of *Oprah* before I tackled finding my Core Self. Was sorry I did – nearly choked on my mid-morning snack when a grim doctor snapped on an extra-long pair of rubber gloves, then casually laid a diseased bowel on a slab so that he, Oprah and the studio audience could have a really good look at it. They then proceeded to talk about how farting is a natural condition and vital for good health. I was appalled. It put me right off my blueberry muffin.

Felt a bit down in the dumps for the rest of the morning, but tried to remind myself that I should be giddy with excitement that I am now free to do *whatever I want* for three whole hours every day. The possibilities are endless. Maybe I could become a bestselling author – everyone knows those chick-lit novels are dead easy to write. Or I could start hosting at-home lingerie parties and make serious cash.

To distract myself, devised my grand plan to befriend Angelica. Am desperate to get a good look at her close up – word at the school gate is that she has the skin of a teenager and the booty to match.

Project Angelica

- Hang around school gate, looking glamorous and approachable. (NB May need to invest in chemical peel and/or tummy tuck ASAP.)

- Engage wife of A-lister in casual chit-chat. (NB Avoid controversial topics, such as Betty Ford visits or recreational drug use.)

- Impress her with my wit and charm. (NB Think of something interesting and educated to say. Do not mention borderline obsession with celeb-and-cellulite exposés in *Heat*.)

- Become her sole confidante. (NB Reassure her that I
  would be the perfect red-carpet date and would never
  upstage her at an awards ceremony – show her my
  bingo-wing arms, if necessary, to prove the point.)

Am sure this approach can't fail to impress her – she'll
probably be delighted that a real-life civilian is trying to
befriend her.

3 September

Spent ages skulking about at the school gate again today,
hoping to put my ingenious plan into action, but apparently
Angelica drops off her little boy on time every morning
(which is a bit anal, if you ask me) so I'd missed them again.

'She's very down-to-earth,' another mother said smugly,
when I asked casually if she'd seen her. 'She chatted to me
for ages this morning. Brandon, her little boy, is coming to
mine for a play date tomorrow.'

Was furious that the jockeying for position of VBF to
the celebrity mom had already started. But then I decided
that the other mothers have no real hope of competing
against me. Once Angelica realizes I'm one of her own, they
won't stand a chance – bet none of *them* knows all the names
of Brangelina's children or has almost every back copy of
OK! in existence.

Mrs H popped round for coffee mid-morning.

'Isn't it great for you now that Katie's at school and Jack's
at playschool,' she said primly, munching a biscuit. 'You'll
have much more time to keep the house in order now you're
free in the mornings.'

Refrained from beating her over the head with the Jaffa

Cakes box. Cleaning the house from top to bottom every day is not on my agenda in any shape or form. This is the year I will finally find myself and my Intrinsic Values. Vacuuming definitely does not count as an Intrinsic Value.

PS Oprah is top of the *Forbes* Rich List. Apparently she's worth a zillion million dollars or something. Obviously the fart talk is working just fine for her.

4 September

Have decided that the only way to cope with craziness of school mornings is to run a tight ship and take no prisoners. Children need a solid, dependable routine with lots of rules – that hunky child psychologist on telly is always saying so. (Also, if I get to the school gate before nine, I may have a decent chance of meeting Angelica Law.)

Rules for a stress-free morning

- Have all children's clothes washed, ironed and ready to go the night before. (NB Bonus points will be awarded for ironing underwear.)

- Prepare nutritious packed lunches and store them neatly in a fridge that has been bleached to within an inch of its life. (NB Slicing carrots and apples in an attractive way will fool gullible children into thinking they are as much fun as Fruit Winders.)

- Present porridge as a viable breakfast option. Discourage yummy choccie cereals and high-sugar fruit drinks – these are unwise choices that contribute to destructive behaviour and should be avoided at all costs. (NB Do not feed to the dog instead.)

- Ban all TV before school – too much high-impact stimulation can lead to disharmony in the morning hours. (NB Ignore full-scale meltdown that occurs when children realize *SpongeBob SquarePants* is no longer an option at six a.m.)

- Have children in car a full twenty minutes before leaving time, then engage in a calm, educational discussion about topics of the day on the road. (NB Discussions of the merits of Power Rangers as opposed to Ninja Turtles is not recommended.)

Feel much better now that I have a foolproof plan to follow. Am sure that the yummy TV child psychologist would be delighted with me. Wonder if he needs a model family to film and judge dysfunctional families by. Must investigate.

5 September

Calm morning routine not going according to plan. Am now regretting emailing yummy TV child psychologist and offering ourselves for filming purposes. Must remember not to be so impulsive in future.

Revised rules for a stress-free morning

- Try to reason with Jack that getting out of bed at five a.m. is not necessary. Bribe him with age-inappropriate baby bottle of milk, if need be. (NB Try to block from my mind that the use of baby bottles increases the likelihood of ear infections and speech disorders in older children — what do those pesky child experts know anyway?)

- Bribe Katie to stay in bed for an extra half-hour by promising she can purchase a new Bratz micro-mini and matching cropped top.

- Once children are up, try to persuade them that eating breakfast is not a waste of valuable cartoon-watching time.

- Convince them that porridge does not look like puke and that it is a very nourishing breakfast option.

- Argue that watching *Playhouse Disney* while eating jam doughnuts is not a reasonable way to start the day.

- Try to locate clean clothes. If desperate, recycle yesterday's grubby specimens. It is acceptable to remove ground-in paint stains from jeans, etc., with fingernails and/or a tea-towel.

- If children refuse to wash, giving them a wipe with the same tea-towel is allowed.

- If children refuse to have hair brushed, do not panic. Dishevelled, just-out-of-bed look *à la* Kate Moss is very 'now'.

- Putting fleece on over PJs to do school run is OK but it is crucial to put on real shoes instead of slippers (matching pair preferable). To look perky and awake, apply bronzing powder in swift deft strokes to pallid complexion. Use shimmer eye-shadow to accent. (NB Remember to remove yellow crust from eyes beforehand.)

- Drive to school like a lunatic on acid to make it before the bell goes. Paste fake Hollywood smile on face before disembarking at the school gate, just in case Angelica Law is about.

PS Have discovered that half-term is definitely only eight weeks away. Am considering writing to the Minister for Education demanding a rethink of the primary-school time-table. Surely it will be very disruptive to yank children out of school when they will only just be getting used to the routine? Also, am very concerned that I'm expected to entertain them for another whole week so soon after the summer holidays.

6 September

Angelica Law waved at me today! Was stumbling blindly out of the gate still half asleep when a massive 4 x 4 careered towards me at high speed. Looked up in the nick of time to see Angelica waving frantically and beeping the horn energetically to get my attention. She was wearing massive designer sunglasses that covered most of her face – but it was definitely her: her bone structure is so exquisite it can't be mistaken. I leapt out of her way and fell to the path as she zoomed by. Feel quite smug. She's bound to choose me as her best friend and confidante now that I'm on her radar. It was almost worth getting run over.

Called Louise to fill her in on latest dramatic developments but before I could launch into the very exciting news about my near-fatal brush with Angelica, she cut across me. 'I'm so *hoooot*,' she moaned. 'This weather's killing me.'

'Em, it's only about fifteen degrees,' I ventured, not wanting to antagonize her – her temper has been unpredictable lately.

'It may as well be thirty-five,' she hissed angrily. 'I'm so fucking uncomfortable. You should try being six months pregnant in the middle of summer – it's torture.'

Refrained from telling her that I had actually been pregnant twice, and that summer is officially over. Louise believes she's the only woman to have been 'with child'. Ever. In the history of the world. Also, her pregnancy hormones seem to be playing havoc with her emotions. If she's not crying, she's ranting and raving. (And using very vulgar language to boot. Jack heard her say the F-word three times last week. It took me ages to convince him she'd been saying 'foot'.)

Suspect she may be in dire need of an intensive anger-management course, but I'm too afraid she might beat me over the head with her genuine Louis Vuitton handbag to suggest it.

'You are *so* lucky,' she went on, sounding as if she could quite cheerfully strangle me. 'You spent the whole summer chilling out in the country while I was stuck in this godforsaken office. If one more person asks me when this baby is due I will suffocate them.'

Was about to joke that it would be simple to suffocate anyone, with her unnaturally large bump and enormous pregnancy boobs, but could hear a distinct wobble in her voice and knew she was morphing from angry woman into sobbing woman and that any joking would lead to waterworks. 'You'll be going on maternity leave soon, Louise,' I ventured, hoping she'd cheer up a bit. 'Then you can come round to mine every morning and we'll have lots of coffee and biscuits.'

'Great – so I can pile on another ten pounds and look even more like a beached whale than I do at the moment,' she cried. 'I can barely see my feet as it is.' She sounded really despondent. 'Anyway, I'd better go, I have a board meeting in five minutes.'

'OK, I'll call you tomorrow,' I said, guiltily relieved I could escape, and deciding that now was not the right time to mention the new celebrity in town.

'Well, I might call you later,' she replied. 'We need to start talking about doing those Lamaze classes.'

Hung up feeling panicky. Why did I ever agree to be Louise's birth partner? OK, so she is my VBF, and the father of her unborn baby has abandoned her, but I had to be knocked out to deliver my two – I'll never cope with seeing her give birth. Especially since she wants an all-natural delivery with as little medical intervention as possible. Hopefully this will change when she realizes how mind-bogglingly painful giving birth is. Luckily, I'll be on hand then to demand multiple epidurals and gas masks on her behalf from hunky obstetricians.

7 September

Confided in Joe that I was nervous about being Louise's birth partner. 'I just don't know if I can handle it,' I said, digging anxiously into a tub of Rolo ice-cream. 'Louise has very high expectations, you know. What if I do something wrong? What if I drop the baby when it's coming out?'

I was in serious mental anguish at the prospect.

'Has her baby started to kick yet?' Joe asked dreamily, his face going all soft and squishy.

'Um, yeah, I think so,' I said, wondering what that had to do with anything.

'Ah, I used to love that – didn't you?' He chortled.

'Remember? Jack used to kick so hard when you were lying in bed that the duvet cover would move.'

'Yeah, I remember,' I said, giggling, 'and you'd pat my tummy and tell him to go back to sleep.'

'And he'd kick even harder!'

We laughed together. Jack still loved kicking – except now it was the living daylights out of his sister instead of my insides.

Then Joe looked at me, a funny expression on his face. 'They were great times,' he said softly.

'Yes, they were,' I said, touched he remembered them with such affection. 'Isn't it amazing how they've grown?'

I smiled fondly at him. But then Katie bounded into the kitchen and threw herself to the ground, gasping and screaming hysterically, and ruined the tender moment.

'Daaaad!' she wailed. 'Jack just peed all over my new Bratz DVD!'

8 September

Mrs H called round. 'I have some big news for you, Susie,' she said, looking delighted with herself.

'What's that?' I asked, doubting it was true. Unless you'd stop the presses for a five-euro win at the bingo leagues, that is.

'David's coming for a weekend visit next month!' Her eyes shone with excitement.

'That's great,' I said, wondering why Second Son David was paying her a flying visit – usually he only came home from London for Christmas.

'Yes, it is, but there's a lot of work to be done,' she said solemnly, biting into a mini-muffin and whipping her to-do list from her pleather handbag. 'I'll have to get the entire house wallpapered from top to bottom.'

'Do you really think that's necessary?' I said. 'I'm sure he wouldn't want you to go to any trouble.'

'Oh, it won't be any trouble,' she said. 'Sure isn't your Joe very good with his hands – he'll be able to do the lot in no time. Anyway, I don't want to disappoint David. He's very up on his interior design, always glued to those home-improvement shows.'

She took another bite of muffin, plucked a paint chart from her handbag and smoothed it out on the table. 'And you'll never guess,' she whispered, glancing furtively over her shoulder, as if the entire country was eavesdropping on our conversation, 'he's bringing a friend with him. But it's top secret, so I really shouldn't tell you.'

She looked at me hopefully, obviously dying for me to beg her to spill the beans.

I perked up. This *was* news. 'A friend?'

'Yes, I can't say too much about it, but it's a famous celebrity.'

'Really?' I was intrigued. Celebrities were ten-a-penny, these days, it seemed.

'OK, then, if you insist on knowing,' she gushed excitedly, 'it's that weatherman from Toxic TV. You know, the really handsome fellow – he was in *Dancing on Waterskis* last year. Well, David's *very* good friends with him.'

Better friends than you probably know, I thought, wondering if David was ever going to admit to his mother that he was gay.

'By the way, you'll never guess who I met in Tesco this morning,' Mrs H went on. 'That Angelica What's-her-name. You know, the wife of that famous actor.'

'You met Angelica Law?' I was dumbfounded.

'Yes, and very nice she was too. She was in the biscuit aisle trying to decide whether to get the Jaffa Cakes or the chocolate Kimberley's. I told her that if she wanted a taste of the real Ireland she should go for the Kimberley's – you can't beat them with a nice cup of tea.'

I sucked in my breath, not believing what I was hearing.

'She was so grateful for the advice she offered me a lift home. Such a nice girl and very down-to-earth. Anyway, I must fly, dear. I have so much to do.'

She waddled off, her to-do list and paint chart under her arm.

PS Am furious Mrs H has somehow managed to befriend a real-life celebrity with so little effort. It's so unfair.

9 September

In a very bad mood. Spent ages just staring at the washing-machine and wondering whether I should try to regrout some of the kitchen tiles. Strongly suspect I may be suffering from empty-nest syndrome. Looked up tips for dealing with it on-line.

Apparently the trick is to allow only good, positive thoughts about how things will be now the children have gone from my life. (Well, from nine till lunchtime.)

From now on, I must remember:

• how happy I am that Katie and Jack are where they need to be to follow their dreams (i.e. in school, colouring, playing and, in Jack's case, beating up other kids);

• how good I feel about having the freedom to pursue dreams I've put on hold for a long time. (NB Must try to remember what my life's dreams actually were. Suspect that watching *Dr. Phil* and *Oprah* uninterrupted no longer counts. Anyway, they have lost their lustre now that I can watch them any time I like);

• what a great job I did raising the kids because now they feel good enough about themselves to spread their wings (and forget all about me).

Joe seemed to sense I was feeling depressed (mind you, that might have been because I called him on his mobile phone to ask him to get a generous selection of chocolate bars on his way home). 'What's wrong, Susie?' he asked, giving me a bear-hug when he came through the door. 'Is it because my mother met Angelica Law? Don't be upset – I'm sure you'll get to meet her soon.'

I explained to him that meeting Angelica Law was the least of my worries (well, OK, it was a top priority but I didn't think I should admit that to him just yet) and that I might be suffering from severe emotional trauma now that Katie and Jack were officially on the path towards adulthood. Soon the only time I would lay eyes on them was when they made duty visits to see me in a bleak nursing-home.

He was very sympathetic as I cried over my oven chips. (Then again, I was a bit unsure if his motives were genuine: I caught him blatantly eyeing my battered cod as he comforted me.)

'You know what could be the perfect answer to all this?' he said softly, wrapping his arms round me as I snivelled into his shirt.

'What?' I snuggled up to his chest and hoped he was going to suggest a whirlwind trip to New York with a quick stop-off at Tiffany's to purchase something very expensive and OTT.

'Maybe we should think about having another baby. Then we could enjoy the early years all over again. Remember how cute Katie and Jack were when they were tiny?' He kissed the top of my head.

For a second, the thought of a sweet-smelling bundle of joy floated through my mind and I felt a definite pang, but then Katie leapt across the table and attacked Jack with the ketchup bottle and the moment was lost.

PS Louise has called twice and left tearful messages about leaking nipples and constipation. Am putting off calling her back – it's very draining trying to be emotionally supportive all the time. Wonder if I should try to track down her runaway ex, Steve, and inform him he'll have to help out more. (Must remember to highlight glowing aspects of impending motherhood and avoid mention of massive leaking boobs or enormous pregnancy-related piles.)

10 September

Things are taking a turn for the worse. Spent all morning crying that Katie and Jack no longer need me in their lives. Well, they do, but technically only to make peanut-butter sandwiches with no crusts and to chuck a couple of Cheese Strings into their lunchboxes.

Emailed Mum to ask how she'd coped with empty-nest syndrome when I'd gone to school. Got one back a few hours later.

> You've given them a great start, Susie. You've devoted years of yourself to them, and now you need to do something for you. But please don't flirt with any unsuitable men this time round –

adultery is not the answer to an empty life. Find
something that fulfils you and commit to it.
  Mum xx

Was a bit cross she had mentioned flirting with unsuitable
men. Why does everyone have to bring up Lone Father
every five minutes? We barely kissed, for God's sake. It's
not as if I had rampant sex with him in as many unusual
positions as we could muster. (Although I did think about
it, I suppose.) Anyway, I've decided to take Mum's advice
and try to find something that fulfils me. The thrill of
sucking the jam from Jammie Dodgers without breaking the
biscuit just doesn't last.

PS Just thought – maybe I should go back to education.
I could easily learn some Latin, or how to arrange a dazzling
display of begonias at very short notice.

11 September

Read extremely interesting article in *OK!* about celebrity
posture and what it can mean. Slumped, droopy shoulders
mean you are downtrodden and unhappy (and have the
added disadvantage of adding five pounds to your frame).
Pert, pulled-back shoulders indicate all is well with the world,
you have a successful career and a good relationship. There
were lots of dead good photos of celebs looking dishevelled
beside other glowing A-listers with their chests stuck out,
beaming from ear to ear. Have decided I may need to re-
adjust my stance to achieve success. In fact, I may need to
get my spine realigned.

Mum thinks it's a great idea. 'You should take up yoga,'
she said, when I called to ask her advice about holding your

bum in and keeping your shoulders back. 'It does wonders for core strength.'

Suddenly I had a searing flashback to my last attempt to take up *t'ai chi* – when I'd found Lone Father and yoga-crone Marita snogging in the parish hall in their Lycra leotards. 'I think I'll stick to carrying a few books around on my head, Mum,' I said, hoping she wouldn't bring up that sorry episode. 'I don't have time for yoga.'

'You should make time,' she lectured. 'If you don't invest in your inner self, your inner self won't invest in you.'

Hung up, confused. Those self-help books have a lot to answer for.

PS In bizarre twist of fate, very interesting email popped into my inbox today asking if I wanted to be a fully qualified life coach. Think this could be the perfect solution to my malaise. If I become a hard-nosed, ruthless businesswoman (who, with kindness and compassion, advises others on ways to find fulfilment and happiness) I could work from home, be fulfilled and still watch *How Clean Is Your House?* in my spare time. It couldn't be more perfect. Have decided to send away for the information pack.

12 September

Katie no longer wants to attend full-time primary education. 'I hate school!' she screamed at the school gate this morning.

'Don't be silly, darling,' I said, trying to remain calm but feeling mortified. 'School's such fun!'

'No, it's *not*!' she roared, going a worrying blue colour. 'It's smelly and stupid and I *hate* it!'

'Hate it, hate it!' Jack shouted, jumping up and down,

thrilled he had a legitimate reason to yell at the top of his little lungs.

I laughed nervously, hoping none of the other mothers would notice Katie's tantrum and jump to the conclusion that she was an uncontrollable monster. 'You're very tired,' I said loudly, in case any of them was listening. 'That's why you're so upset. Or maybe you're getting a fever.'

I hunkered down to feel her forehead, which seemed suspiciously hot (but I think it might have been from the yelling and foot-stamping).

'If you go to school, Mummy will bring you to McDonald's for lunch,' I whispered, praying desperately that this little bribe would make her stop.

'OK,' she grumbled. 'But I only want fries and a burger. None of that yucky fruit or yoghurt stuff.'

'Is everything OK?' I suddenly heard another mother say in a concerned voice. I looked up, feeling hot and sweaty, and there, standing over me, was Angelica Law – glossy hair smoothed into a high ponytail, skin glowing with health and vitality, Juicy Couture tracksuit bottoms clinging provocatively to her minuscule hips. She looked exactly like she did at the Oscars last year – except thinner and even more beautiful. Her son stood beside her, gleaming from head to toe, as if he'd just stepped out of a Gap Kids commercial.

'Absolutely.' I fake-beamed, scrambling to my feet as Katie kicked my shin. 'I'm Susie, by the way.'

'Susie!' Angelica reached out, grasped my hand and pumped it energetically, as if she was really delighted to see me. 'Oh, my gosh! I'm *soooo* sorry about the other morning! I almost ran you over, didn't I? I was in *such* a hurry – you know how it is. I've been meaning to call you to apologize.'

'You have?' I could feel myself blushing with pleasure.

'Sure thing.' She smiled. 'So, you're Mrs H's daughter-in-law, right? She is *soooo* cute! Absolutely adorable. Hey, Brandon's having his birthday party soon – you guys just *have* to come!'

Then, before I could answer, she was off, bleached teeth glinting in the sunlight, ponytail swinging perkily as she went.

Am thrilled. Not only has Angelica expressed genuine concern for me, she has issued a personal invitation to Brandon's party – which is probably highly exclusive. Suddenly feel much brighter. The only blip on the horizon is that Louise has left four messages on my mobile phone about Lamaze classes. Think she's starting to suspect that I may have reservations about being her birth partner.

13 September

The literature for becoming a life coach arrived this morning. It looks very simple. All I have to do is study for two hours every morning while the children are at school and I will be fully qualified in less than sixteen weeks. I can then charge lost souls inordinate amounts of money for 'shaping their lives with a common-sense approach'.

Called Mum to tell her I'm on track to be a trailblazing entrepreneur. She was very pleased. 'That's fabulous, darling,' she said. 'Every woman needs a focus besides her family, and life coaching is a wonderful hobby.'

'But it's not a hobby, Mum,' I protested. 'This is going to be my new career.'

'If you want a career, why don't you go back into PR?' Mum asked, sounding confused.

Spent ages explaining how PR was so last-century, life

coaching was the hot new career of choice and that for once I was ahead of a global trend.

'Right.' She didn't sound convinced. 'Anyway, darling, how are Katie and Jack settling in at school?' Then she said something else, but there was so much noise in the background I couldn't make it out.

'What are you doing, Mum?' I bellowed. 'I can barely hear you it's so noisy.'

'That's the wind, darling,' she shouted. 'We're out on a friend's yacht – we've decided to take up sailing. It's terrific fun!'

'Well, I've become friends with Angelica Law!' I shouted over the static, wanting her to know she wasn't the only one with a glamorous life. But the line had gone dead.

Hung up feeling very hard-done-by. It's most inconsiderate of Mum and Dad to take up another challenging and exciting hobby at this stage in their lives when they should be here, sinking into old age and doting on their grandchildren, like normal grandparents. Maybe I could adopt a granny – someone vulnerable and easily manipulated into providing free babysitting would be perfect.

PS Joe brought home a bumper box of Cadbury's Roses choccies from work. Once the kids were in bed, we snuggled up on the couch together watching *Prison Break*, separating the strawberry creams from the orange slices and feeling really smug about our blissfully happy life. We've become so much more in tune since our recent blip. Which just goes to show that the ups and downs of a marriage only make you stronger as a couple. Maybe I should write to console Madonna – there have been lots of nasty rumours in the press that things are sometimes a bit rocky between her and Guy. I could give her a few tips. On second thoughts, when Angelica and I become bosom buddies and I gain entry to the élite golden circle, I can probably just have a tête-à-tête with Madge over tea and cupcakes.

14 September

Joe discovered that all there was for breakfast was out-of-date Coco Pops and a mouldy loaf of wholegrain bread that the kids refused to touch. (Even the dog turned it down.) For some reason he got quite upset about it. I tried to persuade him that the stale Coco Pops would be fine if he mashed them up with lots of milk, but he just stared at me sadly as if I was letting him and the children down with my lack of culinary skills. 'Did you not go shopping this week, Susie?' he said, shaking the Coco Pops packet and looking desperate.

'I'm trying to budget,' I said, not meeting his eye. 'I've been using the ends of everything in the cupboards to see how long we can last.' I obviously couldn't admit that I'm avoiding Tesco because of the irrational fear of bumping into Lone Father.

'Well, we may be at the end of the line,' he said, surveying the empty fridge. 'There's absolutely nothing left to eat.'

Was tempted to tell him that if we suddenly found ourselves under nuclear attack, we would have to live on tinned soup and stale crackers for weeks, but decided against it. Joe can be quite unreasonable when he's hungry.

Then, in a bolt from the blue, he went on to suggest that life coaching is overrated psychobabble rubbish and that it would be crazy to pay €799 for the correspondence course. (Luckily he didn't realize that the €799 was only for the first term.)

I immediately entered into an argument about him daring to stunt my emotional growth, etc., but privately I feel he may have had a point – the course does look like an awful lot of work, and I don't want to spread myself too thin. Also, I missed the *EastEnders* repeat yesterday because I was flicking through the brochure. Anyway, I almost feel as if I'm over the empty-nest thing now. I'll probably soon be too busy socializing with Angelica to have much time for anything else.

Just to make him feel guilty, I did a late-night run to Tesco after he got home from work. Twenty-four-hour opening is really very handy – especially as on-line shopping is out of the question: the computer is on the blink since Jack tried to feed the cordless mouse a jar of peanut butter. I pulled on a hat and dark glasses before I left, just in case Lone Father happened to be in the store by some freakish act of destiny.

'What are you wearing, Susie?' Joe called, as I crept out, trying to look inconspicuous.

'I'm just trying to keep warm,' I whispered. 'I think I have a bit of a cold – probably a lack of Vitamin C.'

'Right,' he said, seeming confused. 'Maybe you should buy some oranges – they're packed full of it.'

Spent ages wandering around the supermarket, reliving my clandestine meetings with Lone Father in the frozen-foods aisle. Then I loaded up with lots of special-offer mandarin oranges, in case Joe inspected the shopping-bags. Just as I was shoving some instant-cookie mixes underneath them, I spotted Eco-mother, my arch enemy from last year, striding purposefully towards me, wearing what resembled a hemp sack.

'Susie!' she called, as I tried to pretend I couldn't see her behind my dark glasses. 'How are you?'

'Fine,' I mumbled. The last time we'd met we had engaged in harsh words about caring for the elderly in the community.

And I may have fabricated some awful lie about Mum and Dad being disabled so I wouldn't have to volunteer for one of her hare-brained schemes to give something back to society.

'What are you doing here?' I said. 'I didn't think Tesco would be up your street.'

'Actually, Tesco does quite a good selection of organic produce,' she said, glancing over her shoulder in an oddly nervous way. 'How's Katie settling into formal education?'

'Great!' I said, hoping she wouldn't ask about Jack. 'And Zoë?'

'I'm home-schooling her,' she said. 'It's going brilliantly. We're on to next year's curriculum already. Children are like sponges – nurture them properly and they soak up so much.'

She grinned primly and I repressed the urge to hit her with my bag of cut-price mandarins.

Suddenly she gasped. 'Susie, I *do* hope you're not planning to feed that rubbish to the children. Those cookie mixes are packed with colouring and preservatives. Goodness knows what the long-term effects could be on their health.' She clutched my sleeve.

'What? These?' I said, fingering a packet. 'No, they're for the – er – dog.'

'Don't you think it's rather cruel to feed an innocent creature such processed junk?' she asked, even more appalled.

Thankfully, at that moment the store alarm went off and she reacted with such fright that I managed to slink away unnoticed.

PS Feel a lot more confident now I've braved that expedition. It's ridiculous to expect I'll run into Lone Father every time I go to Tesco. Anyway, he's probably way too busy having tantric sex with his muse Marita to be doing grocery shopping at night.

Worked up the courage to call Louise and discuss childbirth classes.

'I'm glad to hear from you, Susie,' she said, in an accusatory way. 'I was beginning to think you'd gone off the idea of being my birth partner.'

'Don't be silly,' I said, feeling guilty that I'd put off calling her for so long. 'It's just that I've been really busy, what with Katie starting school and Jack starting playschool. It's been non-stop.'

I didn't mention Angelica – I felt it might intimidate her to know I was hobnobbing with a very glamorous celebrity mom – one who had done a naked cover shoot for *Elle* when she was pregnant. Especially because poor Louise's bump is now so massive that a photographer would have to use a wide-angle lens to capture even half of it.

'OK.' She didn't seem happy. 'Anyway, the classes start soon. They cover all the basics – deep breathing, holistic massage and alternative pain-relief methods.'

'Great,' I answered, feeling a bit sick.

Hung up vowing to work on getting through to Louise that deep breathing and visualization will be useless when she's in the agonizing throes of labour. Unless you're deep-breathing in a tank of happy gas or visualizing a handsome ob-gyn injecting you with double-strength pain relief.

PS Maybe I should order a birthing tape to show her how horrific and excruciatingly painful the whole process is actually going to be.

PPS Wonder what the alternative to an epidural could be. Maybe some over-the-counter painkillers would work. There was a really interesting exposé on TV recently about how they stuff innocent-sounding painkillers with extra-strength narcotics so they're even more addictive than heroin. Sounds ideal.

16 September

Mrs H called at eight a.m. 'Susie, I'm suffering with my gout again. I need a lift to the supermarket,' she announced.

'Right now?' I asked, digging Joe in the ribs to alert him that his mother needed his assistance. It was his duty, not mine, to tolerate a morning's shopping with her.

'Well, they don't open until nine, but I like to be there early. That way you can make sure the staff don't urinate over the lettuce.'

'What?' I said, sure I must have misheard her.

'Oh, yes, dear, it's a known fact that supermarket staff regularly wee all over the fresh produce. They get some kind of sick kick out of it. Apparently, it's even better than snorting that Charlie stuff.'

'OK. Well, Joe will be over in a bit to pick you up,' I mumbled, giving Joe another dig and making a mental note to get him to talk to his mother about her unhealthy addiction to *Horrors Caught on Camera*.

'Oh, no, dear, it has to be you,' she whispered. 'I need to get a few feminine-hygiene products and I couldn't possibly do that if Joe was with me. Now, if you can't make it I'm sure that nice Angelica Law could come and get me – she gave me her mobile number and told me I could call any time if I needed anything. *Such* a kind girl.'

Couldn't be sure, but felt an implied threat in the air.

I told her I'd be there in ten minutes and hung up. Was absolutely determined to get more information on Angelica

Law. Was also intrigued – what feminine-hygiene products could she have been talking about? She'd had the menopause at least ten years ago. I knew that because she'd used excessive amounts of Yardley talcum powder to disguise every hot flush.

Braved Tesco with Mrs H, even though I was nervous about bumping into Lone Father in broad daylight and him creating some sort of dramatic scene beside the broccoli. Was quite glad I did, though, as I discovered that Mrs H classes hair-removal strips and deodorant as illicit feminine-hygiene products.

'I like to keep myself neat and tidy,' she said, as she whipped a packet of waxing strips and a bottle of Tropical Mist spray off the shelf and into her basket, then covered them with a large cauliflower.

'I have to hand it to you, Mrs H,' I said, in admiration. 'Even I don't bother with my legs or bikini line much these days.'

'Oh, no, dear, no one has seen my legs in decades,' she replied. 'And Mr H, God rest him, never saw *down there*. No, these are for my upper lip. That busybody Mary Murphy has been making snide remarks about someone looking like Adolf Hitler all week at bingo. This'll shut her up. And just *wait* till I tell her that David's bringing a real-life celebrity home for a long weekend. She'll be sick so she will.'

'Right,' I said.

'Yes, he'll be here before we know it, so we'll have to get cracking soon,' she said, as she stopped to look at the hair-highlighting kits.

I didn't get a chance to ask her what she meant – was sidetracked by a charming lady in a white hat and coat handing out delicious free mini-sausages on sticks.

Second Son David called from London. 'Susie, what has Mum told you about Max?' he asked abruptly, not even saying hello.

'Em, that he's a friend?' I said. 'Are you OK? You sound a bit out of breath.'

'I'm fine,' he gasped. 'I've just been warming up to my Abba CD. I'm trying out for a West End production this afternoon and it's crucial to limber up first.'

'OK,' I said, deciding not to ask any more. David had auditioned for a million West End productions and never been offered a part – mostly because he hadn't a musical bone in his podgy body.

'So, you don't think she knows about me, then?' he huffed.

'That you're gay?' I laughed. 'She'll never figure that out – not unless you wear your leotard and leg-warmers next time. Mind you, you'd probably have to add a tutu – just to drive it home for her.'

'Very funny.' David sounded glum. 'This is serious, Susie. Max is really important to me, *really* important. I think he might be The One.'

'Wow!' I was impressed. David had never been serious about anyone before.

'Yes – so I'd appreciate it if you'd take care of him when we come home to visit.'

'Sure,' I said. 'But, David, don't you think it's time to tell your mother you're gay? I mean, you *are* thirty-five.'

'I just keep hoping she'll work it out for herself.' He sighed. 'I don't want a big scene. You know me – I can't handle drama.'

He hung up before I had the chance to ask him if he was going to bring back the Disney DVDs he'd borrowed last year. Can't say I'm hopeful of a happy outcome. Mrs H wouldn't believe David was gay if the Pope put in a special appearance and broke the news to her himself.

18 September

Katie brought home Brandon Law's birthday invitation. According to a handwritten note on the embossed cream card, he's having a clambake fiesta at his house. Not sure what that is exactly, but it sounds exotic and, even more important, very exclusive.

'That's great, Katie,' I said, when she reluctantly fished the invitation out from the bottom of her schoolbag, stuck to a half-eaten peanut-butter sandwich. 'You'll have such fun at the party.'

'It's a stupid party,' she sulked, 'I don't want to go.'

'Why not?' I asked, scanning the card to see if parents were invited too.

'Because Brandon was born in America and his dad is *famous*. He's always talking about it. *And* he's been to Disneyland a million times. We haven't even been *once*.' She glared at me.

'Well, we have a holiday home in the country,' I countered, wanting to boost her self-confidence and give her something interesting to talk about in the playground.

'The country is *stupid*,' she replied, throwing me a withering look. 'Brandon has a holiday home in *Hollywood* – he even knows Hannah Montana.'

Spent the rest of the afternoon trying to convince Katie that going to the party was a fantastic idea – I absolutely cannot miss the opportunity to mingle with Angelica, her famous-actor hubby and their coterie of celebrity friends. It's vital to impress them all. If I do, we may well be invited to LA for half-term. Which would show Mum and Dad that Portugal isn't all that special and that when they get round to inviting us to stay we may be otherwise occupied.

Told Joe I was a bit concerned about Katie's unnerving antisocial behaviour. He thinks there's nothing to worry about. 'She's adjusting to the new routine, Susie,' he said, from behind the *Irish Times*. 'I'm sure you're finding it hard to adjust yourself.'

Not sure what he meant. Suspect he may have been referring to the fact that he has had to iron his own shirts for weeks now. Decided not to ask just in case.

19 September

Went to the first Lamaze class with Louise. I was a little bit nervous that everyone would think we were a lesbian couple who had used a turkey-baster to get Louise up the duff, but no one batted an eyelid, which goes to show how cosmopolitan Dublin is, these days. It's probably quite trendy to take your VBF to birthing classes when her partner has absconded without leaving so much as a forwarding address or other contact details. (Or a DNA profile.)

Gave Louise a comforting pep talk about not being self-conscious just because she's unmarried and a single-parent-to-be, etc., etc. If Ginger Spice Geri can do it, so can Louise. (Although I will advise her not to choose a really outlandish baby name – unless it's guaranteed to snag her an at-home photo spread of the newborn, of course.)

Louise didn't seem impressed with the pep talk so I cut it short. She was definitely nervous even though she was pretending to be tough and fierce.

The Lamaze instructor was calm and spoke in a breathy, gentle voice, obviously to offset any tendency towards hysteria among the expectant mothers. It was a bit disconcerting, though, the way she kept swooping round the room waving her hands and looking meaningful.

'Did you know that a woman's inner wisdom can guide her through birth?' she asked, gazing at me in a really intense (and unnerving) way.

'Em, no, I didn't,' I mumbled, trying to hide behind Louise – which was quite easy because she's so excessively large now.

'Oh, yes, it can,' she went on, in a hypnotic sing-song voice. 'Women are controllers of their own destiny.'

I wasn't too sure about that – what about corporate glass ceilings and centuries of oppression at the hands of men? Didn't say anything, though, as Louise was nodding vigorously.

'First, we will practise taking deep, cleansing breaths,' the instructor went on. 'Then we'll try rhythmic breathing, which maintains the kind of relaxation introduced centuries ago in eastern cultures.'

Was pretty sceptical. Modern medicine has advanced so much, why bother with all this centuries-old stuff? But I gave it a go and it was actually quite comforting, with the heavy-duty breathing and whatnot. In fact, I almost dropped off at one stage, until Louise suffered a panic-attack half-way through and had to sit with her head between her legs, puffing into a brown-paper bag.

'It's all right, Louise,' I crooned, trying to sound comforting and calming. 'Everything will be fine.'

'Oh, shut *up*, Susie,' she hissed, in a sudden fit of uncontrollable rage. 'Everything will *not* be all right. I'm pregnant, Steve doesn't want to know, and I have to raise this baby by myself. You have no idea how I feel.'

Caught the Lamaze instructor giving me a sympathetic look. She must be used to emotional outbursts.

PS Feel that if Louise cannot get through one simple Lamaze class without losing the plot, she has no hope of coping with a natural birth. Didn't tell her that, obviously. However, am very proud of my unruffled composure during the entire episode. Maybe I could retrain to be a professional birthing instructor instead of a life coach. After all, I've given birth twice already. It probably doesn't matter that I used excessive amounts of gas and air and had epidurals each time.

PPS Must ask Lamaze teacher more about that mystical inner wisdom next week. Think I could do with some of that to stop Jack throwing his toothbrush down the toilet every day.

20 *September: Brandon's birthday*

Dropped Katie at the birthday party/clam bake. Was a bit overawed when we pulled up outside a proper mansion-type establishment, with an immaculately groomed lawn and two perfectly pruned spruce trees on either side of the gate, but tried not to let it show. It is a well-known fact that young children are like dogs – they can sense fear at a hundred paces – and Katie was still reluctant to go. (In fact, I think the government should consider allowing young children to sniff for drugs and terrorist devices at the airport and other high-risk areas. Katie and Jack can locate a tube of sour-cream-and-chive Pringles in a heartbeat – I'm sure they could make a massive contribution to homeland security.)

Was greeted at the impossibly clean door, with a proper old-fashioned brass knocker polished to within an inch of its life, by Angelica herself. Was teeny bit disappointed not to see a real live butler in tails, but tried to hide it.

'*Heeeey*, Katie!' she twanged. 'Brandon will be *soooo* happy to see you!'

Katie scowled and kicked the ground with her toe.

'She's a little shy,' I said, nudging her through the door and hoping she wouldn't make a scene.

'I understand,' Angelica said, cocking her head to one side and looking instantly earnest and concerned – just like Bill Clinton, in fact. 'Brandon wasn't a good mixer either but we got him some extra coaching and he *really* improved.'

She beamed at me, revealing the most perfect set of choppers I'd seen since my LA trip last year. I immediately had nightmarish flashbacks of being holed up in a Beverly Hills hotel room with only 239 TV channels for company. I beamed back, unsure if she wanted me to give her a high-five or something.

'Are you all set for the party?' I asked, hoping she'd invite me in so that I could have a good nose round and maybe be introduced to a famous friend, like Bono or someone.

'Well, the caterers were late getting here,' she said, 'you know what it's like, but I think we'll be OK – at least the jugglers and clowns have arrived, right?'

Hearing this, Katie scampered off without a backward glance, leaving me standing alone on the doorstep.

'OK – I'd better get back in there and try to organize the chaos! See you later, Susie.' She closed the door without asking me in and I was forced to trudge back down the driveway alone. Can't be sure, but think I saw the Edge looking out of the window as I left.

PS Came to me in a blinding flash that Angelica's grass looked as if it had actually been *combed*. She must have live-in staff to cater to her every whim. Am more determined than ever to develop a deep and meaningful friendship with her.

21 September

Mrs H arrived at eight a.m., wearing a pair of tight canary-yellow dungarees she had obviously kept from the 1970s and waving some paintbrushes.

'It's painting-party day!' she chirped, whipping a roller and a jumbo bottle of turpentine from her holdall and presenting them to Katie and Jack with a flourish. 'Are you ready to go?'

'Oh, shit,' I heard Joe mutter.

'What's going on?' I asked.

'Didn't Joe tell you, dear?' Mrs H said, fondly tapping his cheek. 'You and the children are going to help me redecorate my house today – just in time for David's homecoming.'

'Is this a joke?' I glared at Joe, who stood, shamefaced, by the yucca plant. (NB Must remember to water it ASAP. Although suspect it may be too late and I may have to purchase new plant – something hardier, requiring less care. A cactus, maybe?)

'A joke? Decorating is no joking matter, dear,' Mrs H ploughed on. 'Painting parties are all the rage – all the best TV designers have them. Many hands make light work. Isn't that right, children?'

Katie and Jack looked dubious, sensing that actual physical work might be involved.

Spent rest of day at Mrs H's house, following her barking orders to strip, sand and paint anything within arm's reach.

'I really don't think David would want you to go to so much trouble,' I puffed, weary from slapping magnolia cream on everything and dying to get home for *American Idol*.

Mrs H narrowed her eyes as she adjusted her paint-spattered headscarf so that a stray hair was called to task. 'I don't think you realize quite how fashionable my David is, Susie dear. He had his colours done years ago.'

'What's his favourite? Pink?' I heard Joe mutter darkly from beneath a dust cover.

Mrs H decided to ignore the barb and stuck her brush into the turps once more. 'Yes, the place must be spick and span. We can't let the Irish down – I'd never forgive myself if things were less than perfect. Never.'

Didn't think the time was right to interrogate her about the true nature of Second Son David's relationship with the weatherman from Toxic TV. Besides, it will probably be much more fun to watch things play out.

PS Had strange dream in which I was covered with magnolia paint from head to toe and Lone Father was rubbing me down with the turps rag in a very seductive way. Am most alarmed that he is still lurking in my subconscious. Thought I had eradicated from my mind all thoughts of him and his come-to-bed eyes.

Katie's swimming lessons started again today. Am a bit worried that, after I've paid through the nose for professional coaching, she can't do much more than paddle from one side of the pool to the other with one foot on the bottom, waving her Barbie armbands about.

'Every child goes at his or her own pace, Mrs Hunt,' the instructor said, twirling his official-looking whistle and acting disinterested, just like Simon Cowell does when some no-hoper belts out 'My Way' out of key on *The X Factor*.

'Yes, but Katie's been attending the class for almost two years now,' I said. 'That little boy is new and he's in the deep end already.'

I pointed to a child diving into the water confidently and then flipping over to do back crawl across the pool.

'Ah yes, *Brandon*.' The instructor sighed. 'Well, he's a special case. He has talent. I fully expect him to be a Big Name in swimming in the future. A Very Big Name, in fact.'

Then I spotted Angelica Law sitting in the gallery, cheering energetically and madly waving an American flag as Brandon started the butterfly stroke, his little Speedo cap glistening under the chlorinated water. All the other parents stood watching, mouths open.

'Susie!' she called, when she spotted me. 'Come sit by me!'

Everyone turned and stared as I picked my way gingerly towards her, blushing furiously, like a lovestruck teenager.

'Who's she?' I heard someone ask, as I wobbled by.

'Maybe she's famous too,' another suggested, and they craned their necks to get a better look as I tottered past, trying to suck in my bum cheeks.

'Thank you *soooo* much for Brandon's cute birthday gift the other day,' Angelica sang, patting the seat beside her and indicating that I should sit. 'I'm real sorry I couldn't ask you in – James's agent was visiting and I had to supervise. Those boys can go a little overboard, if you know what I mean.' She giggled impishly and winked at me.

'So, Brandon likes to swim?' I said, watching as he did another back flip and shot through the water.

'Uh-huh, he had private coaching back in LA – they think he may make the Olympics some day, if he works hard enough.'

She frowned as her phone beeped. 'Sorry, Susie, I have to take this – James is having a bad day. You know how men are.' She raised her eyes to heaven knowingly.

Spent the rest of the lesson trying not to eavesdrop as she chatted to her famous husband but could hear James shouting that his new director was a wanker and that he'd walk off set if he didn't get a new trailer soon. It was so fascinating and I was so busy basking in Angelica's golden glow, smirking in a superior way at the other parents, that I even forgot how pathetic Katie's attempts at swimming were.

Had a huge row with Joe when I got home. He is refusing to train Katie and Jack to be Olympic swimming champions, or all-Ireland medallists at the very least. In fact, he refuses even to wear a tracksuit. Or a whistle. Which is a terrible start. It's bad enough that he wouldn't introduce American football to Ireland last year, but now he's scuppering the children's chances of being gold-medal swimmers. All it would involve is six a.m. training sessions for the next ten years or so.

'Why can't you be more sporty?' I fumed, munching a jumbo sausage roll and feeling really cross.

'I *am* sporty,' he said. 'I love football.'

'Watching Liverpool versus Manchester United on TV doesn't make you a sports hero,' I snapped.

'Well, I'm sportier than you,' he said, as I licked the last of the sausage roll off my greasy fingers. 'Unless eating counts as an Olympic sport, these days.'

PS Am furious Katie and Jack will never be Big Names in swimming and have to defend their good characters against baseless allegations of steroid abuse, etc. Their father is to blame. Also, how am I expected to participate in any kind of serious exercise training? I'm up to my eyes looking after two very demanding children and a dog.

PPS Think the dog has fleas. Caught him scratching frantically this afternoon. Am putting off going to the vet. Can't remember if I still owe for the last visit when Jack tried to tie Spiderman to the dog's back and he ended up with a prolapsed disc.

23 September

Louise called at eight fifteen a.m. 'We've forgotten to do a birth plan,' she squealed. 'You need to get on to it right away.'

'A birth plan?' I asked, wondering what the hell she was on about. 'There's no real planning, Louise,' I ventured. 'Usually you just go into labour, push and shove and the baby arrives.'

'No, Susie!' she screeched. 'You need to make a list of my preferences for the labour ward. We *spoke* about this.'

'We did?' My mind was blank.

'Yes. I'll email you my list. And don't forget the Lamaze class tomorrow night.'

She hung up abruptly.

Received Louise's email. Discovered that, as well as a medication-free birth, she apparently wants a five-star delivery suite with

- Low lighting. (Jack's Thomas the Tank Engine lamp will probably be unacceptable – must double-check)

- A compilation CD of calming, soulful music. (NB *Greatest Pop Hits* may be inappropriate – perhaps substitute with whale sounds?)

- A trained hypnotist on hand to help cope with contractions. (NB Check *Yellow Pages* – do not book magician by mistake)

- A TENS machine. (NB Must find out what this is)

- Round the clock massage – suspect I may be expected to provide this

- Gas and air – for use as a last resort.

Called her back to ask what she needed the CD for – it's not like she's going to be in the mood for boogieing her way through crippling contractions.

'It's to keep me calm and focused,' she said. 'All you have to do is put my favourite music on a disk and have it ready to play when I'm dilating. I probably won't even need a TENS machine if you get the mix right.' She hung up, making some excuse about a crucial presentation and the CEO.

Am at my wit's end. This sort of thing is most definitely not included in the birth-partner job description. Feeding ice chips is *de rigueur*, but setting up a mixing deck and sound system is just asking too much. Feel very shaky. Have no idea how I'll manage to meet Louise's unrealistically high standards of perfection without cracking.

PS Have been getting heart palpitations all afternoon. Am putting this down to the fact that I'm frantic I'll compile a CD of music Louise hates. Spent ages trying to remember acts she likes but couldn't think of one band, except Salt 'n' Pepa from the eighties. And I'm not sure if 'Push It' is an appropriate track to play.

PPS Have broken out in unattractive boils on my chin. Think it may be severe physiological reaction to internal stress and turmoil. Or some kind of allergic reaction to the instant-cookie mix I shared with the dog last night.

24 September

Went to second Lamaze class with Louise.

Was quite looking forward to it – it had been very entertaining last week, what with all the huffing and puffing and touchy-feely conversations, etc. In fact, the only disappointment had been the fruit plate at break. Surely expectant mothers and their life/birthing partners need something more substantial to sustain them. Like blueberry muffins, for example.

Filled Louise in on my fledgling friendship with Angelica on the way there but she didn't say much – think she was a bit annoyed I'd been late picking her up. (As if *I* am personally responsible for *Lost* running over time.)

The room was darkened when we got there so I was all set for lots of lounging around in the candlelight and a spot of aromatherapy massage but instead a video projector jumped into life.

'What's going on?' I whispered, to a couple at the refreshments table as I watched Louise try to lower herself on to an enormous floor cushion. (She's quite ungainly now – it took her three attempts to sit down.)

'It's a birthing video,' they whispered, looking excited. Well, the woman looked excited, the man was glassy-eyed and white with terror.

I settled back to watch and remind myself of the miracle of birth, etc., etc. In my pocket I had a half-eaten packet of cheese and onion crisps that Katie hadn't finished, so I munched them quietly under cover of darkness, delighted that Louise couldn't see me so I didn't have to share. She doesn't seem to understand that eating for two does not extend to other people's food as well.

Was happily enjoying my crisps while watching the spectacle of panting and squealing in the delivery room when, as I was licking the packet to get all the little crumbly bits, the camera zoomed right in to the woman's *private area* and did a close-up shot of the baby *coming out.* Then the midwife was tugging at something, until what looked like an enormous piece of lamb's liver followed.

'What's that?' the man to one side of me squeaked, in a very high-pitched voice.

'The afterbirth,' his wife breathed.

There was a stunned silence, until one couple started a slow clap and everyone joined in.

I turned to comfort Louise, sure she would be inconsolable after the graphic detail. Sure enough, she was sobbing into her limited-edition Chloé handbag.

'I can't believe it, Susie,' she gasped, tears falling down her puffy face.

'I know, Lou,' I said, feeling very weak and woozy. 'It's not a pleasant sight.'

'That's going to be us in a few months!' she went on, a wide smile spreading across her face. 'I'm so *happyyyy*.'

Then she dissolved into floods of noisy tears while I clutched a cushion and tried not to throw up. Suddenly it dawned on me that while I had given birth to two children I had never seen any of the gory detail. Katie and Jack were handed to me after they'd been given a good wipe. No wonder they edit the gore out of *Portland Babies*. Am seeing Joe in a whole new light. After all that, it's a miracle he ever wanted to have sex again.

PS Still feeling very sick. In fact, may well consider suing Lamaze instructor for post-traumatic stress disorder. Also, am consumed with panic that the doctor may ask me if I want to cut the umbilical cord of Louise's baby. What if the scissors slip in my hand and I end up slicing off a body part? Or, worse, give it an outie belly-button? And I definitely don't want to see that gross afterbirth stuff. Have decided that the only way forward is to hire a private investigator to track down Louise's ex, Steve – he'll have to step into the breach and be her birth partner. I don't think I'm up to the job.

25 September

Spent the morning wading through ads for detective agencies in the *Yellow Pages*. Eventually decided on one agency, mostly because it was called Magnum Investigations and the guy in the ad looked like Tom Selleck back in the 1980s, complete with bushy moustache and bright Hawaiian shirt.

Shaking with nerves, I called and explained the situation as best as I could.

'So, you want him *done*, is that what you're sayin'?' Magnum asked excitedly, in an American accent, once I'd told him the whole story.

'Um, what do you mean?' I asked.

'You know, taken care of. This guy ran out on his broad – he deserves it, right?'

I could hear him chewing gum at the other end of the line. 'Em, no, I just want you to find him for me. Then I can go and talk to him,' I said, even more nervous. Was this guy for real?

'You're sure?' Magnum sounded disappointed. 'It doesn't cost much more.'

'I'm positive.' My hands were sweating. 'So, do you think you can track him down?'

'Sure.' Magnum sounded bored now. 'All I need is his name and I'm on the case.'

I gave him the limited information I had – name, last-known place of work – and he told me he'd be back to me in a few days. I hung up, feeling a bit scared. What if Magnum lost the run of himself and assassinated Steve accidentally on purpose just for kicks? He'd sounded like he was perfectly capable of it – in fact, he'd sounded like he wanted to give it a go.

A few minutes later Louise called to ask what I thought the normal weight gain was for this stage in her pregnancy.

'Em, twenty pounds?' I guessed, trying desperately to remember the right answer.

'Yes, you're right.' She sobbed. 'But I've gained forty-five already! What am I going to *doooo*, Susie? I feel like a great big fat BLOB!'

I spent ages telling her she didn't look like a big fat blob and that most of the weight was amniotic fluid and water retention. Did an excellent job – she seemed to believe me. No point telling her that her pelvic floor is now shot and that her hips will never be the same again. Or that she looks like the back of a bus from every angle.

Also decided it was not the time to mention that I have a private investigator looking for Steve. Much better to keep her in the dark until I can talk to Steve and persuade him to become involved. Then I can present her with the PI bill and retire to be supportive from a distance.

26 September

Second Son David called to ask me to pick him up next week. 'I don't want Mum making a song and dance,' he said. 'The last time she came to the airport she brought out an enormous welcome banner – it was really embarrassing – everyone knew I was only flying in from Heathrow.'

'I don't know how I'm going to persuade her, David,' I said. 'She does love to make a fuss.' Immediately had vivid flashback of the time she welcomed Joe and me back from our honeymoon with a brass band.

'Please, Susie,' he begged. 'Max is very sophisticated. He wouldn't understand her ways and I really want to impress him.'

Promised to do my best but am filled with a sense of doom. If Max is so sophisticated, he'll never understand Mrs H's decision to hang on to candlewick bedspreads she's had since the 1970s. Or her creepy obsession with Barry Manilow memorabilia.

27 September

Angelica Law is on the cover of *TV Ireland Today!*. I spent all morning reading about how she's settling into Irish life. 'Everyone has made me feel so welcome,' she said, in an obvious reference to our new-found friendship. 'We feel like we've always been here.'

There were a dozen photos of her lying in various positions round her living room and across her baby-grand piano. Spent ages fantasizing that I could be in the next photo spread as her favourite gal-pal.

Fantasy was rudely interrupted when Louise called to say she wants to bury her placenta in the back garden and plant a rosebush over it.

'What?' I gasped, feeling instantly faint.

'Yes. Do you know that some people like to eat theirs because it's so nutritious? But I'd like to bury mine – it's meant to be a very sacred thing. Do you think the hospital will let me take it home?'

I didn't trust myself to say anything. Am kind of hoping I can develop some mystery illness, preferably before Louise's due date. Unless the PI tracks down Steve soon, it's the only way I'm going to get off the hook.

28 September

Had horrible nightmare last night. Walked in on Louise peeling onions with a Jamie Oliver limited-edition kitchen knife, then tossing them into a sizzling pan with her placenta. 'Nutritious and delicious,' she kept singing, over and over again, as she rocked her baby back and forth, and I tried to escape by clawing with my bare hands at a blocked-up window.

Called PI at nine a.m. for an update.

'This guy's pretty tricky to track down,' he drawled. 'He covers his trail real good, if you catch my drift.'

'What does that mean?' I asked, hoping he'd start talking normally soon. It was really tiring trying to decipher the *Magnum, PI* speak.

'It means, doll-face,' he went on, snapping chewing-gum, 'that he's a player. I need more time.'

'More time? How much more time?' My stomach did a little flip of unease.

'Hard to tell. I'm hot on the trail, though, so it shouldn't be too long.'

He hung up.

Am a bit nervous. This guy charges by the day so the longer it takes him to track Steve down the more it's going to cost. I'm trying to put that from my mind, though – Louise has a great savings plan: what better way to spend it than on tracking down the father of her baby?

PS Watched a very interesting piece on *Oprah* this morning about saving your marriage once the kids are born. A selection of self-satisfied authors spent ages explaining how a couple's happy union can steer into very dangerous territory once children enter the picture. 'You may forget to behave in a romantic and thoughtful way,' one said, smiling into the camera and looking utterly gorgeous while Oprah nodded.

'Before the kids came along you'd cuddle up together on the sofa and watch TV together, but now you sit in chairs at opposite ends of the room and fight over the remote control. Am I right?'

Everyone in the audience clapped wildly as if they'd all had the exact same problem.

'You need to reconnect,' she went on. 'Get off the chair, snuggle up with your partner, hold hands, remember what it felt like to be romantic with each other – even if it's only for five or ten minutes. The effort will pay off.'

Am thrilled that Joe and I are apparently still acting like newly-weds and that lying about on the sofa eating chocolate and watching *Grey's Anatomy* is a sure-fire way to reach our fiftieth wedding anniversary.

PPS Just thought – maybe I should write my own guide to marriage after children. It could be an award-winning bestseller. Maybe then *The Gerry Ryan Show* would take my calls.

29 September

Angelica has asked me for coffee! I knew it was only a matter of time before we really hit it off. Granted, there's no set date or location, but the signs are good that I'm sure to become her confidante soon.

'We must do coffee, Susie!' she called gaily, as she jumped nimbly into her Range Rover Sport at the school gate. 'Call me!'

She held an imaginary phone to her ear, then took off at speed before I had a chance to ask for her number. But, still, it's progress. Could see some of the other mothers looking at me enviously but pretended not to notice. It's very important not to act superior when you're the Chosen One. It will be soon enough to lord it over them when I become Angelica's closest gal-pal and learn the deepest, darkest secrets about the ins and outs of her marriage to her famous-actor husband.

That afternoon, I found myself bragging to another

mother at the school gate that I was going to have coffee with Angelica Law soon.

'Do you mean her charity coffee morning?' she asked, smirking.

'What charity coffee morning?' I was puzzled.

'The one she's holding to raise funds for the children's hospital. It's such a worthy cause – she told me about it when she dropped Brandon to mine last week. It's strange you haven't had your invite yet. Everyone else has . . .' She trailed off, letting me put it together.

'Oh, *that* coffee morning,' I bluffed. 'No, not *that*. This is a personal invitation. You know, just the two of us.'

I stalked away, trying to hold my head high. Am sure it was an oversight on Angelica's part not to invite me to her charity do. I'll have to remind her about it next time we meet.

PS Dad called to ask if I'd remembered to deadhead the roses at the country house. Didn't want to admit that we haven't been back since the end of the summer, or that I have no idea what deadheading roses involves. How can I be expected to juggle all these balls in the air at once? It's not humanly possible.

30 September

Louise called to ask my expert opinion about breastfeeding. 'Why do you want to know?' I said.

'Well, it's vital to breastfeed to build up the baby's immunity, obviously. I've been reading all about it – the research is really compelling.'

'Well, I know nothing about breastfeeding,' I admitted cheerfully. 'I bottle-fed my two – Jack still loves his.' I looked fondly at him. He was happily sucking a half-empty bottle of juice as he lay watching *Bob the Builder*.

There was a cold silence.

'I do hope you're joking, Susie,' Louise said icily.

'No, I'm not. What's the matter?' I was worried she was about to announce that bottle-fed babies were at risk of developing serious psychological problems in later life.

'Everyone knows breast is best, Susie,' she went on. 'That wasn't really fair to Katie or Jack, was it?'

Decided to say I had to rush to the loo so I wouldn't have to answer. 'Weak bladder,' I explained. 'You'll know all about it in a few months' time.'

'I doubt it,' she answered. 'I'm up to a thousand kegel exercises a day. My pelvic floor has never been stronger.'

PS Am quite shocked that Louise, of all people, would even consider breastfeeding, what with the leaking and sagging bosoms it involves. Wonder if she knows she will quite possibly never again fit into a La Perla lace set. Maybe I should tell her.

1 October

This morning I caught Joe scrolling through the texts on my mobile phone. Luckily I had been forced to burst in on him in the bathroom to get my Clinique tinted moisturizer or I'd never have known about his deceit.

'What are you doing?' I asked, aghast that he appeared not to trust me.

'Em, just looking for a phone number,' he stammered, shamefaced and guilty.

I knew instantly that he was lying. 'It doesn't look like that to me,' I said, snatching the phone and dangling it between my thumb and forefinger so I could give it a good clean with a handy Dettox wipe before I used it again. Then I stalked out of the bathroom, leaving him looking mournful on the toilet seat, his trousers round his ankles.

Am suddenly worried that Joe feels the need to check up on me. Am also very annoyed. Just because I almost had an adulterous affair with Lone Father and exchanged some (OK, lots of) sex texts with him, he has no right to violate my personal property.

PS Scrolled through all my old texts to see what Joe could have been reading and found one solitary message from Lone Father from when we were in the throes of our passionate flirtation.

It said: *C u at playgroup.*

Luckily I no longer harbour any feelings for him or I would have been quite upset.

PPS Have decided I should keep the text to remind myself that adultery is wrong in all circumstances and that I must never go down that road again, even if Joe insists on sitting on the toilet for unreasonable periods of time, then forgets to spray the lavender room-deodorizer.

2 October

Last Lamaze class with Louise. Am very relieved. Don't think I can take the pressure of being supportive and kind any longer. Had another horrible dream last night. Louise was in the throes of labour, squealing in agony, while I tried desperately to find her favourite Billy Joel song. Then J-Lo burst through the double doors, waving what looked like a pair of pliers and talking about an emergency forceps delivery.

Clearly I'm in a high state of stress.

Skidded up to the class venue with seconds to spare, Louise huffing and puffing about being late again.

'This is excellent preparation in case you go into labour early and I have to make an emergency dash to the hospital,' I soothed, trying to judge whether I would be able to manoeuvre the people-carrier into a parallel-parking spot by the kerb.

'What do you mean "emergency dash"?' Louise squeaked.

'Don't worry,' I replied, patting her enormous puffy knee. 'First babies always take ages to come. You could be in labour for days. We'll have plenty of time.'

Shuffled into the hall to find everyone sitting cross-legged on the floor, looking scared. Not surprising after last week's distressing video.

'Tonight we'll concentrate on helping birth partners to be encouraging and supportive during labour,' the instructor said.

There were sighs of relief as everyone realized they wouldn't have to witness another actual birth.

I didn't think I needed much coaching in this area but I nodded sagely to show what a good and helpful student I was being.

'OK. So, what kind of supportive things could you say and do while your partner is experiencing labour pains?' she asked.

'You could massage her back and tell her she's doing a great job,' one husband piped up, pleased with himself.

'You could rub her forehead with a damp flannel and play some of her favourite music,' another offered.

I could feel Louise glaring at me, willing me to contribute, so I tried hard to think of something good to say. 'You could tell her that lots of women have children in unconventional circumstances and that it's nothing to be ashamed of,' I said, my voice booming oddly round the room.

The Lamaze instructor nodded vigorously. 'Yes, of course. Your relationship is just as valid as any other.'

All the other couples nodded and murmured their agreement. I could see Louise from the corner of my eye: she looked as if she was going to give birth at any second from the shock of realizing that everyone really did think we were lesbian lovers and *au fait* with all sorts of outrageous sexual antics involving turkey-basters.

'Em, yes,' I mumbled, trying to change the subject, 'and you could bring her something to nibble, a Toblerone, maybe?'

PS Think Louise is feeling down. We travelled home in silence and she got out of the car very quickly when I pulled up outside her house. Well, she tried to. It took her three or four attempts to haul herself out of the passenger door. Must think of some way to cheer her up. Lymphatic drainage to improve her knees' mottled appearance might work.

PPS Am teeny bit worried that we're supposedly officially ready for childbirth. Don't think our *Lamaze Rocks!* stickers will do us much good in the delivery suite.

3 October

Bumped into Angelica this morning. Well, I kind of hung round her Range Rover Sport until she came out of school, but still.

'Hi, Susie,' she called brightly, when she spotted me lurking by the boot. 'How *arrre* you?'

'I'm great, thanks,' I said cautiously, waiting for her to invite me to the charity coffee morning.

'I'm *sooo* glad I met you,' she continued. 'You're just the person I was looking for.'

'I am?' I was thrilled – she was going to ask me to help her organize it. As long as she didn't expect me to make anything, it'd be fabulous.

'Yes, I'm in a bit of a pickle. You see, I have an appointment this afternoon and Brandon's nanny is off.' She sighed. 'You couldn't take him for me, could you?' She batted her eyelashes at me.

'Of course I will!' I almost cheered. This was far better than a dime-a-dozen charity invite. Far, far better. Angelica Law, celebrity mom, was entrusting me with her only child – a child who was ripe for kidnapping. She obviously thought I was VBF material. Things couldn't have been going better.

'Thanks, Susie, you're a sweetheart.' She hugged me and I breathed in what was unmistakably very expensive perfume. Maybe even custom-made scent, exclusively designed for her by a team of perfumiers.

'Can you drop him back by six?' She pressed her mobile-phone number into my hand and then she was off, waving a perfectly manicured hand out of the tinted window.

4 October

Sped round to Louise's this morning to show her the photos I took of Angelica's house on my mobile phone. 'She insisted I came in when I dropped Brandon off,' I explained, showing her one of the downstairs toilet. 'I couldn't say no. She really is so nice, Louise. You'll love her.' I sat back and admired the shot I'd taken of the bidet.

'Well, she's certainly not shy, is she?' Louise said, raising an eyebrow.

'What do you mean?' I cradled my mobile, wondering if I should have grabbed some of the toilet roll as a keepsake.

'You barely know her and she's already asking you to mind her child. I think that's a bit rich.'

'Well, you see, that's how we mothers work,' I explained. 'We help each other out.' I was a bit annoyed. 'You'll see once you have your own baby.'

'Whatever you say,' Louise said. But I could tell she wasn't convinced.

PS David emailed me to make sure I wouldn't forget to collect him and his secret lover Max, the weatherman, tomorrow.

'Can you come in something other than the people-carrier?' he wrote.

'Sorry,' I replied. 'It's either that or your mother – take your pick.'

'OK, but can you at least clear the back seat of sweet wrappers? I ruined my Lagerfeld suede parka last time.'

Sometimes I wonder if I'm too kind for my own good.

5 October

Picked up David and weatherman Max.

'Yummy, yummy!' I whispered to David, as Max lagged behind us, dragging a large Prada suitcase. 'It really *is* raining men!'

'Shut up,' he hissed, but I could tell he was delighted.

Think I've fallen in love with Max. He is *gorgeous*. He has a perfectly chiselled jaw and a six-pack you can actually see through his clothes. *And* he's witty and a bit bitchy – the perfect package.

Mrs H seems to love him too, especially as he shares her

unnatural obsession with cleanliness in the home and spent ages admiring her dust-free surfaces and asking how she got the toilet bowl so sparkly.

'Ammonia and borax,' she declared, with a self-satisfied grin. 'The king and queen of the cleaning world.'

'Talking of queens . . .' Joe muttered in my ear, glaring at David as he spun Katie and Jack round his mother's front room to an Abba soundtrack.

I pulled Max into the kitchen to get the low-down, leaving Mrs H to fill David in on the bingo leagues.

'I was quite nervous about meeting his mother. David said she could be a little overbearing,' Max confessed, as we made another pot of tea. 'But she seems lovely – and so understanding of our situation. I think he may have exaggerated.'

I didn't want to tell him that Mrs H has no clue that there is any 'situation' and if she did she'd probably have a coronary on the spot. No point in upsetting the apple cart. Besides, by tomorrow we'll most likely be best friends and then I'll be able to tell him to run for his life.

6 October

Mrs H is in complete denial about David's sexuality. She now thinks his new habit of wearing a smoking jacket and a silk scarf in the house is an excellent way to avoid getting strep throat.

'Do you have a girlfriend, Max?' she asked, straight-faced, as we sat at the kitchen table, drinking from the best bone china she had taken down specially to impress him.

'Er, not exactly,' Max said, running his manicured fingers through his perfectly coiffed hair.

'Well, I don't know,' Mrs H joked, elbowing him roughly in the ribs so that he spluttered his tea over his Jermyn Street button-down shirt. 'All you young bachelors living the high life. You need a good woman to sort you out – isn't that right, Joe?'

'Actually, Mum, I don't think it is,' Joe said, glaring at his brother as if he could happily have murdered him. 'I think David has something to tell you, don't you, David?'

David looked as if he was going to throw up over the Aynsley tea set.

'Do you, love?' Mrs H smiled indulgently at David, then poured him a fresh cup of tea.

'Yes, Mum,' David stuttered. 'The thing is, I'm not going to get married – ever.'

There was silence as Mrs H processed this information. 'Well, love, I can see your point,' she said at last. 'Why get married when you can live in sin? Maybe you should have done that, Joe.' She glanced at me.

We all gasped. Living in sin had always been a complete no-no, guaranteed to get you a ticket straight to hell if you so much as thought about it.

'Don't be so shocked. I'm not as old-fashioned as you all think,' Mrs H went on, mopping up a stray crumb and giving the teapot a little polish. 'I can get down with the best of them, you know, Max,' she added.

'I'm sure you can, Mrs H.' Max smiled.

Then Joe put his head into his hands and groaned, and I decided to break the tension by showing everyone the photos of Angelica's downstairs toilet on my mobile phone. It's not every day that people get to see a real-life celebrity loo.

7 October

Drove David and Max to see Angelica's house on the way to the airport.

'Why don't we go in if you're such good friends with her?' David asked, as I edged past her mansion.

'That's not the way these things work,' I said, hoping Angelica wouldn't look out and recognize us. 'Surely you know that celebrities don't like to be disturbed out of the blue. You can't just drop in unannounced.'

'This is fab, Susie,' Max said. 'Just like a Hollywood tour!'

I beamed at him, delighted that at least someone appreciated my efforts.

'Can you get a shot of her hubby next time?' David whined. 'He's a honey.'

'What's a honey?' Katie asked.

'You'll find out when you're older.' David giggled, patting her head.

8 October

Only two weeks to Katie's birthday. Luckily we've had a frank exchange of ideas and I've managed to persuade her that parties at home are so last year and that taking a select number of classmates to a movie is a much more mature option.

'I think you're right, Mummy,' Katie said, pausing from brushing her Baby Bratz's hair to gaze enigmatically into the middle distance. 'And that would show Brandon, wouldn't it?'

I pretended not to know what she was talking about, but secretly I had to agree. A movie party is very 'now' and will be bound to impress Angelica. I'm so glad I thought of it.

Confided in Joe how proud I am of Katie's new maturity.

'Yes, she's getting so grown up,' he said, peculiarly misty-eyed. 'They grow so fast, don't they?'

'You're right,' I said, ruffling his hair. 'Before you know it, she'll be using hair-straighteners and snogging boys.'

Joe paled visibly. 'That's not funny, Susie,' he said. 'I'll kill any boy who comes near her with my two bare hands.'

Didn't like to tell him that boys were not the only worry. According to a feature in last week's *Gazette*, being a lesbian is now all the rage when you're a teenage girl.

9 October

Louise called at six forty a.m.

'What is it, Lou? You haven't gone into early labour, have you?' I muttered, half hoping the whole thing was already over and done with.

'No,' she said, in a weird, calm voice. 'I've changed my mind.'

'Really?' I said, trying to sound disappointed but delighted I would no longer have to partner her through a forty-eight-hour labour with no drugs involved. She must have decided she wanted the father of her child to be there instead. She'd be thrilled when I told her a PI was on the brink of finding him.

'I'm glad you understand, Susie,' she said. 'I thought you might be upset.'

'No, of course not,' I said, trying to keep the glee out of my voice. 'Tracking Steve down is absolutely the right thing to do.'

'What are you talking about?' Louise said. 'Why on earth would I track Steve down?'

'Well, you're going to need someone to be your birth partner, and if you've changed your mind about me, then who else will it be?' I was getting confused.

'No, Susie.' She sighed. 'You're still going to be my birth partner. I haven't changed my mind about that. I've changed my mind about keeping the baby. I'm going to give it up for adoption.'

10 October

Am still in shock that Louise has decided to give away her baby. Even to some worthy couple who'll dress it in adorable Baby Dior, give it a private jet and fly in P. Diddy for a concert on its sixteenth birthday, just like those spoilt brats on MTV's *My Super Sweet 16*.

'It's her decision, Susie,' Joe said, when I confided that she might regret this choice for the rest of her life.

'Yes, but I think she's making a huge mistake.' I sniffed into my toast. 'Children bring so much joy into your life, and she'll miss all that.'

I watched Katie and Jack wrestle each other on the kitchen floor for the last chocolate croissant and came over all emotional that Louise was denying herself the wonder and privilege of motherhood.

'Maybe she'll change her mind,' Joe offered. 'Pregnant women have been known to make rash decisions before.'

Suspect he was referring to the time I decided to become a vegan when I was expecting Katie. Little does he know it, but when Louise makes up her mind, there's no going back: if she resolved to be a vegan, she wouldn't be ravenously munching a roast beef and chocolate-spread roll three hours later.

Tried calling the PI for a progress update on finding Steve but I couldn't get through. Have decided to pay him a visit tomorrow – a face-to-face discussion is definitely needed. I have to make him understand that time is now of the essence. Steve may be the only person capable of making Louise see sense.

11 October

Drove to the PI's office this morning. At first, I thought I was lost – the building I found myself in front of was so dingy that there was no way a hot-shot PI, who was a dead ringer for Tom Selleck, would have offices there. I stood on the pavement, looking for a red Ferrari, checking and rechecking the address and then, just to make sure, I asked a shifty teenager standing outside smoking what looked like a cigar if I was in the right place.

'Who's askin'?' he said warily, in a thick Dublin accent, looking me up and down.

'Um, I am,' I said. 'Magnum is doing some work for me.' Was thrilled I was able to say that – it sounded really exciting and dangerous, just like a real-life episode of *Undercover Cops*.

'Is that right?' the teenager answered. 'Follow me so.'

He fished a key out of his polyester tracksuit pocket, opened the door and ushered me in before I had a chance to think about it.

'Are you the caretaker?' I called after him, feeling a bit nervous. What if he was a psycho? But he continued shuffling along the corridor until we came to a grimy door, which he pushed open and walked through.

'Susie, yeah?'

'That's right,' I said, gaping at the shambles before me. 'How do you know that?'

'It's written on your keyring. I wouldn't recommend that by the way. Makes you an easy target.'

I looked at my keys. He was right. There was my name in bright pink lettering on the keyring.

'I'm Magnum.'

'Sorry?' I spluttered. 'Are you having me on?'

'Why would you think that?' His eyes glinted across the desk.

'Well, you're nothing like the picture for one thing. And you're so . . . young.' I pointed at the poster of the handsome dude with the moustache that hung on the wall, with 'Magnum Investigations' scrawled underneath.

'I'm working undercover,' he said.

'But what about your accent?' I asked. 'The man I spoke to was an American.'

'I'm a master of disguise. I use the accent on the phone so people won't recognize me in the flesh. You have to be very careful in my line of work. Very, very careful.'

He pushed a mountain of files and empty crisps packets off a filthy chair and indicated that I should sit. I ignored him. Leaving ASAP was now a priority. There was no way my bottom was touching that grimy seat.

He shrugged his shoulders. 'Your case is interesting,' he said. '*Very* interesting. This Steve is quite a character.'

'What do you mean?' I asked, wondering how the hell I was going to get out of there and whether Magnum was a fantasist who was about to attack me and eat my liver for supper.

'Well, for one thing he's married.'

Then he deftly pulled out the chair for me and I sank into it.

Am at my wit's end. Turns out that Steve is

(a) married;

(b) already a father of three;

(c) living in a housing estate in suburbia;

(d) conducting a secret affair with his dentist.

Magnum gave me a file detailing Steve's comings and goings over the past few weeks. It included some unsavoury photographs of him and his dentist lover partaking in vigorous tonsil tennis.

'Why did it take so long to track him down though? It sounds like he didn't try to cover his tracks at all,' I said, feeling very foolish.

Magnum shifted in his seat. 'Well, the truth is, I was out of action for a while.'

'Really?' I asked, perking up a bit. Maybe he'd been caught in gunfire between rival drugs gangs, or someone had put out a hit on him and he'd had a narrow escape.

'Yeah, my wisdom tooth was giving me gyp so I had to go in and get it taken out. It's still very painful.' He winced.

'So, what you're saying,' I said, as it dawned on me that this teenager was a complete chancer, 'is that Steve *wasn't* tricky to find? That the only reason it's taken so long is that your mammy's been looking after you and your gammy tooth? That I could have just looked up his name in the phone book, gone over there and had a chat?'

'Um.' He was shamefaced. 'I suppose so, yeah.'

'And do you expect me to pay you for this, you genius?'

'I did the investigating,' he said stoutly. 'You have to pay me.'

'Not on your life, buddy,' I said, standing and pulling myself up to my full height. 'This was a complete swindle. You can sing for your money.'

'OK, OK.' He caved in resignedly. 'The truth is, I'm only starting in the game. The real Magnum was my uncle Mick. He got put away for extortion so he gave me the business – to take care of, like. That's him on the poster.'

'This is ridiculous.' I was walking out of the door.

'Tell you what, if you ever need another job done, come back to me, yeah? If your old man's having how's-your-father with a slapper, that kind of thing. We'll call it quits.'

'Right,' I said grimly, 'but I doubt you'll ever see me again. I'll do my own investigating from now on.'

I am so disappointed. It looks like there's no point in even approaching Steve to help Louise. It certainly doesn't seem as if he'd be interested in supporting her through labour, even though he might be familiar with gas and air from the dentist's surgery. And if he's already the father of three unruly brats he'll probably be delighted that Louise is giving the baby away. It's up to me now to convince her she shouldn't part with her child. At least I'm well equipped for dealing with all sorts of emotional emergencies. Being a full-time mother guarantees that.

13 October

I've decided to lure Louise to a secret location so we can discuss, in a calm and reasonable manner, her rash decision to put up her baby for adoption. Starbucks may be the ideal choice. Hopefully a double-chocolate-chip cookie and a decaff latte will lower her defences and I'll be able to make her see sense.

Made a list of points to persuade her that she would regret this decision for the rest of her life:

(a) Adoption is a noble choice for young mothers with no other option, not middle-aged women with an excellent career and a two-storey town-house in a desirable area.

(b) Angelina and Brad seem to have their hands full, so if she's hoping that they're planning to add an Irish child to their United Nations family and allow her to tag along with them as they traverse the globe, going to premières or saving rainforests, she may be in for disappointment.

(c) Nothing can replace the thrill of shopping for fab designer kiddie gear. Giving the baby up means missing out on that. (NB Do not mention breast pumps. *Do* mention amazing designer baby-changing bags, and limited-edition dummies.)

14 October

Got an email from David:

> Hi Susie,
> Thanks for the ride to the airport. Max and I had a little fight on the journey home – he accused me of pocketing all the samples of hand cream they gave out on the flight. As if! I would never use in-flight samples. They're so cheap and nasty. Anyway, we made up and things are going really well now. I took

him to see *Chicago* last week and he loved it so much I bought him a box set of West End show tunes for his birthday! It's so nice to have met someone who understands my passion for the arts. Hope all is well in dreary Dublin!

David xox

PS Have sent Katie hair-straighteners for her birthday – her mop was a bit unruly when we were there and, as you know, it's never too early to start grooming. Please hide it from Joe. xox.

Emailed him back:

Did you steal the Jo Malone hand cream I had in the glove compartment of the people-carrier? It seems to have gone missing and I know for a fact the dog didn't eat it this time.

Susie

15 October

Met Louise in Starbucks for a heart-to-heart.

'Louise, I think you're making a huge mistake,' I said, deciding there was no time to beat round the bush. She's so huge, I'm starting to think she may have got her dates wrong and be about to pop at any second.

'There's no point in trying to talk me out of it, Susie.' She stirred the third sachet of sugar into her decaff latte. 'I've made up my mind.'

'But why?' I asked, itching to remind her that gestational diabetes is rife, especially in pregnant women who put on twice the recommended weight, and that so much sugar was doing her no good whatsoever. 'You're an independent woman, you can go it alone. Loads of people do.'

'I just think that a baby needs a stable family background,' she said, tears filling her eyes. 'With two involved parents. Think about it. You have Joe to help you. I don't think I'd be able to cope on my own.'

I stirred my mocha latte thoughtfully. She had a point. Although surely a live-in nanny would be just as good. And there'd be no sulking if you weren't up for sex.

'I don't think you know how lucky you are, Susie,' she went on. 'Joe even forgave you for that affair.'

'It wasn't actually an affair, though.' I laughed nervously, hoping she wasn't going to lecture me at length. 'It's not as if we had mad, passionate sex.' An image of Lone Father and his piercing blue eyes flashed into my mind and I had to grip my mocha latte tightly to fight a strange urge to cry.

'Well, at least Joe's still in the picture. I could rear this baby on my own but, frankly, I don't want to. It would be better off with a proper family – and, let's face it, we can never be that – not with Steve already married.' A large tear plopped into her decaff.

'You know that he's married?' I gasped.

'Of course I do.' She sniffed. 'Why do you think we broke up? He already has three kids and doesn't want another. How do *you* know about it, though? I've been too scared to tell you the truth.'

I quickly pretended to choke on my mini-shortbread so I wouldn't have to divulge that I'd employed a PI to track Steve down. It worked a treat – Louise was so busy slapping me on the back that she seemed to forget all about it.

PS Am very worried that Louise may be a broken woman. Will have to come up with a new plan.

PPS Am also very worried that I can't seem to get an

image of Lone Father out of my mind, even though I know he's a good-for-nothing cad who never had any real feelings for me. Spent all afternoon fantasizing about his come-to-bed eyes and his sexy corduroy jacket. Finally resorted to tackling a pile of ironing to clear my mind and refocus my priorities.

PPPS Iron seems to be broken. Only managed to do three of Joe's shirts before it blew up in a hiss of steam. Have decided to buy Joe non-iron shirts from now on. At least that's his Christmas present sorted out early.

16 October

Mrs H popped in on her way back from Mass. I explained to her that Louise is considering giving up her baby to someone who can provide it with a more conventional family environment.

'Maybe you should try to fix her up with a nice man,' she said, sipping her tea. 'Our David could be perfect for her.'

Joe spat a mouthful of his tea across the table.

'What's wrong, dear?' Mrs H jumped in alarm. 'Do you need me to do the Heimlich manoeuvre?'

'No, I'm fine, Ma,' Joe said. 'It's just that I don't think Louise and David would be very well suited.'

'Why not?' Mrs H seemed disappointed that her first-aid training wouldn't be coming in handy any time soon. 'David's a very accepting person. I'm sure he wouldn't mind being father to another man's child. It's quite trendy nowadays.'

'I don't think the *baby* would be the problem, Mother,' Joe said sarcastically, chewing a slice of toast mutinously.

I kicked him under the table to stop him saying any more.

One emotional crisis on my hands was quite enough. Now was not the time to disclose David's sexual preferences. Especially when Mrs H has no idea that her second son dreams of donning a powdered white wig, full pancake makeup and a false beauty spot like Elton John did at his extravagant birthday bash a few years back.

PS Joe obviously has unresolved anger about his brother's secret sexual identity. Bit worrying.

PPS Caught Mrs H slipping Jack an age-inappropriate boiled sweet. Am convinced she's determined to try the Heimlich manoeuvre on someone.

17 October

Katie has announced she wants her entire class to attend her birthday movie treat. She went a very funny purple colour when I tried to reason with her that it would be irresponsible to take thirty children to see a Disney flick. For one thing, the cinema complex would need to increase their security staff from one spotty teenager in a baseball cap to at least ten burly security guards.

'You can invite five friends, Katie,' I said, as it dawned on me that she had misunderstood the implications of a pared-down event. 'That's a reasonable number.'

'I don't *want* a reasonable number,' she roared. 'I want everyone.'

I decided to defer to Joe. I didn't think I was adequately equipped with the necessary negotiating skills to deal with this conflict. I was also afraid I might climb down and destroy any shred of respect Katie had for me.

Joe calculated that it would cost an eye-watering five

hundred euro to bring Katie's classmates to the cinema and for fast food afterwards.

'Well, that's it, then,' I said, deciding he would have to break it to her. 'We simply can't afford it.'

'Hang on, Susie,' he said, fiddling with his calculator. 'She's only going to be five once. Let's throw caution to the wind and just do it.'

'But what about tough love?' I stuttered, not sure I was hearing properly. 'You always say I give in too easily and that I should stick to my guns.'

I was puzzled that he was moving the childcare goalposts, but I didn't want to say anything as I knew that taking the entire class to the movies could blow Angelica's clam bake fiesta out of the water.

'Well, maybe I'm mellowing.' He smiled, and my heart melted. 'I did get that big bonus for pulling off the LA deal.'

Hugged him tightly. I really am so lucky to have such a wonderful husband. Can only hope he's not suffering from some degenerative brain disease. Throwing caution to the wind isn't really his style.

PS Just had a brilliant idea! Louise should spend some more one-on-one time with Katie and Jack. It would persuade her that motherhood is full of joyful moments and is not just an endless round of wiping up vomit and trying to dislodge crayons from nasal cavities. I have decided to rope her in to help with Katie's party. She could do with getting out a bit more now that she's on maternity leave. Also, she's so huge that she may come in handy as a body-blocker if any of the kids tries to escape.

Mum and Dad have invited us to Portugal for half-term. Can't be sure but think they finally gave in when I mentioned our lack of plans for the millionth time.

I decided not to accept the invitation straight away – they couldn't expect us to drop everything and visit just because it suddenly suited them to ask us.

But then Dad called back to force me into a decision. 'If you don't want to come, we're going to invite the Glennons,' he announced briskly, on the answering-machine, 'so can you let us know by today, please?'

I really must get Mum to speak to Dad about his inappropriate emotional-blackmail tendencies. May have to threaten to disown him and his five-star villa if this sort of behaviour continues.

Did a quick check on web fares and discovered it was only going to cost us ninety-nine cents each to fly to Portugal (taxes not included, but they're bound to be minimal). I immediately called Mum to tell her we'd be accepting their invitation. She seemed pathetically pleased that we were coming. 'That's wonderful, darling,' she said. 'We can't wait to see you all.'

Suspect she may be very lonely in a strange country, surrounded by people who don't even know what real Irish tea is. Am glad we'll be there to give her emotional support – for a while, at least.

Joe is delighted we're getting away.

'It'll be nice to spend some quality time together,' he said, cuddling up behind me at the kitchen sink as I attempted to peel some potatoes without skinning my knuckles. 'Your parents can baby-sit and we can go out for meals alone together.'

I didn't like to break it to him that Mum and Dad seem to have elaborate social engagements every night of the week. Am not sure they'll be willing to forgo them so we can have a second honeymoon.

PS Have decided that living in the twenty-first century really is a privilege, what with all the fare wars driving down the cost of international travel and giving even ordinary people the chance to travel to far-flung destinations. Like Lagos. Wonder how I can get through to Katie and Jack that they're lucky to be living in an era of prosperity and commercial competition. Maybe I should buy a set of encyclopedias and not make fun of the door-to-door salesman next time he calls.

19 October

Thought I saw Lone Father and his lover/muse Marita in the street today. It was hard to tell as they were locked in what looked like a passionate embrace, but am sure it was them. It was definitely Lone Father's son, Rodney, circling them and whooping gleefully. I'd recognize his destructive, dysfunctional behaviour anywhere. Also, Marita was wearing her trademark hot-pink acrylic nail extensions. Could just make them out snaked through Lone Father's dark curls.

Think I went into shock afterwards because, before I knew it, I'd driven straight to the Centre where, in a freaky out-of-body experience, I walked robotically into Starbucks and heard myself ask for a chocolate-chip muffin with extra cream. Just as I bit into the muffin, I spotted a trim Oprah on the cover of the latest *O* on a nearby newsstand, mocking me. I could actually hear her lecturing me about eating my feelings as I munched. Anyway, I'm sure I did the right thing: sugar is good for shock

PS Louise called to ask about breast pads and leaky nipples. I let her twittering wash over me. All I could think of was Lone Father and the way he used to look at me when I wore my one and only push-up bra.

20 *October*

Had a terrible dream last night: Jamie Oliver was whipping up homemade pizza and organic fruit smoothies for dozens of children, who were happily smacking a *piñata* around his East End loft.

'Fast-food culture is at the root of society's slide into obesity, innit?' he shouted, putting the finishing touches to a magnificent three-tier birthday cake he had made with wholemeal flour and rosewater, while Katie greased a muffin tray and looked accusingly at me. 'You should bring the kids on a picnic for her birthday, mate,' he went on. 'Have a kick-about in the park, then feed them proper food, not ground up testicles and gristle.'

'But chicken nuggets have *real* chicken in them now,' I yelled in desperation. 'Haven't you seen the new ads?'

As Katie turned her back on me and the other kids advanced, twirling *piñata* sticks menacingly in their grubby little hands, I woke up and told Joe I was having second thoughts about the movie party.

'Please, Susie, let's just take them to the cinema,' he begged, when I suggested that maybe having a mermaids-and-pirates party at home wouldn't be complete and utter hell. 'Let's just spend the money.'

He looked so desperate that I gave in. After all, it wasn't as if Eco-mother would be there to condemn me and my bad lifestyle choices.

Gave Angelica Katie's birthday invitation at the school gate.

'Thanks, sweetie,' she gushed, jingling her car keys. 'Listen, can I ask you to help me out again? Brandon's nanny's away tomorrow and I have another appointment. You couldn't take him for the afternoon, could you? I would be, like, *sooo* grateful.' She took my hand and looked at me pleadingly.

'Of course,' I said. 'No problem.'

'Fabulous!' she said, air-kissing my cheek, then jumping into the Range Rover Sport before I could ask if she wanted to grab a skinny decaff (which is all she drinks, according to *TV Ireland Today!*). 'You're a doll, you really are.'

Am delighted Angelica now feels she can rely on me to step into the breach when she needs to. And I'm sure Louise won't mind if I have to put off baby shopping with her tomorrow. It's not as if she's due all that soon.

PS Katie's party invitations have caused quite a stir at school. I definitely heard a few mutterings about over-the-top displays, so I'm bang on track to impress everyone.

21 October

I have discovered that Brandon may have control issues. He spent all of yesterday afternoon putting Katie's books in alphabetical order.

'Wouldn't you like to play a game, Brandon?' I asked, as I watched him stack and restack them.

'No, thank you, Mrs Hunt,' he said politely, his face

scrunched in fevered concentration. 'I have to get this right first.'

Katie threw her eyes to heaven. 'I told you he was weird,' she said. 'You never listen to me.'

Felt really sorry for Brandon. Obviously the celeb life has affected him. It must be hard moving about so much – and I'm sure having paparazzi stalk you isn't much fun, even if it looks like it is.

Dropped him back to Angelica's at six – she answered the door looking a little flushed and out of breath.

'Is everything OK?' I asked, alarmed by her dishevelled appearance. 'You're not feeling unwell, are you?'

'What? No!' Beads of sweat shone on her forehead and her eyes were a bit glassy. 'Thanks so much for taking him – see you tomorrow.'

Then she grabbed Brandon, hauled him inside and shut the door before I could ask if he was coming to Katie's party. Was a little put out but am trying not to take it personally. She was probably coming down with flu and not up to socializing.

PS Katie's birthday tomorrow. Feel quite emotional that my baby's turning five. Also feel quite sick that have so far received twenty-nine RSVPs from her classmates confirming attendance. Strongly suspect that some of the mothers may be taking advantage of my kind nature. The only good news is that a virulent strain of bird flu is apparently making its way to Ireland. Am hoping it gets here by tomorrow and that at least half of Katie's friends will be in solitary confinement.

PPS Hope Louise doesn't get stuck in her cinema seat. Maybe I should call ahead and get them to double-check dimensions.

22 October: Katie's birthday

It was an inspired decision to take Louise to Katie's party. Not only did her hulking frame stop the boys escaping from their cinema seats and making a break for the popcorn counter, she also caused a sensation among the girls and kept them occupied throughout. Once the rumour mill got to work that she wasn't just fat, there was a real live baby in her tummy, they were enthralled. Which was really very handy as it stopped them rampaging up and down the aisles.

'That is *soooooo* cute,' they sang, gathering round her and taking turns to touch her belly.

Thought Louise would be delighted with the attention, but unfortunately she seemed a bit uncomfortable with the touching and the accompanying complicated questions.

Once the movie was over, we spent ages rounding up the children, doing a headcount, then frogmarching them to the burger joint, where some anti-war protesters were congregating. (Obviously to refuel before hitting the streets and reminding the world that they thought George Bush was the devil in a bespoke suit, etc., etc.)

I was getting ready to congratulate them on their good work when suddenly I heard a familiar voice call my name. I spun on my heel to see Eco-mother bearing down on me, her newly dreadlocked hair swinging in all directions.

'You ought to be ashamed of yourself, Susie Hunt,' she shouted. 'Haven't you seen *Supersize Me*? This den of evil is one of the conglomerates responsible for the plague of obesity in the Western world. Not to talk of slaughtering rainforests worldwide.'

'What are you doing?' I stuttered, as the children looked on agog.

'We're trying to raise awareness among the community that fast food is an evil assault on our souls, as well as our bodies and minds. Do you want to sell *your* soul for a double bacon cheeseburger? Do you?'

'She mightn't, but I sure as hell do.' Louise puffed herself out to her full pregnancy weight and stared evilly at Eco-mother. 'Now, I'd advise you to step aside or things will turn *really* ugly.'

Then, in a feat of pure brute force, Louise managed single-handedly to scrum the kids forward into the res-taurant, where a scared-looking spotty teenager was hiding behind the counter, terrified that the protesters were about to storm the place.

'Give me thirty kiddie meals and make it fast,' Louise said, as he quaked before her. 'Otherwise I might deliver on your floor.'

Really admire Louise and her forward thinking sometimes, even if she did eat all of her double bacon cheeseburger and most of mine. Think her maternal instinct kicked in a bit too – she only stole a handful of the kids' fries.

PS Brandon was a no-show – left a voicemail for Angelica in case the date had slipped her mind but she didn't call back. Suspect the flu has kicked in and she's too dehydrated to chat – which is exactly the problem with being a size zero: when you're laid low with a virus, you need a bit of body fat to fight the germs.

Booked flights to Portugal on-line. Total cost: €1499 including taxes, insurance and flight surcharges. Am scandalized. No wonder all the celebs have private jets – it's probably far cheaper than flying commercial. I may investigate leasing a share in a helicopter soon. Maybe Angelica would like to go halves. Will look into it.

Am afraid to inform Joe that the ninety-nine-cent flights were an elaborate con. Hope he's still feeling mellow – that may mean he won't go through the Visa bill with a permanent red marker this month and discover it's costing us a small fortune to go away for half-term.

Louise is not altogether pleased that we will be AWOL for a week in Portugal.

'What if I go into premature labour?' she whined, when I called to explain.

'Well, if you do, ring the hospital and get yourself admitted,' I said soothingly, trying not to antagonize her.

I didn't like to tell her that she'll probably be two weeks overdue and lucky to have the baby before Christmas – her nerves are clearly frayed already. She bleated on about breastfeeding and society's aversion to Mother Nature's honey for ages yesterday. She really is very irritable. Obviously the piles cream I recommended is doing no good.

PS Tesco is doing a special promotion on two-for-one depilatory creams. Found myself buying six tubes today just to get another six free. Not sure I'll have time to use them all before we go to Portugal, though. Maybe I can offload some on Mrs H.

24 October

Can no longer deny that Hallowe'en is coming, for the following reasons:

• All the neighbourhood houses are draped in flashing lights and ghosts.

• Firecrackers are going off at all hours of the day and night, and the poor dog is teetering on the edge of a nervous breakdown.

• Katie and Jack are spending hours debating what goodies they'll receive in their trick-or-treat bags and beating each other senseless over same.

'Mummy, can we have lots of lights and ghosts all over *our* house for Hallowe'en?' Katie asked, as she clambered into the car after school.

'That might be nice,' I said, vaguely, trying to fob her off.

'Brandon says his house will be the best,' she went on, a murderous glint in her eye. 'But I told him that ours was going to be better. *Much better.*'

Instantly I felt nervous. Angelica had had decades of practice at creating elaborate lights displays. A half-carved pumpkin and a string of harmless-looking ghosts flapping on the porch were definitely not going to satisfy Katie's high expectations. Decided to drive past the Laws' mansion to assess the display. The house was festooned from top to bottom with lights, pumpkins and ghouls. There were also dozens of flapping banners, declaring 'Happy Hallowe'en', draped artistically across the front porch, and a life-size witch swaying on the steps. She must have got in the professionals to decorate – there was no way she could have managed it, not in her weakened flu state.

PS Mrs H called round for a quick cuppa. She says she no longer uses depilatory cream.

'I'm converted to waxing, Susie dear,' she claimed. 'A good Brazilian lasts for ages – and it's so hygienic. You should try it.'

She took a sip of her tea and smiled in a very self-satisfied way. I sometimes wonder if Mrs H hasn't got hidden depths. Have put all the depilatory cream under the stairs until I decide how to get rid of it.

25 October

Was called to one side by Jack's playschool teacher this morning when I arrived to collect him.

'How do you think Jack is settling in here at Little Angels, Mrs Hunt?' she asked, gazing at me unflinchingly.

'Em, fine?' I ventured, feeling hot and bothered all of a sudden. It wasn't a good sign that she was calling me Mrs Hunt.

'*Yeees* . . . It's just that he seems to have a little difficulty interacting and sharing with the other children.' She paused meaningfully.

'In what way?' I asked.

'Well, he likes to spend a lot of time pretending to be a dog.'

'A dog?' I laughed, relieved nothing serious was wrong. 'Well, he has a very active imagination.'

'Yes, and we do encourage imaginative play here at Little Angels.' She looked stern. 'But we also encourage more formal group activities and unfortunately Jack is proving to be . . . Shall we say rather disruptive? We think he may need some extra encouragement and tutoring in that area.'

I left clutching a pile of literature on interactive play.

'Why are you pretending to be a dog at school, Jack?' I asked on the way home, trying to catch his eye in the rear-view mirror.

'Woof! Woof!' he barked happily.

Am very worried. What if he develops a serious psychological disorder and stops talking altogether? The only consolation is that they could make a TV movie of his life for the Living Channel.

Spent ages flicking through the brochures that the Little Angels teacher had given me. I have decided to implement a new schedule to improve Jack's social skills.

Plan to Encourage Jack to Share With Other Children, Make Some Friends and Stop Pretending To Be a Dog

(a) Encourage him to talk about sharing and how this makes him feel.

(b) Ask him how it feels when others share with him.

(c) Ask him which is his favourite toy to share.

(d) Draw a picture of him sharing with a friend.

(e) Go to the zoo and explain how animals share food, water and shelter.

Am confident he will be back on track in no time, although the plan does seem to involve a lot of talking and Jack is not a big fan of that.

PS Katie and Jack have given the dog a massage with two

tubes of the depilatory cream I put under the stairs. Luckily, I managed to wash it all off in time and he has just one bald patch on his head, but he's still traumatized. He keeps looking at me with big mournful eyes, as if to say, 'You're a hopeless excuse for a parent.' Have a strong feeling he wants to run away from home so have locked the back gate.

26 October

Spent the day attempting to transform the house into a spooky Hallowe'en cavern, complete with cauldrons, skeletons, cackling witches, etc. Roped Joe in to help. Unfortunately, most of the Hallowe'en stock was sold out in the Centre, so we had to make do with last year's paraphernalia – which fell seriously below par when compared with Angelica's masterpiece.

Katie supervised the exercise with an eagle eye and a sharp tongue. 'We need more pumpkin lights, Mummy,' she said, surveying the front door critically. 'I want people to be really, really scared when they see it.'

'I don't think we'll be able to fit any more in, darling,' I said, while Joe muttered something under his breath about unrealistic expectations and blown fuses. 'Anyway, it would be a bit vulgar to have too many lights.'

'What does "vulgar" mean, Mummy?' Katie asked.

'It *means*, Katie, that if you want any more lights we'll have to remortgage the house.' Joe tried to arrange a skeleton to dangle over the door.

'Well, I like vulgar,' Katie said. 'It's cool.'

May have to explain to Katie that the environment is practically beyond repair and that we should try not to contribute to global warming any more than is absolutely necessary. Maybe I could invite Al Gore round and get him to explain it all to her.

PS Saw clip of Cameron Diaz asking everyone to be environmentally responsible and unplug their mobile-phone chargers every night to save electricity – will have to drop that discreetly into conversation with Angelica next time I see her. Surely as the wife of a big-name celebrity she should be more ecologically friendly and abstain from such an electricity-guzzling Hallowe'en display. She has that 'I'm Not a Plastic Bag' carrier so I know she's eco-aware. Maybe she just needs reminding.

27 October

Annoyingly, it seems that Mum and Dad are turning more Portuguese than the Portuguese themselves.

'Oh, we don't eat any of that stodge, Susie.' Mum laughed, when I called to ask if she wanted any honest-to-goodness Irish produce brought over, like pork sausages or six-pack crisps. 'We practically live on fresh fruit here. Your father has never had so much stamina.'

Hung up quickly before she could go into any more detail. Have decided to sneak some Pringles and custard cream biscuits into my carry-on luggage anyway. It's a well-known fact that too much fruit can cause painful bloating. All that fermentation in the gut can't be healthy.

PS Joe asked what arrangements I've made for the dog when we're abroad. I didn't admit that his existence had temporarily slipped my mind or suggest that he stay home alone for the week. Wonder if Louise would take him. It's not as if she has anything better to do now that she's on maternity leave. Also, she'd probably enjoy some company for a change. It must be very lonely having no one to come home to at night – even if you live in a plush townhouse with a flat-screen TV in every room.

PPS Jack wants to dress as a Super Dog for Hallowe'en. In a collar and lead. I have looked up childhood obsessions on-line. There was some great information about how children can become unusually attached to all sorts of random items, like blankies or dinosaurs. It did not, however, mention a strange preoccupation with doglike behaviour.

28 October

Casually dropped hints at the school gate that we're off to Portugal for half-term. All the other downtrodden mothers listened in envy until Angelica bounced up in her dazzling white sneakers, looking as if she'd just come back from a health spa.

'Hi, you guys, I am *sooooo* exhausted,' she announced, beaming at everyone. 'I was up all night packing for our trip to LA. Sometimes I wonder if it's really worth travelling so far for a week. But I need my fix of sun – this Irish weather sucks!'

There was a murmur of approval as the others moved in to hear more about her fabulously glamorous lifestyle.

'Are you feeling better, Angelica?' I asked, wanting her to know that she'd been in my thoughts when she was unwell.

'Better?' She seemed confused.

'Didn't you have the flu? You looked quite sick the last time I saw you. You were hot and sweaty and . . .' I trailed off because her face was blank.

Then she smiled broadly. 'Oh *yeeees*. Thanks, Susie. I'm much better now. You're so sweet to think of me.'

She linked arms with me and walked briskly back to her Range Rover Sport. 'Listen, would you like to come to a charity gig with me in December? I know it's a long way off but the tickets are like gold dust – it's some environmental thing, you know, reducing our carbon footprints, yawn, yawn. Boring, but the gang will be there so it'll be good fun.'

'I'd love to!' I said, my voice squeaky with excitement at the thought of sharing a top table with *bona fide* celebs. 'What date?'

'Um, I'm not sure. I'll check my diary, OK? Now, I gotta run, my trainer's waiting for me – and you know how they can be.' She giggled.

Then she kissed me – actually *kissed me* – on the cheek.

PS Spent the morning researching the environment, greenhouse gases, etc. – have to be *au fait* with it if I'm going to be sitting next to real celebs at dinner: they're always sponsoring eco-awareness campaigns. I discovered some very scary information about global warming and carbon footprints, etc. Am now a teeny bit anxious that a freak tidal wave may engulf us or that deadly giant mosquitoes could invade Ireland at any second. Also, have calculated that I have a carbon footprint of approximately three zillion and that I'm probably singlehandedly responsible for certain environmental disaster due to befall the earth. Am baffled as to why I rate so highly when I don't have a private jet on standby and don't manufacture CDs or anything else abominable. Perhaps using new Katie's new hair-straighteners so much is to blame.

Louise called in a panic. 'I'm getting stretchmarks, Susie!' she howled. 'How could this happen? I smother my skin with buckets of that bloody body moisturizer religiously every night. *Religiously.*'

'You'll be fine, Lou,' I said. 'Listen, you'll never guess! I'm going to a charity function with Angelica. And she *kissed* me!'

'On the lips? Gross.' Louise was distinctly unimpressed.

'Not on the lips, on the cheek. She has to look the date up in her diary but it's some big environmental gig – loads of celebs are going! I'm *soooooooooo* excited.'

'Great,' she said flatly. 'But what about my stretchmarks? I'll never be able to wear a bikini again.'

She broke into uncontrollable sobs and I had to spend ages trying to convince her that stretchmarks are motherhood's badge of honour and nothing to be ashamed of. Didn't like to tell her that they'll soon be just one of a long list of reasons why a bikini is now completely out of the question. A jelly belly and deflated, saggy boobs mean that a dowdy suck-it-all-in one-piece swimsuit that costs an arm and a leg is now the only viable option going forward.

30 October

Dropped by Louise's to inspect her new stretchmarks. After quite a lot of banging on my part she answered the door with a headset attached to her belly.

'What are you doing?' I asked, transfixed.

'Letting the baby listen to some classical music,' she said, smiling fondly. 'And some French, of course.'

'You're a scream, you really are.' I guffawed, glad her sense of humour had been restored. 'Some of those baby ideas really are crazy, aren't they?' I squeezed past her and made my way to the kitchen in search of the delicious designer nibbles she buys from the gourmet deli for outrageous sums of money.

'Why would you think I was joking, Susie?' She was looking at me blankly. 'Scientific research has shown that babies *in utero* can hear and respond to outside stimuli.'

I knew immediately she wasn't kidding by the way her eyes glinted dangerously off the cafetière.

'Of course,' I agreed, worried that the gourmet latte and brioche might be withheld. 'I did that with Katie and Jack too. That's why they're both so advanced now.'

Don't know why but she looked a bit worried when I said that.

Anyhow, she eventually agreed to have the dog while we're in Portugal, although I'm not sure she's altogether happy about it.

'He *is* house-trained, right?' she asked, when I went through his daily routine of lying around, interspersed with cowering under the table when the children are experiencing their more active moments.

'Of course he is!' I said, relieved I hadn't mentioned his fondness for vomiting on the stairs, then licking it up at his leisure, or his habit of weeing on the sofa now and again.

Am sure she'll be grateful for this learning experience – it'll give her excellent practice in parenthood before the baby arrives: once she's experienced the joy of unrelenting responsibility for another living being round the clock, she'll probably change her mind about adoption. So, in a round-about way, I'm doing her a colossal favour in dumping the dog on her. Must remember to tell her that when we get back.

PS Mum called to say the weather has turned unseasonably cold in Portugal. 'We can't understand it,' she said, sounding baffled. 'It's been glorious for months now.'

Am refusing to be downhearted. Maybe she's become so acclimatized to the heat that she thinks anything below thirty degrees is chilly.

31 October: Hallowe'en

Have decided that Hallowe'en is a stupid holiday that should be banned due to its pagan, devil-worshipping origins.

Katie demanded a homemade costume this year, so I spent the entire afternoon clumsily fashioning a witch's outfit from black crêpe paper and pumpkin stickers, even though she already has a dozen Disney character outfits that cost a small fortune in her dressing-up box, just waiting for a night on the town.

'This looks really vulgar, Mummy,' she said, delighted to use her favourite new word as I tried to pin the paper round her waist and create the over-the-top bouffant look she wanted.

'That's right, darling,' I said, eyeing Jack, as he pranced round the kitchen in his cowboy hat and Power Rangers underpants, lunging periodically at the dog with a plastic lasso. 'It's perfect.'

'Yes, but do I look scary? I want to be really, really scary. I want to be the scariest witch *ever*.'

Spent the rest of the afternoon trying to convince Katie that I was terrified of the very sight of her while simultaneously trying to persuade Jack not to garrotte the dog.

Then, as I was reaching the end of my rope, Joe called to say he'd be late so I had to take the children trick-or-treating myself, while the rain bucketed down and drenched us. Was forced to carry the dog as he was so frightened of the bangers and other fireworks. Limped home after an hour and attempted surreptitiously to replace all the sweets that Katie and Jack had been given with others that I'd bought. Don't think old Mrs Kenny next door would spike any sherbet dips with arsenic, but you never know.

PS Am raging with Joe. Suspect he faked the urgent meeting to avoid the Hallowe'en revelry on the streets. Am also furious that I missed *Strictly Come Dancing* because I was traipsing round in the rain – I was really looking forward to watching celebs tripping round a ballroom making complete fools of themselves. Have hidden all the Hallowe'en treats – Joe definitely doesn't deserve any mini KitKats.

1 November

Spent the day packing for our trip to Portugal. Decided to ignore Mum's warnings about downpours and intemperate conditions. She has a tendency to be over-cautious. Instead, I filled the case with all the clothes we never had a chance to wear because of the ridiculously cold Irish summer. Luckily, I was able to create a classic capsule wardrobe for myself – my stylish new M&S tie-dye multiway sarong goes with everything and is guaranteed to take me from day to night with a simple change of jewellery. Or I get my money back.

PS Dropped dog to Louise's. Hope he doesn't pine for us too much. Mind you, he looked as if he couldn't believe his luck when he saw her designer furniture.

Am exhausted after enduring the flight from hell. As usual, Joe fell into a semi-conscious state from which he could not be roused, snoring loudly all the way there while Katie and Jack ran amok in the cabin and I tried to hide behind the latest edition of *Heat*. (The exclusive revelations about Tom and Katie's marriage were fascinating.)

'Is there anything I can help you with?' the snooty air stewardess enquired, as Jack attempted for the third time to launch himself off the back of his seat and on to the lap of the passenger behind.

I tried to look calm and unruffled while attempting to drag Jack back with one hand. 'Not really, thank you.' I smiled with gritted teeth, praying the plane was about to start its descent.

'It's just that the children seem to be, em, rather, em, boisterous,' she pointed out. 'There have been a few complaints.'

Was instantly furious that our fellow passengers had been judging Katie and Jack's playful antics. OK, so spraying fruit juice across the aisle at the couple in the pristine white cotton suits may have been a bit naughty, but it was done in the spirit of fun, and who wears white cotton on a flight? It's completely impractical.

'Well, perhaps you should remind people that we were all children once and that the Geneva Convention probably protects the right of children to fun and frivolity,' I said, poking Joe's arm so he would wake up and help me. 'What do people expect them to do for three hours? Sudoku?' I glared at the passenger behind, who was now cowering under a newspaper.

'Maybe they'd like another drink,' she suggested, flinching as Jack tried to lick her hand.

'That's a good idea,' I said, trying to sound confident. 'They may be dehydrated. Who knows what damage is being done to their internal organs at this very moment?'

The stewardess raised her eyebrows and sashayed up the aisle while Katie and Jack stuck out their tongues at her. Was quite proud of them.

Turned out Mum hadn't been joking about the weather. High winds whipped round the plane's steps as we disembarked and I almost fell to my death as the children clung to my legs. Joe was manhandling our cabin luggage with some difficulty. 'What the hell's in here, Susie?' he grumbled, as he dragged my holdall along.

'Not much,' I answered, struggling to keep upright against the wind. I wasn't going to admit that I'd smuggled large quantities of Irish confectionery on board. He'll be glad of it when Mum and Dad forcefeed him organic fruit for a week.

Eventually made it to the arrivals hall. Scanned the crowd for Mum, Dad and a huge welcome banner, but there was no sign of them. Called Mum on her mobile to find out where they were and why they weren't waiting for us, ready to relieve us of our luggage and the children.

'Sorry, darling,' she said, sounding distracted. 'The golf ran a little late this morning because of the wind. Why don't you take a taxi to the resort and we'll meet you for lunch?'

Was forced to struggle outside with the luggage and wait, shivering, for a taxi to pick us up. Joe tried to jolly Katie and Jack along, but I was furious at my parents' blatant disregard for my feelings. Have decided to withhold the jumbo tube of Pringles from them.

PS Am seriously considering contacting the Civil Aviation

Authority, or some such body, and demanding that airlines provide better facilities on board for children. Such as in-flight nannies and a designated play area. (Well away from adult seating, obviously.) May even write to Richard Branson and suggest it. Who knows? He may invite me to his private island for a brainstorming session with Kate Moss and pay me a vast sum of money to patent my ideas.

3 November

Raining. Am in despair. Only the Lindsay Lohan revelations in *OK!* are keeping me from losing my mind.

Am also a bit worried about Mum and Dad. They seem to be having some difficulty speaking English and keep breaking into Portuguese. It's most disconcerting.

'Do you think they're going senile?' I asked Joe, as we lay in bed, huddled together for warmth as the wind howled outside.

'Senile?' He snorted. 'That pair have the life. This is exactly where I want to be when we retire.'

Not sure about that. If this is the kind of unsavoury weather you can expect in Portugal, I may prefer a holiday home in Hollywood, just like Angelica Law.

4 November

The weather was better this morning, although still not balmy and tropical or in any way suitable for my M&S tie-dye multiway sarong.

Mum and Dad tried to persuade Joe and me to play a round of golf with them while Katie and Jack spent the afternoon in the on-site crèche. But than I discovered that just driving round the course in a golf-buggy for fun was not an option.

'Don't be so over-protective,' Dad said, when I queried the crèche staff's qualifications and suitability as a way to get out of it. 'We'll only be gone a couple of hours.'

'Come on, Susie,' Joe coaxed, ready and willing to abandon our children for the sake of eighteen holes under grey skies. 'They'd love the chance to play with the other kids.'

'I can't believe you'd just leave them with strangers,' I hissed, annoyed he wasn't volunteering to stay behind and watch over them while I went for a manicure in the on-site beauty salon.

Spent the rest of the afternoon huddled under a blanket, watching Katie and Jack's every move in case they fell into the toddler pool. (Although this was unlikely: they didn't get any further than sticking their toes into the freezing water and squealing in horror.)

Was glad I'd stuck to my guns, even if Katie and Jack were a bit cross when some other resort children marched past us on a treasure hunt, led by two cheerful staff members in red T-shirts and bandanas.

PS May have to make a quick trip to the nearest shopping centre. Am so cold after sitting by the pool that I can no longer feel some of my extremities.

5 November

Almost became tragic young widow *à la* Jackie Kennedy this evening.

At seven, after hours of bickering over Katie's *Dora the Explorer* Scrabble, the only board game to hand, we decided to brave the cold and make a break for the fish restaurant at the marina.

'You won't be sorry!' Mum enthused, as we donned several layers to withstand the hundred-mile-an-hour winds and lashing rain. 'Antonio's serves the best sea bass this side of Lagos. The local fishermen catch it every afternoon.'

Got to the restaurant and Jack went into meltdown when he discovered Captain Bird's Eye's fish fingers weren't available and that he had to eat fresh fish like everyone else.

'I love fresh fish,' Katie announced, in a superior voice, smiling coyly at the waiter and fluttering her eyelashes. 'It makes you big and strong, doesn't it?'

I'd just managed to persuade Jack that sea bass wasn't 'yuk', when Joe suddenly started choking.

'That'll be the bones,' Dad said, as he licked his fingers with relish. 'They take a bit of getting used to.'

Suddenly Joe's eyes were bulging and I realized he couldn't breathe. But instead of leaping to his rescue and saving him, like a heroic intern in *ER*, I was rooted to the spot in horror, unable to move.

Then Mum screamed and Antonio, the owner, leapt to the rescue. He grasped Joe round the abdomen and squeezed hard until a small chunk of bone popped out of his mouth and flew across the table, hitting me in the eye.

Joe spluttered while Dad slapped him violently on the back and Antonio puffed out his chest, looking pleased with himself.

'God, Joe,' Dad said, 'we thought you were faking it. It's a good thing Antonio knew what to do or you'd have been a goner.'

PS Feel quite traumatized. May never be able to eat sea bass again. Also, am worried that Katie and Jack may suffer disturbing psychological flashbacks of Antonio squeezing Joe with enormous force as his eyes bulged from his head. They seem unusually subdued.

PPS Mrs H will be raging when she hears. She's been desperate to try out the Heimlich manoeuvre and this would have been the perfect opportunity.

PPPS Joe seems quite affected by his near-death experience. Half suspect he may be faking it so he can avoid childcare duties.

6 November

Joe has upped the ante on the fallout of his near-death experience. He spent the entire day mumbling about 'reassessing priorities' and 'living in the now'. 'When you have a brush with death, it really makes you sit up and rethink your life,' he said to me sorrowfully, as he tucked into his third croissant.

'I'm not sure it was a brush with death,' I offered, wondering if I could sneak a pastry past without him noticing and whether I should suggest that he could reassess his cholesterol intake while he was at it.

He turned doleful eyes on me. 'Oh, but it was, Susie. If Antonio hadn't saved me, who knows what might have happened? I really thought I'd had it.'

'Yes, but you're fine now,' I said, as reassuringly as I could, suppressing an urge to ask sarcastically if he'd noticed a white light on the other side.

'Yes, but life is short, don't you see?' he went on, looking intense – and a bit wild-eyed. 'It can be snatched away from you at a moment's notice. That's why you have to make every minute count.'

Then he went back to chewing on his croissant and looking thoughtful.

PS Hope Joe doesn't think he can become an inspirational speaker or some such. Not sure he has the charisma to carry it off. Mind you, he could probably make lots of money doing TV appearances to discuss his brush with the spirit world.

PPS Crept back to the kitchen after midnight to find a spare croissant, but all that was left was a trail of crumbs across the tiled floor. Joe's selfishness in the wake of his near-death experience is really starting to grate on my nerves.

7 November

Mum and Dad are seemingly unaffected by our imminent departure. They are also refusing to confirm when they'll next visit us. Or when we can next visit them for that matter.

'It depends, darling,' Mum said vaguely, when I tried to pin her down on her next trip home to Dublin.

'Depends on what exactly?' I said, determined not to be fobbed off with generalities.

'Oh, lots of things,' she said, avoiding my eye. 'Let's just concentrate on enjoying our last day together tomorrow.'

I thought I saw the glint of a tear as she turned away. She's probably gutted that we're leaving her to her own devices again among strangers so far from home, but she doesn't want to show it and is being brave to protect me. Maybe I should encourage her to express her feelings more – I'd love to hear how devastated she'll be.

PS Dad seems unusually jolly now that we're leaving. If

I hear him whistling 'Copacabana' one more time, I'll scream.

8 November

Woke to sunny blue skies so decided to wear my new M&S tie-dye multiway sarong. It provides excellent overall coverage, with no need for waxing of intimate body parts, except ankles. Luckily, fake tans are now so advanced that I'll be able to slap some on when we get back and I don't need to panic that my skin seems whiter now than it was when we arrived. Which is a good thing – it's vital that I'm glowing and healthy at the school gate on Monday and preferably looking a good five years younger than when we left. Especially if I'm going to a glamorous charity gig with Angelica soon.

Dad almost choked on his organic fruit salad when I appeared at the breakfast table with the ingenious sarong wrapped round my bust (turned out the instructions that boasted it would take you from the beach to the boardroom in three simple steps proved impossible to follow so I just tucked it under my arms and hoped for the best).

'What on earth is *that*, Susie?' he snickered, when I shuffled in, hoping it wouldn't collapse round my defuzzed ankles.

'A sarong.' I sniffed, annoyed he found me so hilarious. 'It offers excellent protection against UVA and UVB rays.'

'Well, it's certainly interesting.' He winked at Katie and Jack.

I attempted to storm off, furious that he was ridiculing me in front of my children, which everyone knows can sow the seeds of destructive behaviour patterns in later years. It will be his fault if they turn into disrespectful lager louts who won't listen to a word I say when they hit their teens. Unfortunately, though, I was unable to make a really good sort of storming-off motion as the sarong had wrapped itself round my inner thighs, so I had to shuffle at a hobble, like a geisha (although maybe not as gracefully).

Spent ages on the beach building sandcastles with Katie and Jack and collecting shells. It was just like a proper old-fashioned family holiday. Sadly, it ended in tears when Katie gave Jack's dinosaur sandcastle a sly kick and he retaliated by bulldozing her Bratz sand palace. But at least I captured some fond family memories on camera, even if Joe sat at the water's edge, ignoring us and looking sorrowful.

PS Am dreading the flight back to Dublin tomorrow. Thankfully, I have devised a detailed plan of action to ensure that Katie and Jack are occupied at all times and cannot run amok in the cabin, mortifying me again.

9 November

Detailed plan to keep Katie and Jack occupied during the flight failed abysmally.

10.00 a.m. Presented children with colouring pads (extortionate ten euro in airport shop) and an assorted array of crayons (five euro in same). Encouraged them to draw for at least thirty-five minutes in jolly-hockeysticks way. Children glared mutinously at me.

10.03 a.m. Colouring pads fell to pieces. (OK, Jack ripped them to shreds while he was pretending to be a corgi.) Children threw crayons on the floor with abandon. Attempts to retrieve them proved futile.

10.07 a.m. Proceeded to try to engage unruly children and explain to them how to play old-fashioned game of Hangman.

10.10 a.m. Realized Hangman is difficult to explain. And may be psychologically disturbing for young children.

10.11 a.m. Tried to explain how to play noughts and crosses.

10.13 a.m. Abandoned noughts and crosses when Katie insisted on being the crosses and Jack violently disagreed.

10.14 a.m. Poked Joe's arm with an in-flight aeroplane pen to encourage him to engage with his children.

10.15 a.m. Pretended to fall into deep, impenetrable sleep and ignored chaos around me.

10 November

Think I may be suffering from jet-lag. Feel quite jittery and off-balance – may need Reiki healing to recover from in-flight trauma. Joe says it's impossible to suffer from jet-lag when travelling from one European destination to another but I have to disagree. Who knows what sort of havoc all that magnetic energy can play with your *chi*? He's even acting a bit strangely himself. He asked if I was truly happy over deep-pan pizza this evening. I told him I was, even though I think that lugging my oversized suitcase around may well have dislocated something vitally important that could prevent me finally taking up Pilates.

PS Spent all night carefully applying fake tan to all visible areas. It's vital to look bronzed and youthful for school gates tomorrow. Cannot, under any circumstances, admit that the weather was abysmal and that lugging a bag packed to the brim with flimsy summer clothes was a complete waste of time – and led to ridiculous excess-baggage charge by the airline.

Very humiliating morning. Woke up late – suspect my body clock is all over the place after overseas travel – and barely made it to school on time.

Saw Angelica in the distance, her peroxide teeth flashing against her mahogany skin. Was relieved the hours I'd spent self-tanning meant I was a natural, honey-kissed shade too.

I smiled serenely as the mothers cooed over my glow, until one silly cow piped up, 'Oh, Susie, if you want to get those tan marks off you should try toothpaste. It's really effective.'

She was pointing at my palms, which, I suddenly saw, were a funny orange colour. Rushed away, cursing Joe. If he hadn't distracted me with another meaning-of-life conversation last night I would have remembered to scrub my palms in the brisk, yet careful way outlined on the back of the bottle.

Then Louise called to find out when I was coming to collect the dog. Was a bit disappointed that she hadn't developed a lifelong bond with him and had decided not to give him back. 'He really misses you,' she said, sounding a bit eager to be rid of him. 'He chewed my Persian rug to bits on the first night and insisted on sleeping in my room the whole time. His snoring kept me awake almost every night.'

'Aw, how sweet,' I said, hoping she thought so too. 'He must have been trying to protect you.'

'It wasn't that sweet, Susie,' she said. 'The rug was very expensive, and there's dog hair everywhere. I'm going to have to get a contract cleaner in before the baby arrives.'

'But I thought you were putting the baby up for adoption?'
I said.

'Oh, that – well, I've changed my mind,' she said sheepishly. 'I've decided I'm strong enough to cope on my own.
I think I was just having a crisis of confidence – I'm over it
now.'

'That's great, Lou,' I said, thrilled that my grand plan had
worked. The dog *had* brought out her maternal side, whether
she liked it or not. Decided that maybe the time wasn't
right to suggest letting go of her impossibly high standards,
though. A little bit of dog hair is nothing compared to the
chaos that a newborn's spit-up and poo will cause. Anyway,
was distracted when she asked me to attend her antenatal
scan to give her moral support. It seems her ob-gyn is
concerned about her unusually large bump and wants to
double-check the measurements. Am really looking forward
to hearing all the gory details.

PS I'm not sure but I think the dog may have turned up
his nose at me this evening when I collected him – his eyes
seemed to mock me when I was opening his can of Pedigree
Chum.

12 November

Louise's baby is going to be enormous. It may even break
countrywide records.

'You have a big one there,' the ob-gyn announced evenly,
as he was doing the scan.

'What do you mean by big?' Louise said, sounding
nervous, as I craned my neck to get a better look at her
monster child.

'Conservatively, I would say at least nine or ten pounds,' the doctor said, wiping the jelly off Louise's tummy and making a note on her chart.

'Ten pounds!' Louise turned grey and grabbed my hand in a death-grip, her manicured fingernails digging into my skin. 'How is a ten-pound baby going to get out of me?'

'You've done your Lamaze classes, right?' For a split second the doctor looked concerned.

'Yes, we have,' I said. Louise seemed unable to speak.

'Well, I'm sure everything will be fine, then,' he said patting her hand kindly. 'We have our special tricks for dealing with these things.'

Didn't like to ask what the tricks might be – suspect an industrial-sized pair of forceps and a clamp may be involved.

To cheer her up, I offered to drive Louise to a top-notch city-centre baby boutique to stock up on necessities. Tried first to persuade her that supermarkets do an excellent range of bargain baby gear – now that she has to dress and feed a freakishly enormous baby on her own, she really should start watching the pennies – but she wouldn't hear of it.

'My baby may not have a father in its life,' she pulled her designer cashmere wrap round her and shuddered in distaste, 'but it will have the best of everything else.'

Eventually made it to the shop, where Louise, in a panicked fit of nesting, proceeded to earmark all of the most expensive items. That is, until the very helpful assistant asked her when her twins were due and she dissolved into an uncontrollable bout of sobbing.

She waddled out of the shop without purchasing a solitary item and then cried bitterly in the passenger seat all the way home.

Tried to comfort her by saying it was an easy mistake to

make – not everyone was lucky enough to have neat little bumps like I did – but that didn't help. In fact, she seemed to cry even harder afterwards.

PS Just had a great idea! We should ring round the local shops to get a bit of sponsorship or some free stuff at the very least. The local Spar could make the baby its mascot and give Louise free nappies for the privilege. A ten-pounder is going to need a lot of disposables, not to talk of wipes.

13 November

Joe has dropped a bombshell. He wants to go for counselling. And he wants *me* to go with him. 'That brush with death I had in Portugal has shown me there are issues between us, Susie,' he announced, his eyes searching my face in an unnerving way. 'Issues that need to be resolved.'

'What issues?' I asked, mystified. We hadn't fought in ages. OK, so we hadn't had sex in ages either, but that wasn't unusual. There was no need for this counselling lark.

'I've been ignoring what happened for too long,' he said. 'I think we need to thrash it out properly.'

He was talking about Lone Father. My stomach heaved.

'There's nothing to talk about, Joe,' I stuttered. 'All that's in the past. It was nothing anyway.'

'Don't dismiss it, Susie,' he went on, looking serious. 'We have to talk about it. Otherwise it'll fester. Eventually it could destroy us.'

I said nothing.

'Counselling will give us an arena in which we can air our grievances and try some conflict-resolution techniques to resolve them,' he said. Then he handed me some brochures. 'Think about it.'

Am in a state of shock. Am also seriously concerned by Joe's unusually high grasp of psycho-speak. Suspect he has been sneakily watching *Dr. Phil* unbeknown to me.

Called Mum to tell her that Joe wants to go for relationship counselling.

'That's probably very wise, darling,' she said, plainly trying to be supportive. 'I'm sure things will improve no end once you get a chance to explore your feelings and anxieties.'

Didn't like to tell her it was the exploring-my-feelings-and-anxieties part that I was dreading. I'd honestly felt that our relationship was fine and dandy, that we were happier than we'd ever been. It's been a huge shock to discover that Joe has issues he feels need resolving. And that my semi-adulterous fling is at the top of his list.

14 November

Mrs H popped in for coffee and immediately pounced on the relationship-counselling brochures I'd stupidly left on the kitchen table. (Note to self: must get Joe to build handy A–Z cabinets ASAP so everything can be filed neatly away in alphabetical order and out of reach of nosy mother-in-law. It looked a dead easy job on *DIY Den*. A bit of reclaimed pine and a tin of Farrow & Ball White Tie and Bob's your uncle.)

'What are these, Susie?' she asked.

'Oh, just something that was shoved through the door,' I said, trying to sound casual. 'You know what junkmail's like!'

But it was too late. Before I knew it, she'd fished her

extra-strength glasses out of her handbag (the special ones she uses for checking fine print) and was reading the brochure aloud: 'Relationship Counselling,' she said slowly, taking a fig roll and dipping it into her tea. 'Maybe you and Joe should have a go at that.'

'Why?' I was flabbergasted. Joe had sworn he'd never tell his mother about my little fling. 'Do you think we need to?'

'Well, Joe does seem rather unhappy at the moment, dear,' she went on, beady eyes speedily scanning the literature. 'Maybe you need to spice things up a bit.'

'What do you mean?' I was nearly choking with fear that she was about to confront me about Lone Father and threaten never to make her scones ever again as punishment for my betrayal.

'You know, get some edible underwear, that sort of thing. It's all the rage apparently. You can even order it off the telly.'

I was at a loss for words.

'If you do,' she went on, fig roll spraying from her dentures, 'you should go for the raspberry flavour. The bubble-gum ones look most unappetizing.'

PS Really must have serious words with Joe about his mother's odd behaviour. Getting Sky Digital as her birthday present may have been a mistake: having more than three hundred channels to choose from has obviously unhinged her.

PPS Am very worried that Mrs H thinks Joe looks unhappy. Am I the only one who didn't notice it?

Joe has made an appointment with a relationship counsellor. She's called Rita and has agreed to fit us in tomorrow at ten a.m. He has even arranged for his mother to drop the kids to school. I'm appalled by this sudden turn of events.

Met Angelica at the school gate. She seemed to sense that something was amiss. 'What's up, Susie?' she asked, her amazing green eyes searching my face. 'You look a bit blue.'

For some reason, I found myself confiding in her that Joe felt we needed counselling.

'Is that all? Counselling's nothing to worry about.' She laughed. 'James and I have it all the time.'

'You do?' I was intrigued.

'Sure. James has tons of issues. Without therapy, we'd have been divorced years ago! When are you going?'

'Tomorrow,' I said, feeling much better. If Angelica and her A-list husband went to counselling, Joe and I should definitely give it a whirl. It was probably a really trendy thing to do.

'Morning or afternoon?'

'Morning. Why?' I wondered if she was going to volunteer to pick up Katie and Jack for me.

'It's just that I was going to ask you to take Brandon for me. I hate to ask, but his nanny has a day off – and afternoons are so tricky for me . . .' She trailed off.

'That's OK.' I smiled at her. After all, she'd been so kind about the counselling. 'I'll drop him over to you at six, OK?'

'Could you make it six thirty, honey? We – I mean I should be done by then. Good luck in the morning – remember, everyone does it, right? It's no big deal.'

I tried to believe her but I'm petrified. What if Joe wants

to know the truth about what happened between me and Lone Father? The real truth, not just the sanitized version I've been telling him all this time.

16 November

The morning started badly when Mrs H waved us off, shouting encouragement as Joe reversed out of the driveway. 'I'm sure your marriage can be saved, dears,' she yelled, waving enthusiastically as Katie and Jack clung to her stout legs, looking scared.

We drove in silence to the counsellor's office. Joe cracked his knuckles so I knew he was nervous. I spent the journey trying to remember as many psychiatry buzzwords as I could to impress her. Surprisingly, she didn't seem bowled over when I piped up about emotional intelligence and trust issues in the first five minutes. In fact, she asked me to stop talking and I just had to sit there while she quizzed Joe.

'What do you feel is at the heart of the problem, Joe?' she said, in a calm, measured voice.

'I guess I feel that Susie thinks I'm not enough for her,' Joe admitted, staring at the floor, a red blush creeping up his neck. 'She had a friendship with a man and I don't think she's been truthful about it.'

'Is that so, Susie?' Rita said, turning sorrowful grey eyes on me. 'Was your relationship with this man more than just a friendship?'

'I feel that Joe has serious trust issues,' I protested, flustered. 'I caught him checking my texts recently.'

'Have you given him reason not to trust you, Susie?' she asked, her eyes boring into mine.

'He was very neglectful of me last year.' I pouted. 'It's no wonder I had to look for attention elsewhere.'

'You're not answering my questions, Susie,' Rita said, 'but maybe that's something you can think about before next week's session.'

I gave her my best sulky stare but she locked eyes with me until I was forced to look at the poster on the wall behind her instead – of a happy couple frolicking playfully in the park together, wearing seventies acrylic jumpers and flares.

Have decided I may not go back next week – not unless Rita takes a completely different approach: such as blaming Joe for my adulterous fling and letting me off the hook completely.

When I dropped Brandon back to Angelica's in the afternoon she gave me a special little squeeze on the doorstep so I knew she had remembered our therapy conversation.

'Here are the tickets for that charity auction I was telling you about,' she said, slipping an envelope into my hand. 'Don't worry, you can give me the money tomorrow.'

Had to sit in the car for ages after opening the envelope – have somehow agreed to buy two seats to a December charity auction for the environment, at the cost of five hundred euro apiece.

PS Joe is looking oddly pleased with himself. In fact, he's positively perky. Don't expect it will last once he finds out that I've committed to spending a grand for one six-course dinner, even if it is guaranteed that real celebrities will be there.

Mum called to ask how our first therapy session had gone.

'Terrible,' I said, sniffing with despair. 'Joe's being really unreasonable. He told the counsellor about my innocent flirtation last year. I thought that was a really low blow.'

'But isn't that exactly why you decided to go to counselling in the first place?' Mum asked, sounding confused.

I didn't answer. Felt she might not be all that understanding if I said I wanted the counsellor to focus on Joe's failings, not mine.

'He probably just needs to talk about it to an objective outsider,' she went on, 'express his emotions a bit. Then the healing process can start.'

'What about my healing process?' I grumbled. 'He's really sprung this on me – it's so unfair.'

Got an email from David that depressed me even more.

> Hi Susie, amazing news! I've been called back for a second audition! It's a small chorus part in *The Lion King* with no real lines or anything, but it's a start! Who knows? This time next year I could be tripping the light fantastic on Broadway! I think darling Max is bringing me good luck. He comes to as many auditions with me as he can – of course he's very busy but he really is so supportive when he can make it. He even wants to come home with me for Christmas. A HUGE step. I haven't told Mum yet though so keep it to yourself, OK? BTW, how's the counselling going? Mum told me all about it. You

definitely need it – all you old married couples are as boring as dishwater! Miaow! David xox

18 November

Katie refused to go swimming today. She denied sabotaging her Barbie armbands accidentally on purpose, but I cannot imagine how they got two enormous holes in them otherwise. I think she's overawed by Brandon's so-called 'natural ability'. Tried to convince her that she needs to see through the commitment to swimming and reach her full potential, but she looked at me as if I was deranged and went back to her jigsaw. I decided to go and speak to the instructor to find out how this serious issue could be resolved to my satisfaction – and Katie's, of course. Travelled to the pool to have it out with him.

He looked at me blankly when I suggested he favours some children over others. More specifically that he favours Brandon over every other child there and that this has had a serious and detrimental effect on my daughter's psyche.

'But Brandon is a born athlete,' he deadpanned, as if that was to be the end of the matter. 'I'm even giving him extra training.'

'Well, how do you suggest I encourage Katie to come back?' I said, eyeing Brandon and his freakishly muscular body as he cut through the water.

'Just give her some space,' he said, in a most unhelpful way. 'When the time is right she'll let you know.'

When I got home I asked Joe if Brandon's abnormally toned body could be natural in a boy so young.

'He's a fit little kid,' Joe said. 'It's not unusual for boys his age to have muscles.'

'But Katie doesn't have any,' I said, watching fondly as she polished off another bag of cheese and onion crisps.

'Well, maybe Katie needs to exercise more,' he said darkly, 'and eat less rubbish.'

'Crisps aren't really rubbish,' I argued. 'They're fried in sunflower oil now so they practically count as one of her five-a-day.'

'If she doesn't want to go swimming then let's find her something else physical she likes – how about dancing?'

Think he may be right. Katie probably has natural poise and grace under her puppy fat. And if her uncle David is finally making a breakthrough in the West End maybe she has talent too. Also, her becoming a child star would be a sure-fire way to impress Angelica.

PS Discovered the dog chewing what looked suspiciously like half of Katie's armbands in his basket. He seems to be somewhat disturbed since he came back from Louise's. Am considering getting him psychologically assessed.

PPS Am still too terrified to tell Joe we're going to have to pay a thousand euro to go to a black-tie charity auction (even if the top prize is a Maserati). Found myself chewing my hair this evening. May develop a tic any day now.

19 November

Am scandalized. Called three dancing schools to enquire about enrolling Katie. All of them asked if she had any previous experience.

'Well, she's only five,' I said to the first, a bit taken aback that she would be expected to have any relevant experience other than dancing along to *High School Musical* on DVD.

The second school agreed to put her on the waiting list

after I managed to convince them that she had bags of natural talent and charm.

The third – Vera's Dance and Drama School – reluctantly agreed to see her, but only when I persuaded them that she looked uncannily like a mini Hannah Montana and had much better moves.

'Come along to the next session,' the instructor said, sounding curt, businesslike and not the least bit impressed that she might be bagging the next big star of stage and screen. 'We have one space left, if she's got talent, that is.'

Decided to rent *Flashdance* from the video shop to help Katie brush up on her technique. Preparation is key.

PS Louise called as I was watching the bit where the mechanic-turned-sex-bomb jumps on top of the judges' table and flings herself about in a sweaty frenzy. 'I think my waters have broken, Susie,' she babbled, in a funny, high-pitched voice.

Advised her to relax. As if her waters could possibly have broken! She's not due for another two weeks yet.

20 November

In state of shock. Delivered Louise's baby in the people-carrier in the hospital car park at six a.m. Dargan (nine pounds four ounces) is doing well but the front seat of the people-carrier is not a pretty sight. Bit worried that I'm not covered by insurance for this eventuality.

My heroic car-park delivery has made the national news! Joe said they must be having a slow day – which I thought was a little mean-spirited.

Spent the day at the hospital, being interviewed by TV7 about my role in the drama. Luckily, I was able to nip home and change into my most flattering black-polo-and-bootleg combo beforehand.

'Were you worried that things would go wrong?' the reporter asked, after she had advised me that it would probably be far more interesting for the viewer if I could admit I'd been terrified.

'Yes, well, I was scared,' I said, biting my lip to look sincere, like Tony Blair used to when he was under pressure, 'but I held it together. All I knew was I had to make sure that Dargan was delivered safely, so I put my fear to one side and just got on with it.'

'And was it a *really* difficult delivery?' the reporter went on, just as we had rehearsed.

'Yes, it was,' I said, trying to squeeze out a few tears for dramatic effect like she'd told me to, 'but I helped Louise to do her breathing and we got through it together.'

I didn't think there was any point in mentioning that breathing techniques were the last thing on my mind as Louise roared her way through the birth, cursing me, her ex and the Lamaze coach all at the same time.

'You must be exhausted,' the reporter said, doing her concerned face, the same one I'd seen her practise before the camera started rolling.

'Yes, I am,' I said humbly, 'but I'm so happy I was there

to help.' I did a half-smile to the camera to show how brave I had been.

Then the crew took a few shots of Dargan gurgling in his cot and one of Louise, smiling weakly from her hospital bed.

The piece aired on the evening news, right at the point where they usually do segments on baby ducks trying to cross the road, etc. Was quite pleased with my appearance, although next time I may angle myself a little more to the left. All the nurses think I'm a TV natural. But I'm remaining humble and not displaying any diva-type behaviour yet – such as demanding herbal tea instead of the regular kind in the machine in the lobby or insisting that Louise's room be repainted pink.

PS Do feel quite drained after the interview, though. Finally realize how celebs must feel when they're doing a junket to promote a new film. It really *is* hard to remain perky and upbeat all the time.

22 November

Louise and Dargan came home from hospital today.

Louise was outraged that she was being discharged so soon. She spent ages explaining to a junior doctor that the health service was a disgrace and if we lived in a Nordic country she'd be waited on hand and foot for the next three to six months, getting relaxing spa treatments and intensive massage to tone and firm her post-partum tummy while Dargan was bathed in honey and milk, etc., etc. Not sure that the junior doctor understood what she was on about and I was too busy packing her overnight case to pay much attention. (Tragically her La Perla silk nightdress is now destroyed by baby sick.)

Am a bit disappointed that all the heroic-birth furore has passed. Am also a bit disappointed that Louise doesn't seem especially grateful that I practically saved her life or that I protected her from the worst of the paparazzi – or I would have done if any had turned up.

'I *told* you I was in labour,' she said, as she struggled to breastfeed a ravenous Dargan before we left. 'You just wouldn't believe me.'

'No one could have predicted how quickly your labour would progress, Louise,' I said, repeating what the in-studio doctor had said, word for word, on TV7 news. 'And at least it was natural and medication-free like you wanted.'

'Yes,' she said, a little bitterly. 'I didn't have much choice. Giving birth in a car park kind of precludes an epidural.'

Cannot understand why she is so annoyed about the experience. She's very lucky she delivered two weeks early. Any later and Dargan would have had to be choppered out of her womb, he is so big. Luckily, Louise's mother has flown in from Canada to spend quality time with her new grandson. Am a teeny bit relieved that I can now take a back seat. (Also, things are a bit boring now that the camera crew has disappeared.)

PS Katie says she is more popular than Brandon now that I am a celebrity in my own right. Am so glad that my new-found fame is bringing joy to her life.

PPS Maybe I should consider writing a Kabbalah children's book. That would probably make Katie even more popular – am sure it would be dead easy to do. Must remember to buy myself a red stringy thing for my wrist – that would be an excellent start.

Met Angelica at the school gate. 'I saw you on TV, Susie!' she squealed, bounding up to me. 'You were awesome!'

'Thanks, Angelica,' I murmured, thrilled she had seen the segment.

'Seriously, you're a natural – even James thought so.' She winked at me.

'He did?' I was quivering with excitement that her famous husband (a) knew who I was, and (b) thought I had star quality.

'Sure! You should definitely pursue a career in TV – you have what it takes! Would you like me to hook you up? I met a great producer at a TV awards party last week, I'm sure he'd do me a favour.'

'Oh, I don't know.' I laughed, flattered. 'I have no experience.'

'Experience, schmerience,' she said. 'The camera loves you! I am totally going to put in a call. By the way, you're all set for the auction, right?'

'Yeah . . . About that . . .' I said, trying to pluck up the courage to admit I had made a terrible mistake. This was my moment to back out.

'Listen, don't worry about the minimum-bid thing,' she said breezily. 'People don't stick to the guidelines.'

'They don't?' I was so relieved. The admission ticket had said the lowest possible bid was two hundred and fifty euro.

'Oh, no, everyone starts with at least five hundred euro – it *is* for charity, after all. See you later!' She air-kissed me and took off.

Have decided to lie to Joe and tell him I won the tickets. Only trouble is, I'll have to raid the children's savings accounts to pay for them. Am trying very hard not to feel guilty. Like Angelica said, it *is* for charity.

PS Tossed and turned all night, thinking about Angelica's remark that I am a TV natural. On the one hand I am a happy housewife and don't long for the limelight of a TV career. On the other, the buzz of on-air action was electric and I can't help feeling that having paps secretly photographing my cellulite or trying for shots up my skirt as I get out of my car could be really fulfilling.

24 November

Popped round to Louise's to find out if any journalists had called looking for me. Louise confided that her mother wants to revel in all the publicity of Dargan's dramatic arrival and is refusing to change nappies, help with feeds or do anything even remotely useful.

'She just wants her face in the paper,' she said fiercely, heaving her enormous bosoms out and waving them in Dargan's face. 'She hasn't called me in six months and suddenly she drops everything to be at my side. The whole thing stinks.' (I felt like telling her it wasn't the only thing that stank – those recyclable cloth nappies she's insisting on using may be fashionable and kind to the environment, but they sure don't mask the pong like disposables do.)

Tried to console Louise by reminding her that her mother has probably been too busy to keep in touch. Devoting herself to her wealthy second husband and their estate outside Vancouver is a full-time job. The upkeep on her face-lifts alone must keep her very occupied.

Decided not to tell her that her mother has spent a lot of time asking about camera crews, reapplying her face powder and fire-engine-red lipstick from her limited-edition D&G compact.

'Do you think I should call Steve and tell him?' she asked sadly, as she cradled Dargan in her arms.

'Yeah, maybe you should,' I suggested, hoping she wouldn't ask me to make the call. 'He deserves to know he has a new son.'

'He probably already does,' Louise said, a tear sliding down her cheek. 'He always watches the TV7 *News at Five* – he loves that female newsreader, the one who wears the really low-cut tops.' She sniffed.

'Maybe not,' I said softly, patting Dargan's crusty little scalp. 'Maybe you should text him, just to make sure.'

'No,' she said grimly, fastening her massive maternity bra. 'If he wanted to be in his son's life, he should have made the effort. It's too late now – he can rot in hell for all I care.'

Left feeling a bit unsettled and empty – although that might have been the aftershock from viewing Louise's breastfeeding bra up close and personal. Don't think I have ever seen anything quite so unpleasant in all my life.

25 November

Katie had her first class at Vera's Dance and Drama School today. Was a bit surprised that Vera didn't look fit and supple like the super ballerina Darcey Bussell or any of the toned celebrities on *Strictly Come Dancing*. In fact, wads of cellulite were clearly visible beneath her Lycra dance shorts. (It was a bit comforting to think that she could look like that after hours of dance practice, though.)

'No mothers allowed,' her assistant snapped, when I attempted to accompany Katie into the dance hall. 'It distracts the children. You can wait over there.' She pointed to a dusty area where dozens of other mothers stood nervously.

Luckily, Katie marched in with confidence, swinging her Bratz bag over her shoulder and flicking her hair back.

'See you later, Mummy,' she called, throwing me a dazzling smile.

'Confident, isn't she?' one mother said to me.

'Yes,' I said proudly, suddenly delighted with my child-rearing capabilities.

'Vera will soon knock that out of her,' another mother said, nodding wisely.

'What do you mean?' I asked, instantly alarmed.

'Knock 'em down to build 'em up. That's Vera's motto, love,' the first mother said, offering me a stick of gum. 'It really works. My Beyoncé dances like a pro now. She can do fifty head spins in a row.'

'She can,' the second agreed approvingly. 'She's got a leading part in Vera's next big production – *Be-bop on Broadway*.'

'They're actually travelling to New York?' I breathed, thrilled I'd chosen such a prestigious stage school for Katie.

The other mothers looked at each other in disbelief.

'No. It's on in the community college.' The second mother snorted. 'But it *is* the biggest stage-school production in the city.'

Spent the next hour watching all the mothers pressing their ears to the door to hear how the class was progressing. Eventually felt obliged to try it myself but I couldn't hear a thing. Suspect the hall may be soundproofed to discourage earwigging. Anyway, was very alarmed by their behaviour. Children should be allowed to develop at their own pace, not an artificial one inflicted on them by their over-ambitious parents. Luckily, I watched *Stage School Moms and Dads* last season so I can spot the signs of a parent who is out of control.

Came home and emailed David for tips to help Katie get a starring role in *Be-bop on Broadway*. He wrote back:

> Showbiz is dog eat dog, honey. Try a diamanté manicure and if all else fails get her an all-over spray tan – that should make everyone sit up and take notice. David xoxo

26 November

Called Louise to find out how Dargan was settling.

'OK,' she whispered, 'but he seems to be having a bit of trouble latching on.'

'You shouldn't whisper, Lou,' I said, feeling authoritative and a bit smug that I was qualified to dole out advice on childcare (even if I was a little squeamish about the latching-on talk). 'The baby needs to get used to noise.'

'It's not him I'm worried about,' she whispered again. 'I'm trying not to wake my mother. If she asks me how her bum looks in one more outfit I'll strangle her with the cord of the baby monitor.'

'Well, guess what?' I said, trying to distract her. 'Angelica says she can hook me up with a producer and maybe get me a job on TV!'

There was silence.

'You're not serious,' Louise said eventually.

'Yeah,' I went on. 'She says I have natural talent. Apparently I glow on the screen.'

'She's up to something,' Louise growled. 'I don't trust her.'

'Don't be ridiculous,' I said. 'She's a lovely person – you're just feeling a bit down in the dumps. It's perfectly natural after you've had a baby. You're probably suffering from post-natal depression.'

Then Louise burst into uncontrollable tears.

'You see? I told you.' I tutted. 'Don't worry, it'll pass. And if it doesn't there's always drugs. I hear they can really help.'

Louise howled even louder. 'I'm going to kill my mother if she tells me one more time my boobs will never be the same again. She's enjoying this – I swear she is,' she sobbed.

Hung up feeling uneasy. Irrational rage with a tendency to weep and feel out of control are textbook signs of baby blues. Maybe I should call the health visitor and alert her that Louise is at high risk of causing serious bodily harm to someone. Most likely her mother.

PS Katie has announced that she wants to be a Pussycat Doll. She also wants to launch her own perfume and design a blingin' range of clothes. She spent all day singing, 'Don't Ya Wish Your Girlfriend Was Hot Like Me' to herself in the glass oven door, intermittently pouting and gyrating at the temperature knobs. Was quite alarmed that one session with Vera had reduced her to this.

Told Joe his only daughter wanted to flaunt herself on TV in a tight-fitting catsuit for fame and fortune.

'Do you think she has any talent?' he asked, perking up immediately. 'Those Pussycat Dolls probably earn a fortune.'

Was saddened to see he has learnt nothing from poor Britney's downfall. Having millions of dollars and access-all-areas passes to the best parties is not the key to happiness and fulfilment. Although I'm sure *I* will be able to handle it once Angelica decides that I can be her plus-one on a regular basis.

Second relationship-counselling session was much better than the first. In fact, it was quite fun. Probably because this time it was Joe's turn in the hot seat so I could relax and enjoy myself a bit. Just before the end we made a significant breakthrough.

'What was your childhood like, Joe?' Rita the counsellor asked.

'Fine,' Joe answered, shifting uncomfortably in the battered leather chair.

'His father had an extra-marital affair and his mother smothers him,' I babbled, unable to keep it in.

Rita raised her eyebrows knowingly.

'Let's give Joe an opportunity to speak, Susie,' she said, with a half-smile so I knew she was secretly on my side.

Joe glared at me, but I avoided his gaze. I was concentrating on trying to work out what Rita was thinking. Unfortunately she was very good at maintaining her I'm-an-objective-professional face, even when confronted with the shocking discovery that Joe's dark family skeletons had probably shaped his psyche from an early age.

'My mother is lonely,' he said. 'She only really has me to depend on.'

'So, you're an only child, Joe?' Rita made a note on her jotter.

'Oh, my God!' I burst out. 'I totally forgot – his brother's gay but he hasn't come out yet even though he's *thirty-five*.'

'Susie, you really must let Joe speak. You'll have your turn.'

Rita was obviously shocked by this revelation, which must have been why she was looking a bit tense.

'Yes, but it's a very toxic situation,' I went on. 'His mother is incredibly controlling, which is probably why David can't come out to her.'

I was getting into my stride when Rita's little clock buzzed. It was the end of the session.

'Susie, for next time I want you to think about respect,' Rita said, eyeing me sternly.

'Respect?' I gazed back at her.

'Yes, you don't seem to have much for Joe's opinions. I know it's difficult for you not to interrupt but you must learn to listen to him. Only then can true communication begin.'

I asked Joe in the car on the way home if he thought I didn't listen to him.

'Sometimes,' he said, indicating left even though I'd told him the shortest way home was to turn right.

'But why didn't you tell me?' I asked, a bit shocked he felt that way.

'I suppose I was too busy with work. But that's all changing. Almost dying has made me realize there's more to life than professional success. Communication with your partner is crucial. I'm really looking forward to getting down to the nitty-gritty and trying to find out why we had that blip. Aren't you?' He patted my hand.

'I guess so,' I said, feeling my stomach heave and turn over. Hopefully there'll be weeks of faffing about and talking about our childhoods before we tackle any of that.

28 November

Less than four weeks to Christmas. Have made a detailed Christmas list.

- Joe – a selection of non-iron shirts.

- Mum – M&S tie-dye multiway sarong (she definitely admired mine when we visited last time).

- Dad – self-help book on emotional maturity (ask salesperson for recommendations. Make clear it is not for myself, but for an older gentleman with a penchant for putting his foot in it).

- Katie – stage-school stories and other tales of inspiration for girls, plus assorted array of dance accessories.

- Jack – something other than the dog collar and lead he wants.

- Louise – Trinny and Susannah super-duper Lycra knickers to pull in saggy post-partum tummy.

- Dargan – a baby-walker. His legs are so enormous he may well need the support soon.

- Mrs H – George Michael biography.

- Rita the counsellor – a large box of expensive chocolates. Hopefully that will put her off asking unnecessary probing questions about infidelity, etc.

Joe's firm is not having a Christmas party this year. Not even in January. Am quite relieved after last year's débâcle when I had to endure the attentions of a lecherous eighty-year-old director, but Joe seemed a bit upset.

'But where's the joy?' he asked, when I said I was delighted I wouldn't now have to put up with endless small-talk with old fogeys over a reheated dinner and a swing-along dance session. 'Christmas is supposed to be magical, you know.'

'Well, I may have just the thing to cheer you up, darling,' I said, seeing my opportunity. 'We've been invited to a fabulous charity auction next week. It's very exclusive – the tickets are like gold dust.'

'How did you manage to get some, then?' He was looking at me suspiciously.

'Angelica Law invited us.' I smiled. 'It's a real privilege to be asked, you know. And it's the perfect way to celebrate the season. We have a romantic night out and get to contribute to charity. It's ideal.'

I left out the small detail that we had to pay an enormous sum of money to attend.

'OK,' he said, brightening. 'It does sound fun.'

Then he hugged me and I felt a bit guilty. But I absolutely cannot lose face in front of Angelica. Find myself thinking more and more about her promise to fast-track me to a high-profile TV career.

PS Katie and Jack are suspiciously quiet about Christmas. Think they may already be jaded and bitter. Or they are waiting to launch an offside attack when I least expect it.

29 November

Took Katie and Jack to see Santa in the Centre to capture some Christmas spirit.

He's been there for two weeks already, now that Christmas

is so commercialized. It did not go well. Suspect the project on civil liberties Katie is doing at school may be to blame. She has become quite militant.

She marched into the grotto, stood in front of a petrified Santa and demanded to know if Rudolph was getting enough protein, why Mrs Claus was banned from flying with him on Christmas Eve and whether the elves were on the minimum wage. Jack, meanwhile, concentrated on pulling Santa's nose hair to see if it was real. 'Women have the right to work as well, you know,' Katie announced, as she stared levelly at Santa. 'They aren't just slaves in the home. Mrs Claus could have a discrimination case against you. And the elves could too.'

'Of course, dear,' Santa agreed timidly. 'Now, what would you like me to bring for Christmas?' He looked at me pleadingly to intervene.

'I would like an iPod,' Katie said, staring him down. Then she leaned in close and whispered something in his ear. 'Do you think you could manage that?' she said. He nodded at her in terror.

Later she quizzed me in the car. 'Would you like to work outside the home, Mummy?'

'Um, sometimes I think I might,' I admitted, Angelica's praise about my star quality ringing in my ears.

'But what could you do?' she asked, her face crumpling in puzzlement. 'Unless maybe they need mummies to pack lunches in an office?'

Katie has been assaulted at Vera's Dance and Drama School!

'A mean girl kicked me,' she wailed, as she limped through the door after her lesson, a shamefaced Joe trailing behind.

After detailed questioning, Joe admitted he had sat in the car for the entire lesson, instead of pressing himself to the door and trying to ascertain what was going on inside or patrolling the parents' area and eavesdropping a bit at the very least.

'I did stay for a while,' he grumbled, when I reminded him how important it was to keep a close and vigilant eye on events, especially when there were showbiz mothers about. 'But it's like bloody boot camp – they take it way too seriously. Some of them were putting makeup on their kids and everything.'

I was outraged. No wonder the other children had looked so groomed last week. I had underestimated showbiz mothers, with their underhand use of cosmetics. David had been right – I'll apply lip-gloss and bronzing powder next week. It's obvious that Katie's rhythm and natural ability are causing jealousy – which is then manifesting itself in physical assaults. Can distinctly remember hearing that poor Christina Aguilera was bullied as a child because of her enormous talent. Luckily it didn't stop her becoming a multi-award-winning singer-songwriter – although it may have impinged on her fashion judgement just a bit. Those bumless leather chaps definitely erred on the side of bad taste.

Must remember to watch her *Behind the Music* special more closely next time it's on for tips on how to deal with this outrageous behaviour. Must also remember to have a quiet word in Vera's ear and discuss her bullying-on-the-dance-floor policy.

PS Louise called in a hysterical panic at eleven p.m. 'You don't think there's anything wrong with Dargan, do you?' she wailed. 'He won't stop crying.'

'All babies cry, Louise,' I replied, trying to sound comforting. 'It's probably colic. He'll get over it soon. By three months anyway.'

'Three *months*?' she screeched. 'If I don't get a full night's sleep soon, I'll lose my mind. And my eyes are so *puffy*. I think I'm actually developing *crow's feet*.' She broke into heartrending sobs.

'Don't worry, pet,' I said, taking charge. 'I'll get you some eye cream when I'm in town.'

I am definitely much more in tune with Louise again now that she knows motherhood doesn't consist of dressing a baby in cute designer outfits and pushing it about in a Bugaboo, with oversized shades on your head and a mocha latte on hand. Suspect she regrets packing her mother back to Canada so soon, even if she was no help whatsoever and spent her days filing her nails and applying neck cream. Am glad I can help – Louise will start to look her age soon, if she's not careful. Her skin is already starting to look grey and less dewy.

1 December

Katie and Jack have launched their pre-Christmas frenzy. I was almost relieved to hear them arguing over who would get most toys, who was on Santa's black list, who was Rudolph's favourite, etc., etc. At least it meant they had retained some childlike innocence. They spent the afternoon writing their Christmas lists to Santa. Had good intentions of creating a perfect festive atmosphere by baking a complicated Christmas cake and letting the aroma of soaked fruits waft about the place while carols played in the background but I abandoned this idea when I discovered that the recipe was more than a page long. Instead, I lit the open fire in the living room to create a Christmassy feel and scattered some pine-scented pot-pourri about. Am sure the deli in the Centre needs all the custom it can get at this time of year so am really being very selfless in deciding to support their gourmet cakes again.

Jack spent ages sprawled on the floor drawing the Power Ranger ensemble he wants. Meanwhile, Katie sat in the corner, scribbling furtively on a scrap of paper.

'What are you asking Santa for, darling?' I asked fondly, as she frowned with concentration.

'I can't tell you, Mummy,' she answered primly. 'It's a secret, remember?'

'But you could whisper to me, pet,' I said, feeling the first stirring of panic. If she didn't tell me what she wanted I'd have to take a wild guess.

'No, Mummy.' She was adamant. 'You can see it on Christmas morning.'

Then she marched straight to the fireplace and chucked in the list. I watched in horror as the flames licked it up.

'Now,' she announced, with glee, 'no one will know what Santa's going to bring me until Christmas morning. You are going to be *very* surprised, Mummy.'

She winked at me and turned on her heel and left the room as I tried not to hyperventilate. This was all Mrs H's fault. If she hadn't told the children that the traditional way to contact Father Christmas was to throw your list up the chimney, it would never have happened.

PS Have decided to revisit Santa at the Centre to ask what Katie wants – he's bound to remember her.

2 December

Trudged to the Centre to talk to Santa. Luckily I didn't have to queue for long.

'I need to know what my little girl wants for Christmas,' I said, eyeballing him so he'd know I was serious. 'It's vital.'

'Listen, lady,' he sighed, looking bored, 'I see hundreds of squawking brats every week. There's no way I can remember what yours wants.'

Patiently explained to him that Katie had been the bright child who had quizzed him at length on gender equality in the workplace.

'Oh, *her*.' He paled a bit under his beard. 'Yeah, I remember *her*. She wants a flatscreen TV for her bedroom. And an iPod.'

'What?' I said, feeling faint.

'Yeah, she's quite a character,' he sneered. 'Good luck with that.' He reached into his pocket and pulled out a packet of Nicorette chewing-gum. 'If I don't have a smoke soon I'll swing for one of them kids,' he muttered.

Am at my wit's end – how will we afford a flatscreen TV? Maybe I could try eBay or a friendly local criminal.

3 December

Mum called to confirm that she and Dad will be spending Christmas in Portugal with their new friends on an over-sized yacht. Was determined not to let her know I was furious so I did an Emmy-worthy impression of nonchalance. 'That's fine, Mum,' I said bravely. 'We'll be quite busy ourselves this year, what with Katie's dance show. And we have that charity auction tonight – there'll be dozens of celebs . . .' I trailed off deliberately, hoping she'd ask lots of questions.

'Oh, that's wonderful, darling.' Mum sounded relieved. 'Dad said you'd kick up a terrible fuss if we didn't come back for the holidays, but I knew you'd be fine.'

Bit my tongue to stop an acidic retort escaping. No point proving Dad right.

Told Joe I'd get my own back by accidentally-on-purpose posting Dad's Christmas present late to teach him a lesson.

'That's not what Christmas is about, though, is it?' he said, in a faraway voice, looking sad. 'Where's the joy?'

Was tempted to suggest that if he was still looking for joy he could whisk us away to Lapland for the three-night magical experience I'd seen advertised on the back of the *Gazette*. 'Well, we have the auction tonight,' I said. 'That'll be lots of fun.'

'Oh, yeah, I forgot about that,' he said, cheering up.

Didn't feel the time was right to tell him he'd have to squeeze into his old tux – he's definitely put on a few pounds recently and that might only depress him more.

4 December

Am in a state of shock. Last night, at the glamorous charity auction dinner, I managed to buy a bespoke Harley-Davidson motorbike. Joe is not speaking to me.

I tried to explain at breakfast that it was the excitement of being surrounded by the rich and beautiful that made me raise my hand at a critical moment in the proceedings, but he refused to believe me. 'You were jumping up and down and shouting so the auctioneer could hear you, Susie,' he pointed out. 'Other people gave up.'

'OK,' I admitted, 'but I never thought for a second that my bid would be accepted. I presumed one of the celebs would wade in and double the offer.'

'They couldn't get a word in edgeways,' he said, his head in his hands, 'and now we're five thousand euro down and stuck with a Harley-Davidson we'll never use.'

'Yes,' I conceded. 'But at least the food was good.'

'That's true. It was to die for – those garlic prawns were divine.' Then he looked off into the middle distance, a dreamy expression on his face. 'I often thought I'd like to be a chef.'

I snorted with laughter. 'What? Like Gordon Ramsay in *The F Word*?'

'Gordon Ramsay is very highly respected.' Joe sniffed. 'I'd do anything to be able to cook like that.'

I shuffled off, still laughing. As if he could ever cook like a pro – he can barely boil an egg.

Meanwhile Angelica's delighted with me.

'Buying the Harley was *sooo* generous of you, Susie,' she said, throwing her arms round me and hugging me warmly at the school gate. 'Are you going to ride it?'

'Um, I don't think so,' I mumbled, not wanting to admit that Joe wanted to get rid of it on eBay. I was relishing the hug and the way the other mothers were gawking in open jealousy.

'You're gonna keep it as a memento, huh?' She narrowed her eyes. 'That's a *greeeeat* idea. Listen, I was wondering if you could do me another favour?' She hooked her arm through mine and led me away from the other mums.

133

'Um, OK, I suppose so,' I said, as their eyes burnt into my back.

'James and I really need to get away. Just to have a weekend to reconnect, you know how it is.' She stared intensely at me, her perfectly plucked eyebrows framing her radiant complexion.

'Sure,' I said, transfixed by her curled eyelashes and wondering if she had them professionally dyed. 'Alone-time is very important.'

'That's right!' She grasped my hand. 'I just *knew* you'd understand. The thing is, though, everywhere we go the goddamn press follow us. It's impossible to get any privacy.'

'That must be awful,' I said, patting her hand. 'Fame can't be easy.'

'Ain't that the truth,' she said, hauling her massive Chanel tote on to the other shoulder. 'Anyway, I remember you telling me that you had a little hideout in the country. I was wondering if we could maybe shoot down next weekend – no one would think of looking for us there.'

'Of course!' I said, not having to think twice about it – her using the country house as a celeb retreat would be an honour. 'I'll get you the keys.'

'You're such a good friend, Susie,' she murmured, hugging me again. 'I knew I did the right thing getting those auction tickets for you. By the way, you can't write a cheque for them, can you? My accountant's screaming for it. He's so controlling.'

PS Called Joe to tell him we'd be spending this weekend in the country. He didn't seem very enthusiastic about the idea. But what's the point in having a country retreat if you never spend any time there? Also, it's vital to clean the entire place from top to bottom before Angelica and James use it.

Wonder if I could rope in Mrs H to lend a hand. She loves a good cleaning challenge.

5 December

Next time I decide to visit our country retreat, I will remember the following.

- Attempts to fill the car with all the necessary equipment for a flying visit (smoky bacon crisps, wine, packets of instant mash, etc.) will mean at least a two-hour delay before set-off.

- Attempts to create old-fashioned fun in the car on the way by playing I Spy or singing nursery rhymes will be met with strong opposition and loud clamouring for the Pussycat Dolls CD from both children.

- Attempts to indulge in cosy chat with husband will be met with frosty silence and grunts about 'bloody traffic' and/or comments about the rat race.

- Attempts to rustle up a nutritious dinner upon arrival will fail abysmally when it is discovered that all provisions have freezer burn.

- Attempts to placate children and spouse will not work until they have visited the local chip shop for batter burgers.

- Attempts to stick to dietary principles by refusing to eat said batter burgers will result in fierce hunger pangs and eventual devouring of entire six-pack of smoky bacon crisps in one sitting.

'Maybe we should get someone to look in on the house every now and again, Joe,' I said, wondering how I was going to get the place looking shabby chic/rock starry before Angelica and James used it.

'Give someone a key you mean?' He looked thoughtful. 'That's probably not a bad idea, let them air the place – that sort of thing.'

'Um, I was thinking of something more permanent, actually,' I suggested. 'You know, like a live-in butler.' I was busy imagining a friendly old caretaker who would get the house ready at a moment's notice if we decided to visit on a whim. Someone who dressed in an old-fashioned uniform and served Pimm's on the lawn would be perfect.

Joe roared with laughter, which I thought was a bit rude. Bet Becks never laughs at Posh when she tells him she needs a bit more domestic help.

'Don't be ridiculous, Susie,' he snorted, 'we can barely afford the repayments on the house, let alone get a live-in butler to take care of it.'

'Well, what about a Range Rover, then?' I wheedled. 'Everyone who has a house in the country has a Range Rover. It's practically required.'

'Well, we won't be getting one,' he said, 'so you can forget about it. We already have a Harley we can't get rid of. Anyway, those four-by-fours are an assault on the environment.'

Was very annoyed. All this talk of environmental protection was pure bluff – Joe was never concerned about the environment before. In fact, if I recall, he always said that global warming was quite handy as it meant he could play more golf.

PS Have come up with the perfect solution: a Range Rover Sport. They are cheaper *and* Angelica drives one.

6 December

Katie and Jack spent the afternoon moving a bucket of mud from one far corner of the garden to another. I'm so glad they're getting to experience true country living and will grow up knowing where milk comes from, etc. Am seriously considering getting a small cow.

Meanwhile, I spent the afternoon scrubbing the toilet and trying to brighten the place up for Angelica and James without Joe cottoning on that soon they would be frolicking in our chipped bath and having a *9½ Weeks* moment with the mayonnaise in our fridge.

PS Am trying not to panic about the overgrown garden. Luckily the wild-country-cottage look is all the rage – it was in the *Gazette* gardening supplement last week. People spend years trying to achieve what I seem to have managed in just a few weeks. Maybe I should be a gardening columnist – there's nothing to it, really, just let things run amok a bit and *voilà* – I could be charging people entry at the gate!

PPS Dog is behaving like a frisky puppy. I do feel he's truly happy in the country – he spent ages out and about roaming wild and free, as Nature intended.

7 December

Travelled back to the city in silence. The children were furious that they had been forced to clear the country house of all sorts of rubbish. Joe was furious that he had been made to repaint the kitchen at very short notice. I was furious that Joe had stupidly purchased lime green paint instead of reliable golden cream in the hardware shop because it was on special offer, and the dog was furious that he was headed back to a tiny city garden and no longer had free run of the countryside. It was all very bleak. The only bonus was that at least there was relative silence for the entire journey – except for Katie and Jack exchanging an occasional insult in the back seat.

As soon as we got back Mrs H came bursting through the door.

'David's bringing Max home for Christmas!' she bellowed. 'What am I going to do?'

Joe and I looked at each other. Was it possible she'd finally put two and two together and realized they were more than just good friends?

'His family are all dead, God rest them, so David said he has nowhere to go,' she wheezed. 'But Max is used to very glamorous events – I'll have to lay on something really special . . . and as for the food! Do you think we could get caterers in? I'm in a tizzy – David really is very naughty not to have given me more notice.'

Then she collapsed in the Queen Anne chair and Joe had to make a gin and tonic to revive her.

'A mother's lot is not an easy one, Susie,' she said, once she'd come round a bit. 'You'll have to help me.'

'What about Westlife?' I heard myself say. 'They're doing a special Christmas concert – I heard there were tickets left.'

'Westlife? Oh, I do love a bit of Westlife. Are they glamorous enough, though, do you think?' She looked doubtful.

'Absolutely!' I reassured her. 'Those boys are glamour on legs.'

'Yes, they *do* look good in those white suits.' Mrs H was getting a funny look in her eye. 'Almost as good as Barry Manilow, in fact.' She took another slug of her gin and tonic.

'You should book the tickets,' I said. 'Max won't know what hit him.'

I could feel she was starting to cave in and I felt a smidgen of shame for encouraging her but I was desperate – the chance to see a delicious boy band up close and personal didn't present itself every day and there was no way I could afford tickets, not now I had the charity dinner *and* a Harley to pay for.

'Maybe you're right, Susie,' Mrs H said, whipping a lined jotter out of her bag and beginning to write. 'Let's make a list.'

I knew instantly that she meant business – she was using her permanent marker, the one she saves for very special occasions.

'She'd better still be having us for Christmas dinner,' Joe muttered darkly later. 'I want proper roast potatoes this year.'

Think this was a veiled reference to the pre-prepared potatoes I served last year but decided not to say anything. Am also hoping to get a proper roast dinner this year – one I don't have to make myself.

8 December

Got an irate call from a farmer, who informed me that the dog had been caught frolicking with his pedigree sheepdog bitch at the weekend. He has threatened to shoot on sight if he ever catches him having his wicked way with her again. The dog is hiding under the stairs, looking very guilty.

Also got an email from David.

> I think Max is going to propose! He dragged me
> down to Hatton Garden yesterday to look at

diamond-stud earrings, just like the ones David
Beckham wears (OK, maybe not as big). Do you
think that's a good sign?
David xoxo

---

9 December

As if I don't have enough on my plate! Louise has asked
me to complete her Christmas shopping. Apparently, she's
too exhausted to get out of her pyjamas and go into town
to do it herself. Sadly, my heavy hints that she could mind
Katie and Jack for the afternoon while I sorted it out fell
on deaf ears so I was forced to battle my way through the
city-centre crowds with them complaining loudly all the
way. I tried to interest them in the magical Christmas display in the Brown Thomas window, but instead of putting
dancing polar bears and laughing Santas out, the store had
gone for half-dressed mannequins, dripping with diamonds
and lying suggestively on what looked like a mound of fox
furs.

'Where's Santa?' Jack roared. 'I want Santa!'

Tried to explain to him that in Celtic Tiger Ireland Santa
is not as important as selling luxury goods for lots of money
to harassed customers.

He was not impressed. Happily, Katie was overawed by
the Mac makeup counter and seduced the assistant into
giving her a full makeover, including shaded brows and lip
liner, leaving me to complete Louise's list in record time.
Unfortunately, I was then forced to purchase two hundred
euro worth of Mac products out of guilt.

PS I noticed that there was no expensive gift for me on
Louise's list — maybe she's ordered something exclusive

from overseas. Like a top-of-the-range Marc Jacobs handbag from New York.

10 December

Louise called to ask me for brunch. Was delighted – she was obviously going to rustle up something gorgeous to thank me for the Christmas shopping.

'So you can come round tomorrow at ten-ish, then?' she asked.

'Great,' I said. 'Would you like me to bring anything?'

'Bring anything? No, just yourself,' she replied, sounding confused.

Am so looking forward to having a scrumptious plateful handed to me – feel I may be lacking in essential minerals and vitamins and a gourmet meal could be just the remedy.

PS Found myself watching the TV7 tape about Dargan's dramatic car-park delivery again tonight. I really do look good on screen. Maybe Angelica's right and I *do* have star quality.

11 December

Arrived at Louise's to discover she had not rustled up Eggs Benedict and freshly squeezed orange juice. She had, in fact, made an appointment with the hairdresser and intended to leave me in sole charge of Dargan while she hotfooted it to the salon for a full head of highlights, lowlights and a deep-conditioning treatment.

'Thanks, Susie. The time has come for me to get my act together. I've moped about for long enough and I really need to get my roots done,' she said, as she pulled a sheepskin coat over her shoulders and checked her reflection in the hall mirror. 'I don't want to be one of those mothers who let themselves go and slob around in their tracksuits all day. Do you know what I mean?'

She stared at me intensely, obviously waiting for me to say something in response.

'Well, it's OK to wear tracksuits sometimes,' I mumbled, thankful my handy fleece was preventing her from seeing the mismatch of old sweatpants and bobbled jumper I had on underneath. 'Looking after a baby isn't all glamour. You have to be practical as well.'

'Ah, yes, it may be OK for you,' she said sympathetically, 'but I firmly believe that you can take pride in your appearance and still be a good mother – the two don't have to be mutually exclusive. And who knows? I may get back into the dating game as well – what man will look at a woman with a saggy jelly belly and grey roots?'

She handed Dargan to me and gave herself one last glance in the mirror.

'I've left detailed lists of instructions on the fridge,' she called, slamming the door behind her and disappearing up the front path before I could say breast milk.

Decided not to be annoyed with Louise. She is obviously still in the first deluded stage of motherhood, when you actually think you will get back to normal some day. Also, her hair did need doing. Which is precisely the trouble with having high-maintenance hair. It needs looking after.

It was quite nice to spend some nice quality time with Dargan, though – it almost gave me a broody pang. Except it was a little disconcerting when he kept burrowing into my chest area looking for milk. Was just settling him for his nap when Louise burst through the door, hair dripping.

'What happened?' I gasped.

'Nothing,' she cried, snatching Dargan from me. 'I just missed him *soooo* much I couldn't stand it.'

I smiled at her and switched on the kettle. She's also at that stage when you can't bear to be parted from your child – a fuzzy feeling I can just about remember.

12 December

Met Angelica at the school carol service. 'Did you get those house keys for me, Susie?' she whispered, as the kids warbled their way through 'Little Donkey' completely off-key.

'Yes,' I whispered back, passing them to her with written directions to get there. 'It's nothing fancy, though,' I said. 'I hope you won't be disappointed.' I was terrified she'd be repulsed by the modest house, even if the pared-back look *was* in.

'Don't worry, honey.' She slipped the keys and the directions into her cashmere coat pocket. 'This little getaway is exactly what the doctor ordered.'

Then she joined in the singing lustily before I could ask her if she had been serious about my star quality and if she really could get me a high-profile TV job. (With maybe a PA, a personal trainer and a makeup artist on standby 24/7.)

13 December

Mrs H has bought the tickets! We're going to see Westlife live in concert for Christmas!

'I HATE Westlife,' Katie moaned, after Mrs H announced the happy news when we dropped by. 'They're really *old*.'

'Don't be silly, Katie.' I rushed to cover her *faux pas*. 'That's very kind of you, Mrs H,' I said, nudging Katie to say thank you. 'We'd love to go.'

'Yes, well, I thought I'd better organize some kind of entertainment,' she said, obviously thrilled with herself. 'Thanks for the tip, Susie dear.'

'Not at all,' I said, pretending to be embarrassed. 'It was the least I could do.'

'Yes, and I love that fellow with the sparkly eyes,' she went on. 'What's his name? Oh, yes, Kian. He's gorgeous and *such* a gentleman. I'll bet he'd put up a few shelves for his mother if he was asked.' She threw a dagger look in Joe's direction while he hid behind the paper. 'I just hope Max isn't disappointed by my modest surroundings. He's probably used to very starry affairs.' She peered at the kitchen critically.

In a rush of foolhardy sympathy, I suddenly found myself agreeing to bring her to Habitat to buy a few key accessories to brighten up the place for the holiday season.

'Nothing too garish, mind,' she said, 'I know your taste can be a little eccentric, Susie dear. I'd favour more classic lines myself – muted, subdued shades. Taupe, maybe.'

PS Hopefully Mrs H's new muted, subdued self will refrain from buying me another hideous red dressing-gown for Christmas.

14 December

Called Angelica to see if she'd got into the country house all right.

'Is everything OK?' I asked, when she eventually answered her phone.

'Everything's just perfect, Susie, thanks, honey,' she purred. 'This place is *soooo* cute and the break is doing us both the world of good.'

I could hear James giggling in the background.

Am really pleased I have been instrumental in rejuvenating a celebrity marriage. If only I had been on hand to help Britney and Kevin things might have turned out very differently for them.

PS Louise called. 'Dargan just smiled at me!' she half sobbed down the phone.

'Really?' I said, not wanting to burst her bubble and break it to her it was probably wind that was making him grimace.

'Yes! Oh, Susie, it was so adorable. I feel like we really connected, you know? It's as if all the sleepless nights are worth it now.'

She rambled on for ages while I half listened. Highlights of *I'm a Celebrity Get Me Out of Here* were on – Z-list celebs battling over a campfire is compulsive viewing.

It's nice that Louise has mellowed and is allowing herself to enjoy motherhood instead of worrying about her general appearance or her roots, though. This sort of stance has worked very well for me over the past five years.

15 December

Jack has a lead role in the playschool nativity production!

'Your Jack is going to be such a cute shepherd,' another mother said, as I tried to unhook Jack's arms from their vice-like grip on my leg and propel him through the door this morning.

'Sorry?' I said, wondering what she was talking about.

'He's one of the shepherds in the play. Didn't he tell you?'

'Jack, is that right?' I asked, incredulous that he hadn't shared this nugget of information with me.

'I *hate* shepherds!' He gave the other mother an evil stare. 'They're for *babies*.'

I quickly decided to downplay the subject before his rage escalated out of control, gave a weak smile and ran for the people-carrier, trying to conceal my distress that my only son was not confiding his innermost thoughts and secrets to me. God only knows what else is going on that I'm unaware of. Am going to tackle the Little Angels' head teacher about her worrying lack of communication ASAP. This type of slip-up is simply unacceptable.

PS Louise is becoming positively matronly.

'Dargan gurgled at me this morning,' she said, when she rang to ask if it was possible for such a young baby to lift his head off a pillow, or if she should contact *The Guinness Book of Records*. 'I really think he's very bright – don't you, Susie?'

Agreed with her just to get her off the phone. Thankfully I was never as boring about Katie and Jack.

16 December

Little Angels' head teacher says she sent a note to all parents updating them about the nativity play. She also said that Jack is still being quite a disruptive force in the classroom. 'I did try to speak to you about this earlier in the year, Mrs Hunt,' she said coolly. 'He's still reluctant to participate in group activities, which is why we gave him the shepherd role – to encourage him.'

'But you never told me he had a part,' I stuttered, wondering what she meant by disruptive. 'I didn't even know you were having a nativity play this year.'

The head teacher sighed loudly. 'The note was distributed in October,' she said. 'We've been having dress rehearsals for some time now. Maybe you should consider becoming more involved in Jack's learning here at Little Angels. It might help his socialization skills.'

I slunk away, utterly humiliated.

PS Have found half a dozen notes at the bottom of Jack's Power Rangers backpack. They were hard to decipher, what with all the dried-in yoghurt and mushy banana. Am very ashamed.

17 December: Joe's birthday

Had long one-to-one chat with Jack last night about his communication issues. Tried to make him see that holding back his emotions does not help matters. He must confide in me and share any concerns he may have. Think I may have got through to him, although he continued to play with his Hot Wheels toy car as I talked. He did glance in my direction every so often, though.

Joe says I'm panicking about nothing.

'Jack is just an active little boy,' he said, when I confided that he might be heading for some sort of juvenile-delinquency centre if he doesn't start to toe the line. 'He has lots of personality and that's what counts at the end of the day. Would you want him to be submissive and quiet all the time? That would be no use when he grows up and learns how unforgiving the world is and how you have to give up your dreams to fit in. The meaner and tougher he is the better.'

'What do you mean, give up your dreams?' I asked, a little concerned that he looked so forlorn.

'When I was a boy I didn't want to be a director, you know, Susie,' he said, hanging his head. 'I wanted to be something much more creative. But life gets in the way, doesn't it?'

'You know what?' I said slowly. 'We should probably talk about this in counselling. I mean, I didn't want to be a house-wife when I was a child, I wanted to be Wonder Woman. There's probably loads of issues we need to explore.'

'That's a good idea.' He smiled. 'I'm so glad you're taking the counselling seriously. It means a lot to me.'

Felt a bit guilty when he said that but I'm secretly delighted that I can now introduce a new topic to the sessions – anything to divert attention from Lone Father and me. And who knows? I may even get some insight into how I ended up picking fluff off the hall, stairs and landing for a living instead of saving the day in a pointy bra and shiny pants.

PS Think Joe was a little disappointed that I hadn't organized a surprise birthday bash for him, but it's probably better to ignore the whole day at his age. Have decided to dress up as Wonder Woman some night soon to make it up to him – just have to practise my twirling moves first.

18 December

Went to the third counselling session with Rita.

'So, today we're going to talk about your affair, Susie,' she announced, before we had even sat down.

'Eh?' I said, horrified. 'What about my childhood? I've loads of really damaging stuff to talk about. And Joe had a breakthrough last night. He feels he had to give up his childhood dream,' I gabbled.

'Yes, and we'll get to that,' she said gently. 'But first I

want to ask you why you felt the need to look outside your marriage for a relationship.'

'Well, it wasn't exactly a relationship,' I stuttered. I could feel Joe staring intensely at me. 'He was just a friend, really.'

'A platonic friend?'

'Um, mostly.' My face was starting to burn.

'So, what do you think drove you to seek out his company?' Rita was like a dog with a bone and she wasn't letting go.

'He paid me attention, I suppose,' I said, looking at my feet. 'Joe was busy with work. I was lonely.'

'But you have lots of friends, Susie,' Joe said. 'How can you be lonely?'

'Full-time motherhood is hard,' I answered, glancing at him out of the corner of my eye. 'Sometimes I need more.'

'Do you feel fulfilled by life, Susie?' Rita asked.

'Um, yes,' I said, guessing that was what she wanted to hear.

'Why don't you think about it before you answer?' She smiled kindly at me.

'Well, I suppose I can get a bit bored and down at times.' Tears pricked the back of my eyes. 'Sometimes I think there's got to be more to life – every day it's the same endless round of thankless tasks.'

I stopped, feeling a bit funny and out of breath.

'I never knew you felt like that,' Joe said softly.

'It's OK,' I whispered. 'I never knew I felt that way either until just now.'

'And are you fulfilled, Joe?' Rita asked.

'Well, I do feel as if I'm searching for more. I had a near-death experience recently and it's changed my perspective.'

'So how can you both resolve these issues, do you think?' Rita was chewing her pen thoughtfully.

'Take a holiday to the Caribbean?' I suggested, feeling a flicker of excitement. A week on a deserted beach was bound to do us the world of good.

Rita smiled. 'Yes, that would probably be nice. But what I'm getting at is that you have to find inner fulfilment to be happy with yourself and others. Why don't you think about that over the Christmas break?'

Didn't like to tell her that we were going to be too busy concealing David's true sexuality over the Christmas break to do anything else – thought it might have deflated her a bit.

19 December

Mrs H has gone into a Christmas frenzy. Spent more than an hour this morning trying to talk her out of a decision to buy a live turkey and wring its neck in the backyard to create the right seasonal atmosphere.

'But Max is mad about all those organicals, or whatever they're called,' she said, looking worried. 'David says he goes to a farmers' market every weekend – although I can't understand where all the farmers are in central London.'

'It's "organic", Mrs H, and don't worry – you can buy an organic turkey in the supermarket,' I soothed. 'You don't have to slaughter one on the premises to get the same effect.'

She didn't look too convinced. 'Do you think so?'

'Absolutely,' I reassured her. 'And we'll buy nice organic vegetables as well. Everyone will be delighted.'

Am quite annoyed that Christmas at Mrs H's is starting to be such hard work – may as well have had it at home.

Jack continued to express himself today by not participating in the nativity play in any way, shape or form. In fact, he ripped off the cute little tea-towel headscarf in the first five minutes, refused point-blank to say his lines and stomped off the stage at the first song.

Am at my wit's end. Despite what Joe says, if Jack doesn't learn to be a team player how will he ever become an international sports legend? Also, I could see the other playschool mothers blatantly nudging and whispering to each other as Jack screamed blue murder off-stage. Wonder if Vera the dance teacher could take him in hand and groom him to be the next Justin Timberlake? Her knock-'em-down-to-build-'em-up policy could be just what he needs.

Meanwhile, Mrs H announced that she needs a new outfit for Christmas Day and wants me to accompany her into town to choose something appropriate. Was quite flattered that she valued my good taste and eye for fashion, although I was also concerned that battling through the crowds in the week before Christmas wasn't a good idea. I was still quite traumatized from completing Louise's shopping.

'Yes, I'll need someone to help me with the bags, Susie dear,' Mrs H said, dusting imaginary dandruff from my shoulders as she spoke, 'especially if we're going to Habitat as well. You have a nice strapping pair of arms so you'll do nicely.'

PS Have just realized that have not had an invitation to the Christmas drinks do from Evil Anna and my other former work colleagues. They have finally forgotten that I ever existed.

Next time I agree to accompany mother-in-law on a shopping trip I will remember the following.

- Do not offer an opinion on any outfits tried on. (NB Absolutely do not suggest that revealing too much cleavage is unsuitable for a woman of her years or that she suffers from VPL.)

- Ditto suitable colours or fabrics. (NB Never say that sequins can make a person look a bit bulky.)

- Ditto dress size. (NB Do not laugh out loud when mother-in-law insists she can squeeze into a size twelve, when she is patently a good size eighteen.)

- Do not laugh at enormous girdle worn by mother-in-law.

- Ditto bunions.

- Do not agree to barter with the shop assistant to get a better price for chosen outfit.

- Do not argue with mother-in-law when she insists on buying hideous retro velour cushions in Habitat.

- Do not agree to carry all purchases from shop to shop due to fictitious back problems of mother-in-law.

- Do not agree to take mother-in-law for 'quick pick-me-up' in local hostelry, resulting in much merriment and flirting with barmen (hers) and lots of embarrassment and heartache (mine).

Called round to Angelica's with a poinsettia plant – the only one that Jack hadn't torn to shreds with his plastic Transformers sword.

'Susie! What are you doing here?' she said, looking a bit flustered when she opened the door.

'Happy holidays!' I said, hoping she'd ask me in for eggnog or something else Martha Stewartish. 'Did you have a great time in the country?'

She stepped out and closed the door before she answered.

'Yes, we did, thanks.' She glanced over her shoulder. 'Listen, Susie, James is in a really bad mood – the movie isn't going well and he's very upset. Would it be OK if we chatted another time?'

'Oh, sure,' I said, a bit disappointed. I'd been hoping for a sing-along with a few big names in entertainment round her baby-grand piano. 'It's just I wanted to ask you about the TV thing.'

'The TV thing?' she said blankly.

'Yes ... My counsellor says I need to find something to fulfil me and you said you might be able to hook me up with a producer and stuff ... I thought maybe a job might help.'

'Oh, yeah! I talked to a contact in TV7 about that – he *sooo* wants to meet you.'

'Really? When?' I was thrilled.

'Soon – probably first thing in the new year. See you then!'

She grabbed the poinsettia and disappeared inside.

Am over the moon. Soon I'll be mixing in all the best

circles! Who knows? I could be hobnobbing with the entire *Ugly Betty* cast this time next year.

23 December

At the last minute Joe announced he couldn't go to the airport to pick up Second Son David and his friend/secret lover Max the weatherman. He asked if I could battle my way through the airport crowds and do it.

'Why can't they take a taxi?' I was a bit put out that I'd be missing the excellent Christmas movie on TV7 and the chance to read in *Red* magazine how to create the perfect Christmas (which, of course, I do not have to do as Mrs H is taking care of most things).

'I'm sorry, Susie, but Mum wants to give them a proper Irish welcome.' He sighed, then explained that he was about to go to a top-level management meeting and couldn't be disturbed under any circumstances. 'She won't hear of them getting a taxi.'

'So I'm supposed to drop everything and get them?' I fumed, feeling totally taken for granted and very aggrieved.

'Well, I'd love to do it, Susie,' he said, 'but unfortunately I'm stuck here doing a thankless job that's sucking my soul dry.' Then he paused. 'I'll make it up to you, if that helps.'

Informed him, in no uncertain terms, that making it up to me would involve buying a bumper hamper of Bliss beauty products (to include the miraculous blackhead-removing stick thingy), a Burberry hat and scarf set and a cappuccino-maker, with the special gadget for perfect frothing (and a jumbo pack of mini-marshmallows to accompany same).

Took Katie and Jack to pick up David and Max from the airport.

I didn't recognize David at first – he was so bronzed and glowing.

'Are you wearing makeup, Uncle David?' Katie asked, eyes like saucers.

Suddenly it dawned on me why he was so orange round the gills. 'It's fake tan!' I burst into laughter. 'David, you are hilarious.'

'It's just a little tinted moisturizer,' he said, pursing his lips. 'Wearing black can be very draining when you have such a pale Celtic complexion. Isn't that right, Max?'

He turned to Max, who was dragging an array of matching suitcases behind him and was struggling to stay upright. 'Sure,' he said, winking at Katie. Then he leant down and whispered, 'But he may have gone a touch overboard.'

'Makeup is *yuk*!' Jack shouted, jumping at David's thigh and trying to hold on.

'Men don't wear makeup.' Katie giggled. 'It's for girls.'

'Well, *this* man does.' David stuck out his Pringle-clad chest and in one swift movement peeled Jack deftly off his leg. 'Now, darlings, did I ever tell you that naughty little girls and boys only get coal in their stocking for Christmas?'

He strutted away, the children following open-mouthed in his wake.

'You're lucky,' Max said, handing me a suitcase to carry. 'That's his pared-down look – he *was* going to highlight his cheekbones with peach blusher.'

24 December

Spent the evening displaying a vast assortment of toys under the Christmas tree. Luckily, I'd managed to persuade Joe that a flatscreen TV would be an excellent long-term investment. (Although he doesn't yet know that it will be hanging on a wall in Katie's room and unavailable for watching Sky Sports round the clock in the living room.)

PS Am very nervous about Louise joining us for dinner at Joe's mother's. Really hope she doesn't breastfeed at the Christmas table – Mrs H simply does not believe in any kind of bodily exposure – even if Dargan's nutrition does depend on it. Also, suspect it would put me right off the sage and onion stuffing. Wonder if it's too late to buy her an electric breast pump for Christmas.

25 December: Christmas Day

All hell has broken loose. Last night Mrs H found David and Max in a very compromising position underneath the mistletoe and has taken a funny turn. Christmas dinner is hanging in the balance.

26 December: St Stephen's Day

Everything is still in upheaval after yesterday's events. Mrs H took to her bed in protest at the discovery of illicit homosexual activities under her roof and all Christmas festivities decamped to our house. David was a sobbing mess and kept cornering me in the kitchen to say that Max was his one true love and that if Mrs H couldn't accept him he may never get a cut-price Ryanair flight home ever again.

Meanwhile Max kept that famous English stiff upper lip and just got on with things. (I suspect that the 'miracle' serum he applies every hour on the hour may have had something to do with it. In fact, the entire area from his lip to his forehead seems strangely frozen.) He was a whiz with a potato-peeler and turned some of the mouldering carrots in the veg compartment into very fetching flowers for the table while I tried to concoct a meal from the remnants in the freezer. (Sadly, *Red* magazine's Christmas special did not have an article on how to deal with this eventuality – may write and suggest it for next year.)

Was almost tempted to send Joe on an undercover mission to Mrs H's, where a fridgeful of organic delights was going a-begging but decided against it. Apparently she had freaked out when she'd caught Max and David snogging with abandon in her living room.

Was teeny bit embarrassed that Max would now have to consume freezer-burned steak and oven chips for Christmas dinner but decided to adopt a 'together under siege' mentality, just like an old second world war movie. Strangely, it seemed to work – we definitely bonded in the kitchen while Joe played with Katie and Jack in the living room, Louise nursed Dargan and sipped goat's milk and David watched *The Lion King* and snivelled into his monogrammed hankie.

'I'm so sorry this has gone so badly wrong, Max,' I volunteered, as he lit some of the scented candles he had whipped out of his man-bag, 'but I'm sure you must be used to dealing with repression by now.'

'What do you mean?' he asked, turning his finely chiselled face towards me and cocking one eyebrow, just like a gorgeous gay James Bond.

'Well, you know . . .' I stuttered. 'Your people weren't allowed to marry for so long. It must be very annoying.'

He laughed uproariously. 'Susie, I wouldn't marry David if he were the last man in the world,' he said, shaking with mirth. 'He's a lovely guy, but he's not my soul-mate or anything. I do love his accent, though – it drives me wild, know what I mean?' He winked and licked his lips, grinning.

'Oh,' I said, thinking it was probably just as well that David didn't know this. I didn't think he would be too thrilled to hear that his one true love was using him for his cute Irish accent. 'But didn't you bring him to Hatton Garden to look at diamonds?'

'Yes, I did.' Max grimaced. 'I was hoping he'd get the hint and buy me some for Christmas, but guess what – I got another bloody CD collection.'

PS Played lots of Kylie to cheer David up. It didn't seem to work all that well. Perhaps I should invest in a Barry Manilow CD.

PPS Mum and Dad called. Had very hurried conversation with them – am determined not to confess that Christmas has been an unequalled disaster.

PPPS Joe doesn't seem happy with the Lycra slim-fit non-iron shirts I bought him in M&S. Granted, they do cling to his love handles in a very unflattering way but maybe he could keep his jacket on a bit more.

27 December

Have decamped to our country retreat to escape the high drama and tension at Mrs H's. Louise has gone home but we brought Max with us. (We were kind of forced to as Mrs H is continuing to accuse him of turning David into an unholy disgrace and condemning him to eternal damnation with the hounds of hell, etc., etc.) David stayed behind on Joe's instructions to patch things up with his mother. 'I'm not going to listen to her bang on about unholy acts and immorality for the rest of the year, David,' he warned. 'Sort it out with her once and for all. It's gone on far too long – you should have told her years ago.'

David gave a long, dramatic sigh, then squared his shoulders and left the room, a determined glint in his eye. Can now see why he thinks he should be in a West End production – he really does know how to make a dramatic exit.

Journey to the country was quite tense as weather conditions were appalling. Also, I was worried that Angelica and James had left evidence of their secret dirty weekend – I still hadn't told Joe they'd used it as a love-nest and for some reason I wasn't too convinced he'd be happy about it.

'Why didn't you warn us it was going to bloody snow?' Joe complained to Max, as he sat squashed between Katie and Jack in the back seat, the dog lounging against his pure cashmere coat.

'How would I know that?' Max asked, plainly confused.

'You are a weatherman, aren't you?' I said, wondering if he really was some sort of character actor David had hired.

'Oh, that – yes, of course,' he said, 'but they fax me the weather stuff. I'm hired for my looks, not my weather expertise.'

'That's lucky,' Joe muttered, as I turned up the fan heater.

I bounded into the house ahead of everyone else to check for signs of Angelica and James but, thankfully, everything seemed in perfect order. (Was a teeny bit disappointed, actually – kind of hoped I'd find a stray G-string somewhere that would give me an insight into the ups and downs of their passionate relationship.)

Had nice one-to-one with Max when the children were tucked up in bed and Joe was busy doing Sudoku.

'David should tell his mother the truth about his sexuality,' he said, as we sat in front of the roaring log fire. 'You have to be honest about yourself or what's the point of life?' Then he dipped his chocolate flake into his Bailey's coffee and sucked it suggestively.

Thought he had a point, although not sure Joe agreed. Caught him glaring in Max's direction at least half a dozen times. Suspect he may be bitter that he missed out on a proper Christmas dinner again this year. Or maybe he needs to get in touch with his feminine side a bit more. Will buy him the box-set of *Queer Eye for the Straight Guy* in the January sales. Am sure that will help him be more sensitive.

28 December

Am very worried that the Westlife concert is off. I really wanted to get up close and personal with a toned, tanned and beautiful boy band and this may be my one and only chance. Called Mrs H to determine if we're still welcome to go now that she has disowned her second son and his lover.

'I'll leave the tickets under the mat,' she said, when I called. 'You can all go if you like. I couldn't possibly face it after what I've been through.'

'But you love Westlife,' I protested. 'Maybe we should forget about the silly row and go together.'

There was a silence.

'You're right, Susie,' she said. 'I do love Westlife, and this may have been the only time I would have got to see them before I die, which will probably be any day now, but if David is going with that – that *person*, I will not.'

Hung up, bone weary. No wonder Dr. Phil's looking a bit drained – it's exhausting being an emotional crutch for people all the time.

David arrived at midnight. Max and I were still up watching a Shirley Temple movie and drinking cappuccino with tiny marshmallows while Joe was lost in his jumbo cross-word-puzzle book in the corner. (Another excellent present I'd bought at the last minute in the Centre.)

'How did you get here?' Max asked, sounding not altogether pleased to see him, it has to be said.

'I hired a cute little convertible and drove.' David sniffed. 'Oh, Maxie, Mum says she doesn't want us to cross her threshold ever again,' he said sorrowfully, as Max stroked his arm and looked sweetly concerned (although I suspect he was a bit annoyed he was forced to miss Shirley doing her cute tap dance – I definitely caught him discreetly rolling his eyes at me over David's head).

'You can hardly blame her,' Joe said scornfully. 'There are ways of breaking it to her that you're gay. Getting it on with your boyfriend in her living room probably wasn't the way to go.'

David immediately broke into loud sobbing so I told him we were going to see Westlife and he cheered up considerably. 'Do you think they'll sing "Mandy"?' he asked, sniffing.

'I'm sure they will, David,' I said. 'I'm sure they will.'

I could hear Max making a strangled sound as I put my arms round David and he cried softly on my shoulder.

29 December

The Westlife concert was amazing. The boys were so manly in their pristine white suits and silver shoes (may get Joe to try that look – it really is very sexy). Am sure Shane was staring straight at me when he sang 'Flying Without Wings' – his puppy-dog eyes are so *soulful*. We definitely had a special connection. Suspect David may have felt the same thing, though – I caught him swaying madly, tears running down his cheeks, when they sang 'Mandy'. It was quite touching, even if some of the crowd were unruly and insisted on throwing knickers at the stage, etc. Luckily, the boys took it in their stride and completely ignored all the pants flying through the air – which I thought was very dignified of them.

Felt a bit bad that Mrs H had missed the excitement, but tried hard to forget about it – I'm not responsible for her feelings. Also, she may have been outraged by the knicker-throwing – although she would have loved the flashing neon bobble headsets that everyone was wearing.

30 December

David spent the morning giving Katie a French manicure, then packing to leave. 'Remember that nails are an indicator of how much pride a person takes in their appearance, Katie,' he said, his eyes filling with tears. 'My mother always told me that.'

'OK, Uncle David,' Katie breathed, as he filed and clipped her cuticles while I looked in dismay at my own scraggy, chipped specimens. 'I'll remember.'

'Are you going to call her, David?' I asked later, as I watched him expertly apply tinted moisturizer to his face.

'No,' he said sadly, checking his jawline for a tidemark. 'I always thought Mum understood me, but I was wrong. If she can't accept me for what I am, our relationship is a lie.'

'Maybe that's a bit drastic,' I said. 'You have to give her a chance to get used to the idea. I'm sure she'll come round.'

'I doubt it,' he said, snapping his Jo Malone makeup bag shut. 'She's very set in her ways. She still washes her face with soap – and *everyone* knows how harsh that can be on the skin.'

PS Had a very strange dream about Lone Father. He was leaning nonchalantly against a weather chart and saying things like 'Bright and breezy,' and 'Westerly gales coming in from the Atlantic.' Then, suddenly, he stripped off to a pair of Hawaiian shorts and started singing, 'Hot, hot, hot,' and wiggling his hips about. Woke up sweaty and confused.

31 December: New Year's Eve

Mrs H is refusing to talk to me for harbouring 'godless sinners' and 'condoning immoral behaviour'. Suspect she is secretly furious we went to Westlife without her.

'I cannot believe you tolerated such carryings-on in your house, Susie,' she barked, when I called by to invite her to our New Year's Eve celebration (a bottle of Babycham and an assortment of nuts in the living room at midnight). 'What must Katie and Jack think?'

'Think about what?' Katie asked.

'Nothing!' we chorused.

'Well, it is the twenty-first century, Mrs H,' I murmured

sheepishly. 'Being gay is no big deal any more. Haven't you ever watched *Will and Grace*?'

'I most certainly have not,' she said primly. 'I restrict my TV viewing to educational programmes.'

Spied the TV guide on the side table, with things like *Pimp My Ride* highlighted in neon yellow, but I didn't say anything.

'Granny, are you cross because Uncle David and Max are in love?' Katie piped up.

The colour drained from Mrs H's face and she gripped her chair to keep steady.

'What are you talking about, Katie?' I asked, hoping she hadn't witnessed any man-on-man action under the mistletoe or anywhere else.

'I heard Uncle David telling Max he adores him and wants to be with him for ever and ever.'

I looked at her, unable to speak.

'Mummy, can I be a flower-girl at their wedding?' she went on. 'I want a princess dress and flowers in my hair.'

Left Mrs H sipping brandy at the kitchen table, her rosary beads gripped in her clammy hands.

PS Am glad I didn't tell Mrs H that I read in the *Gazette* supplement that you're nothing in Primrose Hill if you haven't had some girl-on-girl action. It may have sent her over the edge.

1 January: New Year's Day

Have decided not to make any resolutions this year. They are a pointless waste of time, designed to make you feel much worse about yourself and your sagging, stretchmarked body than you do already. Luckily, I am busy concentrating on not devouring the last chocolate selection box so my mind is fully occupied.

PS Found a note rammed between the pages of the jumbo crossword-puzzle book I gave Joe for Christmas. It had lots of silly things scribbled on it, like

• Find myself.

• Retreat in Himalayas?

• Organic cookery course?

Obviously he'd been trying to work out some clues. Threw the lot in the fire – am determined to be clutter-free this year. Hope he doesn't notice.

2 January

Joe has announced that he wants to be the next Jamie Oliver.

'What do you mean?' I asked, not sure if he meant he wanted to grow his hair shaggy and get a few blond streaks or wear Converse trainers with bright shirts.

'I've always wanted to learn how to cook. This year I'm going to do something about it. I'm signing up for a cookery course,' he said. 'Rita said to do things to enrich our lives. I think this could be it.'

Then he handed me a brochure: 'Cooking With Passion', an eight-week evening course with trained chefs.

'That's great,' I said, wanting to be supportive but thinking it sounded faddy and that he'd never last the pace. 'Does that mean you'll be doing the family meals from now on?'

'Maybe,' he seemed doubtful, 'but I'll probably be more concerned with creating food with flair.'

Didn't like to tell him that food with flair is all very well, but unless it's cooked to Katie and Jack's specific instructions it will end up in the stainless-steel bin.

3 January

The children are very restless. Katie attacked Jack with her safety scissors today. Decided to do some crafting-type activities to keep them occupied. Some lolly sticks, glue, glitter, and they'd be occupied for hours. And at least the safety scissors would be used for their official purpose and not to gouge out each other's eyes.

Went to the Centre and bought lots of crafting paraphernalia. Naturally none of it was reduced to half-price in the January sale. Asked the snooty sales assistant why this was so.

'Crafting is a year-round activity,' she said, eyeing Katie and Jack suspiciously, as if they were mini-shoplifters. 'We never reduce our stock.'

Lugged it home. Children played with it for approximately five minutes before Jack poured the glitter over Katie's head and she lunged at him with a glue stick and tried to ram it up his nose.

4 January

Jack shoplifted from the crafts shop in the Centre! Found a glue stick in his jeans pocket just before I was about to throw them into the washing-machine. (The only new-year resolution I made was to search pockets before washing –

that time my mobile phone ended up in a boil wash has taught me a lot.)

Am horrified Jack is now practically a juvenile delinquent. Who knows what could be next? Firecrackers through pensioners' doors? Mugging little old ladies on the street?

Told Joe we may have to send our only son to reform school to nip his burglary habits in the bud.

'He's only little, Susie. He doesn't understand the meaning of stealing.' Joe sighed.

Am inclined to disagree. Didn't tell Joe but I also found two packets of coloured beads stuffed into Jack's duffel coat.

5 *January*

Decided that Katie and Jack needed some fresh air (and not just the sort they get sticking their heads out of the car window as I'm driving) – they're starting to look quite grey and not at all like the cheerful, ruddy-faced children on the Christmas cards. Spent ages muffling them up in coats, scarves, mittens, etc., then bundled them, kicking and screaming, into the people-carrier and drove to meet Louise and Dargan in the park, trying to placate the sulking dog on the way.

Was very conscious that Katie and Jack were not dressed in designer gear and instead wore unwashed, mismatching, unironed articles and looked nothing like the cute kids in the Benetton ads. Meanwhile, Dargan was dressed from head to toe in Dior Baby, with matching bib and blanket draped across his gleaming Bugaboo buggy. Hordes of people stopped to admire and coo over him – the same hordes who seemed to go out of their way to avoid Katie and Jack and their hilarious mud-slinging game.

Was quite worried about Louise – she seems to have lost an unnatural amount of weight.

'That's the breastfeeding,' she said smugly, lifting her Prada knit to reveal a flat belly. 'The weight just falls off. And guess what? Dargan slept for twelve hours straight last night – and he's so young!'

'Well, it could just be a one-off,' I snapped, furious that her baby was now officially sleeping longer at night than Jack. 'They can revert to their old patterns at any time.'

'Really?' She sounded worried.

'Oh yes,' I said. 'Children are very unpredictable. You should look it up on-line.'

Felt a bit mean, but I had to regain the upper hand. Parenting is my only speciality and I cannot have her trying to gain control. Maybe I'm starting to resent Louise and her unnatural adjustment to motherhood, just a little.

6 January

Joe started his cookery course tonight. He arrived back after three hours, flushed, excited and very happy.

'It was amazing, Susie!' he gushed, flopping on to the sofa with a huge smile. 'I'll be making perfect pastry soon! Danni says I have a very light touch.'

'Who's Danni?' I asked, flicking the channels to find *Farm of Fussy Eaters*. Watching people throw up after touching a tomato is genius programming, in my opinion.

'The teacher – she's Italian. She has such a passion for good food. She's going to show us how to make risotto next week.'

'Is she like one of those wrinkly Italian *nonna*s?' I asked, imagining a silver-haired granny in an apron, waving a wooden spoon.

'No,' he laughed, 'she's only twenty-three – but she's got such charisma and presence in the kitchen you'd never know it. I really think this course will change my life.'

Was a bit unsettled by Joe's enthusiasm. Still, as long as he keeps bringing home samples from class I'll keep quiet.

7 January

Spent nice family day at the sales. Suspect Joe may need some sort of multi-vitamin booster, though. He had no stamina and could barely carry half a dozen bags at a time.

'Are we almost done, Susie?' he kept moaning, as I tried to decide between two non-stick frying pans, both reduced to an amazing half-price. 'My feet are killing me.'

Was very annoyed by his selfish behaviour and informed him in no uncertain terms that if he wants to cook like Nigella we still had her entire range to purchase with 25 per cent off in Debenhams. Meanwhile Katie and Jack spent ages hiding in the changing rooms and practising commando-style attacks on all fours. It was quite cute until Jack went missing and store security caught him in the shop window, wrestling a life-size mannequin to the floor.

PS May consider developing party-feet gel inserts for men's shoes – there could be a huge, untapped market for them. Saw quite a few men with pained expressions today.

8 January

Katie had the dress rehearsal for her dance show tomorrow. Dropped her at the community college, where gangs of stage-school mothers were standing about, looking fierce and competitive. Was convinced someone was about to pull a lethal weapon or maybe even suggest a dance-off to the death.

Tried to calm Katie by telling her it was all going to be great fun and nothing to be worried about.

'Are you sure, Mummy?' she said. 'Britney said last week that if I steal her limelight she'll strangle me.'

'Who's Britney, darling?' I asked, deciding the time was right to tell her that she had to stand up to bullies and stick up for herself.

Katie pointed to a chubby little girl in a cut-off T-shirt, muffin belly hanging over the waistband of her pink glitter trousers.

I instantly changed my mind. 'Just keep out of her way,' I whispered, out of the side of my mouth in case her mother heard me. 'Don't rock the boat.'

Not sure I did the right thing – but I was a teeny bit afraid of Britney myself. Not altogether convinced that the tattoo on her left shoulder was a fake.

9 January

Arrived early at the community college to settle Katie's nerves before the big performance. Saw Britney and her mother in the hall doing complicated breathing exercises. 'You're not concentrating, Britney,' her mother screeched at her, stamping her foot with rage. 'Do you want to make a holy show of yerself in front of Angelica Law?'

'No.' Britney pouted. Then she spotted Katie. 'You're supposed to have yer hair in a plait,' she sneered, hers swinging across her rouged cheeks. 'It's part of the performance.'

'Um, excuse me,' I called, 'is Angelica Law here today?'

Britney's mother eyed me. 'Yeah, she's introducing the show. What's it to you?' Then, without waiting for my response, she hauled Britney off to practise some a-cappellas.

I tried not to panic as I attempted to plait Katie's hair under extreme pressure backstage. I hadn't known that Angelica was going to be there. She would be judging Katie on her dancing ability and general stage presence. I cursed myself for not practising the 'Twinkle, Twinkle' routine with her.

Before I had time to coach Katie on pasting a smile to her face and keeping her head up, the lights went down and I rushed to my seat, just in time to see Angelica standing centre stage making a speech about how the arts were crucial for personal development. Then the music started and Katie was pirouetting wildly across the stage, her hair flopping about in time to the music.

She was spectacular. Am sure Angelica thought so too. I really think she may be gifted. Unlike Britney – whose mother stood in the front row, doing all the actions and mouthing the words to the songs while Britney shook with fear under the spotlight.

Tried to chat to Angelica afterwards, but she was surrounded by swarms of mothers begging her to take a look at their child or asking if they could get a walk-on part in James's new movie.

'Will Britney be OK, Mummy?' Katie asked, as we made our way home.

'Of course she will, darling,' I said. 'She just had stage fright. She'll be fine next time.'

'I don't think there'll be a next time.' Katie smirked. 'The teacher said she'll never trust her with a lead role again. *And* she was sick in a bucket behind the curtain.'

10 January

Katie and Jack went back to school today. Felt quite lonely and bereft with only the dog for company (and he seemed quite happy just to lie about licking his bits).

Then the doorbell rang at eleven. It was Angelica, hopping from foot to foot in her spotless white sneakers. 'Hi, Susie.' She smiled weakly. 'I was just passing so I thought I'd call in and surprise you.'

'Angelica!' I was lost for words. She'd obviously come to tell me she thought Katie was the next Beyoncé and should go to a proper stage school ASAP.

'*Sooooo*,' she peered past me into the hall, 'is this a good time?'

'Of course.' I motioned for her to come in, kicking myself I hadn't vacuumed in more than a week.

'Your place is adorable,' she said, as she picked her way over the toys scattered in the hallway and into the kitchen. 'It's so . . . rustic.'

'Can I make you a coffee?' I asked, hoping desperately we had some milk that wasn't curdled.

'Well, actually, I can't stay. I just wanted to ask you a favour.'

'Right,' I said, feeling a bit cross that she hadn't thought Katie had been the star of the show.

'I'm sorry, Susie. You must be totally sick of me. I know I've been very demanding.' A tear suddenly slid down her perfectly sculpted cheek. 'It's just that James and I are going through a difficult patch and I'm finding it hard to cope.'

'Really?' I felt terrible for my momentary annoyance. I was also intrigued. Their marital problems hadn't made the papers yet.

'He's been messing around with an extra from the movie.' She laughed bitterly. 'I don't know why I'm surprised. It's textbook. Most actors get involved on sets.'

I was dying to ask for more juicy information, but I thought that might be insensitive so I kept quiet.

'Anyway, I just thought if we could get away again, maybe to your country retreat . . . You know, we could bash out a few issues, spend some quality time together. Of course, I'll understand if you want to say no – you must think I have a nerve, asking you for so much.' She hung her head sadly.

'Of course not, Angelica,' I said. 'I'd be delighted to help out – you have only to ask. In fact, why don't you keep a key? Then you can use the house any time you like – we never get down there.'

'Really, Susie?' Her eyes shone. 'Thank you so much. You're such a precious. I don't know how I can ever repay you.'

'You can get me that TV job,' I joked.

She stared at me blankly.

'Sorry?'

'The job, um, with the producer, and TV . . .' I trailed

off, feeling like an idiot. She hadn't meant what she'd said about me glowing on TV. It had probably been a line to make me feel better about myself.

'Oh, my God – of course! I'm such a shmuck.' She smacked her forehead. 'I totally forgot to tell you. He'll be calling you *real* soon.' Then she took her BlackBerry from her bag and punched in something at speed.

'Really?' I spluttered.

'Yes! Isn't it fabulous? It's for that new show – *Chat with Dee and Fran*. All you have to do is go in and have a little talk with him – you're sure to get the job. Unless you really screw up, of course.'

She threw back her head and laughed, showing off her perfectly capped teeth, and my knees went weak.

11 January

Tossed and turned all night. On the one hand I'm really excited about the prospect of going back to work and being mentally challenged and stimulated; on the other, I'm tortured that I'll probably miss lots of special moments in the kids' lives – I wouldn't trade seeing Jack getting that potty stuck on his head last year for anything. Also, am unsure how Joe will take the news. The only bonus is that at least I don't have to worry about childcare – Mrs H is bound to jump at the chance to spend more time with her grandchildren. It's not as if I'll have to employ a complete stranger to come into the house (just a chronically nosy mother-in-law who will spend her time rifling through my bedside-table).

Called Louise to discuss my anxiety.

'Is this so-called producer actually going to call, though?' She sounded doubtful. 'Maybe there is no job.'

'Why would Angelica tell me there was if there wasn't?' I said.

'I dunno,' Louise said. 'There's something about her that I just don't trust. She seems a bit me-me-me.'

'Louise,' I said patiently, 'I know you're suspicious of her, but that's because you only ever see her in the celeb magazines. Honestly, she's just like us. She isn't self-involved at all – she's very giving, actually.' I decided not to tell her that I had given Angelica the keys to the country house in case she misunderstood her motives.

'Maybe,' Louise said. 'But there's just something that doesn't add up.'

'Look, it's quite simple,' I went on. 'This producer is looking for someone with pizzazz and personality. Angelica says I have plenty of both. The only thing I have to decide is whether or not I want the job. Do I really want to be a working mother again?' I felt a knot in my chest when I said it out loud.

'I guess you have to weigh up the pros and cons,' Louise answered. 'If you feel it's right to go back you should do it. You've devoted years to raising the children. Maybe it's time to do something for yourself now.'

'Will you be going back to work?' I asked, hoping she'd give me some more insight.

'Definitely, in some capacity,' she said, 'but that doesn't mean I won't miss Dargan every second.' She paused. 'But I need work to keep me sane. I couldn't do what you do, Susie – I really admire you.'

'Admire me?' This got my attention.

'Yes – you really give motherhood your all. I'd go slightly

mad if I stayed at home.' She laughed quietly. 'You're a brilliant mother.'

'Well, I enjoy it,' I said, realizing that I did, for the most part. 'It's just that sometimes it gets lonely – and it can be boring . . .'

'What does Joe think?' Louise asked.

Made a quick excuse to get off the phone before she could pursue this line of questioning. Didn't want to admit that I haven't discussed it with him yet. I'm saving the news for our next counselling session – in case he takes it badly and we need a third party to intervene.

12 *January*

Called Mrs H and asked her to pop round. Was desperate to butter her up so I could ask her to mind the kids if I went back to work.

'I don't know,' she said stiffly. 'I'm not sure I want to talk to you.'

'Oh, come on,' I wheedled, 'you can't give me the cold shoulder for ever. Anyway, Joe baked chocolate-chip muffins last night – they're really good.'

'Well, all right, then,' she said, 'but only because the bingo leagues aren't on today.'

Ten minutes later the doorbell went.

'Have you spoken to David?' I asked, making a large pot of tea and wondering if I should discreetly slip in some sort of sedative in case things turned ugly.

'I most certainly have not,' she replied icily, holding her cup to the light and rubbing the rim with her handkerchief. 'He's made a complete fool of me – if the bingo crowd ever gets to hear about it I'll be the laughing-stock of the city.'

'Being gay really is no big deal, Mrs H,' I said, wonde
if I should break the news to her that most of her favo
singers and quite a few of her favourite movie stars were
batting for the other team.

'*No big deal?*' she exclaimed. '*No big deal?* You may have
no morality, Susan, but I most certainly have. I no longer
wish to discuss it.' She took a large bite of a muffin.

'These are quite good,' she admitted. 'Did you say Joe
made them?'

'Yes, he's started a cookery course. He thinks it'll fulfil
him.' I nibbled my third muffin of the morning and let the
chocolate chips melt on my tongue.

'A cookery course?' Mrs H sprayed muffin crumbs across
the table.

'Yes, "Cooking with Passion",' I said. 'He's really enjoying it.'

'Stop right there, Susie,' Mrs H said. 'I've heard quite
enough for one day.' Then she quickly bundled three muffins
into her bag and left. Thought better of asking her to look
after Katie and Jack before she went – I'll have to pick my
moment more carefully.

13 January

Phone rang at eleven fifteen a.m., at critical moment when
Dr. Phil was about to tell another deadbeat dad to shape up
or ship out.

'Hi there,' the voice said. 'My name is Mike and I'm
calling—'

'You can save it, Mike,' I said, furious that another double-
glazing call had interrupted a crucial psychological breakthrough. 'We already have lots of insulation, thank you, so
you're wasting your time.'

I slammed down the phone, thrilled to have put my foot down and spoken my mind for once.

It rang again.

'Hi, em, this is Mike again.'

I was so outraged he'd rung back that I proceeded to inform him I would be calling the consumers' watchdog authority, or whatever it is, as well as his employer and possibly *The Gerry Ryan Show* hotline to inform them of his ruthless and aggressive cold-calling tactics.

'Em, I'm not a double-glazing salesperson,' he said eventually. 'I'm the producer of *Chat with Dee and Fran*. Angelica Law gave me your number.'

It dawned on me then that Mike had never mentioned anything about double-glazing.

'I'm so sorry,' I heard myself babble. 'It's just that we get a lot of cold calls . . .' It was hopeless. I'd already scuppered my chances of a prime-time career. I was never going to be on camera with glossy hair and perfect makeup now.

'OK. When can you come in?' He cut across my histrionics, sounding a teeny bit bored.

'Any time!' I shrieked, probably a bit over-enthusiastically, but it was hard to contain my excitement. This was a real live TV producer, who knew real live famous people.

'Right. How about next week? I'll get my PA to set it up.'

Then he hung up before I had a chance to ask what the role involved and whether they'd be throwing in a company car and an enormous wardrobe allowance.

Spent morning fantasizing about huge wage packet and public exposure soon to befall me. I'll be driving a posh 4x4 and wearing designer sunglasses on my head at all times very soon.

PS Just thought – maybe I should get an agent.

Went to fourth counselling session with Rita.

'So, today we're going to talk about how we can bring joy back into our lives,' Rita said. 'Joe, let's start with you.'

'Well, I'm doing a cookery course – I'm really enjoying it.' He beamed at her.

'Great.' Rita made a note on her jotter. 'What about you, Susie?' she asked.

'Well, I'm happy for him,' I said, 'and the muffins he made weren't half bad either.'

Rita smiled. 'No, I mean what are you doing to fulfil yourself?'

I paused. Maybe now was the right time to tell Joe I was on track for a dazzling TV career and that our lives would never be the same again. 'I'm thinking about going back to work,' I muttered.

'What?' Joe said. His mouth fell open.

'Yes. Angelica says she might be able to hook me up with a TV producer. She says I have real star potential.'

'That sounds very interesting, Susie,' Rita said. 'And you think this would be helpful?'

'Yes, I do,' I said, looking at Joe. 'I think I need to grow a bit as a person – you know, use my unique talents.'

'That's great, Susie,' Joe said slowly.

'It is?' I was astonished.

'Yes. Now we can both live our dreams! I'll support you a hundred per cent.' He took my hand and squeezed it tightly so I knew he meant it.

'You're not annoyed?' I asked, a little shocked that he had absolutely no objection whatsoever.

'Of course not,' he said softly. 'Life's too short – that's

why I want to pursue my cooking now before it's too late. If going back to work is right for you, you should do it. It's all about self-fulfilment, after all.'

Rita was nodding approvingly and my heart soared. Maybe I *could* be a TV celebrity. I could do tell-all interviews with celeb mags about my loving, supportive husband. It'd be brilliant.

PS Went home and made a list of all my unique talents. Have decided that being able to name all of Jennifer Aniston's exes counts.

15 January

Mum is not convinced I should talk to the *Chat with Dee and Fran* people. 'Maybe you're being a bit over-ambitious, Susie,' she said, when I told her I was going to be like Barbara Walters, the American entertainment legend. 'Maybe you should set up a nice little work-from-home business if you want outside interests.'

Poor Mum doesn't realize that most of those work-from-home businesses are elaborate scams where you get paid fifty cents a day to stamp and seal five thousand envelopes. Which just goes to show that she really needs to keep up with current affairs and do less hobnobbing on yachts with property developers.

Then Dad came on the line. 'Susie, you'd better get walking,' he laughed, 'the camera adds at least ten pounds, you know.'

Hung up, furious. Also, a little panicky. Maybe I should hire a personal trainer to get me into peak physical condition ASAP. Or I could buy one of those all-in-one sweat-it-out boiler-suit things you get in spas. It would probably be much more cost efficient.

16 January

Met Angelica at the school gate. Was thrilled. Now I could fill her in on recent developments and she could offer to lend me any number of expensive tailored suits that would be perfect for the interview with Mike the producer.

'I'm going in next week!' I called, as she gazed into space, twisting her silky hair round her ring finger.

She looked at me blankly. 'Going in where?' she said.

'To meet the producer, of course!' I threw myself at her. 'Thank you *sooo* much for organizing it.'

'Oh, that ... Right ... fabulous. Let me know how it goes,' she muttered. Then she disentangled herself from me and darted across the road.

Felt so sorry for her. Obviously things are still not going well with her cad of a husband. Which just goes to show that being rich and famous doesn't guarantee success in your private life. I wonder if the Range Rover Sport makes up for it in some small way.

Spent ages hanging around at the school gate, feeling superior. Little do the other mothers know that I may be on the brink of a brand new career that will catapult me to fame, fortune and air-brushed publicity shots in the very near future.

PS Had very vivid dream in which I was sitting on a cream-leather couch in a designer grey cashmere turtle-neck, just like Oprah's, interviewing Jennifer Aniston and showing the audience photos of the two of us laughing together in my summer retreat.

Feel I may have found my true calling at last. As soon as the producer's PA rings, I can finally start realizing my potential.

17 January

Mrs H called round again. 'I've been thinking about what you said the other day, Susie,' she remarked, as she dipped a chocolate finger into her tea. 'Maybe I should have known that David was, you know . . .'

'Batting for the other team?' I ventured, wondering when I could get round to talking about the childcare arrangements that urgently need to be put in place.

'Yes.' She glared at me. 'He was always such a nice, affectionate boy, so artistic. Not a bit like Joe. I should have known something was up.'

'Maybe you did, deep down,' I said, 'but you didn't want to admit it to yourself.'

'I most certainly did not,' she declared. 'How can you say such a thing?'

'OK.' I backed off and offered her another chocolate finger. 'Anyway, it'll all be fine. Now you know and everyone can move on.'

'Move on? What do you mean, Susie? I won't rest until I turn him back to the natural course of things. And you must help me.'

Then I somehow found myself agreeing to help Mrs H turn David into a straight, woman-loving Casanova.

Joe is furious with me. 'How could you agree to this?' he choked, when I told him I'd promised to try to persuade David to date women. 'David's gay and that's that. Mum will have to accept it.'

Patiently explained to Joe that his mother is operating in a delusional state and that not even Elton John could get through to her now.

Sent David an email.

> You wouldn't consider pretending to be straight for a bit, would you? I don't think it would take much – just pay some girl to come home with you next time to keep your mother happy. I really need to get her on-side if I'm going to persuade her to take care of the kids while I forge a TV career. Let me know what you think.
>   Susie

Got a reply:

> What's in it for me? And a ride in your god-awful puke-mobile is not an option. BTW I think Max is having an affair – smelt Brut on him last night and he claims he's lost the Kylie CD I gave him. Do you think that's a bad sign?
>   Hugs xoxo

18 January

Still no call. Have decided to turn to religion for help. Rang Mum to see who is the patron saint of hopeless cases.

'Em, St Jude, I think, darling,' she said. 'I'm not altogether sure. Now that we're non-religious, I've forgotten all that superstitious mumbo-jumbo.'

'What do you mean, Mum?' I asked.

'Well, your dad and I have decided to ignore Church

doctrine. It's been very freeing. Worrying about what some decrepit old men think about your life choices can be very damaging.'

'But what about the saints?' I stuttered. 'Heaven and hell? All that stuff?'

'Yes, well, now we believe that you have one life and you must live it to the full. Of course, we're still very spiritually aware, but that doesn't mean we have to be dictated to by the Church's limited views. You should think about it.'

I listened in shocked silence as she babbled on and on about toxic energy, blah-blah-blah, and hung up feeling disoriented. Also, am a bit annoyed that she has refused to pray to St Jude for me. If I'm ever to establish a fascinating new career I need all the help I can get. Am quite worried that Mum and Dad are mixing in the wrong sort of circles in Portugal. They seem to be getting quite Bohemian and hippie. What next? Drugs and all-night orgies?

PS Had terrifying dream – Mum and Dad were strolling down the beach, completely nude, as Mrs H raced after them waving a Bible about. Am very annoyed that my vital beauty sleep was interrupted by subconscious worrying about parents and their ridiculous notions. Vow never to embarrass or cause a moment's worry to Katie and Jack when they're older. I will simply continue to be a loving, supportive mother who always puts their needs first.

19 January

Louise has taken up running, and is now sprinting about, pushing Dargan along in a three-wheel jogging buggy. She arrived on the doorstep this morning, reeking of health and vitality, just as I was about to consider vacuuming the stairs.

'Hi, Susie,' she trilled, twisting off the top of her sports water to take a drink. 'I'm converted to running! My energy's up, I feel great, and Dargan loves being pushed about, don't you, honey?'

Dargan gurgled up at her, his chubby little cheeks aglow.

'It's a bit cold to have him out, don't you think?' I said, cross that she looked so good in skin-tight Lycra leggings so soon after giving birth.

'His immunity system's in fantastic shape, actually,' Louise said, bending to stretch her calf muscles and show off her depressingly pert bum. 'The breastfeeding takes care of that. Why don't you come with us some morning? Running's great for toning up – it's so hard to get rid of that jelly belly, isn't it?'

I pulled my fleece even tighter round me, not wanting to admit that I wouldn't run for the bus. Anyway, I'm not sure I want to get rid of my jelly belly – I've grown quite fond of it. And my boobs might not take to jogging – even an industrial-strength sports bra wouldn't stop them swinging over my shoulders as I ran.

Spent the rest of the morning watching Dargan eating his fingers while Louise hovered over him, capturing it all on her latest mobile phone. Was quite annoyed she outstayed her welcome – although it meant I didn't have to do any vacuuming. (NB Some day soon must investigate how the complicated Hoover attachments actually work. Then I will finally be able to vacuum curtains and other hard-to-reach corners with minimal fuss and disruption. Also, if the attachments are long enough I may get the children to participate – it's important to teach them how to do household chores at a young age to create socially responsible people who will not have ASBOs brought against them, etc. Also, if they're doing household chores, it will free up some valuable me-time.)

20 *January*

Told Katie, Jack and Joe that we were going to Mass. None of them seemed altogether happy about the situation so I decided not to inform them that we had to pray specifically that I would impress the TV producer and snag a high-profile TV job.

Katie immediately threw herself on the floor wailing. Had to promise to let her choose her own outfit, *all by herself*, before she would stop. Meanwhile, Jack crawled under the sofa and refused to come out until I gave him a chocolate biscuit and promised he could take his Roboraptor to show the priest.

'Why the sudden devotion?' Joe asked, after I'd informed him that his tatty jeans were not suitable for church and he would have to pull on a non-iron shirt quick smart.

'I've always been spiritual,' I answered haughtily, annoyed he was questioning my deep and abounding faith.

'I never noticed before,' he said, smirking in a very annoying way. 'Has this something to do with *Chat with Dee and Fran?*'

'Not at all,' I lied, trying to hold Jack under my arm to scrub chocolate and dust balls off his cheeks. 'It's only right we give the children some sort of religious instruction. They're at a very impressionable age.'

Screeched up outside the church gates in the nick of time and spent an hour trying to persuade Jack that it was not

OK to attack the boy behind with his Roboraptor, and Katie that dancing up and down the aisle was not part of the deal and the priest would not be handing the mic to her to perform a quick musical number. Maybe I could just start listening to religious services on the radio like the elderly and infirm. It's probably far better for the soul.

21 January

I finally told Mrs H that I will be meeting a top producer and snagging a sparkling new TV career.

'I often thought about going back to work when the boys were young,' she said, looking wistfully into the distance when I broke the news. 'Sometimes I think my life has been rather wasted. I could have been something big in the corporate world, like that nice Donald Trump.' She slurped her tea sorrowfully.

'But you devoted your life to your boys, Mrs H,' I said, feeling a bit sorry for her. 'You've done the best job of all – being a mother.' I patted her hand fondly, just to show I really did care.

'Yes, you're probably right, dear,' she said, brightening up. 'You should probably take a leaf out of my book. There's no point hankering after what you can never have.'

Then, before I could ask if she would take care of Katie and Jack, she decided she wanted to 'help' me choose my interview outfit. 'You should definitely consider getting your colours done, dear,' she said. 'You look rather drained in that mournful black you wear all the time.'

Informed her that black was considered chic and stylish and perfect for almost every possible occasion.

'That nice fashionable girl on TV7 said that women over

a certain age should never wear black against their faces,' she went on, ignoring me. 'It's so ageing. I think you're more of an autumn.'

She chewed one of the scones she'd brought with her while surveying me from head to toe.

'What colours should *I* wear, Granny?' Katie asked.

'You, my darling, are most definitely a spring,' Mrs H said, rooting in her handbag for a chocolate treat. 'Which means you can wear nice bright colours and stand out in a crowd. Your mother couldn't carry off pastels – browns are more her style. Maybe even a nice grey.'

Katie marched off, happy that she could still wear neon pink with style, while I tried to hold my tongue.

Later, I confided in Joe that his mother seems to regret some of her life choices.

'That's probably because she's on a losing streak at bingo,' he said, shovelling Chinese takeout into his mouth. 'Her arch enemy Mrs Murphy's won practically every game for the last three weeks. The competition's getting to her.'

Mulled this over while watching Jack try to scoop some chicken fried rice into his mouth and fail spectacularly. Not sure I'm convinced by Joe's evaluation. Bingo could be the trigger, but I suspect darker issues are at play. After all, she did dabble with alcohol addiction last year. Maybe she's having a proper crisis and will go off the rails any day now. Or else she's stopped the HRT. It's unusual for her to show any sign of weakness.

22 January

Louise called round again this morning on her way to the park to do her daily five-kilometre run. Almost pretended I wasn't in. If I'd had to listen to one more story about how ankle weights were super for toning calf muscles I might have attacked her with her energy drink. I think she's become a bit unhinged – she's come up with some hare-brained idea to design and market maternity clothes for businesswomen.

'It's brilliant – and so simple!' she enthused, as she did her warm-up lunges. 'I found it really hard to get sharp, polished maternity suits when I was pregnant with Dargan. The market's there – it's just waiting to be tapped.'

Told her it was a brilliant idea, sure to succeed, etc., etc., but I wasn't really listening. Watching the phone and checking to make sure Jack hadn't unplugged it again was taking up most of my time.

23 January

Possible reasons why TV producer's PA has not called to set up interview:

(a) she has inexplicably lost my number;

(b) she has collapsed due to some seriously debilitating disease and is in a coma;

(c) the show has been put on hold due to unforeseen circumstances – such as Dee and Fran killing each other in a bitter feud;

(d) a computer virus has attacked TV7's telephone and computer systems.

I haven't heard anything about these possibles on the news but they're probably keeping it from the public in case there's widespread panic that new episodes of *EastEnders* will go missing in the mayhem.

PS Just thought – could make my fortune by calling the *Gazette* and informing them that TV7 is falling apart at the seams. Wonder how much they pay for revealing exclusives, these days. Would probably have to throw in a bit of kinky sex and a sordid love triangle to make any real cash.

24 January

I'm going to meet top-producer Mike tomorrow! His PA Elaine called this morning and informed me the meeting was set up for ten a.m.

'Um, ten – that's a bit early,' I stuttered, freaking out that I was getting such short notice. I couldn't possibly lose a stone overnight.

'Take it or leave it,' she snapped. 'It's all he has available.' The threat hung unmistakably in the air.

'I'll take it,' I said decisively. 'I'll be there.'

'Great,' she sneered. 'We can't *wait*.' Then she hung up. Can't be sure, but I think there was a hint of sarcasm in her voice.

Spent the rest of the day trying to decide what to wear to the meeting. Am terrified they'll do a few test shots – I know from my experience of appearing on *Doyle Tonight* last year, when I was dragged from the studio audience, that you can look twice your actual weight on camera and that's not just something TV stars say to disguise their flabby bottoms. I even attempted a brown/grey combination as per Mrs H's specific instructions to dress like an autumn person but tossed it to one side when I decided I looked like a rotting leaf.

'Just go as yourself,' Joe advised, when I asked him what look I should try.

Little does he know it, but going as myself will be completely useless. I must sex up my image at all costs.

Called Louise to inform her that the interview was going ahead and that I may not be available for *ad hoc* coffee mornings much longer.

'That's OK,' she said, sounding unconcerned. 'Some of the women from the breastfeeding support group are taking up boxercise. Apparently the instructor's absolutely divine. With that and my new business idea, I'll be busy every morning from now on. Anyway, good luck tomorrow!'

PS Have decided to wear fail-safe black bootlegs and polo-neck combo, with a bold red scarf draped about my neck to indicate I'm serious, but willing to take risks. Think it works well.

PPS Joe says I look like a Spanish bullfighter. Am reconsidering the outfit.

25 January

Day did not start well. In a stupid, misguided attempt to appear groomed and high maintenance, I decided to pluck my overgrown eyebrows to get rid of the Neanderthal unibrow look. This turned out to be unmitigated disaster as

(a) I could only find a very old pair of tweezers that were quite possibly rusty;

(b) the bathroom-mirror light wouldn't switch on and I had to work in almost dark conditions (Joe's fault for not replacing bulbs as I requested at least two weeks ago);

(c) my hand was inexplicably shaky, perhaps due to onset of serious and debilitating illness.

'Joe!' I cried, when I realized I looked permanently surprised on the left side of my face. 'Do you notice anything peculiar about me?'

He opened one eye and assessed me from our bed. 'Not really.'

I breathed a sigh of relief that I was just being too hard on myself.

'Hang on, do you mean your eyebrows?' he piped up. 'Are they supposed to look like that?'

Was anguished. If Joe had noticed they must have been terrible – he never notices anything. Spent ages attempting to redraw half an eyebrow on the left side of my face with one of Katie's crayons as I do not possess a real eyebrow pencil – a serious disadvantage of being low maintenance.

Fortunately, the deformed look did not go against me in the interview. In fact, I don't think the top producer even noticed, although I caught his PA Elaine sniggering a few times. Tried hard not to be myself but to be confident, sassy and cheeky, just like the presenters on *Chat with Dee and Fran*. Unfortunately, I didn't have much hair to flick around with charisma (pesky feather-cut still growing out), but I did manage to pull as many different facial expressions as possible to show them that I was a versatile, fun-loving type who could quite easily present a cooking segment if the need arose.

'*Sooo*, Susie,' Mike the producer said, 'why do you think you'd be an asset to the team?'

'Well,' I said, trying to sound confident, 'I appeared on TV recently and was well received – would you like to see the tape?' I fished it out of my handbag.

'Em, maybe not just now,' Mike said, as Elaine laughed into her hand. 'You do understand that the role is more behind the scenes, right? Not that it makes the position any less important, of course – our support team is critical. Without them nothing could run properly, isn't that right, Elaine?'

He winked at her and she smiled up at him. 'That's right, Mike,' she simpered, 'we pride ourselves on the support we provide.' Then she giggled again.

'So, Elaine will be showing you the ropes and getting you settled in,' Mike went on. 'Shall we say you'll start in a couple of weeks or so?'

I swallowed. How on earth was I going to organize everything in that amount of time? 'No problem,' I stuttered, sensing he didn't want to hear about childcare issues or other such trivialities.

Then he swept from the room, clipboard in hand, Elaine panting behind him, taking notes.

Came home, exhausted after the effort involved in smiling so much, to find Joe making risotto while Katie and Jack watched in disgust. Have horrible sense of foreboding that they will suffer from malnutrition or develop rickets when I start my new job.

26 January

I will soon begin my fabulous new career. Am a teeny bit concerned that the role may not be as glamorous as I'd previously thought but I'm sure I'll work my way to the top of the heap in no time. Absolutely must not admit to anybody that it appears I'll be working in an administrative capacity initially. Am sure it is only very short-term.

Joe is delighted by my success but keeps grilling me about irrelevant details, such as contracts, hours, weekend working, salary, etc. Am outraged he can't understand all that stuff is irrelevant and what's really important is that I will soon be a household name.

To placate him, found myself telling a tiny white lie about my salary and how it would be enough to buy a new car and take at least three sun holidays a year.

He perked up pretty quickly when he heard the fictitious pay packet I came up with on the spur of the moment. In fact, he became positively animated. 'Oh, my God, Susie, that's fantastic!' he screeched. Then he grabbed me by the waist and twirled me round with glee. 'It'll take so much pressure off me!'

Am worried I may have overshot my salary by quite a lot. But once I start climbing the ranks at TV7 I'll be earning close to it in no time. And I'm sure Dee and Fran aren't two bitchy, overpaid hags, like that exposé in the *Gazette* said.

'Who do you think we should get to look after the children when you're at work, Susie?' Joe asked over breakfast, spooning Cheerios into his mouth and pretending innocence.

'Your mum, of course,' I said, chopping a banana and trying to hide it in Jack's Coco Pops so he might eat even one of his five-a-day.

'Do you think she'll want to do it?' Joe said, his forehead creasing.

'Of course she will,' I answered, smiling wisely at him.

Joe has no idea how empty Mrs H's life is. Am sure she will be delighted to become a second mother figure to her grandchildren. It's bound to give her a new lease of life. Added bonus is that we won't have to pay her a cent and she'll probably do lots of home baking, cook evening meals and do the ironing as well.

PS Wonder if I could rent a luxury house for a day if TV7 eventually want to do a celebrity photo spread of me. I don't think the peeling magnolia walls in my musty old kitchen would have quite the same cachet.

PPS Have not told Katie and Jack about my new career move, childcare arrangements, etc., just yet. Fear they may not take it well. Which is what happens when you devote your life solely to your children. They have trouble readjusting.

Mrs H is refusing to mind Katie and Jack while I carve out an illustrious TV career.

'I'm sorry, dear,' she said, flicking through her Sacred Heart calendar and shaking her head when I called in to discuss it with her. 'I'm too busy to be taking on extra commitments.'

'But, Mrs H, who am I going to get to mind the children while I'm at work?' I asked, put out that she hadn't grabbed the opportunity to spend more quality time with her grandchildren.

'Maybe you could advertise,' she said. 'I believe there are lots of reliable foreigners who'll mind children, these days. You could even get someone who'd run a Hoover round for you as well.'

Decided to call Louise to see if she would step in. She's still on maternity leave, after all.

But she point-blank refused. 'You *are* joking, Susie?' She laughed.

'Em, not really,' I said, wondering why on earth she would have a problem with it. 'Katie and Jack are no trouble, you know that. You probably wouldn't even notice they were there.'

There was a choking sound at the end of the phone. 'No, Susie, I really don't think it's a good idea,' she gabbled, in a funny, high-pitched voice. 'I'm up to my eyes with my new maternity-wear venture anyway. You should advertise. Put an ad in the newspaper.'

Am at my wit's end. This must be how poor Posh feels all the time – may write and extend my sympathy. Being a working mother is no joke. And I haven't even started yet.

Spent the morning composing advertisements for a reliable childcare worker/substitute mother. Decided on following wording. Think it hits the perfect tone.

> Successful career woman seeks nurturing person to care for her two young children while she does TV work. References absolutely essential. Please call Susie on the number below.

Rang the *Gazette* and dictated it to the small-ads department. Was quite surprised when the dopey girl at the other end did not ask any searching details about my television work. Would have expected her to be impressed by talking to a real live TV personality. But she did sound excessively stupid. I had to spell 'nurturing' for her at least three times.

Mrs H popped round in the afternoon. 'Have you found a nanny yet, Susie?' she asked, arching an eyebrow at me.

'No,' I admitted, not wanting to say I'd been hoping she'd change her mind.

'Well, you'd want to be careful,' she advised. 'There are some real weirdos out there, people who pretend to be nannies and are really raving lunatics, that kind of thing.' She looked dead excited at the thought of meeting some bona-fide loonies.

'Well, I'll be asking for references, Mrs H,' I said feeling a bit sick. 'Everyone has to provide those nowadays.'

'Ah, yes, but how do you know the references will be real?' she asked. 'I read a story where a pretend nanny had written them herself, saying how amazing she was. Turns out she was out on bail for assault and had never changed a nappy in her life.'

'Well, Joe and I will check out everything,' I said, feeling even sicker but trying not to let it show.

'Yes, but what if she has an accomplice?' Mrs H continued, obviously having thought through all the scariest possibilities. 'She could put a fake telephone number on the reference and her partner in crime could pretend to be her former employer. These gangsters can be very cunning, you know.' She munched a biscuit reflectively.

Really think Joe was wrong to give his mother the box-set of *Law and Order: SVU*. It's simply playing on her already overactive imagination.

30 January

Bought the *Gazette* on the way home from the school run. It read:

> Successful career woman seeks nurturing person to care for her two young children while she does transvestite work. References absolutely essential. Please call Susie on the number below.

Immediately called the dopey girl in the ad department and demanded an explanation as to why she would possibly think I'm a transvestite.

'You *said* TV,' she whined. 'I wrote it down.'

'I meant *television*.' I wanted to wring her neck.

'Oh, sorry. I'm new and the fact sheet the manager gave me says "TV" stands for "transvestite" so I thought I'd better put it in.'

'How could you think I was going to work as a trans-vestite?' I shouted. 'I live in the suburbs, for God's sake. I want to speak to your manager.'

'Oh, please don't tell her.' She started to sob. 'I'm in enough trouble as it is.'

'Why? What did you do?' I asked, suddenly intrigued.

'We get all sorts of weirdos ringing up,' she said. 'I had an American guy last week who put in an ad for ladies shoes in size thirteen. I asked him if he was mental and he went mad. I'm on my last warning.'

Proceeded to have long conversation with ad girl about the Yank and his secret love of dressing up in his wife's underwear. 'Tell me where he lives,' I begged. 'I might know him.'

'Sorry, I'm not allowed,' she said. 'It's more than my job's worth. But give me a ring at the end of the week and if anything else funny happens I'll fill you in.'

Hung up feeling mollified. At least I'll get some excellent scandal out of the mix-up. And I'm sure no one will notice the mistake – hardly anyone reads that rag anyway.

PS Maybe I should ask Angelica for her advice – if anyone should know about childcare she should. Rumour has it that they've had three nannies already this year.

PPS Have received five lewd messages on my mobile phone, none about providing satisfactory childcare. Am shocked at the goings-on of ordinary-sounding people in the suburbs. Who knows what old Mrs Kenny next door is up to?

31 January

Spent the afternoon registering with an au-pair agency on-line. According to the website, I will have, in no time at all, a young girl with lots of energy to care for Katie and Jack, do some light housework, cook meals, and will pay her next to nothing. The bonus is she can teach the children her native language over supper – everyone knows kids can be trilingual if they're taught at an early age. Can't remember why I didn't think of it sooner. On-line questionnaire was ridiculously detailed, though, so decided to fabricate a little to stand out from the crowd – everybody does that so it's perfectly acceptable. And there's no possible way an au pair can seriously expect a mansion with a separate wing for staff, especially not in suburban Dublin.

1 February

Have received five responses to my on-line application. All sound delightful – don't know how I'll be able to choose between them. Spent ages sifting through, then cut down to three possible candidates. The other two were eliminated for having odd hobbies.

- Pole dancing may be all the rage with celebs but not sure I need my au pair to be performing it in my home at all hours of day and night. Plus, am sure installing a pole would be financially prohibitive – not to talk of damaging the polished floorboards.

- Morris dancing is just plain weird.

Called Louise to tell her the good news.

'Just be careful,' she cautioned. 'A lot of those girls have never looked after children before – they lie on their forms all the time, which is such a disgusting thing to do.'

'You're right,' I agreed solemnly. 'It should be illegal to lie on an official form. But how am I going to choose one? They all sound lovely.'

Louise laughed. 'Just make sure whoever you get isn't too lovely, Susie. Remember, you'll have to look at her a lot . . . and so will Joe.'

'You've lots of experience recruiting, haven't you?' I'd suddenly had a brainwave.

'Well, yes, in the technology sector,' she said.

'You'd know how to spot a nutter, then?' I asked.

'I'm not sure about that.' She giggled. 'Sometimes it's hard to tell who's sane and who's not – especially on a first meeting.'

'Come on, Lou, help me out,' I begged. 'I really trust your judgement.' (I threw that bit in for good measure although privately I felt it might not be that great – especially as the father of her child was still nowhere to be seen.)

'Oh, OK then,' she sighed, 'but we'll have to do it properly. I don't do things by half-measures. First, you have to draw up a wish list of candidate characteristics, then come back to me.'

Am so relieved I've persuaded her to help me choose the best, most reliable and least psychotic girl to take care of Katie and Jack in my absence. However, I'm a bit worried she insisted that fabricating on an official form is fraud and can result in five to ten years behind bars. Which can't possibly be right. Celebs who are jailed for violating parole only ever get a few days in the slammer – and lots of lucrative TV deals afterwards.

2 *February*

Have made a comprehensive list of candidate qualities, as Louise advised.

<u>Qualities to look for in a childcare candidate</u>

• Candidate must demonstrate firm handshake and maintain eye contact at all times (but not have creepy over-intense stare that makes you want to run away screaming).

• Candidate must be clean and presentable, but not tarty or too made-up. (Hint: nails bitten to the quick may indicate that the candidate is a nervy type who will not perform well when required to cook three different evening meals on a whim.)

• Candidate must not crack when faced with tricky questions. (Beads of sweat running down face may be an indicator that a candidate will have difficulty coping with stressful situations and may not take well to coaxing Jack off the table at least three times a day.)

• Candidate must provide evidence that she has carried out similar duties effectively in a previous role. NB Serving burgers in a fast-food emporium does not count as childcare.

• Candidate must demonstrate a sense of humour. Any experience as a stand-up comic, juggler, circus performer is a bonus.

Tried to practise my interviewing technique on Katie, but she refused to co-operate and continued to do intricate dance moves in the living room while Jack spun round her doing his best to do the splits.

3 February

Louise arrived at nine thirty, clipboard in hand, Dargan strapped to her chest in his BabyBjörn.

'I want to do a dry run for the morning,' she said, looking serious and professional when I told her she was a day early. 'Where are you conducting the interviews, Susie?'

'Um, at the kitchen table?' I wondered if I should have bought a pull-down screen to do a PowerPoint presentation.

'Maybe we should try the living room,' she said, narrowing her eyes. 'I'm not sure the kitchen strikes the right tone.'

'But this *is* where we spend most of our time,' I said.

'Yes, and it shows,' she admonished. 'We want to project the right image, and a pile of dirty dishes and half-baked drawings doesn't really cut it, do you know what I mean?'

She strode off to the living room, and I trailed in her wake, thankful I'd given it a quick tidy earlier and shoved the piles of useless gossip magazines behind the sofa.

'This will have to do, I suppose,' she announced, sitting down and pulling a manila envelope from her bag.

'What's that?' I asked.

'A dossier of the candidates,' she replied. 'I've Googled them to make sure they don't have any criminal convictions.'

'Criminal convictions?' I spluttered.

'Of course. They seem pretty clean, but we'll make notes as we go along, follow up their references, then make an informed decision based on quantifiable statistics at the end.'

PS Am worn out. Am also very worried. Had completely dismissed Mrs H's notions of the possible seedy past of au pairs as one of her fanciful ideas that could be ignored. Turns out she had a point. I'll have to be on my guard tomorrow.

4 February

Points to remember when conducting interviews in future

- Do not wear sunglasses in an attempt to look tough and menacing.

- Do not ask the candidate if she minds being frisked.

- Do not position a living-room lamp to shine directly into the eyes of a candidate and intimidate her.

- Do not turn up heating to make a candidate feel hot and sweaty and so confess that her qualifications are bogus.

- Do not grill a candidate about extra-marital affairs or ask her if she has ever engaged in inappropriately flirtatious behaviour with husbands (even if it would be helpful to know this).

- Do not force a candidate to make a snap decision between Ricki and Oprah (although this can reveal a lot about a person).

- Do not accuse a candidate of child-smuggling and/or engaging in slave-trade activities.

In despair. I start work in less than a week and I still have no childcare arrangements in place. This is all Louise's fault, or possibly Mrs H's, for making me so paranoid. Or the government's for not providing adequate childcare arrangements like they do in Sweden. Or is it the Netherlands? Some civilized European country where the powers-that-be provide free crèches until a child is practically a teenager. Anyway, I may now have to inform TV7 that I can no longer pursue international jet-setting career because I have to remain a downtrodden stay-at-home mother.

Joe was too busy worrying about his cookery course to pay any attention to my crisis.

'Danni may have to stop teaching,' he said mournfully when he came home from class and emptied a batch of fresh bread on to the kitchen table.

'Really?' I said, not caring if Danni had to be deported back to wherever she came from but pretending to listen.

'Yes, she's struggling to pay her rent because her teaching gig's only part-time. She needs a second job but she can't find anything suitable so she may have to leave – everyone's devastated.'

Suddenly a lightbulb went on in my head. 'Does she like kids?' I asked.

5 February

I'm on cloud nine. Joe's cookery teacher, Danni, has agreed to be our childminder. Turns out that as well as being a fully qualified chef, she loves kids *and* she has a first-aid qualification so if any of us happens to choke on a chicken nugget she'll know just what to do.

Was really impressed by her when she called over to chat.

'I *loooove* kids,' she said, as Katie and Jack eyed her from the living-room door. 'And these *bambini* – they are *sooo* cute, yes?'

'Um, yes,' I said, wondering how much information Joe

had given her. 'Do you have any experience of working with children?'

'Of course!' she exclaimed, fishing piles of paper from her bag. 'Here are some references for you.' She gave me a dazzling smile. 'I used to do the babysitting for lots of families at home. Of course I can do some cooking also.'

She's starting tomorrow on a trial basis – a girl who loves kids and can cook is hard to find. And her letters of reference look excellent, even if they are mostly in Italian and I can't understand what they say. I'll just have to overlook the fact that she looks like a supermodel and has the most enormous breasts I've ever seen in my life.

PS Maybe I should start night classes in Italian – that would come in handy when I'm telling her what to make for dinner, and I could eavesdrop on her while she's talking on her mobile phone.

6 February

Danni arrived as Joe was chasing Jack round the kitchen because he had fed the dog a full jar of Tesco Finest marmalade. The one without peel, which is his favourite. He quickly composed himself before he opened the door.

'Good morning!' she sang, her perfect skin gleaming, her glossy black hair swinging in a high ponytail, and her enormous breasts jiggling under her little yellow T-shirt.

'Oh, hi, Danni,' Joe said, smiling widely. 'Please come in.'

'OK,' she said, politely ignoring the enormous pile of dirty clothes that had somehow found their way into the hall.

'Hi, Danni,' I called, wondering how I would be able to ignore that she was so incredibly beautiful.

'Hi, Susie.' She beamed. 'Why don't I make breakfast and

get the *bambini* ready? Then you have nice long shower.' She shooed me up the stairs, past the dog, who was being violently sick into another pile of dirty washing.

Then she disappeared into the kitchen, Katie and Jack trailing admiringly in her wake.

Came downstairs half an hour later to find a mound of ricotta pancakes and freshly sliced fruit waiting to be eaten, the children dressed and munching happily at the table for the first time in three years. They usually sit on the floor in front of *Scooby Doo*, whining that fruit is evil.

'I take children to school, yes?' Danni said, scooping some warm pancakes on to my plate and spooning fruit on top. 'Then you can have morning to shop for new clothes for new job. Yes?' She smiled, and a warm, fuzzy feeling enveloped me.

'Um, yes,' I said. 'I suppose I should get some new things for work.'

'Oh, yes. Lots of people will see you, no? You must shop – buy lots of new things.' She winked at me, shook her ponytail and wiped Jack's chin as he gazed at her adoringly. Then he popped another slice of fruit into his mouth as if it were the most natural thing in the world, and eating five portions a day was an ordinary occurrence.

On my way out I caught sight of my reflection in the mirror and was shocked to the core. I looked at least ten years older than I am. All this worry about childcare had aged me terribly. Immediately decided I had to have luminous, dewy skin for my new TV career so I marched to Boots, where I informed the skincare specialist I needed a complete transformation ASAP.

'Well, I'm a beautician, not a magician.' She laughed, punching my arm playfully. She stopped when she saw the dismay on my haggard face.

'OK. Let's try some highlighter,' she said, whipping out

an impressive stick and applying it deftly on my cheek-bones. She dabbed and swabbed for ages until eventually she shoved a magnifying mirror under my nose so I could examine my reflection in detail.

Heard a scream gurgle in my throat before she whipped away the mirror and adjusted it. 'Ooops, sorry!' She chuckled. 'Wrong side . . . Those mirrors can be a little over-realistic.'

Was quite pleased with new, dewy, glowing self so proceeded to purchase €145 worth of skincare products. Felt a bit sick as the grinning assistant swiped my credit card, then spent ages reasoning with myself in the car park. Ridiculously overpriced makeup is an investment purchase that will guarantee viewers do not turn off their sets when I make it on-screen in a few weeks' time. Also, if Eva Longoria, the little one from *Desperate Housewives*, is worth it, so am I.

7 *February*

Feel Danni may transform our lives. No wonder Angelica has gone through so many nannies – they're so useful. Came home from shopping yesterday laden with glamorous purchases for my new job to find her making real, not from a packet, pasta with the children. *And* real, not from a jar, tomato sauce. *And* the children were not beating each other over the heads with the rolling-pin, but were happily taking turns to roll the pasta into tiny little sausage shapes and stir the bubbling pot of delicious-smelling sauce.

Called Louise to tell her that Danni has fitted right in and I can no longer imagine my life without her.

'She's only been there a day,' Louise said. 'She's still on her best behaviour. Wait until you find her stealing from your purse or making a move on Joe. Remember when that actor was caught on the pool table with the nanny?' She laughed cynically.

'Very funny,' I said, a bit annoyed that she was raining on my parade. 'Anyway, she's brilliant with the children,' I bragged, 'and Joe's right – she's an amazing cook. Her pasta is to die for.'

'She sounds great,' Louise admitted. 'Did all her references check out?'

'Of course,' I lied, not wanting to say that I still hadn't got round to calling her previous employers. Anyway, am trusting my gut instinct – which is telling me Danni is perfect and must stay at all costs.

PS Must remember not to let Mrs H near Danni. She could traumatize her in no time.

PPS Keep thinking about the pool-table thing but am trying not to worry. Don't think our Subbuteo toddler football table would be sturdy enough for any shenanigans.

8 February

Joe found the Boots receipt and was not happy. (Blast my hapless, disorganized ways. May have to purchase an accordion folder and start alphabetizing invoices and receipts in an anal manner – it might be worth it if it means Joe is none the wiser about my *ad hoc* beauty expenditure.)

'You spent how much?' he squeaked, when he spied the total.

I informed him that I was now a marketable commodity and that I needed to invest in myself to reap success. (I didn't bring up the working-behind-the-scenes thing obviously.) 'I need to look good off duty as well as at work,' I said. 'I can't go to the supermarket looking haggard any more. I have to be *on* all the time. People will be watching me. Maybe even taking pictures. Do you want your wife looking old and scruffy when she meets her public? Anyway, we can afford it now – remember?' I threw in the last bit to fob him off.

'You're right,' he said visibly relaxing. 'I'm so used to being worried about money. Now that you'll be earning as well we can afford these little luxuries. I'm sorry, Susie.' He reached across and stroked my face happily.

I tried to keep my expression composed and not let it show that I was experiencing a sick sinking feeling in my stomach. Think I pulled it off quite well. Anyway, I only have to lie for a little while – just another week or two at the very most. By then I'll have impressed the producers so much that they're bound to put me on-screen. In the meantime I have volunteered to look after all the pesky household bills. That way Joe won't cotton on that anything's amiss.

PS Just thought – I might get my own personal stalker. At last I'll have something in common with Hollywood celebs.

PPS Lots of brilliant photos in the tabloids of Dee from *Chat with Dee and Fran* stumbling out of a nightclub, her left breast half falling out of her Roberto Cavalli mini-dress. Suspect she will not be pleased.

9 February

Came home from another shopping trip to find Mrs H sitting at the kitchen table watching Danni bake *biscotti*. 'Ah, Susie,' she called, as I struggled through the door under the weight of my many bags. 'I'd like a word with you please. In P-R-I-V-A-T-E.'

She raised her eyebrows and made a face at Danni's back.

'We go to other room,' she shouted at Danni, in pidgin English. 'You stay here, OK?'

'Mrs H, you don't have to shout at her. She's not deaf,' I said, dropping my purchases on the floor and wondering how long she had been on the premises without my knowledge – or consent, for that matter.

'I wasn't shouting, dear,' she said, pushing me into the living room and closing the door. 'I was speaking clearly. That's what you're supposed to do with these people – otherwise they won't understand you. And that could lead to all sorts of trouble. Do you know what I mean?' She stared hard at me. 'What made you choose this particular girl, Susie?' she asked.

'She just seemed the best,' I answered doubtfully, not wanting to tell her that Danni had been the only real option.

'But, Susie,' she said, shaking her head, 'have you not noticed her, ahem, chest area?'

'You mean her boobs?' I replied.

'Yes.' She glared at me. '*And* she can cook.'

'Meaning?'

'It's a dangerous combination. Very dangerous indeed.'

'What are you talking about, Mrs H?' I said wearily.

'I am talking about Joe, dear. Your husband. A figure like that on a girl who can make tiramisu from memory is a lethal cocktail. The way to a man's heart is through his stomach. Which is why I never understood why Joe went for you.' She patted my hand sympathetically. 'I know you try, Susie dear, but you're no great shakes in the kitchen, are you, pet?'

I nodded mutely, knowing it was pointless to argue.

'Anyway, try not to worry, dear. I'll do my best to keep my eye on her while you're at work. Make sure there are no shenanigans or funny business.'

'But I thought you'd be too busy during the day,' I said, remembering the excuses she had made not to look after Katie and Jack in the first place.

'Well, that's true,' she seemed flustered, 'but your marriage is of the utmost importance, Susie. I'm willing to sacrifice some of my social life to protect that holy bond. You can take yourself off to that little job at the TV station with a clear conscience. I'll be here to keep guard.'

She waddled off back into the kitchen to try some of Danni's delicious *biscotti*.

Had words with Joe when he came home. Told him he must inform his mother that she cannot drop in to check on Danni whenever she wants.

'Ah, she's probably a bit lonely,' Joe said, snuggling into me. 'Don't stress out about it. And sure she can keep an eye on Danni – make sure she's being good with the kids, that sort of thing.'

Fell asleep wondering if I should get spy cameras fitted in Katie's teddy bears – not to keep an eye on Danni but to make sure Mrs H isn't snooping round the house all the time.

10 February

Called Angelica to see if she had any advice on my new role at TV7. The signal was really bad.

'Oh, hi, Susie, I was about to call you!' she said, when she answered.

'Really?' I was delighted – she'd been going to wish me luck.

'Yes, we're down in your country place and one of the fuses has blown – you don't know where the box is, do you?'

'Um, behind the kitchen door,' I said, trying to hide my surprise. She hadn't called to tell me she was going to use the house.

'I hope you don't mind us being here?' she went on. 'You *did* give me the keys.'

'No, of course not,' I said, realizing that, as an American, Angelica had taken my offer literally. 'Another romantic getaway, eh?'

'Something like that.' She giggled.

Hung up, feeling glad that Angelica is comfortable enough with me to use the house whenever she wants. Anyway, I can't possibly be annoyed. I would never have got this new job without her help.

11 February

Spent the entire night retching over the toilet bowl. 'Do you think it's something serious, Joe?' I gasped, as I threw up for the umpteenth time.

'I don't think so,' he mumbled, from underneath the duvet. 'I'm sure you'll be grand tomorrow.'

Then he proceeded to snore happily in a most annoying way.

Shook him awake and informed him that he should be holding my head and mopping my sweaty brow with a damp washcloth, etc., or at least pretending to be awake in my hour of need.

'Aw, Susie, I'm wrecked,' he groaned, 'and there's nothing wrong with you – you're just sick because you're nervous about the new job.'

Suddenly cold dread washed over me. He was right. What have I let myself in for?

Am exhausted. Not sure I can do this every day. Unless I get a driver who will pick me up and drop me off at the studios so I can snooze all the way there and back. (NB Must check contract to see if this is a possibility.)

Spent the day being introduced to dozens of fresh-faced teenagers who apparently run TV7, none of whose names I can now remember. (NB Fear I may have early-onset Alzheimer's. How could my memory have deteriorated so much in the few short years I've spent out of the workplace? Maybe I could call everyone 'darling' to cover it up.) PA Elaine ignored me completely.

Came home shell-shocked and weary to find Katie and Jack cuddled up on Danni's lap as she read them an old Italian fable. Realized it was vital they knew that just because Mummy was now a successful career woman working outside the home it didn't mean they were any less important to me. 'Hi, guys!' I said, as cheerfully as I could, injecting enthusiasm and love into my voice, even though I felt like crawling straight under the duvet and never coming out again.

'Hi, Mummy,' Katie said casually. 'Danni made cookies with us today and she taught us some Italian. She's the best minder ever.'

Felt a twinge in my stomach before I devoured an entire lasagne that Danni had made. Not sure if it was hunger pangs or an intense, inexplicable urge to kill her. Shooed her home, then tried to some spend quality time with the children before they went to bed. Trouble was, they had no interest whatsoever in spending any with me.

'I want to watch *That's So Raven*,' Katie whined, when I

said she could sit on my lap and I'd read her another story. Then I tried to bribe Jack to play Lego with me, but he crawled under the sofa to hunt for rabbits.

Suddenly I have a new understanding of working mothers. I had somehow forgotten it wasn't all Gucci handbags and long corporate lunches. It really can be quite a juggle. But I'm sure, once I get into the swing of it, everything will fall into place.

13 February

Spent all day answering phone calls from irate viewers enraged by Fran's on-air comment that liposuction should be tax-deductible. PA Elaine wasn't much help when I asked her what I should say.

'How should I know?' She scowled. 'Make something up.' Then she went back to updating her Bebo page and ignoring the phones.

Arrived home, emotional and overtired, to find Joe, Danni and the children baking in the kitchen. Joe had flour on his nose and Danni was wiping it away with a teacloth when I burst through the door, sodden with the rain that was pouring down outside. Felt thoroughly miserable.

PS Had horrible dream that I was at TV7 and couldn't remember anyone's name. Called Elaine 'darling'. She slapped me across the face and screamed she was going to sue me for sexual harassment. Then arrived home to find Danni wearing my clothes and holding hands with Joe across the table as Katie and Jack recited Italian nursery rhymes. Fear I may have taken on too much. Maybe I'm not cut out to be a working mother.

14 February: St Valentine's Day

Out of the blue Joe called me at work. I thought it was to surprise me with an extravagant Valentine's Day token, but he wanted to ask about our counselling sessions. 'We have one pencilled in for tomorrow, Susie,' he said, apparently forgetting he was supposed to be showering me with expensive romantic gifts rather than harassing me about therapy.

'You'll have to cancel it,' I said, terrified Elaine would figure out what I was talking about and somehow use the information against me. 'In fact, cancel them all for the immediate future. I won't be able to take time off work to go.' I hung up before he could argue. Was quite pleased, actually – it's not as if anyone can question my motives. Busy career women don't have time to devote to extra-curricular activities like marriage therapy.

15 February

Spent the morning opening letters from irate viewers who feel Dee and Fran are insensitive to the needs of the common person and that wearing designer bling on a chat show for housewives is vulgar and in bad taste. Asked PA Elaine what I should do with the letters.

'Chuck them in the bin,' she snapped. 'That's what I do.'

'But surely they'll be expecting a reply?' I said.

'Well, if you care so much, Miss Goody Two Shoes, why don't you send them one?' She was staring at me in a very funny way.

Spent the rest of the day replying to housewives, and other under-represented minorities across the country, and trying to reassure them that Dee and Fran really did care about the issues and not just what they would be wearing to the TV awards. Some of the letters were trickier to reply to, though.

Dear Dee and Fran,

I was disgusted to hear you suggest that 'If you can't fit into a size ten then you are a fat heifer'. I think you should apologize.

Jo from Tyrone

Dear Dee and Fran,

I like your programme but I do not want to watch award-winning makeup artists making ye up to look like common tramps in the street. I would prefer to see some moral, upstanding people being interviewed. Daniel O'Donnell is very pleasant. Please send me tickets to the show.

Mary in Belturbet

Dear Dee and Fran,

Have you ever considered having a threesome? I am up to the challenge.

Frank in Wexford

Asked PA Elaine when she thought I'd be moving on from opening mail to doing some on-camera work. She spent a long time laughing loudly and telling everyone in the other cubicles that I wanted to be a TV star. Am a bit worried about her. She has the wild look in her eye that Britney had just before she went in for her 'rest'.

PS Must request an industrial-strength pair of medical gloves ASAP. There was only one pair of pants in today's batch of mail, but still.

PPS There were rumours at the water-cooler that Posh is coming on the show soon. I am beside myself with excitement. Am sure to pick up some excellent styling tips.

16 February

Arrived home to find Joe cooking up a storm with Danni in the kitchen again.

'What are you doing?' I asked, as he beat something in a Tupperware bowl frantically, a glint in his eye and beads of sweat hanging off his brow.

'I'm making focaccia,' he gasped. 'I have to keep my rhythm up or it won't work.'

'That's eet, Joe,' Danni encouraged, clapping her hands excitedly, Jack hanging off her hip and cuddling into her heaving bosom. 'You can do it.'

'Thanks, Danni.' He looked delighted with himself. 'If it wasn't for you, I wouldn't have a clue how to do this.'

'So, what's for dinner?' I asked hopefully.

'Oh, we haven't had time to do dinner as well,' Joe said, offended. 'We've been kind of busy here, you know.'

He rolled his eyes at Danni, who smiled indulgently back.

'I fed the *bambini*, Susie,' she said, 'but they were so hungry there's nothing left for you. Sorree.'

She shrugged her shoulders in the special Italian way that made me think she couldn't have cared less if I starved to death or had to eat beans on toast for the third night running.

PS Feel very unsettled. Don't think I've seen Joe look so alive and happy in years. Maybe even ever.

PPS Katie is refusing to speak with a normal Dublin accent and keeps saying things like '*sì*' and '*ciao*'. It's getting very irritating.

17 February

Top producer wants me to do my first piece to camera! 'The idiot junior broke her foot doing that bungee jump yesterday and we're stuck for a slot,' he announced at my cubicle, while PA Elaine glared venomously at me behind his back. 'You're going to do a quick piece to camera tomorrow, Susie. I'm thinking something fluffy – what the average housewife reads maybe? What do you like to read?'

'Em, nineteenth-century feminist authors?' I suggested, trying to sound plausible.

He roared with laughter. 'You're a tonic, you really are. Now, come on, tell me the last book you read.'

I listed off three millionaire chick-lit authors and he nodded approvingly. 'Perfect. Go to a shopping centre with the crew and ask women on the street who they like and why. We're looking for about four minutes of airtime.'

He stalked off before I had a chance to ask when I'd be receiving my training to prepare me for camera work. Asked Elaine if she knew.

'Why don't you go fuck yourself, Goody Two Shoes?' she snarled.

'Have I upset you in some way, Elaine?' I asked, shocked by her outburst. Maybe I'd used her coffee cup by mistake or taken her favourite stapler.

'Why would I be upset?' she spat. 'Let me think . . . Maybe it's because you got this job because of your good friend Angelica. Could that be it?'

'She only got me an interview!' I spluttered. 'Mike wouldn't have hired me if he didn't think I had potential.'

'Yeah, *right*. And it has nothing to do with the fact that Angelica shagged him, I suppose?'

I gasped. 'That's not true.'

'If you say so. Listen, honey, some of us have worked our arses off to get where we are now and we don't appreciate wannabes like you bulldozing your way in, thinking you own the place. Why do you think he's giving you that slot? His little American tart probably told him to. So, take my advice and keep out of my way, OK? *Sweetie.*'

She eyeballed me and I hung my head, terrified she was about to leap across the partition and attack me with her nail file.

PS Am in shock. There's no way Angelica slept with Mike – especially since she's been using my country house to reconnect with her husband. Not that I can divulge that top-secret information to anyone, of course. Elaine is obviously just insanely jealous of my soon-to-be meteoric rise to stardom. Suspect she wants to be on camera herself. Unfortunately her buck teeth mean there's very little chance of that happening any time soon.

18 February

Got up before even Jack had woken (i.e. the crack of dawn) to blow-dry my hair with lashings of anti-frizz serum. Took so long to get it tamed (giving up the hair-straighteners in an effort to preserve the environment may have been a rash decision) that I was late and skidded up to the studio doors in a panic that the crew would have left without me. Was very nervous. Was also quite sweaty. (NB Must purchase extra-strength deodorant advertised on Lifestyle TV ASAP. Or get sweat glands removed in a painless, cost-effective op.)

Found a solitary cameraman waiting for me in a battered old van, smoking a dubious-looking cigarette and drinking a can of Red Bull.

'So, where are we off to?' he said.

'Em, I'm not sure,' I answered, trying not to gag at his bad breath. 'The producer should be here any minute.'

'He won't be coming, love,' the cameraman drawled. 'It's just you, me and Quin today. I'm Sam, by the way.'

'Who's Quin?' I asked, squinting through the smoke in an attempt to make out anyone else.

'The sound guy – he's asleep in the back.' Sam shrugged.

'Right,' I said nervously. 'But I thought a producer always went along.'

'Not unless you're top TV totty,' he said. 'No offence.'

'OK, let's go to the nearest shopping centre,' I said, trying to take control and sound as if I knew what I was doing.

'You're the boss,' Sam said, and started the engine.

When we got there, I fumbled about for ages trying to get my mic on while Quin and Sam sniggered. I spent the rest of the morning trying to persuade harassed women to talk about their favourite authors. Most ignored me completely. Others threw evil stares at me. More actually hissed at me, saying things like, 'Reading? Do you think I have time to be reading?' as they shoved their buggies away from us at high speed. Wanted to call out that I didn't have time for proper, intellectual reading either and that I was really there under false pretences but nobody would listen to me.

I eventually persuaded one dishevelled mother to discuss her favourite authors, but only when I offered to buy her an outrageously expensive mug of coffee and snag her tickets to the show. This ploy worked so well that I decided to use it for the rest of the afternoon. I managed to get some excellent, top-rate footage. Sam says it's all good stuff and I think he meant it. Shared a can of Red Bull on the way back and he confided he'd never wanted to be a cameraman, he'd always fancied himself as a roadie, but his controlling wife won't let him live his dream. Which seems completely unreasonable to me.

19 February

Katie woke me at six a.m. to ask what I'd made for the school bake sale. Apparently I was supposed to have rustled up an array of home-cooked delicacies to raise money for the school's sports-equipment fund.

'When did this happen?' I screeched, panicked. I'd never heard of it.

'Danni got the note.' Katie pouted. 'It was given out ages ago.'

Stumbled downstairs to find the note hanging prettily from the noticeboard, Danni's neat handwriting telling me what to do.

Proceeded to tell Katie that we'd have to stop off at the deli on the way and buy cakes to donate. Her bottom lip trembled. 'Buying stuff's no good, Mummy,' she wailed. 'You need to bake it. With your hands. Otherwise it's cheating.' She dissolved into tears.

I caved in immediately – working-mother guilt is very hard to shake off. After I'd convinced her that I wouldn't be able to make an elaborate three-tiered Bratz monster gâteau and that fairy cakes would have to do, I spent another hour trying to locate adequate ingredients. Had to substitute good old-fashioned granulated sugar for caster but otherwise it went surprisingly well. Just in case they didn't taste perfect, though, I decided to creep in discreetly and leave them in the school hall without drawing attention to myself.

This plan was scuppered when we arrived to find Angelica standing by the door in designer shades, clipboard in hand, making a note of what everyone had brought and handing out name badges to prop beside the baked goods.

'Hi, Susie,' she called. 'What did you make?' She had wrestled the cake tin from me and prised off the lid to take a look before I could stop her. 'Oh, fairy cakes – how sweet!' 'Now, I presume they're organic, right?'

'Em, not exactly,' I said, wondering how I could corner her and confide Elaine's allegations about her and Mike the producer without the other mothers hearing.

'Oh, really?' She looked shocked. '*Ooookaaay* . . . Well, there is a non-organic stall, although you may be the first to contribute to it. Anyway, why don't you take your name badge and go drop them off?'

Slunk to the back of the hall and found the stall, a huge sign with 'NON-ORGANIC PRODUCE' written on it dangling precariously from the awning. It was empty except for an offering of Rice Krispie cakes that had patently been assembled by a five-year-old.

I watched as other mothers swept into the hall and arranged dainty plates of cakes in impressive displays while Katie glared at me murderously. 'Why didn't you make something organic, Mummy?' she demanded. 'Don't you care about global warming?'

Left, cursing the modern education system and its insistence on teaching impressionable children about carbon footprints, etc. Surely they should be concentrating on memorizing their times tables and learning to tie their shoelaces.

20 *February*

Top-producer Mike came to my cubicle to say my work shows potential but that I need more experience and may not be ready yet to progress from answering the phones. Thankfully Elaine was on a doughnut run so she wasn't there to witness my humiliating feedback.

'The footage was quite good, Susie,' he said, leaning across my desk earnestly, 'but your technique needs work. You probably need more training here before you can expect to move on.' I tried to listen to what he was saying, but really I was assessing whether Angelica would ever have had an affair with him. Didn't think it was very likely. He has an awful lot of hair on the backs of his hands – and coming out of his ears as well.

Then he gave me a written list of things to consider before I try again (on some unspecified date in the future). Going forward, I must remember that:

(a) Bribing harassed mothers with expensive coffee and muffins to get them to talk on camera is against company policy. (If I have to bribe people, I must use supermarket-brand crisps and fizzy pop and stay within budget.)

(b) Also, if I do bribe people, make sure they're attractive and not complete mingers who need their roots done (unless I'm interviewing for a makeover show, then the worst mingers are to be rounded up like cattle and told to act as downtrodden and unattractive as possible).

(c) Dressing in a corporate navy suit is completely unsuitable. If I am ever to appear on TV again (a distinct improbability) I must try to look dowdy so as not to intimidate the viewers.

PS Fear I am losing touch with the children. Katie tripped on her *Shark Tale* DVD tonight and wanted Danni to put a Bratz plaster on the cut – not me. How could I have been replaced so quickly? Apparently, endless years of sleepless nights, handholding and household drudgery can be replaced in an instant by an olive-skinned slip of a girl who smells of coconut oil nearly all the time. Am bereft.

21 *February*

Word has leaked out to Elaine that I may never be put in front of the camera again. She seems inordinately thrilled by this news.

'You screwed up big-time,' she jeered across the dividing partition this morning. 'You'll be answering viewer letters for the rest of your life. You're not Little Miss Perfect now, even if you *are* friends with that slag Angelica Law.'

Then she laughed, her enormous buck teeth glinting dangerously under the fluorescent lights.

I tried not to mind, but I have a sinking feeling she's right. I was really convinced when Mike arrived at my desk with another sackful of mail and told me it needed answering as soon as possible.

Louise says I should tough it out and slowly but surely work my way to the top. 'Corporate life is dog eat dog, Susie,' she said, when I called to moan. 'If you want to make it to the top you have to put in the work.'

Didn't want to admit to her that putting in the work really wasn't in my grand plan and that I was hoping to be catapulted to the top with little or no effort on my part.

PS Came home to find that Joe had bought dozens of recipe books at half-price from the bargain bin in the book-shop. Am trying to tolerate his new-found passion for cookery but it's starting to grate a little – especially when most of his concoctions end up in the bin. Wonder if Jamie went through this phase or if Jools ever felt annoyed when he used all the milk on making some experimental recipe and there wasn't any left for a cup of tea. May write and ask her.

PPS Found myself shouting at Tyra Banks tonight, I was so tired and grumpy. But, really, as if *America's Next Top Model* is going to be a cross-eyed no-hoper who can't even strut properly.

22 February

Met Dee and Fran in the corridor and they blatantly ignored me. Mind you, they blatantly ignore everybody (including each other) when the cameras aren't rolling so I decided not to take it personally. Instead I'll keep my head down and come up with some excellent award-winning ideas to impress them. Am sure it won't take long.

Spent the morning devising clever segment ideas for possible pitch:

(a) fly-on-the-wall documentary about a put-upon stay-at-home mother (huge pool of talent waiting to be unearthed at playschool);

(b) fly-on-the-wall documentary of celebrity mom struggling with everyday tasks such as grocery shopping, etc. Discuss with Angelica;

(c) exposé of ridiculously overpriced organic foods on supermarket shelves;

(d) documentary on real lives of children's entertainers – fairies, clowns, magicians, etc. (NB Consult *Yellow Pages* for unsuspecting participants);

(e) exposé of underworld of children's dance schools, and stage mothers. (NB If proceed with this, a recording device secreted about my person will be absolutely necessary. It will also be crucial to wear an elaborate disguise in case any stage mothers set about me with their makeup cases.)

Am very pleased with my ingenuity. At least no one can accuse me of being out of touch with current events.

PS Came home to find Joe carefully scooping pastry into a plastic bag to sweat it. Am getting quite worried about him.

23 February

Received my first pay cheque. Was so appalled by the paltry sum that I spent it all at lunchtime on inappropriate things I cannot afford (although I definitely deserved the too-expensive hand moisturizer. I still can't find my Jo Malone stuff and I don't want to develop veiny claw-hands like some celebs on the cover of *Heat*).

Joe smiled benignly at me when he spotted some of the carrier-bags I lugged in. 'I hope you haven't spent too much, Susie,' he teased. 'You should put some aside for a rainy day.'

'Oh, I will,' I mumbled, wondering if now was a good time to admit that I was earning a fraction of what I'd told him and that the rainy day might be just round the corner.

'That reminds me,' he went on, 'will your salary go straight into the joint account?'

'Um, yes, I think so,' I said, remembering that he checked it in a very anal-retentive way every month.

'Great! That'll make a big difference.' He smiled again. 'What would I do without you?'

Must remember to hide all joint-account details from Joe at all costs.

PS Mrs H called. 'I need to meet with you, Susie,' she whispered. 'I have important information to pass on.'

Agreed to see her in the Tesco café tomorrow after work. Am intrigued, although she probably only wants to tell me that the local priest has a love child.

24 February

Bang in the middle of the Tesco café, Mrs H told me she thinks Joe may be 'turning'.

'What do you mean?' I asked, wondering if she meant he was going to abandon his lifelong obsession with Liverpool FC and declare himself a Man United fan.

'It's the cooking, Susie.' She sniffed into her non-fat latte. 'He was never into cooking before.'

'So?' I said, dunking a KitKat finger in my cappuccino and wondering what she was wittering on about. 'If he ever gets the hang of it, it'll be great.'

'But men aren't supposed to cook,' she cried. 'It's a sign. A G-A-Y sign. Our David always loved cooking too. I think Joe may be gay.'

I almost choked. 'Mrs H, Joe is not gay,' I spluttered. 'He has just found a new hobby and he likes it. We should encourage him.'

But she wasn't listening. 'If the bingo crew finds out both my boys are gay I may as well emigrate right now.' She broke into distressed sobbing.

'Don't be silly, Mrs H,' I said. 'Joe's *not* gay. He's just discovered a passion for Italian food.'

'Well, he never had a passion before.' She gulped. 'How do you know he's not turning into a homosexual?'

'I just do,' I said.

'When was the last time you performed . . . you had . . . you know . . .' She grimaced at me and I realized she was asking when Joe and I last had sex.

'Mrs H!' I was outraged. 'I refuse to answer that.'

'Mr H and I did it every Friday night, like clockwork.' She was staring into space. 'We never missed – except when I was afflicted with my bunion problem. It was then he had his affair with that common tramp.' She was sobbing again. 'Haven't I suffered enough?' she demanded. 'Peggy Gorman never does the novenas but her two boys are the biggest Casanovas in town – they'll do it with anyone. And my David's been leading a secret double life all these years . . . Now Joe. I just can't take it. All I want is for them to be sluts like everyone else.'

I shoved a KitKat finger across the table to comfort her.

PS Have decided to ask Joe to stop cooking. Cannot sit through another sob-fest with Mrs H any time soon. I managed to head off an inquisition on how my 'straightening of David' was going, but only because she was in a weakened state. I won't be so lucky next time.

25 February

Tried to have heart-to-heart with Joe last night. Unfortunately he refused to be parted from Nigella's *Forever Summer* long enough for me to talk any sense into him. In fact, I caught him stroking it dreamily on quite a few occasions.

'Your mother's worried, Joe,' I said, nibbling a tiny madeleine he had concocted earlier. 'She thinks you may be walking a fine line between heterosexuality and the devil.'

'That reminds me!' Joe shouted, with a wild look. 'Devil's food cake – that's what I'll bake next!'

Wonder if there's a medical term for Joe's new obsession. Must look it up on-line.

Emailed David to ask his opinion.

> Do you think it's possible that Joe is gay? Your mother seems to think so and I'm starting to have my doubts. Can it be possible for a truly straight man to love whisking so much?

Got an almost instant reply:

> A man who thinks washed-out straight-leg chinos are stylish is most definitely not gay. But he could be turning metrosexual. Has he been using your moisturizer recently?

Think David may be on to something. My Beauty Flash Balm has been disappearing at a very rapid rate recently.

26 February

Went round to Louise's to discuss the likelihood that both Mrs H's sons are now homosexual. 'I'm going to ask him to pack in cooking,' I told her, as she half watched the Oscars countdown.

'Are you?'

'Yes. It's really started to take over his life. He hasn't paid me or the kids a blind bit of attention in weeks.' Suddenly I felt very sorry for myself. 'Maybe Mrs H is right. Maybe he *is* gay.'

'That's ridiculous!' Louise laughed. 'Sure you two are probably at it morning, noon and night. I don't think you've anything to worry about. Not like me. I'm practically a virgin again, it's been so long since I had any nookie.' She sighed sadly.

I said nothing. There was no point in telling her that Joe and I had no real sex life to speak of – especially now that he seems to prefer his new Krups mixer to me.

PS Am sick of Oscar build-up everywhere. All the gossip mags are full of useless tips about achieving red-carpet glamour in ten easy steps. May write to editor of *OK!* and inform her that trying to get a starlet look is the least of my worries. I need advice on looking groomed, professional and efficient. Mind you, this week's mag has excellent coverage of celebs looking dowdy – and if A-listers can't manage to rock the red carpet after being styled from head to toe, I know there's still hope for me.

Joe has refused to stop cooking. In fact, in a shocking turn of events, he has announced that he's considering leaving his job to find himself. He thinks he might do this by becoming a Master Chef.

'Have you lost your mind?' I shrieked, when he said that he'd thought long and hard about the direction his life was taking and he wasn't happy. 'How are we going to live?'

'Well, you could be the breadwinner for a while,' he said silkily, whipping up another Tupperware bowlful of batter. 'Lots of modern couples do it.'

'Do what?' I spluttered, fear gripping my heart.

'Swap roles for a while.' He paused. 'Just because I'm a man it doesn't mean I can't explore my creative side, Susie. You've wanted a satisfying career for years and now you have one. Luckily for us, it's well paid. So what's the problem? I could step back for a while and take another direction. People do it all the time. Anyway, before you know it I'll be running my own cookery school and making millions. Not that it's about money, of course.'

I was dumbfounded. Didn't Joe realize that it's *all* about money, especially when you don't have much? Decided to say nothing yet, though. He's obviously going through some sort of psychological meltdown. It's bound to pass soon, although I'm worried at this strange role-reversal development. Really feel Joe should stick to what he knows best instead of taking an unpredictable route. Even if his happiness is at stake.

PS Have decided to stop buying the *Gazette*. Joe is getting all sorts of weird ideas reading about alternative lifestyles in the weekend supplement. It may be trendy for men to give up work and go back to nature but that doesn't mean he should *do* it.

PPS Have discovered that most of the sherry has disappeared. Suspect there may be some connection between that and Joe's personality disorder. Or else he has been using too much alcohol in his Italian trifles.

28 February

Louise says I have made my own bed and now I must lie in it. 'You wanted a career, Susie,' she said matter-of-factly, when I called to confide in her, 'and there are consequences. All working mothers have to juggle and deal with issues. It's never plain sailing.'

I felt like strangling her with her prototype breastfeeding bra.

'Surely the consequences shouldn't be quite so dramatic, though?' I whispered so that Elaine wouldn't hear me. 'I'm not ready to provide for my entire family. I've only been back at work for a couple of weeks or so.'

'Well, you'd better concentrate on making a good impression, then,' she said, 'because it sounds as if Joe's made up his mind.'

Meanwhile, Danni thinks Joe's outlandish plan to chuck in a perfectly good career on a silly whim is a great idea. 'But Joe has gift, Susie,' she said, when I told her we must stop complimenting his baking or he'd lose the run of himself. 'We must celebrate, yes? He could cook like Italian if he had more training.'

This did sound tempting, although of course I couldn't tell her that if Joe gave up work he wouldn't be able to afford the ingredients to make even the perfect boiled egg.

PS Found myself hankering for the golden days when I hung around outside the school gate hoping to see Angelica. Things were so much simpler when all I had to worry about was sucking up to a celebrity mom.

1 March

Just back from A and E. Katie fell over in the playground today and cut her bottom lip. Am racked with guilt. If I'd been at home, instead of trying to fulfil myself with my new job, it wouldn't have happened.

Complete sequence of events was as follows:

11.16 a.m. School principal called to inform me that my daughter had had a terrible and possibly life-changing accident.

Her precise words were 'Mrs Hunt, Katie has had a little accident' or thereabouts. She definitely sounded nervous and quite jittery even though she was trying to play it down.

11.17 a.m. Almost collapsed in state of fear at daughter's plight. Heart palpitated very alarmingly. Think I screeched something like 'Accident?' imagining lost fingers or toes. 'What kind of accident?'

Principal responded, 'She slipped in the playground and cut her lip. We think it may need stitches.' She cleared her throat at this point. Feel this may have indicated she was lying.

11.18 a.m. Informed principal I would be there forthwith.

11.19 a.m. Felt so faint had to sit with my head between my knees while Elaine laughed across the partition.

11.20 a.m. Forced myself to be brave and put daughter first. Rushed to the school – possibly ran a few red lights on the way and broke some speed limits. Obviously if I get some sort of legal notice in the post I will be informing the authorities of the mitigating circumstances in case I make the front page of the newspaper for all the wrong reasons.

11.25 a.m. Arrived at school. Gang of infants told me that Katie was inside 'dying'.

11.30 a.m. Found Katie lying in the staff room, surrounded by anxious teachers. She was crying loudly and looked severely distressed. Teachers seemed to be arguing about what had happened – someone mentioned monkey bars. They went quiet when they saw I was in the room.

12.00 p.m. Arrived at A and E after horrendous journey trying to console a crying Katie who was bleeding all over the back seat and her Bratz schoolbag.

12.01 p.m. Demanded to be seen immediately.

12.02 p.m. Had blazing argument with lowly junior doctor, who suggested Katie's disfiguring cut may be just a surface wound.

12.03 p.m. Demanded to see attending consultant.

12.05 p.m. Attending consultant turned out to be the doctor who removed the potty from Jack's head and fixed Dad's ankle when he fell over the Teletubby last year.

12.06 p.m. Demanded to see another consultant.

12.07 p.m. Kind nurse made me a cup of tea and gave Katie a lollipop, which she attempted to eat as blood streamed from her mouth. Kindly nurse informed me that cuts to the lip area often appeared worse than they really were. Asked kindly nurse if Katie might need plastic surgery in years to come. She did not reply, but she definitely looked shifty.

12.10 p.m. Called Danni and told her. Danni started crying and speaking very fast in Italian.

12.12 p.m. Called Mrs H and informed her that her

granddaughter was under observation in A and E. She sounded quite excited.

12.15 p.m. Called Joe, who told me to calm down and stop panicking unnecessarily.

12.20 p.m. Returned to car.

12.21 p.m. Discovered car had been ticketed by heartless traffic warden.

1.00 p.m. Had blazing argument with heartless traffic warden about disgraceful discrimination while I was attending to my seriously ill child.

Traffic warden said, 'There doesn't seem to be much wrong with her now. You shouldn't have parked on a double yellow.' Katie was munching a packet of cheese and onion crisps, which I had been forced to purchase from the hospital shop as she was suddenly ravenous.

1.03 p.m. Wrenched car doors open and bundled Katie inside. Shook fist at traffic warden.

1.05 p.m. Called Elaine to tell her I would be off work for a few days to care for my seriously ill daughter. Elaine snorted violently and hung up.

1.15 p.m. Proceeded home. Jack, furious he'd missed the entire episode, attacked Katie with his *Ice Age* sippy-cup. Katie retaliated by taunting him with her empty crisps packet (probably not relevant).

2 March

Stayed at home to care for Katie. Danni said she could manage perfectly well, but I gave her a few days off. Was sure Katie wanted me, her real mother, even if she kept asking where Danni was and if we could play Italian I Spy.

Mrs H called to say that I should bathe Katie's wound in Epsom salts every hour or it would become gangrenous. 'If that cut gets infected, you never know what could happen,' she said, in a doom-laden voice. 'The infection might enter the bloodstream and she could end up on a life-support machine in Intensive Care. I heard about a case of that once.'

Joe dismissed his mother's advice when I called him, crying hysterically. 'That's another of the urban myths she's always repeating,' he soothed, trying to calm me. 'It never happened, believe me. She makes all sorts up.'

PS Poor Katie is insisting on having all her food liquidized and presented to her in a Bratz sippy-cup. The smoothie-maker is finally coming into its own.

3 March

Mrs H arrived at the crack of dawn with a press clipping showing a young child hooked up to all sorts of tubes and devices, lying prone in a hospital bed. 'Small Cut Leads to Tragic End,' the headline read.

'Here it is!' She waved it triumphantly. 'I knew I had it somewhere. I like to keep these titbits – you never know when they might come in useful.'

'What's that?' Katie asked, slurping the third smoothie of the morning through the corner of her mouth. (She may have been playing up just a little bit – caught her munching a packet of salt and vinegar when she thought no one was looking.)

'This, darling, is what you could end up like if Mummy and Daddy don't follow my instructions to the T,' Mrs H said.

Katie paled and put the smoothie back on the table. Mrs H whipped it away. 'I'll finish this for you, dear – too much fruit is bad for your digestion.'

PS Jack is now refusing to eat solid food and is insisting on having smoothies like his sister. Luckily, the smoothie-maker is standing up admirably to round-the-clock pressure.

4 March

Angelica called as I was trying persuade Katie that chocolate buttons did not count as a nutritious meal. 'Oh, my gosh, Susie!' she said. 'I heard all about the accident. Is Katie OK?'

'Thanks, Angelica,' I said, touched that she had thought to call and taken time to do so out of her hectic schedule of floating about, looking good and organizing charity events. 'She's on the mend, thankfully.'

'Are you guys going to sue?'

'Sue?' I didn't know what she meant.

'Yeah, the school. They're at fault for not watching her properly, don't you think? Do you want me to hook you up with a lawyer? Our guy's an animal.'

Spent the rest of the afternoon surfing the Internet to check previous legal cases involving school accidents. Was astounded to discover there are lots. Apparently schools across the country are negligent on a regular basis.

Called Joe to tell him we may pursue litigation.

'Don't be ridiculous, Susie,' he said. 'You can't sue the school because Katie fell off the monkey bars.'

'Why not?' I replied. 'Angelica says she should have been supervised properly.'

'She should have been more careful,' Joe said. 'Hanging

off monkey bars by the tip of one finger isn't exactly playing it safe.'

Am very annoyed with Joe for scuppering my grand plan. Was quite looking forward to lording it in court and putting my case to the prosecution, etc. In fact, I should possibly have read law instead of doing a useless arts degree back in the eighties. At least then I could wear a tight-fitting black suit, cover my bird's-nest hair with a grey wig, and look imposing and fierce, like the sexy one in *Law and Order*.

5 *March*

Katie is almost fully recovered. Was worried she'd be reluctant to go back to school, where she was so badly traumatized, but she bounded in today, just like the brave little soldier she is.

'Now, there's no need to be nervous, Katie,' I said, anxious she wouldn't want to return to the scene of the crime.

'Whatever, Mummy,' she said, wriggling to get out of my grip. 'I can't wait to show the others my massive scab. They'll be so jealous!' She shoved past me and ran over to a gang of round-eyed infants.

I bumped into Angelica at the gate. 'You poor thing!' she said, hugging me. 'You look absolutely exhausted.'

Was a bit taken aback – had spent ages applying tons of tinted moisturizer and bronzer to look less washed-out, but I supposed I was still a bit hollow-eyed – all the waiting hand and foot on Katie had taken it out of me.

'You probably need a break away,' Angelica observed.

Was hoping she'd suggest whisking me off somewhere exotic as a little treat, but before I could even drop a hint she piped up again: 'Speaking of breaks, honey, would you mind if I used your country cottage again? We really need to get away – you know how it is. And I'm sure you guys won't be getting down there much, not now you're working.'

'Um, yes, I suppose you're right,' I said, suddenly yearning for a holiday – any kind of holiday.

'That's what I thought,' she said, rubbing my arm, 'so why don't I whiz down, water the plants, that kind of thing? I'm practically doing you a favour.' She giggled girlishly.

'OK, then,' I mumbled, a little put out, but not sure why.

'Great!' She beamed. 'Now you just have to fill me in on how your new job's going – the next time we meet for sure!'

She bounded off, leaving me trailing morosely in her wake.

When I eventually got to work Elaine had no sympathy for me.

'You're back, then, are you?' she said loudly, when I slid into my seat. 'That's the trouble with working mothers – they're always taking time off. I mean, really, if I had as much leave as you I'd have been sacked years ago.' Then she waddled off to gossip with the guys in the post room.

Am very worried. What if Elaine bad-mouths me round the building and gets me fired just as I'm making inroads and developing a worthwhile career? I must get her on my side at all costs.

6 March

Have come up with an elaborate plan to get Elaine on my side and ensure a meteoric rise to the top.

1. Pay her.
2. Offer to do all her photocopying.
3. Shower her with expensive gift baskets.
4. Shower her with Joe's cooking. There is now so much

home-baked produce floating about that even the dog doesn't bat an eyelid any more.

7 March

Plan to seduce Elaine is not proving altogether successful. I brought in a large basket of Joe's muffins today and encouraged her to have one with her morning coffee. Next minute she was on the floor, clutching her throat and turning blue. Then everyone was screaming and crying, two (quite hunky) ambulance men arrived, gave her an injection and she was taken away. Turns out she's allergic to macadamias, and by some awful coincidence Joe had used some to spice up his muffin mix. Everyone in the office spent the rest of the day whispering in my direction. How was I supposed to know? It's not like I did it on purpose.

Joe took grave exception when I accused him of lacing his muffins with nuts to get me into trouble and is now not speaking to me. Am worried he has developed a sensitive side. Maybe Mrs H is right, after all – maybe he is 'turning'.

8 March

Danni is acting strangely. I caught her crying into the minestrone this evening, although she tried to say the onions were making her eyes water.

'What's wrong, Danni?' I asked, trying to be sympathetic, even though it was obvious that she still hadn't done any vacuuming as I'd hinted she might; balls of dust were rolling cheekily across the hall in plain view.

'Nothing.' She snuffled. 'Sometimes I get leetle homesick, that's all.' She snuffled even louder.

'Why don't you go and see your mummy, then?' Katie piped up innocently.

I held my breath, horrified. Danni paying an unscheduled trip to Italy was not in my grand plan and would not suit at all.

'You are sweet, my leetle Katie,' she smiled through her tears, 'but I would miss you too much, yes?'

'But if you did miss me, you could bring me back a big present,' Katie suggested, turning on her prettiest smile. 'That would probably make you feel much better.'

9 March

Elaine has lodged a formal complaint with Human Resources about the macadamia incident. Apparently her official email said, 'I cannot work with someone who has blatant disregard for my delicate health requirements.'

Word on the street is that I deliberately tried to kill her. Am attempting to keep a low profile.

PS Mrs H left incoherent message on my mobile phone – something about Joe, pastels and flower-arranging.

10 March

I am a hero at work! Was accosted by a colleague this morning. I cowered in fear, terrified he was about to berate me for what had happened to Elaine, but instead he threw his arms round me and lifted me off the ground in a massive bear-hug. 'It was so simple, but so brilliant,' he said. 'I should have thought of it years ago. How did you get the recipe just right so it floored her but didn't actually kill her?'

Spent rest of the day fielding queries from people wanting to know how I'd done it and if I could do the same thing for their annoying relatives, mothers-in-law, husbands, etc.

Have given up trying to deny that it was anything other than an accident. The masses are looking for a hero figure – who am I to deny them?

11 March

Elaine will be on sick leave for the foreseeable future. I now have to combine her job with mine. Why did I have to be a leader? Why? People have stopped bringing cappuccinos to my desk without me asking them to. How quickly they forget. Am feeling quite sick and really sorry for myself. Combed *Heat*'s special on celebs with mental-health issues and it turns out I have all the symptoms:

• pallid and/or spotty complexion

• listless expression

• severe weight loss/weight gain (latter in my case)

• hunched shoulders

• excessive party-girl lifestyle (N/A)

All I'm missing is the impossible-to-get handbag and I'll tick *all* the boxes.

Decided to leave the magazine lying about and hope Joe reads it. He might want to whisk me away for a romantic weekend before I start binge-drinking or going out without any underwear, like celebs on the edge do.

12 March

Arrived home early. Danni and the children were nowhere to be found. Tried calling Danni on her mobile phone a zillion times but couldn't reach her. Was starting to panic when they breezed through the door laden with bunches of spring flowers.

'Where on earth were you, Danni?' I hugged Katie and Jack to me. 'You really scared me! You should have answered your phone.'

'Sorree, Susie,' Danni said, stricken. 'We were picking flowers in the park.' Then she burst into tears and rushed away before I had a chance to explain. But it *was* irresponsible of her to lose track of time. Have resolved to check her references properly, once and for all. Maybe a previous employer can tell me why she has become so emotional all of a sudden.

13 March

Called two of Danni's former employers in Italy today but couldn't understand a word they were saying so decided to Google her name instead. Couldn't find anything about her. The only D. Genovese on-line was a Sicilian mobster on the run from allegations of drug-trafficking and general warlording. Spent ages reading about his exploits until Mike the producer snuck up behind me and I had to pretend I was doing important customer-care research.

PS Joe is being very quiet about changing his career path and chucking in a perfectly good job to follow his outlandish dream of becoming an award-winning chef. This is a good sign. Hopefully he has given up on the entire idea.

14 March

Still feeling very off-colour. Called Louise to tell her I might be suffering from some kind of yuppie flu. I have all the symptoms – lethargy, aching joints, desire to sleep all day. I haven't experienced any significant weight loss, though (in fact, my jeans may even be tighter than usual), so it can't be anything life-threatening – unless abnormal weight gain is a symptom of a progressive, fatal disease.

'Maybe you're a bit depressed because of your birthday,' Louise said. 'Turning thirty-five can't be easy. Or it might be your thyroid, I suppose. You should get it checked.'

Called Joe to tell him I might have a dysfunctional thyroid or something even worse and could be dead in six weeks.

'You look pretty healthy to me,' he said. He sounded as though it wouldn't bother him if I dropped dead there and then.

'But what about the inexplicable weight gain and lethargy?' I said. 'All the signs point to something serious.'

'Em, maybe you've been over-indulging,' he suggested. 'Everyone puts on a few pounds now and again.'

Am outraged that Joe thinks I'm simply a greedy fatty and am not suffering from a serious, debilitating disease that could snuff me out in no time. He practically insinuated that if I stopped gorging on biscuits I'd be much better off. He'll be sorry when he's a single parent and I'm pushing up daisies.

15 March: My birthday

I am thirty-five. Which means that my life is probably half over already. No wonder I'm suffering from the onset of some serious illness. I'm already midway to certain death.

Mum and Dad called to sing 'Happy Birthday', as they do every year, but this time I interrupted them before they could finish their off-key warbling. 'Is there any history of thyroid disease in the family, Mum?' I asked.

'No, darling, I don't think so,' she said. 'Why do you ask?'

I explained my symptoms to her but she dismissed them and so did Dad.

'It sounds like you're having a mid-life crisis, Susie.' He laughed. 'I had one at your age and then I took up cross-training. Lots more exercise would get the endorphins pumping. You should start rock-climbing.'

Went home. Katie and Jack gave me a sweet homemade birthday card and Joe had baked an elaborate triple chocolate cake, but I still felt down in the dumps. Sometimes I find myself hankering for something a bit more glamorous – like a night in a junior suite at the Four Seasons or an all-expenses-paid trip to New York. Am sure either would be better than hanging off a cliff face and staring death in the eye.

16 March

Called the doctor from my desk to explain my mystery symptoms. Unfortunately I couldn't get through as the power-crazed receptionist insisted he was busy and couldn't be disturbed.

'I need to speak to him,' I said, trying to sound authoritative.

'Mrs Hunt, half of Dublin needs to speak to him,' she retorted. 'I'm afraid you'll have to make an appointment like everyone else.'

Hung up in annoyance. Apparently, unless you're in danger of dying within the next twenty-four hours you're not considered an emergency. Have drafted letter to Minister for Health to demand that the health service be overhauled immediately.

Dear Minister [*NB Find out who is Minister for Health. Maybe Google?*]

I am writing to you to express my dismay at the state of the health service in Ireland today. I am suffering from a litany of serious mystery ailments that obviously need to be assessed as quickly as possible. Imagine my disquiet when I called my doctor today only to be informed that the next available appointment is not until late next week (at which point my symptoms may have deteriorated even further – if I'm still around to tell the tale). I know you are a very busy person [*NB Google minister-type activities and insert here*] but I feel I must remind you that, as a voter, I am, in a roundabout way, your employer. Not that I am telling you this in a threatening way, of course, but I do pay your wages and I may be forced to vote for a different political party at the next general election if things do not improve. That is, when I get round to registering to vote, which I will soon, when I have the time.

I would appreciate it if you could get back to me with your thoughts as soon as possible.

Yours truly,
Susie Hunt

PS I realize you are not personally responsible for the acerbic wit of doctors' receptionists – but have you ever thought about getting the profession regulated? I fear lots of unsuitable types are slipping through the net.

PPS You might consider introducing free massages on the street for stressed-out working mothers. I'm sure they would work a treat and probably stop lots of nasty road-rage incidences as well, so it would be a good investment and kill two birds with the one stone so to speak.

17 March: St Patrick's Day

Was too downhearted to risk the parade. Instead, I decided to watch it on TV in the comfort of the living room as Katie and Jack waved the Irish tricolour about.

'Why did St Patrick drive all the snakes from Ireland, Mummy?' Katie said, tugging at the green ribbons she had demanded I put in her hair.

Felt that the time was not right to explain that snakes were a euphemism for mortal sin, etc., etc., so I encouraged her to watch the samba dancers shaking their booty instead. Will get Mum to explain it to her some day soon.

PS Have just remembered that Mum is now practically an atheist and probably thinks St Patrick didn't even exist. Her lack of sensitivity is really very inconvenient.

18 March

Told Joe I had written to the Minister for Health to demand a complete overhaul of the health service. He looked at me as if I'd gone crazy. 'Susie, don't you ever read the papers?' He groaned. 'There are dozens of people on hospital trolleys all over the country because they can't get a bed. People with *real* illnesses.'

Suspect Joe thinks I'm faking my sickness. Suspect he also thinks I'm not clued in on current affairs. OK, so I usually only read the Style and Home sections of the papers. But at least I know what 'chartreuse' is. And who knows? My mystery illness might make an excellent programme segment on *Chat with Dee and Fran* – especially if I die a tragic and untimely death. Then it really *would* be newsworthy.

19 March

Elaine is back from sick leave. She has agreed to work with me again, but only until she can be moved to a better position. She has instructed that I am not speak to her under any circumstances, not even if Brad Pitt walks into the office and I need to warn her to take her dental retainer out.

Came home and Katie announced that she wants to be a vegetarian.

'Brandon doesn't eat meat now,' she said, with steely determination. 'He says he's going to concentrate on his carbs to improve his swimming.'

'But, Katie, you don't even like swimming any more,' I said, wondering what she would eat if I couldn't feed her sausages.

'That doesn't matter, Mummy.' She pouted. 'I want carbs, like Brandon.'

Am scandalized. I was at least twenty-five before I knew what a carb was.

20 *March*

Joe says he's searching for his signature dish.

'What do you mean, signature dish?' I asked. Perhaps he wanted to develop a range of bestselling cookware to get us out of our financial pickle. The one he still doesn't know about.

'You know, a signature dish,' he said slowly. 'Something that's mine alone, something with the wow factor.'

'Oh, right,' I said, losing interest. 'Well, Häagen Dazs has a lot of wow factor. Maybe you could do something with that.'

'Susie,' he said witheringly, 'my signature dish cannot involve ice-cream. I'm not five years old.'

Am very annoyed. Was only trying to help. Sometimes think Joe is developing a fiery cook's temperament to go with his new vocation.

PS Katie has taken to saying she will eat nothing that has a face. Luckily, she has agreed that frozen potato faces are still acceptable fare.

PPS Jack is being suspiciously quiet. And he hasn't tried to flush his toothbrush down the toilet in at least three days. Something is definitely up. Hope he isn't feeling hard done by because I haven't organized an OTT party for his birthday tomorrow.

Jack's teacher called when I was at work. She wanted to see me urgently. Told Elaine I had to leave unexpectedly and that I'd make up the time.

'You're missing *so* many days, Susie.' She smirked. 'I hope management doesn't have to take it up with you. But that's working mothers,' she announced loudly as I scrambled to find my bag. 'They're never dedicated to the job at hand. Do you know what I mean?' Then she went back to updating her Bebo page.

When I eventually made it to the school Jack's teacher looked grim.

'I'm afraid, Mrs Hunt,' she said, her face stony and unmoving, 'that if Jack's socialization skills do not improve we will have to ask him to leave Little Angels.'

'Why?' I asked, horrified that they were considering expelling him and officially black-marking his educational record for ever. 'What happened?'

'His behaviour is deteriorating day by day,' she said coldly. 'He refuses to sit on a chair for any length of time. He does not colour within the lines. He needs to work on his concentration skills. Do you want me to continue?'

'But it's his birthday,' I pleaded, incredulous that colouring outside the lines was now a criminal offence.

'That's as may be,' she said sharply, 'but we think he may need a psychological assessment.'

'Well, I hardly think that's necessary,' I countered, worried that Jack would be labelled a delinquent so young.

'You're not an expert, though, are you, Mrs Hunt?' she said, tapping her pen. 'We'll give him another week or two, then reassess.'

Left feeling very depressed. Fear she may have hit the nail on the head – I'm *not* an expert. But surely I should be by now? Bought enormous *Bob the Builder* birthday cake for Jack on the way home, then let him mush it any way he wanted to, to cheer him up. Am positive all the negativity is affecting him.

22 March

Mum says playschool must be emotionally stifling. 'It sounds very restrictive, darling,' she said, when I explained that Jack might be expelled. 'Is it really good for him, do you think?'

'What do you mean?' I asked, wondering if I could persuade her to leave Portugal and move home to help out.

'Well, if he's being forced to conform so young, it might lead to problems later in life. Of a sexual nature, I mean. It's all very repressive. Have you considered home schooling?'

Quickly made my excuses and hung up. Think I may prefer Jack to be a cross-dressing transvestite than have to give up work so soon and endure teaching him things of an educational nature in the confines of my own house. Besides, he probably needs social interaction, and lots of it.

23 March

Joe says Jack will have to learn to fit in. He also thinks we need drastically to modify his diet. 'We should cut out refined sugar, Susie,' he said. 'I've been reading up on the subject and foods with a high sugar content can have a very negative impact on children's behaviour. Especially boys'.'

I was so relieved he was going to take control of the

situation that I hugged him spontaneously. It might have led to more, but Jack stormed in at the crucial moment demanding a bowl of Sugar Pops. Still, am very heartened that Joe is devising practical ways to deal with the situation, ones that don't involve me setting up a *Little House on the Prairie* type school.

24 March

Am in a tailspin. Found Joe dumping perfectly good food into the rubbish bin this morning. Including all the children's breakfast cereal.

'What are you doing?' I yelled. 'If Jack doesn't get his Sugar Pops he'll go mental.'

'I thought we agreed, Susie,' Joe said calmly. 'No more sugary foods.'

'What do you propose we eat for breakfast, then?' I asked.

'Porridge, of course,' he said, producing a box of organic oats from behind his back with a flourish.

Went and hid in the bathroom until the worst was over. Could hear lots of shouting and crying from the kitchen but when I resurfaced all three were at the table, happily eating hot bowlfuls.

'How did you manage that?' I asked, gob-smacked.

'I simply explained that porridge has lots of healthy good-ness that would make them grow up to be big and strong,' he said proudly.

'*And* he said we could go to Disneyland if we ate it,' Katie smiled, 'even if it does taste like puke.'

'Puke!' Jack roared happily.

I think Danni may have a secret boyfriend, which would explain all the tears and emotion lately. Caught her whispering into her phone today. Well, actually, I was earwigging outside the toilet door when she locked herself in to take a call, but only because I'm concerned for her welfare. Could hear lots of '*Sì . . . Sì . . . Sì*,' and huge sighs, but that was about all. I really must take up Italian. I'm sure it's easy to learn. All you have to do is wave your hands about a lot and you're halfway there.

Louise thinks there's been something suspicious about Danni's behaviour of late. 'How's she getting on with the children?' she asked, when I confided I was worried about her red-rimmed eyes and loud (quite annoying) snivelling.

'Fine,' I said, wondering if this was altogether the truth. 'They seem to really like her.'

'Hmm . . .' Louise said. 'Of course, you can never be certain.'

I panicked immediately. 'What do you mean? Katie would tell me if anything was wrong.'

'Not necessarily,' Louise said ominously. 'Children can bottle things up, you know.'

Was tempted to ask when Louise had done a degree in child psychology but thought better of it. Will keep a close eye on the situation.

Joe says I'm overreacting to Danni's mood. 'She's probably just homesick,' he said, when I told him how grumpy she was. 'Maybe you should have a chat with her, see how she's coping.'

Didn't say anything, but am worried. What if I have a

heart-to-heart with her and she confides that she's miserable and wants to leave? Then my career's down the toilet before it's even begun.

Have prepared a manifesto of comprehensive guidance points to assist me in getting to the bottom of the matter.

1. If cause of her distress is heartbreak – rejoice. Then act compassionate and dole out the chocolate.
2. If cause of her distress is homesickness – rejoice. Then act consoling and dole out some *gelato*.
3. If cause of her distress is wild and uncontrollable children – do not panic. Reassure her that children will immediately behave after stern talking-to from their father. Promise to increase her salary if she agrees not to jump ship.

26 March

Danni has confided in me that she is not

(a) broken-hearted;

(b) homesick; or

(c) sick of the kids.

However, she *is* on the run from her Mafia relatives, who have disowned her because she refused an arranged marriage with a nice thug who has good mob connections. Also, her Don father has promised to track her down, haul her back to Sicily and punish her for dishonouring the family with her disobedience. Oh, and he has also promised to 'deal' with anyone harbouring her. Instantly knew that this would not involve a civilized discussion about how best to resolve an awkward situation.

'Why didn't you tell me before?' I gasped, grisly scenes from *The Godfather* flashing through my mind.

'Because I thought you not hire me, Susie,' she sobbed. 'I wanted to live free from my family, but now they find out where I am and they come to get me back.'

Have consulted my comprehensive guidance list for advice. Do not seem to have made any provision for this eventuality.

PS Really wish Danni would take her anxiety about her impending doom and do something constructive with it – like playing with the children or spring-cleaning the house.

27 March

Spent a sleepless night tossing, turning and having vivid dreams about Mafia bosses hanging us by our fingernails or throwing us into the nearest river with bags of cement attached to our necks. Decided to email David – he has the full box set of *The Sopranos* so he'd be sure to know what to do.

> Hi David, If, hypothetically, you found that you had inadvertently employed the daughter of a Mafioso what would you do?
> Lots of love,
> Susie xx

He replied straight away:

Hi Susie, you are too funny. Can you imagine?
Horses' heads on the pillow and all that! Hope all is
well with you? How's the job going? Taken over the
broadcasting world yet?
David xoxox

28 March

Elaine caught me Googling 'Mafia info' on my PC today.
'Why are you doing that?' she asked, squinting suspiciously
at my screen.

'Just some research,' I said, trying to sound nonchalant.

'For what?' she asked.

'Um, a programme segment?' I ventured.

'Reeeeally?' Her voice was like acid. 'Your job, Susie, is
not to research programme segments. Your job is to answer
the mail and do errands for the rest of us. What makes you
think you're even qualified to do research?' She narrowed
her eyes at me until I lowered my gaze.

Spent the rest of the afternoon listening to her chatting
to her friends and loudly discussing how some people had
ideas above their station and needed taking down a peg or
two.

PS Wonder if Joe and I could apply for the witness-
protection programme. Am sure we would qualify.

29 March

Have discovered there is no witness-protection programme
in Ireland. We are doomed.

Joe asked if I'd sorted things out with Danni. Mumbled that I had. Definitely don't think he needs to hear that we're all in mortal danger and may be assassinated at any second. Especially when he seems to be going through some sort of identity crisis.

Lay awake all night wondering how I'd convince Danni's Mafioso father not to shoot us all dead in cold blood for harbouring his wayward daughter. Cannot think of any way out of it. Have decided to hire some gangster movies for inspiration on dealing with the situation. Meanwhile, Danni's mood has improved. She's no longer clutching rosary beads and looking anxious all the time. Have taken this to be a good sign. Maybe her father is calling off his international daughter-hunt.

PS Wonder if I have attention-deficit disorder instead of a thyroid dysfunction. I definitely cannot focus on or finish a task properly. Maybe I could use that in my defence when Danni's family come knocking.

31 March: Louise's birthday

Joe says his mind is made up. He is handing in his notice and setting out on the rocky road to becoming the next Gordon Ramsay. (He is way too old to be Jamie Oliver, even if he thinks differently.)

'I've been accepted into a very prestigious cookery school, Susie – Danni helped me with the application,' he said, admitting that he had gone ahead without my knowledge and consent and would be starting any day. 'I'm over the moon. This is my chance to do something I feel passionate about.'

'Don't be too hasty, Joe,' I begged. Without his salary to depend on we'd all be left destitute on the street. 'Think about it for a while. Passion is very overrated, you know.'

'If there's one thing my brush with death in Portugal taught me, Susie,' he said, looking deep into my eyes, 'it's that we have only a finite time here on earth. We have to make the most of it.'

Which is all well and good, but when he's making the most of his time here on earth who's going to pay the gas bill? Am suddenly regretting lying about my new salary. In fact, am seriously considering telling Joe the truth: my wages wouldn't buy an allotment in the inner city to grow organic vegetables, never mind support a family of four.

Have decided Mum and Dad are to blame for this unlikely turn of events. They recommended that stupid fish restaurant where Joe almost choked to death and saw his life flash before his eyes. On the up-side, I'm sure he'll never realize his dream to become a top-notch celebrity chef with his own TV show and book series, and will be forced back to his real job within days. He doesn't have the bad language required to order commis-chefs around with any authority – and there's no way he could hurl vile abuse at anyone – he's way too polite.

PS Was too overwrought to do anything special for Louise's birthday – hopefully, the Lottery scratchcard I bought her won't be a winner. It would be just too awful if she won loads of cash instead of me.

1 April: April Fool's Day

Joe has handed in his notice at Pyramid Consultants.

'What did they say?' I gasped when he broke the news, hoping they had

(a) thought it was an April Fool's joke;

(b) begged him to reconsider and doubled his salary to convince him to stay;

(c) begged him to reconsider and trebled his salary to convince him to stay.

'Maurice hugged me and said he wished he had my courage,' Joe said, looking pleased with himself. 'His dream is to fly a single-pilot aircraft across the Indian Ocean. He'll never do that now, of course. At least I'm still young enough to try to live my dream.'

Refrained from telling him that

(a) thirty-seven is way too old to be thinking about dreams when mortgages need paying and when the new Prada bag costs a month's salary;

(b) living the dream is way overrated – all the celebs in rehab are proof of that.

Instead, I tried not to panic and played for time.

'Well, let's just see how it goes,' I said soothingly, plotting to speak to Maurice as soon as possible and persuade him, by any means necessary, to talk Joe out of this madness.

'No, it's all settled,' Joe said evenly. 'They've agreed to let me go on gardening leave.'

'Gardening leave?' I said, unsure what planting herbaceous borders had to do with it. 'What do you mean?'

'That today was my last day. They're paying me till the end of the month, of course.'

Can't remember any more. Suddenly felt faint and weak and had to lie down with a HobNob.

2 April

Last night I had a blinding revelation. Joe is having a mid-life crisis, not me. That's why he thinks he needs to be the next Gordon Ramsay. What he *really* needs is to buy an expensive sports car, have an innocent flirtation with someone unsuitable and get it out of his system instead of musing on the merits of organic, locally grown produce and trying to decide if beef should be hung for two weeks or three. Am barely functioning at work. Thankfully, Elaine is too busy on Bebo to notice and report me.

3 April: Good Friday

Louise agrees that Joe probably *is* having a mid-life crisis but that an affair with someone unsuitable will not help.

'It didn't work for you, did it?' she asked, watching Dargan as he kicked his legs in his Tommy Hilfiger Babygro and matching bib.

'I did *not* have an affair, Louise,' I snapped, annoyed that she kept insisting Lone Father and I had ripped each other's clothes off and got down to it against the washing-machine in the utility room.

'Ah, yes, but you did in your head!' she argued. 'That's just as bad. In fact, it's probably worse. Emotional infidelity is a complete and utter betrayal of a relationship. When you open yourself up to someone emotionally, you may as well shag him all over the country.' Then she grinned at me and went back to making notes about her new maternity and breastfeeding fashion line on her leather-bound jotter.

Have decided to stop calling round to see Louise for a while. She doesn't deserve my unconditional support. Plus she has annoyed me by buying into the size-zero obsession. It cannot be healthy to have lost so much weight and look so good only a few months after giving birth. Have also decided not to tell her anything about Danni's secret past. She might blow it out of all proportion.

4 April

Couldn't sleep last night. Just lay there wondering how would I explain to Katie and Jack that we were no longer able to afford life's necessities – like the new Bratz DVD or Spiderman underwear. Feel very resentful towards Joe that his selfishness will result in the children missing out on the material goods they patently need to compete with their peers. Katie will be a laughing-stock if she doesn't get heelie trainers soon – and they cost a hundred euro. Which means selling a lot of *tarte Tatins*.

PS Jack wedged his red Power Ranger in the toilet again tonight. It overflowed all over the landing but Joe refused to look because he'd hit a critical moment in *crème brûlée* making. Not sure how much more of this I can take.

5 April: Easter Sunday

Have a head cold. Spent the day lying in bed, eating Easter eggs and pondering the twists and turns of my life. Decided I have enough material to make a for-TV movie or, at the very least, a true-life-story mini-series. Wonder if Reese Witherspoon would consider playing me. Spent the afternoon catching up on the Sunday papers and read that Trinny and Susannah are now doing on-line makeovers. Decided to write to them to applaud their efforts to help the ordinary woman on the street.

Dear Trinny and Susannah,

I am writing to express my delight that you are now doing on-line consultations for no-hopers with zero fashion sense. It is really commendable that you are getting back to your roots and trying to transform harassed and dowdy women. That recent show was not your best idea. Putting naked couples behind a screen and asking them to review each other's best bits was always asking for disaster. If my husband told me I had lovely elbows because he couldn't think of any other body part he found remotely attractive I would whack him across the head. Telling someone their elbows are attractive is patently a nice way of saying that their arse is the size of a bus. Also, I did feel for you when that guy got a massive erection behind the screen and you had to avert your eyes. Some men have no sense of occasion. Anyway, congratulations again on the new venture.

Yours,
Susie Hunt

PS Please feel free to send vouchers as a token of your appreciation.

6 April: Easter Monday

Mrs H called round with extra Easter eggs for Katie and Jack. She was delighted to find me snuffling into my un-ironed sheets. 'Susie, I'm glad you're here,' she said. 'I've something to tell you.' She smoothed the duvet cover and perched on the edge of the bed.

'Have you?' I said, not really caring.

'Yes, and you mustn't be shocked. Brace yourself, dear.' She paused dramatically. 'I've decided to join a support group for the parents of homosexuals.'

'OK,' I said, wondering if I could convince her to do a bit of ironing now she was here.

'Yes. Apparently David's sexuality doesn't reflect on me or my parenting skills. It's just one of those things and should be embraced, not mocked or feared.'

'That's nice,' I croaked.

'You're not disappointed?'

'Why would I be?'

'Well, I know you felt you could turn David straight, dear, but apparently that's a very old-fashioned idea. And you haven't made very much progress, have you, pet?' She patted my hand, as if I was a child and she was trying to explain the facts of life as delicately as she could. 'Anyway, I've decided I'm not the type of woman to let life trample her underfoot so I'm going to take charge and try to understand David's lifestyle choices. Rumour has it that Nuala Connor's young fella is bisexual – so my David's no news at all, really.'

'Great,' I said, wondering how I could get her to leave if she wasn't going to make herself useful.

'Would you not change the sheets, Susie dear?' she asked suddenly, wrinkling her nose. 'How can you expect Joe to be turned on by you when everything's such a mess? It's not *gay* he is, it's repulsed.'

7 April

Mum and Dad have announced they're coming home for a week's flying visit. 'We haven't seen the children in so long, darling,' Mum said, when she called. 'Dad booked the flights on the Internet last night. Isn't it fabulous? We can all spend a cosy few days together.'

Am dreading it. Have not yet confided in Mum that Joe has had a funny turn and is no longer supporting us. Hope I can carry off impression of happy home so they don't suspect anything. They're bound to notice all the home baking now readily available in the house – and they know cooking isn't my strong point.

PS Smell on the landing from toilet overflowing is unbearable. Spent ages on my hands and knees trying to dry the wet patches with the travel hairdryer. Absolutely pointless. Not talking to Joe. He starts his ridiculous full-time cookery course tomorrow but I'm determined to ignore the entire stupid charade.

Joe set off this morning, looking happier than I've seen him in years. Have to admit that the chef's hat is very cute and the way his hair flops out underneath is adorable. Didn't say that to him obviously. He must be discouraged from pursuing this ridiculous dream at all costs. Didn't wave him off at the door either, but could hear Danni saying encouraging things in broken English as he left.

Day got even worse when Louise called me at work to say she had won some utterly pointless poll: Yummiest Corporate Mummy of the Year.

'Who nominated you?' I asked, feeling too sick to finish my second sausage roll at my desk.

'I nominated myself, of course,' she crowed. 'It's a brilliant advertising ploy for my new business. They'll be doing a full-page spread on Dargan and me in the *Gazette* in a couple of days. It's the perfect launch-pad.'

Cannot help but wonder if Louise and I have one of those toxic relationships that Oprah's always talking about. She seems to feed off my insecurities, while I'm nothing but supportive of her goals and ambitions. And she seems to want to do better than me all the time. It can't be a coincidence that I'm finally succeeding at a career I enjoy (sort of) and she suddenly has this great idea for a new business. It's a bit too convenient for my liking.

PS Joe came home delighted with himself. He was also wearing a striped apron with 'Born to Cook' emblazoned across the front. Completely ignored him.

PPS Have worked out that my monthly salary is enough to pay for approximately one-fifth of our outgoings. Am hoping I've made some serious mathematical error – Joe's all-singing all-dancing monster calculator *is* very complicated to use.

Danni is urging Joe on in his outlandish endeavours to be a top-rate chef. 'This *pain au chocolat* ees wonderful, Joe!' she enthused, when he brought home his latest offering from cookery school. 'Try some, Susie.' She offered the buttery (and fairly delicious-looking) *pain* to me.

'No, thanks,' I snarled, frowning to make her understand that Joe must be stopped.

'But, Susie, Joe has the gift!' She threw up her hands and waved them about passionately. 'He ees a maestro, a talent!'

Then Joe blushed and I felt wretched for my deceit. If he wasn't so distracted by the cooking, he'd have been on to me weeks ago. This is the first time in years that he hasn't balanced the cheque book on a weekly basis. As it is, he has no idea how dangerously low our bank balance is.

The only consolation is that I got two numbers in the midweek lotto. Must be sure to invest heavily in tickets in case my lucky streak is round the corner.

Louise and Dargan are splashed all over the Lifestyle section of the *Gazette*. Suspect she practised her photo pose beforehand – she looks just like Paris Hilton in her teeny top and Seven jeans, Dargan dangling off her hip with a grin on his face. The by-line read – 'Yummiest Corporate Mummy of the Year' and the article explained how Louise is set to transform maternity and breastfeeding clothes in the greater Western world. 'Women shouldn't have to look and feel unattractive because they're pregnant or breastfeeding,' she simpered, in the text. 'My new range will be stylish and affordable so now everyone can be a yummy mummy and do the best for their baby as well!'

Then she called to tell me that the *Gazette* is going to pay her extortionate amounts of money to write a yummy-mummy column for them. Tried a few deep, cleansing breaths to quell the strange jealousy that bubbled up within me, but they were useless. Maybe, like Oprah, you have to be a multi-millionaire with your own private jet for them to be effective. Ate a full packet of Jaffa Cakes after I'd hung up. Suspect my sugar levels may have dropped due to my mystery illness. Or else I'm clinically depressed about VBF's new stardom.

PS Lots of bills arrived in the post today. Threw them behind the bread bin until I can figure out how we're going to pay for electricity or to have the rubbish collected. Am regretting not getting a compost bin now. It would have come in handy to destroy all the evidence in an ecologically friendly way.

11 April

Mrs H has morphed into someone unrecognizable. She arrived today wearing a T-shirt that said 'Proud Gay Momma'. She has also started carrying bottles of spring water everywhere and is wearing a fanny-belt stuffed with Gay Pride literature.

'Why are you wearing that T-shirt, Granny?' Katie asked, fingering it in awe.

'It's important to stand up for your rights, dear, remember that,' Mrs H said.

'OK,' Katie said doubtfully. 'But can you get me a T-shirt too?'

David called. 'I think Mum's gone a bit mad,' he said.

'Why's that?' I asked, wondering if the time was right to ask if Joe and I could take a little mini-break to London soon.

'She keeps calling to pledge support,' he said. 'If I have to listen to one more rant about the Church and its hypocrisy, I'll go ex-directory.'

'She's only trying to be supportive,' I told him. 'She feels really guilty about the way she acted at Christmas.'

'Well, I nearly prefer that to this,' he grumbled. 'All this support's freaking me out. I can handle her better when she's being difficult and judgemental. At least then I know what to expect.'

12 April

Louise's first column ran in the *Gazette* today. Her picture was nearly half the page and the by-line read, 'Is this the Yummiest Mummy in Ireland?' The article went on to explain how to look glamorous and well-groomed, even with a newborn.

She'd want to be careful – looking lean and sexy like she does so soon after Dargan's birth might impact negatively on her commercial success. May mention that to her next time we speak.

PS Wonder if we could get solar panels installed – they'd probably cut our energy bills, which, worryingly, seem to be arriving every five minutes.

13 April

Spent day coaching the kids about what to say to Mum and Dad when they're here to stay. Under no circumstances are they to find out about our current position of instability and discord. I made a grand list of topics to be avoided at all costs and pinned it to the noticeboard. (Would probably have been more effective if Katie and Jack could read, but I think they got the general idea.)

Topics To Be Avoided At All Costs

1. Joe's current obsession with rolling handmade tagliatelle
2. Joe's endless attempts to make the perfect *crème brûlée*
3. Joe's creepy obsession with celebrity chef Heston Blumenthal
4. In fact, anything to do with Joe's ridiculous idea to abandon a high-flying career on a whim to follow his dreams in a stupid attempt to find meaning in his life.

Am not sure it will work. Joe is refusing to co-operate. 'I think we should tell them, Susie,' he said. 'I have nothing to be ashamed of – cooking is a noble profession.'

Didn't tell him that it may be a noble profession if you're a cultural phenomenon and doing ads for Sainsbury's, but it's a stupid profession if you're an amateur in a Dublin suburb who has thrown away a perfectly acceptable job because of a mid-life crisis.

PS Hid the new kitchen utensils in the garage. Mum and Dad will never believe they belong to me.

PPS Am also hoping they won't notice the boxes of home-baked goodies lying about the place. To distract them, have decided to encourage them to undergo an intensive detox programme while they're here. If they insist on eating, we'll go to McDonald's. Am sure this will be a treat for them – they must be sick of fresh fish by now.

14 April

Collected Mum and Dad from the airport. Almost didn't recognize them now they're the colour of mahogany. Also, Dad was wearing a ridiculously oversized pair of sunglasses and an inappropriate pair of ultra-short shorts. They spent the entire journey to the house marvelling at the motorway and pointing out new high-rise developments.

'Honestly,' I snapped, 'you're acting like you haven't been here in years. Things can't have changed that much in a few months.'

'You're very edgy, darling,' Mum said, eyeing me in the rear-view mirror. 'Is everything OK?'

'Of course it is,' I said, raging that I'd let the happy mask slip so soon. 'Did you see the new thirty-storey high-rise over there?'

'She's cross because Daddy cooks too much,' Katie piped up.

'Joe's cooking?' Mum asked, raising an eyebrow. 'Since when?'

'He never stops,' Katie said, as I gripped the steering-wheel and tried to look unconcerned. 'Mummy says she'll put *him* in the oven soon.'

NB Must remember to curb my little witticisms when Katie's in earshot.

Mum is watching me like a hawk and keeps making me mugs of herbal tea for my nerves. Even worse, she's determined to find out if Lone Father has tried to contact me recently and renew our passionate flirtation of last year.

'I'm fine, Mum,' I complained, when she plonked another mug in front of me as I tried to watch *Desperate Housewives* in peace. 'And I haven't heard from Paul in months, honestly.'

'I'm not too sure about that, Susie,' she said, in a low voice. 'I've seen you like this before – when you took that funny turn last year. You're very pale. Do you want to practise some deep breathing with me?'

'Not really,' I said, wondering if I could nip outside to sneak a packet of cheese and onion. 'Things are fine. I'm just busy with work, that's all.'

'Ah, yes.' She nodded wisely. 'Trying to have it all can backfire in mysterious ways. No one is Superwoman, Susie.'

At least Dad's keeping off my case – he seems to be enjoying spending time with the children. Apparently he took them to the park today with Danni when I was at work.

PS Fear I may be secretly heartbroken that Lone Father wiped me out of his life without a backward glance. Quite like the idea of him pining in a lovesick way for me.

16 April

Dad has taken an unlikely shine to Danni. Came home to find them sharing a bottle of Chianti at the kitchen table while Mum practised chanting in the front room with the children.

'What's going on, Mum?' I asked, dumping my bag on the ground and hoping someone had cooked something decent for dinner.

'Your dad's bonding with Danni,' she answered. 'He thinks she's got a very wise old soul and may have been here before.'

'Really?' I said, craning my head round the door and watching Danni flick her hair about as Dad refilled her glass. 'How old can it be? She's only twenty-three.'

'Old souls can live in the youngest of bodies,' Mum said.

Couldn't be certain but am not sure Mum sounded too thrilled by this.

PS Joe is still smiling incessantly. Tried to instigate depressing conversation about global warming this evening but he wouldn't take the bait. Nothing and no one can bring him down.

17 April

Work was a complete nightmare today. Viewers' letters are coming thick and fast. Am not sure why ordinary people become so involved in celebs' lives – it really is quite sad. There are so many that I don't know where to begin.

Elaine is still refusing to help. 'All those crazies give me the willies,' she said, filing her nails when I asked her opinion. 'Anyway, you need to be on their level to be able to sympathize.' She glared at me pointedly.

Dragged myself home to discover that Danni and Dad are now bosom buddies. Found them in the living room discussing old Italian movies. They were so engrossed that neither had noticed Jack had lassoed Katie and was leading her around on all fours.

Found Mum in the kitchen, preparing vegetables to dip in hummus. Asked her if she didn't mind that Dad seemed so taken with Danni.

'Don't be silly, darling,' she said, in an odd voice. 'Of course I don't mind. I'm not possessive or jealous. It's nice for your dad to have a new friend.'

Then she continued to chop carrots aggressively, slicing them right down the middle.

18 April

Mum is refusing to come out of her room. Dad says he isn't talking to her until she apologizes for telling Danni that losing some weight would do wonders for her cholesterol levels. Luckily, Danni doesn't seem to mind the drama. In fact, she has perked up considerably – probably her Italian upbringing: she has obviously found things dull till now and would probably love it if we started flinging some crockery around passionately.

19 April

Mum and Dad are talking again but only because Joe told them last night that he has given up work to follow his dream and I am now the sole breadwinner.

'I knew you'd understand,' he said, as they sat open-mouthed at the kitchen table.

'Why would we understand?' Dad said, looking dark and murderous.

'Because you're following your dream by relocating to Portugal, of course.'

'We did that when we hit our sixties!' Dad roared, sending the dog cowering under the table. 'We spent most of our adult lives in complete misery!'

'What do you think, Susie?' Mum asked.

'Susie is being very supportive,' Joe said, before I had a chance to answer.

'Yes.' I smiled weakly, wondering if the Pinot Grigio was all gone. 'I'm being very supportive.'

'Supportive my arse!' Dad bellowed. 'How are you going to live?'

'Susie has an excellent salary,' Joe told him, 'and my cookery course will equip me with the skills I need to make a successful business. In five or ten years I'll probably be turning a profit.'

Felt instantly sick. Tried to hide behind the wine bottle but only succeeded in tipping most of it over my beige linen skirt. Luckily, this distracted everyone from the crisis that is patently at hand.

20 April

Mum and Dad have gone back. Am quite glad – felt so stressed by keeping up façade of devil-may-care that have developed worrying eye tic.

'This is utter madness, Susie,' Dad said, hugging me when I dropped them off at Departures, my eye pulsating madly. 'If you need money let me know.'

Was tempted to ask him to slip me a few thousand euro if he had it handy but tried to look brave instead.

21 April

Have had a terrible shock. My only consolation is that Mum and Dad were not here to witness it. Was leafing through the newspaper when was stopped dead in my tracks by a small photo in the book-review section. I couldn't mistake the intense eyes staring back at me. It was Lone Father, his chin resting on his hand and his eyelids drooping sexily. Recognized the pose instantly – I'd drooled over it so many times at the mother-and-toddler group last year.

'Saucy New Writer Takes Book World By Storm!' the headline screamed. The article read: 'This sensational début novel is set to be an instant bestseller. The story of a passionate secret relationship between the main character, who is married, and his lover, a dowdy housewife with hidden depths, is based on real events. Be warned – the graphic sex scenes are explosive!'

I quickly shoved the review into the kitchen bin before Joe could see. Am gripped by fear. Surely he can't be talking about me?

22 April

Have been struck down by another mystery illness. Feel it could be connected in some way with the terrible shock of seeing Lone Father and his come-to-bed eyes in the paper. Spent the morning feeling fluey and miserable at work, battling my way through dozens of letters that Elaine fired across the partition every five minutes. Suspect she is rallying the general public to write to me. In fact, she may be writing most of them herself – some of the handwriting is eerily similar.

Limped home exhausted and found Joe studying textbooks at the kitchen table while Danni and the children watched MTV in the living room. Took him to task that Katie and Jack were watching half-naked girls cavort across the screen but he just nodded and proceeded to ignore me. He is so happy with his cookery course that he's in a world of his own, these days. Which is probably a good thing. Not sure our marriage would survive if he knew that Lone Father's tell-all fictionalized autobiography was in the offing.

23 April

Felt sick and dizzy this morning. Think the stress of hiding my deceit from Joe is getting to me – I might start having terrifying panic-attacks (apparently lots of celebs get them so I'll be in very good company). Called Elaine to say I was practically dying and would not be going into work.

'I'm sure you *are* sick,' she sneered. 'Got anything to do with your darling friend Angelica, has it?'

'What do you mean?' I asked.

'Try looking at the front page of the *Gazette*, you fool,' she snapped, and slammed the phone down.

I stumbled downstairs to get the paper. There, on the front page, was a grainy black-and-white photograph of Angelica, her arms wrapped round a man who looked nothing like her A-list husband.

'Is Angelica Playing Away From Home?' the headline asked. The piece went on to say that she had allegedly been using a secret country retreat for illicit liaisons with a mystery man, thought to be her personal trainer. 'James and Angelica have had their problems,' a close personal friend was quoted as saying, 'but this could be the final straw. James has such a fiery temper that he might throw her out and start a custody battle for their only child, Brandon (5).'

There was a tiny photo of Brandon coming out of school, his face blurred out.

I stumbled back to bed to let it all sink in: Angelica had not been using our country house to rebuild her relationship with her husband but to get up to all sorts of sexual antics with her Adonis trainer and God knows who else. She had been lying to me for months. I immediately called her to ask what was going on, but there was no reply so I rang Louise.

'I never liked her,' she said.

'But you've never even met her,' I replied.

'Yes, but I have a sixth sense for this sort of thing. I always felt she was taking advantage of you and now it turns out she was using your country house for sordid liaisons – it's all very tacky.'

'Don't you think it might be a complete fabrication, though? The paparazzi are always making things up to fill column inches. Sure they have poor TomKat driven demented.' I really didn't want to believe the worst.

'I guess so,' she said, not sounding convinced. 'But something's up – or she would have called you, surely.'

Hung up, confused. There must be an explanation. I'm sure there's a perfectly logical reason why Angelica seems to have her tongue rammed down her trainer's throat in the photo – all she has to do is call and tell me what it is.

PS Just in case, I hid the paper from Joe – am sure he would recognize the overgrown garden as ours and that could lead to all sorts of problems: such as me having to explain what they were doing there in the first place.

PPS Just thought – there might be a steamy sex tape of Angelica and her lover on the Internet already, which means our house really will be infamous. Wonder if that would triple its value overnight.

24 April

Went back to work. Elaine spent the day smirking across the partition at me and making whispered comments about common tarts sticking together.

Then Louise called. 'Any news?' she asked. 'Has that slut called you yet?'

'Em, not yet,' I said, trying to be circumspect in case Elaine was listening, 'but I'm sure it's only a matter of time.'

'Yes, I'm sure. Anyway, I need a model for my breast-feeding-range catalogue,' she said. 'I was wondering if you'd do it.'

'I'm not breastfeeding, though, Louise,' I said, wondering if she'd lost the plot and if being voted Yummiest Corporate Mummy of the Year had unhinged her.

'That's OK,' she said. 'We'll just shove a baby into your arms – your boobs are big enough to make do.'

Was quite chuffed she thought I was attractive enough to be a catalogue model (and she was right: my boobs *are* quite perky again) and was fantasizing about getting an enormous pay cheque when she unwittingly dealt a lethal blow to my already nil self-confidence.

'Of course, I can't afford to pay you but I'll give you some samples. Oh, and by the way, we'll shoot you from the side so don't worry about your face, OK?'

Discovered letter from the library under the doormat. Suspect it may have been there for quite some time (at least a month, according to the postmark). It says if I don't return the *Postman Pat* book which Jack borrowed three months ago, they're going to take legal action. Spent an hour searching for the book everywhere I could think of – even in the hot press where Jack likes to hide assorted stuff – to no avail. Have reconciled myself to spending time behind bars. On the up-side, I may be entitled to free legal aid.

Called random legal firm from the *Yellow Pages* to see if I have to declare bankruptcy before I can get free representation. Horrible, condescending man told me to stop time-wasting – they were only interested in genuine cases that would make them serious amounts of money.

'So what you're saying is that I have to be the victim of some serious and dreadful crime before you're willing to represent me?' I said.

'That's exactly what I'm saying,' the lawyer replied. 'That or a crippling accident. Call me back if you fall off a ladder at work.'

Have decided to try to engineer some sort of serious workplace mishap – something that would make me temporarily immobile would be perfect.

Am looking on the bright side: at least things can't get any worse.

26 April

Sunday papers full of sleazy allegations about Angelica's personal trainer. Pages 22–6 of the *Gazette* were entirely devoted to his voracious sexual appetite and habit of dressing up like Zorro in the bedroom. There were dozens of quotes from ex-girlfriends, all of whom claim he is a passionate tiger in bed.

One, who looked like her massive breasts were trying to escape from her satin top, said, 'It's no wonder Angelica fell for him. His mask and boots were *soooo* sexy, and when he speaks with a lisp it drives me crazy.' Then she went on to explain that she had met him at the local gym where he used to work and that pelvic-floor exercises had been his speciality.

Tried calling Angelica again to discuss the implications of these allegations but still no reply. I am trying hard to believe that this is all a misunderstanding, but the evidence is starting to stack up. A man who can work wonders with a sagging pelvic floor could be hard to resist.

27 April

My world is falling apart. Lone Father is going to be a guest on *Chat with Dee and Fran*, which means he will get lots of publicity and his book may actually sell a few copies. Or, worse, become an instant bestseller.

'Look at this hunk of spunk!' Elaine squealed excitedly this morning, waving his promotional photo over the partition. 'I wouldn't throw him out of bed for eating crisps – do you know what I mean?'

I felt all the colour drain from my face as she explained that he'd be coming in on Friday to discuss steamy details from his début novel and explain why he cannot under any circumstances reveal the identity of his secret married lover.

'Are you OK?' she asked, when she'd finished. 'You look a bit funny.'

'I'm fine,' I said. 'I just haven't had any chocolate yet today and I need my fix.'

'Well, get me a Mars Bar when you go,' she ordered, immediately losing interest in me and swooning over Lone Father again. 'I need to keep my energy up if I'm going to seduce this hottie!'

Spent all day figuring out how to stop Lone Father appearing on afternoon TV and revealing the sordid details of his secret love trysts with me. Wonder if I could hire a hitman to inflict bodily harm on him – nothing too serious, just a few broken limbs to make sure he misses his slot.

Asked Danni if she knew anyone who could help and now she isn't speaking to me. 'I don't believe you ask thees of me, Susie,' she snapped, when I suggested that maybe one of her Sicilian mob connections could do me a favour at short notice. 'I come to Ireland to escape my family's heritage. You have wounded my sensibilities.'

Joe wants to know why Danni is slamming things about so violently. Told him her period is due to keep him off the scent.

PS Am taking comfort in the fact that Lone Father has vowed never to reveal his married lover's name. Maybe I *will* be able to remain anonymous. Also, at the rate my abnormal weight gain is going, I'll soon be unrecognizable anyway, even to close friends and family.

Office is abuzz with excitement because Lone Father is due in tomorrow to tape his segment for the show. Elaine persuaded everyone to throw their names into a hat for the chance to sneak on set and watch. 'Only one person can go,' she barked, 'and it'd better be me!' Then she laughed, throwing her head back and showing off her unnaturally large Adam's apple.

'Have you got your name in, Susie?' someone said, as I hid behind my partition and buried my head in a mound of complaint letters.

'No, thanks,' I answered, trying not to throw up. 'He's really not my cup of tea.'

'Not your cup of tea?' Elaine screeched. 'I think that should be the other way round, don't you? Let's face it, Susie, he's way out of your league. I'll put your name in for you – even if you have no chance.'

She scribbled my name on a scrap of paper and threw it in and I watched, horrified, as it was drawn from the hat and people crowded round me to congratulate me on my good fortune. I had won the chance to watch Lone Father reveal all on air.

Katie gave me a special kiss when I came home. 'I love you more than Danni, Mummy,' she whispered in my ear, when she met me at the door.

'Thank you, darling,' I said, trying to hold back tears of gratitude. I was filled with wonder at the special unbreakable bond between mother and daughter. It was as if she knew I needed encouragement to keep going and had reached deep inside to try to comfort me.

'Yeah, her bum's much bigger than yours,' she said, 'and yours is GINORMOUS.'

Then she planted another kiss on my cheek and scampered off.

PS News everywhere that Angelica has gone into hiding – possibly in rural Wales. The reports say that there have been unconfirmed sightings of her wearing a zip-up fleece and drinking tea from a chipped builder's mug in a village café so it can't possibly be true. Not unless she's had some sort of breakdown. I know for a fact she wouldn't touch a fleece with a bargepole and only ever drinks skinny decaffs.

29 April

Spent the morning considering faking my own death to avoid seeing Lone Father. Then I tried to persuade Elaine to go in my place. 'I'm not feeling too good, Elaine,' I said. 'You'd like to go, wouldn't you?'

She assessed me through slitted eyes. 'Why would you want me to go?' she asked, instantly suspicious.

'You think he's hot,' I said, 'and I'm snowed under.'

'You've never done me a favour before,' she railed. 'Why start now?'

'It's not a favour, really,' I back-pedalled. 'I just don't want to go.'

'Well, you'll have to,' she snapped. 'I've already committed to another morning meeting. We're not all consumed with lusting after celebs, you know – some of us actually do some work around here.'

Crept down to watch the taping so as not to arouse her suspicions even more and stood hiding in the set wings, trying not to draw attention to myself. Then I saw him. He strolled in, deep in conversation with his agent. His lover/muse Marita was trailing behind them, carrying a tote bag and looking tired. They were closely followed by Dee and Fran and their entourage.

I stood shaking against the wall, my heart pounding in my chest as I watched him chat suavely with everyone, running his hands through his hair when he made a point, just as he used to do at the mother-and-toddler group. Then he excused himself, saying he had to go to the gents', and strode purposefully in my direction, a frown of concentration etched on his forehead. In a panic, I fell to my knee and pretended to fiddle with my laces so he wouldn't spot me, but it was too late.

'Susie,' he said, stopping in front of me as I studied the floor and pretended it was the most interesting thing I had ever seen, 'what are you doing here?'

'Nothing.' I cursed his unnatural ability to make me quake at the knees. 'I'm not stalking you or anything. I work here now.'

'Really? That's interesting.' His eyes roved across my face and down to my chest area, which was heaving inexplicably. 'Have you read the book?'

'No, and I don't intend to.' I was furious his presence made me feel so out of control.

'Why? You know it's about you.' He whispered the last bit, leaning forward to brush the hair from my eyes. 'I've missed you, Susie,' he said softly, his breath hot on my cheek.

'Well, I haven't missed you.' I hoped my heart wasn't going to explode. 'You're a sleaze and if you tell anyone it's me you've been writing about I'll sue you for every penny you have.'

'Feisty, feisty,' he purred. 'I always did love that about you.' Then he pushed open the door to the gents' and disappeared inside.

Turned on my heel, enraged, and bumped straight into Elaine, who was standing directly behind me.

'Well, well, well.' She smirked. 'I knew something was up, but even I couldn't have imagined this little scenario.'

30 April

My life as I know it is over. Spent yesterday afternoon begging Elaine not to tell anyone that I am the mystery lover in Lone Father's new book.

'Why should I keep that little nugget of information to myself?' She was examining her chipped nail polish under the fluorescent lights. 'A lot of people would love to know all about it.'

'He's lying,' I said, and quickly changed tack. 'All the sex bits are made up. We never had sex. We were just friends. I'm a pawn in his sick little publicity game.'

'Now, Susie,' she tutted, shaking her head, 'you're forgetting that I was witness to the chemistry between you. The air was thick with sexual tension. Sparks were flying. Don't try telling me that nothing ever happened . . . But I may be willing to forget about it.'

I breathed a sigh of relief.

'Tell you what, you scratch my back and I'll scratch yours. Deal?' She winked in a very unattractive way and wobbled off in her cheap stilettos.

PS Feel as if I have just sold my soul to the devil. And it's not Prada she's wearing.

The Lone Father interview was aired today. Had to watch it on the office TV surrounded by everyone else, all jostling to get a good view of his piercing blue eyes and dark curly hair.

'So, how did the relationship between this housewife and you develop?' Dee asked, leaning forward so the camera could get a good shot of her surgically enhanced breasts.

'The chemistry between us was electric,' Lone Father said, gazing at her with hooded eyes. 'We couldn't help ourselves.'

'Oh, God, he's a fine thing,' I heard someone say beside me.

'So, it got physical quickly, then?' Dee said.

'Oh, yes. It was a very sexual relationship,' he said, looking directly into the camera. 'We couldn't keep our hands off each other.'

I felt a blush creep up my neck.

'And would you say this type of behaviour is typical of mothers who go to mother-and-toddler groups?' Dee enquired.

'I would say many mothers are frustrated and lonely, yes. That was certainly my experience.' He leaned closer to her and stretched his arm across the back of the studio sofa.

'Will you ever reveal her identity?' Fran was practically drooling over him.

'Never, Fran.' He smiled seductively. 'I'm a man of honour. And she is still married, of course. Although I can't believe they're happy. Not after what we shared.'

Then the camera panned to lover/muse Marita, who was looking murderous in the front row.

2 May

Am at my wit's end. Today, following the TV interview, the *Gazette* published a huge article about Lone Father and his mysterious lover on the front of their entertainment section. The headline read, 'Adultery In The Twenty-first Century – Sex Antics Rock Mum-and-Toddler Group'. There was a very large picture of Lone Father looking smug and gripping a copy of his book. I almost fainted with fright when I saw it. Spent rest of the day cursing immoral hacks and their habit of sexing up stories to sell more newspapers. Composed stiff letter of complaint to the editor, then realized that this tactic might draw even more attention to me so scrapped it. Fortunately Joe is now baking round the clock so he didn't notice my state of despair.

PS Just woke up from horrible nightmare. Was back at mother-and-toddler group, playing Ring a Rosie with Lone Father, when dozens of paparazzi burst through the door and took candid snaps of us. Woke in a sweat – Joe reciting the best method for making the perfect meringue beside me.

3 May

Mrs H called round. 'Have you seen where that poor Angelica Law has ended up?' she asked, plonking the Sunday supplement under my nose. 'It's tragic.' She pointed to a grainy photograph of a woman in dark sunglasses and hat coming out of a rundown B-and-B on the front page. It was hard to tell if it really was Angelica or not, although it did look exactly like her pert bum in real Rock and Republic jeans. 'Imagine the poor girl is reduced to staying in a B-and-B.' Mrs H tutted, shaking her head. 'Her life is destroyed.'

'Well, it's not exactly destroyed,' I said, feeling sick. Things were going from bad to worse. There was no way Angelica would cross the threshold of a grotty guest-house unless she was really desperate.

'Oh, yes it is,' Mrs H replied knowingly. 'That trainer fella has sold his story – he has pictures of them at it and everything apparently, the dirty gurrier. Mind you, I wouldn't throw him out of bed for eating crisps – I can see why she was tempted.' Then she winked lasciviously at me while I gripped the paper and tried not to cry.

4 May

Elaine is blackmailing me. This morning she asked if I'd get her a coffee. Might have been imagining it, but thought 'or else' hung in the air.

This afternoon she wanted some croissants. Traipsed all the way to the canteen and back again but when I gave them to her she said she'd meant the chocolate ones, not plain. Then she arched an eyebrow at me. Found myself traipsing all the way back. Despise myself but have to keep her on my side at all costs.

PS Joe left a message on my mobile phone to say he wants to talk to me. Felt fear grip my heart when I heard his serious voice – the one he hasn't used since he found himself and started this cookery lark.

Joe has found the household bills hidden behind the bread bin. 'What are these, Susie?' he asked, waving them (neatly bound together now with an elastic band) at me before I'd even had a chance to get my coat off.

'Thank-you letters?' I answered, playing for time and wondering why on earth he'd been rummaging there.

'Susie, it's not funny!' he shouted. 'By the look of all these overdue notices, we're in serious trouble. The electricity board is about to cut us off. I knew I should never have trusted you with this stuff.'

'I was getting round to it,' I stammered, unable to meet his eye. 'Administration's never been my strong point, you know that.'

'Then why did you volunteer to deal with it?' Joe said, his voice now icy and strange.

'Because you said I wouldn't be able to manage it,' I spat back, thinking on my feet. (Obviously couldn't say I'd only promised to do it so I could hide the evidence of our financial difficulties from him.) 'Turns out you were right. What do you want? A medal?'

Then Joe said the worst thing possible. 'I'm very disappointed in you, Susie. You've landed us in the most awful mess and now I'll have to sort it out when I'm supposed to be studying how a four-oven Aga works.' He turned on his heel and left, still clutching the bills.

Am living in dread. Cannot imagine how disappointed he'll be when he discovers I also lied about my salary and that I earn approximately one zillionth of what I told him I did.

PS Joe wants to see our joint account statements. Told

him I'd call the bank and get them posted to us. Am considering leaving the country.

6 May

Joe has uncovered my trail of deceit and lies in a surprisingly short time. He didn't wait to see the bank statements. Instead he went on-line to uncover the truth about our debt.

'That was a complete invasion of my privacy!' I yelled, when I discovered he had gone through the account electronically. 'And it was probably illegal. I could report you for identity fraud.'

'Illegal? What the hell are you on about?' he said. 'It's a joint account, Susie, either of us can check it at any time. Looks like I should have been checking it a lot sooner. You've lied to me for weeks. You don't earn a quarter of what you said you did – I'll have to give up my dream and go back to my old job.'

And then he put his head in his hands and sobbed, with real live man-tears. Am racked with guilt, although I do feel that Joe is playing down his role in the tragedy just a bit. He should have put away at least two years' salary before he chucked in his job for a pipe-dream that has no hope of ever becoming reality. That's what all the financial gurus advise.

7 May

Elaine is being suspiciously nice to me. She offered to help answer the mail today. She actually stopped filing her nails to suggest it. Am so riddled with anxiety I accepted.

PS Joe found another of my pay slips this evening. He immediately went to lie down in the spare room.

PPS Mrs H dropped by. She definitely senses something's wrong but is too involved with organizing the Gay Pride bingo night to do anything about it.

8 May

Am toying with being officially sick for at least two weeks, maybe more. Cannot possibly deal with other people when I'm under so much pressure. Am sure the doctor will sign me off when I explain I had palpitations this morning so am probably on the verge of a massive coronary any second – *and* I'm nauseous nearly all the time. Also feel I need to spend some quality time with Katie and Jack. They have mounted a campaign to attend a ridiculously overpriced art summer camp, which tells me they definitely suspect something is awry.

Katie almost knocked me to the ground when I came home from work, brandishing the camp brochure hopefully. I am racked with guilt that she will probably be denied the joy of hours spent messing about with finger paints for twenty-five euro a morning because I've screwed up so badly.

Tried to explain to Danni why there is such tension in the house (and why Joe is stamping about looking mournful). 'We're having some small financial troubles, Danni,' I said, 'but don't worry, you will be paid as usual.' (Wasn't sure this was true, but had to throw it in in case she was tempted to pack her bags.)

'Financial troubles?' she echoed, looking confused. 'But you very rich now, Susie. You have big job – Joe told me so.'

'Well, not exactly,' I murmured. 'There may have been a little misunderstanding ... You see, I'm not earning that much as it turns out.'

'You mean you lie about your pay, Susie?' she said.

'Not *lie* exactly.' I was a bit annoyed that she would challenge me, what with her being staff and all.

She gave me a searing look that cleaved my soul in half (although that may have been indigestion from the six-pack of smoky bacon crisps I had inexplicably felt compelled to devour earlier). 'I must feed the *bambini*,' she said, and then turned on her heel and left.

I was eating my third bag of Maltesers, watching *Dragon's Den* and wondering how I was going to get out of this sorry mess, when the doorbell rang.

Angelica stood on the step, wearing massive designer sunglasses and carrying a large holdall. 'Quick, Susie, let me in,' she hissed. 'I think I'm being followed.'

9 May

Angelica has begged me to let her stay with us until the press stop hounding her. She has also confessed that

(a) she had drunken sex with top-producer Mike in a broom cupboard at a TV awards party and that was why he gave me the job; and

(b) she *has* been using our country house to conduct a passionate affair with her personal trainer.

'Please, Susie,' she cried, 'I need somewhere safe to stay. James is furious with me – we had another terrible argument this morning and he won't let me in the house. You've always been a friend to me, won't you help me now? I'll kill myself if I have to go back to Wales.'

'I don't know,' I said, wondering if she was a fully fledged sex addict and needed to get to the Priory ASAP. 'You weren't very truthful with me in the past.' Then I spotted her holdall and wondered if there was anything in it that she might want to pass on to me if she stayed – like a Juicy Couture tracksuit or anything from last season's Gucci collection.

'I'm sorry, honestly I am, Susie,' she said. 'I didn't *mean* to have sex with Mike – it was a one-off. It only happened because James was flirting with everyone at the awards show and I drank too much wine.'

'And what about the personal trainer?' I asked.

'Well, he's different,' she admitted. 'He has an *eight*-pack.'

I gasped. I'd thought eight-packs were an urban myth.

'Please help me,' she wept, 'everyone makes mistakes, don't they?'

I found myself thinking of how I'd lied to Joe about the TV7 job.

'I just felt so trapped. Everyone thinks I'm perfect – the perfect wife, the perfect mother ... The pressure was too much. It was starting to crack me up. Besides, James has a few secrets of his own. He's always sleeping with extras *and* he's not averse to dressing in women's clothes. I turn a blind eye to it all. Why shouldn't I have a little fun?'

'That's as may be,' I said, a sudden image of James Law in size-thirteen stilettos flashing into my mind's eye. 'But you shouldn't have used my country house to have your fun in. And you roped me in to take Brandon when you were having your flings. That was really low.'

'I'm sorry.' She had the good grace to look ashamed. 'I'll

make it up to you, I promise. But I *did* help you get that job – even though you had no experience.' She eyeballed me and I decided to forgive her – at least this drama was taking my mind off my own worries. Even better, her presence would distract Joe and maybe make him put down his calculator. Suddenly I was confiding in Angelica that I was in a bit of a pickle myself, what with Lone Father, Joe and the financial mess.

'That's terrible, Susie.' She patted my hand. 'We'll find a way out of it. There must be something I can do.'

'Not really,' I said, wondering if she would just whip out her cheque book and put everything right. 'My career's in tatters, my marriage is on the rocks and my finances are in shreds.'

Felt despondent when I said it aloud like that. Celebs have ended up in rehab for less.

Told Joe that Angelica had to stay for a day or two – just until the furore blew over.

He was very understanding about it. 'That's OK,' he said. 'Those paps are scum of the earth – they only ever print rubbish anyway.'

Didn't tell him that the press had got it right for once. Felt he wouldn't take too kindly to this information.

10 May

Angelica shook me awake at the crack of dawn. 'Get up, Susie,' she whispered in my ear. 'I've come up with a brilliant plan to solve all your problems – come on, I need to talk to you.'

I doubted she could do anything concrete to help, but I dragged myself downstairs anyway.

'You know I've been having trouble with rumours of my infidelity?' she asked.

I nodded. They weren't exactly untrue rumours, but that was a technicality.

'Well, I think you should do a top-secret interview with the *Gazette* to tell my side of the story. "Close friend tells all" – that sort of thing. They'll pay loads so that should sort your finances out. Then I'll go on prime-time TV to follow up. It's brilliant!'

'But I thought you didn't want any more publicity?' I asked, confused. 'I thought you wanted to lie low until the whole thing blew over?'

'Yeah, but that was before my LA agent called me this morning. Going into hiding has been fantastic for my profile – his phone is ringing off the hook with offers. I could be more famous than James soon.' Her eyes shone.

'So having affairs has actually been good for your image?'

'Exactly!' She looked triumphant. 'People are starting to think I'm a bit of a sexpot instead of a do-gooder. Isn't it brilliant? Publicity's all mind games – there are probably paps out in the bushes as we speak. My PR firm tipped them off this morning.'

I dived behind a curtain in case any lurking paparazzo got an unflattering shot of me with greasy hair in my unwashed PJs.

Angelica spent the afternoon on a call to her hotshot LA agent, trying to organize it. She asked to use our phone and I didn't like to say anything, what with her mobile probably being tapped and all. Really hope this works – Joe will have a heart-attack when he sees the phone bill.

PS Spent ages practising my Donald Duck voice – vital I disguise my identity for the top-secret interview. All I have to do is speak to a hard-nosed journalist, tell the truth and be paid for spilling the beans. Then maybe this whole sorry mess will be sorted out.

11 May

Angelica says that under no circumstances am I to tell the truth about her alleged affairs.

'But I thought that was the whole point,' I said, wondering if I was going slowly mad.

'The whole point, Susie,' she explained, her voice high and tight, 'is for me to get maximum publicity out of the allegations. You are not to confirm or deny *anything* – OK? We have to spin it out a bit longer.'

'So what should I actually say, then?' I stuttered, feeling panicky.

She paused for a beat. 'Say that I'm in anguish about the allegations. That I've lost lots of weight and am finding it impossible to eat, that sort of thing.'

I watched as she took a bite out of another of Jack's Pop Tarts and licked her lips. 'Why would I say that?' I asked.

'Because then they may do a diet tie-in in a women's magazine. I might even get a fitness video out of it.' She was clearly delighted with herself.

PS Interview set for tomorrow. Top LA agent negotiating fee. Have not disclosed anything to Joe in case it's not big enough to cover our current difficulties. Do not want to raise his hopes.

Have completed newspaper interview. Had to do it at my desk at work so I felt a little self-conscious but think I did OK, even when the journalist kept pressing me for details of Angelica's sexual antics and saying things like, 'Were they at it day and night, then?'

Thankfully, I remembered to keep repeating the mantra that Angelica had practically beaten into me. (I had scribbled it down on the back of a Tesco receipt so I wouldn't forget and cave in under serious journalistic interrogation.)

'Angelica is devastated by the allegations – she hasn't eaten in days. We're really worried about her. She's lost so much weight she may have to be put on a drip soon.'

Angelica is thrilled. Her LA agent has promised that great things will come of the scandalous publicity – and I get half of the cheque. Hinted to Joe that I'll be treating him to a massive wedding anniversary gift very soon. 'I'd love a set of handmade carving knives,' he said dreamily. 'They're meant to be exquisite.'

PS Elaine was being extra nice to me this afternoon – am sure she's up to something but am trying to put it from my mind.

13 May

Worst day of my life ever. The *Gazette* article ran today, but not with the poor-starving-celeb tone Angelica had been angling for. The front-page headline blared, 'Author's Secret Mistress Speaks Out About Famous Friend's Affair'.

Today, the *Gazette* can exclusively reveal the identity of a best-selling author's secret lover – Susie Hunt, a thirty-something housewife from the suburbs. Inside, Susie, best friend of Angelica Law, tells all about her alternative deviant sex life and that of her adulterous gal-pal Angelica.

There were loads of made-up quotes, alongside a picture of me coming out of work, looking at least fifteen years older than I am.

Now I know why Elaine was so nice to me yesterday – she must have eavesdropped on my telephone interview, then tipped off the journalist about my identity. Was forced to confess the whole sorry tale to Joe and explain that I only did the interview to pay off our debts (and maybe snag us a family holiday to Disneyland with any leftovers).

He was furious. 'This is so humiliating, Susie,' he said. 'Everyone will know about our private life now.'

'But half of it's made up!' I pleaded. 'You know that. You said yourself hacks have no morals – they'll write anything for a good story, even if they have to fabricate the details.'

Not sure he was convinced. He retreated to the kitchen and spent the afternoon whipping up the most difficult recipes in Jamie's cookbook so I knew he was really upset.

Meanwhile, Angelica was appalled that she wasn't the main focus of the article and took to her room to apply multiple face masks and call her LA agent for advice.

Then Mrs H burst through the door, wearing her Gay Pride T-shirt and looking fierce. 'Susie, are you gay?' she asked, taking me by the shoulders.

'Of course not,' I said, wondering if stress had brought on some kind of hallucination.

'Are you sure?' She looked a bit disappointed.

'I'm positive,' I said.

'Well, you and that Angelica girl *are* quite friendly and the paper said you were up to all sorts between the pair of you. If you are gay, you can talk to me about it, you know. I'm very accepting of deviancy, these days.'

She sat beside me and took my hand. Suddenly I felt a bit sniffly. 'I'm not gay,' I said, as tears pricked my eyelids. 'I love Joe, but I've really messed things up and I think he's lost patience with me.'

Mrs H nodded sympathetically and stroked my arm. 'All is not lost, Susie dear,' she murmured. 'Everyone knows those good-for-nothing rags print nothing but rubbish. We'll sort it out.'

Am taking comfort from this – she did look very determined.

PS Received text from Lone Father: 'Thanks for the publicity, Susie! Let's meet some time. XX'.

14 May

Angelica has come round and is now insisting that every-thing will be all right, but I'm having my doubts. I think she has only cheered up because there are paps camped on the doorstep outside, demanding to speak to her.

I eventually got so angry with the endless ringing of the doorbell that I wrenched the door open to demand they leave.

There, standing on the step, was Magnum, the teenage PI I'd hired to track down Louise's ex. 'Hi, Susie.' He grinned. 'Give us a quote, will ya?'

'What the hell are you doing here?' I sighed. 'You're not a journalist.'

'I am now,' he said. 'Being a pap is much better paid than

being a private investigator – and I have a special skill that makes me stand out from the crowd. My long-lens work is second to none.' He puffed out his chest and looked dead proud of himself.

'But I'm a nobody,' I said. 'Why are you so interested in me?'

'Nobodies are really hot right now.' He adjusted his camera. 'Blame the reality-TV wannabes – it's nothing to do with me.'

'But those people are on TV,' I argued. 'At least they have some sort of profile. Some even have their own perfumes, for God's sake.'

'So could you, if you played your cards right.' He winked. 'Why don't you let me get a shot of you with your dressing-gown a bit undone? Then my editor would get off my back and I could go home.'

He looked so drained I almost felt sorry for him, but my inner sense kicked in before I was tempted to get out a droopy boob for public display. 'I don't think so.' I was annoyed I'd almost let myself fraternize with the enemy. 'I wouldn't stoop that low.'

'Well, I guess I'll have to hang around for a bit longer, then,' he said, sounding bored. 'But I have to warn you, your Venetian blinds are practically useless. An amateur could get a good shot through those.'

Am now practically a prisoner in my own home and unable even to pop down to the local shops without causing a near riot with the paparazzi. (The up-side is I cannot possibly go back to work until the fuss dies down and at least I'll be able to watch the complete DVD set of *Friends* that Joe bought me for Christmas so all is not lost. Also, living in semi-darkness with the blinds closed isn't that bad – it hides the dust quite effectively.)

Angelica's LA agent has advised that we should leave the house soon, holding our heads high, so the press can get some good shots of us and the story will stay on the front pages.

'We need to act dignified,' Angelica said, slapping on a face mask, 'like we have nothing to hide.'

I was tempted to tell her that I have quite a lot to hide, actually, and that I really would appreciate it if she just upped sticks and left before my sordid past really caught up with me, but I didn't like to say anything in case she was offended.

Meanwhile, Katie seems to be enjoying the paparazzi attention. She changed her outfit five times this morning and has been practising holding a newspaper across her face.

'Why are you doing that, darling?' I asked.

'I want to hide from the paps, Mummy,' she answered, as if I was a complete moron. 'That will really hook their interest.'

'Why do you think that?' I asked, bemused.

'Angelica told me,' she said. 'She said I have to treat 'em mean to keep 'em keen.'

Tackled Angelica in the kitchen about turning Katie into a media wannabe at the age of five.

'The sooner she knows some of the tricks of the trade, the sooner she'll make it in Hollywood,' she explained patiently. 'I wish I'd known all this when I started. Then I could have been a proper celebrity, not just married to one.'

At least Joe's mood is improving – he has even started passing out some cookery samples to the paparazzi. 'I may as well do a bit of research while I've got the chance,' he said, whipping up another batch of vol-au-vents, and wiping beads of perspiration from his brow. 'Hungry paps are vicious critics so at least I'll know if I'm on the right track.' I didn't dishearten him by saying that vicious paps will eat anything as long as it's free. Although have already spotted quite a few feeding their chicken-curry sandwiches to the dog.

PS Mrs H has decided to camp on the doorstep, holding a flag that reads, 'Gays are people too.'

'What are you doing, Mum?' Joe thundered, when he spotted her handing flyers to the fed-up journos at the front gate.

'This is an excellent opportunity to get some positive coverage for homosexual rights,' Mrs H huffed, smoothing her pink T-shirt over her bosom. 'I've persuaded some of the Gay Alliance parents to come over later – we're going to launch a new initiative. We're bound to get on the front page.'

Joe was furious, but I was quite pleased. The more issues the press have thrown at them, the less chance there is of even more scandalous details about me leaking out.

16 May

Things have gone rapidly downhill. Lone Father arrived this morning, battled his way to the front door and banged on it, shouting that I should come out and needn't be scared. I could hear him bellowing through the letterbox that he had the situation under control so I peeped through the Venetian blinds to see him waving his book while Marita stood, looking smug, on the path beside their car.

'What's going on out there now?' Joe asked, popping a tray of cookies into the oven.

'Nothing,' I said, shutting the blinds again. 'It's just another nutter trying to climb on the publicity bandwagon.'

'I hope that's not a dig at me, Susie.' He sounded wounded. 'We have to make the most of the opportunities we have if we're ever to get our heads above water again. And the journalists seemed to like my last batch – maybe they'll give me a good write-up, you never know.'

Then he peeped out of the window, saw Lone Father on the step and, before I knew it, had charged through the front door and assaulted him with his cookie-cutter, hitting him over the head with it and roaring at him to get lost or he'd mangle him in his mincer.

'I'll see you in court!' Lone Father shouted, clasping his cut cheek as he backed up the garden path. 'You've ruined my face. If I lose my sponsorship deal with Makeup 4 Men you're to blame.'

He jumped into his car, Marita at the wheel, and sped off.

'Now *this* is more like it!' I could hear Magnum saying, as I struggled to get Joe back inside. Can't be sure, but I don't think he was referring to Joe's new chocolate and raspberry cookie mix.

When the kids had gone to bed, and Angelica was on the phone to her LA agent again, I had a heart-to-heart with Joe. 'Honestly,' I said, 'I know he claims the book is based on real life – but he made it all up.'

'I know that,' he smiled, 'but it felt good to rough him up a bit. What a pansy.' Then he pulled his apron on carefully over his head. 'Scram,' he said. 'A man has work to do, you know.'

Don't think I have ever loved him more.

PS Mum emailed to ask why half of her old neighbours were leaving messages about me.

Breda Lyons seems to think you are being
door-stepped, darling. I told her she must be
mistaken. Really, as if the press would ever be
interested in you – no offence. But isn't it funny?

PS Dad has taken up windsurfing. He's become
quite good. Even the instructor said he may have
natural ability!

17 May

Just as I thought things were improving, the front of today's
Gazette read: 'Lusty Sex Triangle – Angelica, Me and My
Secret Housewife Lover!' And there was a picture of Lone
Father, smouldering out of the front page, manly and
seductive in a pale blue lamb's-wool polo-neck. Then there
was a completely fabricated story that the three of us had
enjoyed romps together.

'That low-down creep!' Angelica screamed when she read
it. 'How dare he drag me into your sordid little affair? Sorry,
Susie,' she mumbled, when she saw my face drop, 'but he
really is downright sleazy.' She proceeded to use our phone
yet again to call her LA agent and discuss it with him.

Decided to smuggle the children to the park for some
fresh air and leave her to it. Encouraged Jack to bring his
favourite Power Ranger with him to assault the photographers – one swipe with a vicious red Ranger can cause
permanent damage.

'How are plans for the perfume going, Susie?' Magnum
asked nonchalantly, as he rattled off some shots of us battling
down the path to the gate.

'Just fine, thank you,' I answered, with as much dignity as

I could muster, then bundled the kids into the car and took off at high speed to the park.

PS Am considering building a tunnel under the house – am sure it wouldn't take long.

PPS Got home to find Angelica still on the phone to her LA agent. Am really dreading the next phone bill – wonder if I could get some tax back on all these expenses. Must investigate.

18 May

Was woken this morning by thumping on the front door. Decided to ignore it, hoping that Joe would abandon his dawn baking and get it, but was eventually forced downstairs when the vibrations of the thudding got so violent my teeth started to chatter. I wrenched the door open in a daze to find three vicious-looking men standing on the doorstep. I knew instantly who they were – the tailored Italian suits and gold jewellery gave it away. Danni's family had tracked her down and were here to wipe me out. For a split second, I was quite relieved: at least there would be no more newspaper stories about my alleged sexual antics if I was mown down in cold blood.

'Is Daniela here?' the fattest one asked, in a thick Italian accent – quite politely, it has to be said.

'Er, no,' I answered. 'She doesn't start work until eight.'

'OK, we wait,' he said, as the other two looked about shiftily and rubbed their meaty hands. 'We have time.'

I wasn't sure if I should invite them in for a cup of tea, or maybe some strong alcohol, so I stood there gaping at them until Joe stuck his head out of the kitchen and Angelica appeared on the landing to see what was going on.

'Whata sorta place you got here, lady?' the fattest one asked, looking fierce.

'Em, this is my husband, and this is my friend and, um, it's not like that,' I stammered, stuck for words to explain how not only did it seem like I was harbouring Danni but it looked like I was having three-in-the-bed romps with all and sundry too. Just then Danni arrived, her face like thunder. 'Papa,' she shouted, 'I told you not to do this. Please go away.'

'Daniela,' the fattest one said, 'I'm here to take you home.'

'I'm not going,' Danni sulked. 'You can't make me.'

They started yelling wildly at each other in Italian, waving their hands about. Then Magnum appeared and took endless snaps of them and Angelica threw herself into the fray to break it up. 'I'm fluent in Italian,' she called, 'and I've got excellent negotiating skills. Please let me help.'

Later I asked her why she'd wanted to get involved in such a bitter domestic dispute. 'My agent thinks I could be a female Jerry Springer,' she said. 'This was the perfect opportunity for the press to capture that side of me.'

I didn't like to say that frolicking in a see-through nightie on the front step may have given the wrong impression – am not altogether sure that she didn't let the shoulder strap slip to give a flash of her boobs on purpose.

Later

Danni's father and his two henchmen are parked in the kitchen and refuse to move, Danni is locked in the spare bedroom and won't come out, Joe is making finger food to keep up morale, Angelica is on the phone to her LA agent *again* and the kids are taking photos of the paps from the living-room window.

'This is fantastic!' Joe said, as Danni's father and his henchmen gave instructions on how to make the perfect cannelloni. 'This kind of one-on-one coaching is priceless. It's really helping me hone my skills.'

'Yes, but what will we do about Danni?' I hoped her father couldn't understand me. 'They're not going to leave until she agrees to go with them.'

'Could we persuade her to stay upstairs a bit longer, do you think?' Joe whispered excitedly. 'You never know, her father might tell me the old Italian secret for making the perfect Bolognese sauce next.'

19 May

Mrs H has persuaded Danni's father that Danni must be allowed to make her own choices in life, even if that means she refuses to marry the heir to an Italian mob family. 'You can't force your children to do what you want them to, Don,' she said, offering him a fig roll as she made a pot of tea. 'Look at me and our David. I wanted him to be a common slut like everyone else – and what did he do? He turned homosexual, that's what.'

'*Mamma mia.*' Don crossed himself.

'Yes, that's right,' Mrs H went on. 'I got a terrible shock, terrible, but then, I picked myself up, dusted myself down and decided to get on with it. Your children are still your children, even if they destroy your life.' She took a sip of tea and looked sad.

'You are a strong woman,' Don said. 'A very strong woman. Maybe you are right. Maybe it is time for me to let Daniela live her own life.'

'That's the spirit!' Mrs H said. 'Get involved in other

things and stop focusing on her so much. Bingo's very good here on a Tuesday if you're going to stay around for a while.'

Am not sure but could have sworn she batted her eyelashes at him.

PS Angelica and her LA agent have decided that the time has come for her to do an in-depth interview on prime-time TV. It has been set up for *Chat with Dee and Fran* tomorrow. 'It'll be brilliant for my profile,' she purred, as she painted her toenails neon pink in preparation for her appearance in front of thousands, all of whom would be gagging to know the juicy details of her alleged affairs.

Am very relieved. I never realized how draining high-octane drama can be. I have no idea how poor Kate Moss keeps it up *and* manages to look good. Maybe that twenty-four-hour makeup really can work wonders. Must purchase ASAP.

20 May

Angelica has informed me that, as well as talking about our close friendship live on air, she will be discussing, in depth, my secret affair with Lone Father during her *Chat with Dee and Fran* interview. 'I plan on calling you my rock, that sort of thing,' she said, as I stood with my mouth open, wondering if I could lock her under the stairs to prevent her appearing on the show and dragging my name through the mud. Again.

'But you can't say anything about him,' I cried, distraught. 'You'll only make it worse.'

'Don't worry,' she soothed. 'I'm going to tell everyone that the whole thing was a complete fabrication, a publicity stunt to pump up sales of that sleaze-bag's book. I'll destroy him for you. He won't know what hit him.' She flicked her ponytail and threw me a dazzling smile.

Was very impressed. Never knew she could be so ruthlessly cold and calculating.

21 May

Angelica has exposed Lone Father for the fraud he really is. Even better, she has done it while approximately a hundred thousand people were tuned in. Can now see how talented she is – she is definitely not 'a bimbo with artificial boobs and a trout pout', as the *Gazette* claimed. She really does have a more serious sensitive side and is probably very well suited to hosting a Jerry Springer-type show. She would definitely be able to converse with trailer trash of all ages.

With not a glimmer of irony, she

(a) denied all allegations of infidelity on her part;

(b) told Dee and Fran that I had been her rock and constant source of strength throughout the whole horrible ordeal;

(c) poured scorn on the idea that Lone Father and I were ever anything more than passing friends;

(d) suggested that Lone Father's book may have been ghostwritten and that her legal team was keen to sue over allegations of threesomes in the press.

'Books have been pulled off the shelves for less,' she said ominously, smiling at Fran and crossing her long legs. 'And people need to get their facts straight before they go talking to the papers and spreading malicious rumours.' Then she laughed throatily, flashing a smile directly at Camera One and baring her Rembrandt-white teeth to the audience. 'Luckily,' she went on, 'Susie has a very supportive husband, Joe, so none of this gossip is having any effect on her whatsoever. By the way, his new cookery venture is *soooo* hot. It's going to be huge – you heard it here first!'

She crossed her legs again and winked at Dee, who immediately agreed to post details of Joe's new business on the website for anyone who wanted more information.

22 May

Overnight, my world has changed. Angelica has flown to LA to consider some of the offers flooding in, the *Gazette* is launching a top-level inquiry into the veracity of Lone Father's sordid claims about three-in-the-bed romps, Joe's mobile hasn't stopped ringing with requests for catering, and Magnum and the paps have upped and left.

'We're off to Lone Father's house,' Magnum said, when I popped my head out to see if he'd like a cup of tea. 'We'll give him a hard time for you, don't worry, Susie.'

Was just starting to feel that things were finally improving and starting to go my way when top-producer Mike called. 'Can you come in tomorrow, Susie?' he said, sounding very serious. 'We need to have a chat.'

He obviously wants to fire me for immoral conduct or missing so much work. Am bracing myself for the worst.

Top-producer Mike doesn't want to fire me. Instead he wants to give me a massive promotion and pay rise.

At a top-secret emergency meeting, which Dee and Fran attended, he told me they want me to be a proper housewife correspondent on the show and quadruple my current salary.

'But I thought I wasn't ready for camera work?' I ventured. Why had they suddenly developed an interest in me when for so long they had ignored my very existence?

'Things have changed.' Mike smiled.

'Yeah, she could work,' Dee said to Fran, eyeing me as if I was a piece of meat.

'Hmm, I'm not sure about the dishevelled look, though,' Fran said, talking over my head as if I wasn't in the room.

Felt quite panicky when she said that. It had taken me approximately two hours to get groomed and polished that morning. If she thought this look was dishevelled, what would she think of my usual trackie-and-crusty-T-shirt combo?

'Yes, but that look is very street,' Dee replied. 'It could be exactly what we need.'

Then Mike went on to explain that, even though they were hugely successful, Dee and Fran felt they needed an extra dimension to the show.

'We want to attract all the jelly-bellies stuck at home, eating biscuits,' Dee said. 'That's where you come in. Now that you have a media profile, you might be just the ticket.'

'Well, I could try,' I said, wondering if it was politically incorrect to call housewives jelly-bellies. Decided now was not the time to bring that up.

'Yes, all those saddos are our bread and butter,' Fran said.

'Well, until we get a prime-time slot on Friday nights. Then we can stop pretending we care whether or not they stick their heads in the oven with their home-baked bread.'

They roared with laughter while Mike looked on, twitching nervously. 'I think what the girls mean,' he coughed, 'is that you'll fit right in.'

'So, what do you see me doing?' I asked, irritated that they'd been so derogatory about their core audience.

'Oh, you know, housewifey stuff,' Fran said airily. 'It'll be great.'

'Yes, just be your dowdy self.' Dee patted my arm. 'That'll be perfect.'

Told Joe that I had been offered a proper hosting spot on the show.

'That's great, Susie,' he said, hugging me. 'Isn't that what you wanted?'

'Well, I'm not sure,' I admitted. 'I don't know if I could handle the media intrusion.'

'I see what you mean,' Joe said. 'Why don't you have a think about things for a while? You've been through a lot. Maybe you need time to mull it over.'

I didn't want to admit that mulling it over might not be an option. The large salary is tempting, and we could do with the money if Joe is to pursue his cooking dream. Especially as there's still no sign of the cheque from the tell-all interview. Am very confused. If this is what I've always wanted, why do I feel so empty inside?

24 May

Have made a comprehensive list of pros and cons to try to decide whether I should become a national household name or remain an anonymous civilian.

Pros of being bona fide TV celebrity

- Getting invites to swanky showbiz events
- Being stared at in the street
- Being asked for autographs
- Getting good tables in restaurants
- Getting lots of free stuff

Cons of being bona fide TV celebrity

- Having to look best at all times when in public (and also when at home in case of long-lens photographers)
- Having to learn how to get out of a limo without accidentally flashing women's bits
- Having to resist drink and drugs binges
- Having to see less of Katie and Jack

It's strange – I think I could cope with remembering to wear underwear all the time or saying no to cocaine, but I'm not sure about spending less time with the children. How am I supposed to decide? Louise says I should listen to my inner voice, but I can't hear it saying anything – except maybe, 'Polish off that packet of HobNobs, oats are good for you.' Really wish something would happen that would take the decision out of my hands.

25 May

Very faint and weak today – probably the stress of the last few weeks catching up with me. Called the doctor to schedule appointment and, once I had explained my elaborate range of symptoms to the power-crazy receptionist, I was actually put straight through. The doctor advised me to come in for blood tests immediately. I was distraught – he obviously suspected something was seriously wrong.

'What will you be looking for?' I asked, feeling sicker by the minute.

'Oh, you know, the usual things,' he said, in an overly casual way to hide his concern. 'Cholesterol, kidney and liver function, absorption of B12 minerals, that sort of thing.'

'So you think there may be something seriously wrong with me?' I asked, wondering who I should give my precious collection of *Hello!* magazines to.

'Well, it's hard to say until we take a look,' he said, not ruling out the possibility that I was at death's door. 'Just pop in and let the nurse do the bloods. We'll take it from there.' Drove at speed to the surgery.

Blood sampling was excruciatingly painful, especially as they only had really old copies of *Heat* and *OK!* in the surgery – issues that I had already read a million times.

'Do you think it's anything serious?' I asked the nurse, as she drew off another vial to be sent to the lab.

'Let's just wait and see, shall we?' she said, with an expression that was impossible to read – although I'm sure I saw sympathy flicker across her face. She was obviously thinking, Those poor children, losing such a devoted mother so young – that sort of thing.

Limped home. Have not told Joe yet but we probably

need to appoint another guardian for Katie and Jack in case I *am* at death's door.

26 May

Doctor left a message to come in and see him straight away. Was terrified. Things were obviously even more serious than I'd thought – everyone knows doctors only call back promptly if your time is limited.

Asked Joe if he knew what kind of funeral service I wanted when my time came.

'Um, why are you asking me that?' he said.

'Never mind why,' I said, as my eyes welled. I was really going to miss his insensitivity. 'Just tell me, do you know?'

'Eh . . . a private one?' he suggested.

Which proved he never listens. If he didn't know by now that I want an over-the-top display of his love for me then he never would. Must write down detailed instructions ASAP.

Was also very worried how to tell Danni that soon we would no longer be able to afford her services as I was dying and Joe had no income to speak of. Was really anxious that her Sicilian blood meant she would attack me with a kitchen knife out of rage. (Although that could be a good way to put me out of my misery if I was to endure a long, painful death.)

Sped to surgery and asked the doctor if I was dying. 'Just tell me straight,' I pleaded. 'There are arrangements that need to be made.'

'Well, we're all dying, Mrs Hunt,' he said, which I thought was most unhelpful, 'but you're not on the way out just yet. However, you *are* pregnant. Congratulations.'

Then the room went fuzzy and I blacked out.

I am pregnant with my third child, which probably explains the nausea, forgetfulness and weight gain.

Joe was over the moon when I told him I was having one of those hidden pregnancies – the kind you read about in trashy magazines and never believe are true.

'That's fantastic, Susie!' he whooped, sweeping me into his arms and swinging me round the kitchen – until I told him I'd puke if he didn't put me down. Then he stopped dead in his tracks. 'But how do you feel about it? Are you happy?'

I paused while I tried to work that bit out. I'd just been offered a prime TV slot with excellent prospects and now I was expecting a baby that hadn't been planned – the timing couldn't have been worse. Surely I was meant to be devastated. I searched around deep inside to find out how I felt. Finally I knew.

'I'm not happy, Joe,' I said, and his face fell. 'I'm ecstatic!' And I really was. Yes, I wanted a career, but not this one. Being a prisoner in my own home while the paps had been camped outside had made me realize that celebrity had its disadvantages. Disadvantages that not even glamorous bits like red-carpet appearances or luxury goody-bags could compensate for. Suddenly I knew that I didn't want fame or an at-home spread with *OK!*, I just wanted the work-life balance the lifestyle gurus were always harping on about. I needed a Plan B. Now all I had to do was figure that part out.

28 May

Called top-producer Mike to inform him that the new house-wife correspondent position was not going to fulfil me in any meaningful way, even if it had a dedicated parking space and subsidized lunches in the canteen. Also told him that I wouldn't be back to answer mail either.

'But, Susie,' he begged, 'Dee and Fran have decided they want you on board. How am I going to break it to them that you've turned them down? No one ever does that.'

'Just bite the bullet,' I advised, feeling powerful and free. 'What can they do?'

'Um, fire me?' he said, sounding like he was crying.

'Well, maybe it's time for you to stand up for yourself, then,' I suggested. 'Living a lie isn't really living, is it?' I hung up, feeling really happy for the first time in ages. All I have to do now is come up with a way to combine motherhood with another, more satisfying, career. How hard can that be?

29 May

Joe cornered me at breakfast. 'Susie, you know I've been having some really good feedback ever since Angelica mentioned me on *Chat with Dee and Fran*?' he said, spooning some organic flapjacks on to my plate and smothering them with honey.

'Yesh,' I mumbled, spitting flapjack everywhere.

'Well, I'm getting enquiries about catering and classes from all over the country. I feel the time is right to branch out and go for it. The thing is, I really need new premises as a base. So, I was wondering . . . how would you feel about moving to the country house and setting up there?'

'For the summer?' I said, imagining myself lying about, pregnant and blissful, while Joe fed me grapes. 'That sounds like a great idea.'

'No, Susie, not for the summer.' He was staring at me in a very intense way. 'For good. If we sell the Dublin house we'll have enough to tide us over until I start turning a profit, which will be very soon if all these contacts follow through.'

Was gob-smacked. Moving to the country had never been on my agenda. Although it would mean I'd have a legitimate excuse to get a Range Rover Sport.

Immediately called Louise to tell her that Joe had come up with an outlandish plan to escape the city rat-race. Surprisingly, she was enthusiastic about it. 'That's a fab idea, Susie,' she said. 'Relocating is huge.'

'But don't you think it's a bit unrealistic to leave everything behind and start afresh on a whim, Lou?' I was wondering how I'd manage in the middle of nowhere without Sky Digital for company.

'What's keeping you in the city?' she asked. 'You don't want the TV job and Joe's catering business can be based anywhere. The children are young enough for you to go now. If I could, I'd move in a heartbeat – all the best people are doing it.'

'They are?' I said, feeling the first stirrings of interest. If Louise thought the idea had some merit maybe it wasn't as stupid as it had first sounded. She always knew what was 'in' and out.

'Oh, yes,' she said. 'Of course, I'd have to be able to get my non-fat grande lattes round the clock, but I definitely would otherwise. By the way, if you do take the plunge, do you think we could do the photo shoot for the new catalogue there? It's so hard to find somewhere that conveys the right atmosphere. We'll pay you, of course. Now the maternity range is going to be stocked in Harvey Nicks, I'll be back in the money.'

Have decided that maybe it's not such an outlandish idea, after all – Louise might have a point. Also, moving to the country would mean I could forget about Lone Father and the book that seems to mock me from every bookshop window in the city.

30 May

Have just had a brilliant brainwave. If Louise is willing to pay to get a country setting for a photo shoot for her catalogue, others might too. It might, in fact, be a viable business idea. (And I would be able to hang out with artistic types, such as photographers and stylists, all the time.) In fact, the more I think about it, charging city slickers to be photographed in an overgrown garden for extortionate amounts of money could be the perfect way to combine a career with parenting. *This* was my Plan B. *And* I would have an excuse to buy a ride-on lawnmower. Called Mum and Dad to find out what they thought.

'It's a wonderful idea, darling,' Mum said. 'City life can be so spiritually draining. I'm sure the country would suit you so much better.'

'Yes, and we can have their Dublin house,' Dad chimed in, on the other phone. 'It's ripe for development.'

Not sure what he meant exactly – probably that he would rearrange the sitting room.

The *Gazette* has printed a full retraction of its allegations that Angelica, Lone Father and I enjoyed three-in-the-bed romps on a regular basis.

'What did you do?' I asked Mrs H, when she admitted she had been responsible for this latest turn of events.

'Well, dear,' she replied as she patted some pressed powder on her nose, then straightened her Gay Pride T-shirt, 'I simply called the journalist responsible and asked him nicely to take it back that you were a two-timing whore with no moral compass.'

'*What?*'

'Oh, I know he didn't actually say that,' she smiled, 'but the implication was there.'

'And how did you manage to persuade him?' I asked.

'Well, that's my little secret,' she said, 'but let's just say I have my ways and means.' She snapped her compact shut and put it into her bag. 'Now I'm off to the march – maybe you'll join us on the next one. Homosexuality needs all the support it can get.'

Feel I'm becoming much closer to Mrs H. Was almost tempted to confide in her about my surprise pregnancy. Just managed to stop myself in the nick of time.

1 June

Made trip to Tesco to load up on fruit and vegetables. Have decided to start buying organically now that I am eating for two. (However, will also indulge cravings for Lion Bars if necessary.)

Felt so light-hearted as I pushed the trolley up the aisles that I almost mowed down Eco-mother again. She was skulking about and looking shifty.

'We must stop meeting like this,' I joked, as she disentangled herself from my trolley.

'What do you mean?' she asked grumpily.

'We always seem to meet in Tesco,' I reminded her, wondering why she looked so sweaty and uncomfortable. 'Anyway, you'll be glad to know I'm changing my ways. I'm going to be eating healthily from now on.'

'Bully for you.' She shuffled away.

Cannot understand her reaction – thought she would have been overjoyed that I am finally converted to her outlandish green ideals.

2 *June*

Had wonderful dream that we were living in the country and I was hoeing my vegetable patch as the children, barefoot and happy, played at my feet. Woke feeling euphoric and shook Joe to tell him that maybe moving lock, stock and barrel to the country wasn't such a bad idea, after all. But only if

(a) we can employ a gardener and a live-in butler;

(b) we can get a Jamie Oliver outdoor stove and matching BBQ set for impromptu *al fresco* dining;

(c) we can buy a Range Rover Sport and become part of the horsy set.

Feel very smug that we are leaving city life behind. Soon I will be growing my own organic vegetables and strangling my own chickens for Sunday dinner. In fact, I will be just like Felicity Kendal in *The Good Life* – even if my bottom is nowhere near as perky.

One month later

- Angelica has got her new Jerry Springer-type show. She says she owes it all to me – apparently her efforts to break up the Italian fight in our front garden clinched it for her.

- Danni has gone back to Italy. Turns out the Mafia heir her father wanted her to marry is very cute, so she is reconsidering her options.

- Mrs H has snagged a high-profile position with the Gay Alliance. She did a tell-all interview with Dee and Fran describing how David's homosexuality had been the making of her. Apparently they wanted her to be their new roving lifestyle reporter but she turned them down. She prefers to keep her weekends free to visit Danni's father in Italy.

- Louise's new business venture is going from strength to strength. She got even more publicity when Dargan won the Bonniest Baby in Dublin competition – although I strongly suspect it was rigged.

- Elaine was fired after the libellous remarks she made about Dee and Fran on her Bebo page became an Internet sensation.

- Eco-mother appeared in court on charges of shop-lifting Starburst sweets from Tesco. She claims a voice told her to slip them into her recycled backpack.

- David and Max broke up. David says he can no longer tolerate Max mocking his West End obsession.

- Lone Father's book was pulled from the shelves and pulped. Lone Father is in hiding. His lover/muse Marita has received a six-figure advance to write a memoir of their rocky affair.

- We are moving to the country next week and are set to live a blissful, carefree rural existence on a permanent basis. The bonus is that Joe can set up his business with the cheque for the tell-all interview that finally arrived so we don't have to sell the Dublin house any more. All I have to do is convince Katie and Jack that the country isn't a hell-hole for losers and life really will be perfect.

Dear Reader,

When Niamh Greene asked me if she could put an extract from her new novel back here (see next page) I was furious. Bad enough that she'd been plagiarizing my diaries for so long; wanting to shamelessly plug her own book at my expense was simply outrageous. But then she promised that if I gave her book a glowing personal endorsement she would tell everyone I was her creative muse and inspiration – and take me for a slap-up meal somewhere very posh and expensive.

And so, with hand on heart, I want to tell you that Letters to a Love Rat *is an unforgettable work of staggering genius that will change your life for ever. It's bound to win many important literary awards. It will probably also be made into a smash-hit Hollywood movie and win an Oscar for Best Picture. That's how good it is. Really. (By the way, it'll also make you cry with laughter – reading how three women cope when a love rat ruins their lives is hilarious.)*

Anyhow, I'd better go, now that I'm moving to the country I have lots to do – an organic vegetable patch won't grow itself, you know.

See you next time.
Susie xxx

Letters to a Love Rat (sneak preview)

Dear Charlie,

I know I vowed that I wouldn't talk to you ever again, but
technically I'm writing, so this doesn't officially count. The
thing is, I saw your wedding photo the other day and I
kind of had a funny turn and now I'm seeing a therapist
and she's told me to write secret letters to you to deal with
issues that I never knew I had about you leaving.

What happened was this: I was in the supermarket,
waiting to pay for my measly basket of groceries for one
when I picked up the latest copy of *Hiya!* I wasn't going to
buy it – I'm not that sad – I was just leafing through
it to pass the time. I was quite enjoying looking at the
photos of all the VOPs (Very Orange People) with very
white teeth in very short dresses grinning out at me from
the pages. It was really entertaining. Especially the close-up
shots where you could spot the streaky bits of fake tan
round their knuckles or the chips in their nail polish where
chunks of diamanté had fallen off.

But then, just as I was chuckling over a VOP's VPL,
there you were staring back at me from page forty-seven,
your arms wrapped round a ravishing blonde in a couture
wedding dress, and, in a flash, I felt really strange. All
light-headed and dizzy and like I was going to pass out. I
don't know if it was the shock of seeing you and another
woman looking so smugly happy and in love or the fact
that you were wearing a tuxedo (which, by the way, I don't

think suited you all that well: you looked like you were about to serve a good Sauvignon Blanc or pass round a platter of hors d'oeuvres). Either way, I came over all funny.

I don't remember much of what happened after that, but apparently I threw the magazine stand to the ground and started dancing on your head and then I flailed about with my shopping bag and it caught the checkout girl on the cheek. I vaguely remember a security man trying to calm me down (well, getting me in a headlock and threatening to handcuff me to the sweet counter), but other than that it's a blur. Mind you, the store captured it all on CCTV so my solicitor says I'll be able to watch the entire thing soon.

Anyway, after I got home, Anna called round unexpectedly and caught me crying into the ironing. She knew that I hated ironing, but it had never reduced me to tears before so she was able to put two and two together and I was forced to tell her what had happened. I know you think she's an interfering busybody who likes to stick her nose in other people's business – isn't that what you called her at that dinner party all that time ago? – but she is my oldest friend so I value her advice. She insisted that I should be completely over you at this stage and that this little episode proved what she had suspected all along – that I wasn't. Then she convinced me to see a therapist. She says it worked a treat for her and Barry. Of course, Barry did attend the sessions with her so they could understand why he suddenly wanted to wear women's G-strings under his electrician's boiler suits, but still.

Isn't it hilarious to think of me having a therapist of my very own? (Well, it's not exactly hilarious, but if I don't laugh I'll probably cry and I've done enough of that – and gone through enough waterproof mascaras – to last me a lifetime. None of those worked, by the way – obviously the formulas were never properly road tested by truly heartbroken women before they hit the production line.) I'm a bit shocked about it myself to be honest. I mean I always thought that only mad people who wander round in their pyjamas talking to themselves needed counselling. I never, ever thought, not in a million years, that I would have a counsellor of my own. One that I am on first-name terms with and who knows all about me and my 'issues'. I always thought therapy would be plain embarrassing. And you know what? I was right. It's absolutely mortifying to have to admit your deepest, darkest, innermost thoughts to another person. The only way I can do it is by lying on the couch (yes, there is a real couch), clamping my eyes shut and gripping the velvet upholstery to stop myself from sprinting out the door. I'm getting used to it though and Mary (that's my therapist's name) says I'm making good progress – apparently my inner rage is beginning to subside a bit, which sounds hopeful at least.

Truth be told, I don't think I had all that much inner rage to begin with. Unless you count how I feel about people who skip the queue at the deli counter when I'm waiting to get a wedge of that fresh parmesan you used to love so much (can you believe I'm still buying that? Force of habit I suppose . . .) Those types really make my blood boil, although I didn't admit that to Mary, of course – I was afraid she might think I was a bit unstable. Mind you, she says you'd be very surprised at what lies beneath the surface of most normal-looking people. According to her, even the most controlled of us can go bonkers given enough provocation.

She says that's what happened in the supermarket when

I saw that photograph, and that was only the tip of the iceberg – it could take decades for *all* the negative emotions to bubble to the surface but then the suppressed anger could come gushing out in an unstoppable torrent of violence. So watch out, Buster. (Only joking!)

I did explain to her that it's been two years since you left and that really, if I was to experience all this rage, then surely I should have seen some of it by now. But Mary says that these things are unpredictable and that you never can tell when I could lose the plot completely. I thought I'd been coping quite well but Mary says that my insomnia and obsessive cleaning are both direct results of the trauma of our break-up and that it's not acceptable to be so attached to the vacuum cleaner.

So here I am writing to you.

Mary says that I don't actually have to post these letters – if I write any more, that is – I can just store them all up and then have one enormous bonfire at the end when my mental health is fully restored. (She says this may take quite some time, but I'm trying to stay optimistic.)

On a more positive note, did I mention that the features editor at *Her* magazine has commissioned me to do a series of relationship quizzes? She saw some of my work in the *Gazette* and liked my style so called me out of the blue. I did tell her that I didn't have any kind of psychology degree and that maybe I wasn't qualified enough but she said that didn't matter and that I can bluff it if I have to. I felt a bit uncomfortable at first but it pays really well and the bonus is that with my tragic relationship history I certainly won't have to do any research. Here's my first one:

Is He a Cheater or a Keeper?

According to recent research, fifty per cent of all men cheat on their partners. Would you know if your man was playing away from home? Take our simple test and find out!

(1) Your man calls and says he has to stay late at the office to prepare an important presentation. Do you:

   (a) Tell him he's working too hard, then whip up his favourite meal and pop it in the oven to keep warm? The poor guy'll need feeding up when he makes it home.

   (b) Call a girlfriend and head out for a night on the tiles – it's a pity he has to work but it's certainly not going to affect your social life?

   (c) Pull on your biggest shades, jump in the car and race round to his office to make sure he's where he says he is? Excuses about working late could be the first sign of infidelity.

(2) You find a receipt in your man's pocket for a sexy underwear store. Do you:

   (a) Go get a bikini wax immediately? He's obviously going to present the set to you tonight and you want to look your best for him.

   (b) Presume he's gone and bought another gift for his ungrateful mother? He's way too thoughtful to the old bat.

   (c) Hear alarm bells? The last time he bought you sexy underwear was years ago – when you were actually having sex with each other.

(3) Your man keeps getting mystery texts in the middle of the night. Do you:
   (a) Suspect he's organizing a surprise birthday party for you? He's such a rascal!
   (b) Wonder if he's ever going to cut those apron strings and then roll over and go back to sleep?
   (c) Try to get your hands on his phone? You have every right to read his messages.

(4) Your man has been losing weight. Do you:
   (a) Feel proud of him? It hasn't been easy cutting back – you really admire his discipline.
   (b) Ask him how he did it? Maybe if you lost a few pounds that hunky waiter in the Italian wine bar would finally sit up and take notice.
   (c) Suspect he's up to no good? He never minded being porky before now.

Results

Mostly As – Your man could have a dozen women on the side and you'd still be oblivious – you have to wise up.

Mostly Bs – Your man is likely to be playing away from home, but you probably won't be bothered. He's not your type anyway.

Mostly Cs – You're suspicious and with very good reason. This guy is making a fool of you – dump him now!

Letters to a Love Rat is published in May 2009.

Acknowledgements

Thank you to:

My wonderful editor Patricia Deevy and everyone at Penguin Ireland – especially Michael McLoughlin, Cliona Lewis, Brian Walker and Patricia McVeigh – for all the hand-holding, brow-mopping and non-stop hard work that goes on behind the scenes. I feel truly lucky to have you all on my side!

Tom Weldon, Naomi Fidler, Ana-Maria Rivera, Tom Chicken, Keith Taylor and all the fantastic sales, marketing, publicity, editorial and creative teams at Penguin UK. Hazel Orme for her copyediting and words of wisdom.

My agent Simon Trewin and his right-hand woman Ariella Feiner – who know just when to send M&Ms and flowers!

All the booksellers who supported my first novel and gave me such a lovely welcome into the publishing world – it has been a real pleasure getting to meet so many of you.

My friends – strong, funny, and always there for me. You know who you are!

Mam and Dad, who give me so much help and encouragement every day. And Martina and Eoghan, my own personal PR SWAT teams!

Darling Caoimhe and Rory, who are so patient when I have to travel and don't complain (much!) when I lock myself away to write – you mean everything to me. And most of all, Oliver: none of it would happen without you – you're the best!

Finally, a huge thank you to all my readers. I hope you enjoy this book and that it makes you smile.